D1216619

Small Town Secrets

SHADOWS
OF THE
NIGHT

JULIE ANN KEADY

For permission requests and ordering information, email:
info@TwoPennyPublishing.com

Paperback: 978-1-950995-64-6
eBook also available

Library of Congress Control Number: 2022906252

FIRST EDITION

For information about this author, to book event appearance, or media interview, please contact the author representative at:
info@ twopennypublishing.com

To Cody who never believed I would actually finish this. And to Hannah who always believed I would. Together, you pushed me to success. I love you both!

To Cynthia, you gave me the most important tool to complete the first book. We all miss you so much!

table of contents

introduction

Small Town Secrets is a purely fictional story. The seeds were planted in my overactive imagination while I lived in a small town, considered to be a village. The culture shock of living in a small rural community was a warm welcome after living in more densely populated areas where it could take as long as two hours or thirty minutes to travel the same thirty miles, depending on the day of the week and time of the day.

I loved the slower pace with the friendly atmosphere. Many of the homes were built well over a hundred years ago. And on a street close to the heart of the town were a few houses so grand, I often joked about living in the grandest one. I agreed with my friend, I could never afford it. These few houses were so majestic as they appeared to weather many storms over generations. How could anyone ever afford to live in these homes that were once built to hold many generations and servants? Such elaborate houses are no longer made like these.

And as I continued to plan my walks past these homes, I imagined the history of these families and the secrets they held. I wondered if there were secret passageways and if the current home owners were friends, family or enemies. Were they the founding families of the town? Were the current occupants related to the original owners? Were there skeletons hiding literally or fictionally deep inside that only a few knew any of the details?

Many years later, I finally organized my thoughts and Small Town Secrets, Shadows of the Night was created. The name and state is never mentioned because Small Town Secrets could be anywhere in the United States. And like Clara Noelle, I am also hearing impaired and a physical therapist. But that is where our similarities end and her story (totally fictional) begins.

SHADOWS OF THE NIGHT

prologue

Susannah was slow to awaken. She felt stiff and sore as if someone had dragged her all over the mountainside. She noted the ringing in her ears and the wetness on her face and neck. She was met with unexpected resistance when she tried to lift her arms to better explore her surroundings. They seemed to be snug at her sides with her hands together over her stomach. She could not move them.

As panic started to seep in, she realized her legs felt as if they were tied together, but she did not feel any actual binding. Her breaths were shallow as if she was lacking air. Her body was tightly wrapped as if swaddled like a baby.

Where am I? Why can't I breathe? The sudden alarm facilitated the fight response. Susannah tried to move her extremities. Instead, the tight cocoon seemed to keep her secured as she felt the increased heaviness on her body. She tried to scream, but only a groan came out. Her mouth was filled with dirt and blood. She smelled the dampened ground and remembered the recent rainstorms that had threatened to flood her beautiful valley.

Her body slowly calmed as she thought of the multiple colors of the wildflowers brought on by the rain and warmer sunshine. She distantly heard scraping sounds. A part of her mind registered the shovel as it plowed into the ground and the gentle sounds as dirt sprinkled over her body. Fortunately, the panic had diminished her air supply causing her drowsiness to settle. Her brain was able to disregard the terror of her current circumstances. She thought of the falling rain as she continued to smell the sweet scent of lilacs. Oh, how she loved her valley...

The older woman slept deeply. She first dreamed of a young woman who had just stepped out of the tub, feeling relaxed as she debated what to do with the remainder of her evening. Her child had fallen asleep just after reading a chapter together. Her husband told her earlier he would not return home until early morning.

She sighed as she thought about calling her lover but realized it wouldn't be wise. She sat on the small bench to apply her lotion as she smiled to herself, thinking of their last time together. She imagined the soft caress of his lips, the tenderness of his touch, and the musical laughter of his voice. He could always make her laugh, see the good in any situation.

Glancing at the clock, she realized it was getting late. She usually settled in for the night with her evening tea an hour ago. However, she needed to lock the downstairs doors and windows. They had all been opened after the afternoon showers to bring in the cool air. As she arrived downstairs, she smiled at the wonderful smell of the azaleas that had been planted outside the front windows when she was a young girl. She lingered as she slowly strolled through her grand family home. Her husband had a habit of leaving everything unlocked. Soon she would not have to deal with his "everything will take care of itself" attitude. He never cared to plan for the future beyond the coming weekend. He lived as if money were about to drop into his lap. Their marriage was ending, and both were well aware it was beyond saving. He just didn't know what she had planned.

She paused as she entered the kitchen, shocked to find her neighbor standing there. He smiled the moment her eyes met his. He kept staring at her with a look of lust one would expect from a secret lover.

Unprepared for his visit, she stepped back as he advanced toward her. The moment he leaned in to kiss her, she had sudden flashes, as if from a nightmare, of him lying beside her, touching her and kissing her.

She shook her head as he slowly leaned down to kiss her gently on the lips. His arms surrounded her waist as he placed his hands on her lower back to pull her in towards him. She shook her head again and pushed her hands out toward his chest in a puny attempt to hold him off and bring distance between them. He said her name softly as he pulled her even closer with a firm hold. She tried to step back further but found she was up against the counter. She tried to sidestep away from him but he just followed as if they were but one unit.

Distracted by his behavior, the first blow came as a surprise. Her ears rang loud as her tongue tasted blood. She could feel it trickle from the side of her mouth. She froze, staring in shock at the sudden change in the man she had known all her life. Their families had been so close over the years! She was too astounded to prepare for, let alone defend herself from the second blow. It knocked her clear off her feet, causing her to fall back onto the kitchen table, tipping it over and sending her to the floor. A sudden sharp pain shot up through her bottom and up her back, but she braced herself for the next and final blow. She slipped hopelessly into total darkness.

The older woman suddenly opened her eyes from the startling terror of her dreams. She was breathing heavily as if she was the one caught up in the confrontation. The nightmare was so uncanny and very realistic. It was as if she knew the people and the kitchen. Drops of sweat slid down her temples as her heart raced. She felt as if she had been fighting for her life. She slowly lifted the covers and slid to the edge of the bed. She focused on slowing down her breathing, in through her nose and out through her mouth. Feeling her body relax, she tried to recall the events of her nightmare, but her mind drew a blank. All she could remember was the panic brought on by pure evil.

It was odd she would have such a dream. She hadn't had nightmares like that in a while. She thought a nice cup of tea would help calm her nerves and relax her for the remainder of the night. If she started stirring too much now, her granddaughter would wake up asking for breakfast. As energetic as she was, she needed a few more hours of sleep. *Or maybe I am the one that requires the extra solitude*, she chuckled softly to herself. She was getting too old and slow to keep up with the young. But she did enjoy the company and the unexpected drama in the lives of those still so innocent.

She made her tea and grabbed a few biscuits, then calmly climbed the stairs. She decided to sit in her rocker by the bay window, in the sitting area of her room. If nothing else, the slow-motion would relax her. It seemed too much to hope for any more sleep tonight. In the dark of the night, she slowly moved back and forth, staring out into the hills behind the house. She loved this place. The green grass gradually gave way to the trees as the yard turned to deeply wooded areas up the gentle slopes.

Movement caught her attention. As she glanced over to the edge of the yard a few houses down, she expected to see a deer. Instead, she was startled to see what looked like the outline of a man. Was he dragging something behind him? She wasn't sure. But when she blinked and looked again, there was nothing. *I must have been dozing off*, she rationalized to herself. Who would be out at this time of night working in the yard? She continued to rock as she planned her morning, her eyes looking out into the night searching the shadows…

• • • •

Evil saw the low light in the kitchen, the signal for him that the idiot is again away for the night. He shook his head over the injustice in the world. The proof of their love was so obvious it still surprised him how no one seemed to notice. It was a shame they had to keep it secret. All the nights they shared, warming her bed. The gift she gave him, even in secret, meant everything to him. He treasured her with every fiber of his being. He understood she was afraid to leave her ridiculous husband. This being a small town, the malicious talk would bruise her tender feelings.

He closed his eyes to recall the scent of her and sighed as he quietly made his way through the dark and up the narrow stairs. He entered the dark room on the second floor, pleased the lights were all off as he made his way towards her room. When he realized the bed was empty, he sighed in frustration. He hated having to wait. He made his way down to the kitchen.

As he entered, he turned to see her standing in the doorway with a slow surprised smile on her face. Her hair was down and flowing over her shoulders. He walked over to wrap his arms around her and kiss her. Oh, the smell of her has always been the same, jasmine and vanilla.

The feeling of betrayal was unexpected as he felt her resisting his embrace. What is she doing? Why does she not understand their love is what keeps him going? Why was she fighting this?

He only meant for the first slap to yield her attitude towards him. When she just stood there staring at him with the blood seeping from the corner of her mouth, it was as if she was mocking him. The second blow was to wipe that smirk off her face. Instead, it bounced her off the table and onto the floor. She looked up at him with a look of such pity and contempt. He could not help the final blow.

As she lay there with blood dripping onto the floor, he felt a bit of panic. What did he do? He did not mean to hurt her. Only a few ever understand the way things are meant to be. The night was not supposed to go this way, not when the big reward was so close. How is he going to explain this?

As he looked down at the beautiful woman, a plan formed. Quickly glancing at his watch, he saw he had time. He could fix this. And with the ease of someone used to altering facts, he grabbed the table cloth to spread out on the floor. Then he lifted her gently up into his arms and lowered her onto the blue material. He wrapped it carefully around her body. He touched her cheek tenderly before he stepped out.

He went in search of a shovel. He slowly dragged her out into the cool night. Then through the soft grass, he made his way up the slope into the woods. He had already decided on the perfect spot.

Hours later, he returned. He removed all his clothes, placing them into the washer before using the utility sink to wash the dirt and sweat. Finally, he grabbed a towel from the basket of clean folded laundry to dry off.

With only a towel around his waist, he stepped into the kitchen to survey the mess. Once the table was upright, he placed the chairs evenly around it. He used another towel to slowly wipe up the pool of blood. A soft ding in the background alerted him the wash was done. He went to switch his clothes into the dryer and placed the towels into the washer. It's a good thing the towels are white, he thought to himself as he added bleach with the detergent. Leaving the door open to the washer, he returned to the kitchen to wash the table and floor with bleach. He was sure to wipe all the areas he touched.

The kitchen looked as good, if not better than when he first entered hours before. But, hmmm, it's still missing something. He opened a few drawers and pulled out a pretty white lace tablecloth to place on the table. Now it's perfect, he thought.

A glance at his watch told him it was later than he expected. He stepped back into the laundry room, placed the remainder of the towels to be washed, and removed his clothes from the dryer. He quickly got dressed and made his way to the stairs. He still had time to fix this. It's time to start on plan B.

He never saw the pair of green eyes watching from above.

A few days later, he was working in the yard. He loaded the weeds and trimmings onto a tarp to haul off into the woods. As he dragged his load behind him, he suddenly came face to face with the old lady. She had a sudden look of surprise and recognition as if she knew everything that had transpired in the last few days. She cannot possibly know, he thought to himself. She looked down at the load he was dragging behind him and gasped as she looked back into his eyes.

Crap! She does know! How the hell does she know?

The old lady suddenly turned to run down the slope. As he followed, he was amused at the speed and agility of the older woman. She made it all the way to the patio steps when he pushed her from behind.

She slammed down, hitting her head on the corner of the step. Blood immediately colored the ground. At first glance, she looked to be dead. He paused just long enough to see no one was looking out the window of the big house. He heard young voices moving around inside. Recognizing the one, he thought it best not to let her see him. He slowly stood up and retraced his steps back to his tarp, and continued with his chores.

an unexpected death

20 Years Later

*E*vil slowly walked up the steps, pausing to listen before he walked past the closed door. The lights were already out, but he knew from experience, lights off doesn't mean everyone is sleeping. Confident all was as it should be, he continued down the hall. Again, he paused before slowly turning the doorknob. He gently tapped the door open. He waited a moment before cautiously entering the room, remaining in the shadows as he listened. The rhythm of her breathing assured him she was asleep. When he lifted his foot to step forward, her cell phone on the nightstand chimed. He faded back into the darkness as she reached for it. She read the message and sent a reply. She returned the phone to its charger and allowed her head to fall back onto the pillow. As he waited for her breathing to signal she was once again asleep, he pulled out the syringe, removing the cap as he slowly advanced towards her bed. She rolled over onto her side, away from him as he remained standing, watching. It dawned on him for the first time that Elizabeth MacKenzie really was a beautiful woman. He wondered, briefly, if he would have done anything differently. It was a shame she would die young from too much insulin in her body.

A week later, Evil could not believe his luck. Initially irritated at the delay in his evening, he was suddenly grinning like a young lover at the surprise before him. He remained in the seat of his car, forgetting all about his initial rush to get to his destination.

Nothing had prepared him for the unexpected sight of his Babydoll as she stood behind her car. Her trunk was open as she gracefully stood on one leg, switching from the warm winter boots into elegant black pumps. He grinned with appreciation at her muscular calves. He was partly annoyed at her proper upbringing, preventing her skirt from being above her knees for the occasion. But the slit in the back allowed her to balance on one leg as she lifted the other foot. Once unzipped, the boot easily slipped off. She carefully guided her foot into the shoe with the agility of a dancer. She slowly squatted down to retrieve the boots to place into the trunk. Next, she pulled off her bulky coat, revealing her curves in a fitted but appropriate dress over her petite muscular body.

Hidden in the shadows, he was able to fully appreciate her beauty. Her brown curly hair was pulled back into what his wife called a "french twist." The few curls that escaped framed her smooth face. She wore simple makeup accenting her bright green eyes and full lips. Lured in by her graceful movements, he continued to watch, ignoring the ringing of his cell phone.

To his delight, she bent forward, giving him a wonderful view of her backside as she reached for her small bag. When she stood up, she placed the strap over her shoulders as she pulled her dark dress at the waist. He sighed with contentment as she climbed the steps to the funeral home.

Clara Noelle slowly headed up the steps of the funeral home with mixed emotions. She was furious with Jay for not returning any of her calls. He can't be angry with her. She didn't do anything wrong. Just because someone had sent flowers doesn't mean she was cheating. How can he believe she would even consider doing such a thing? They had decided on a temporary separation.

Well, Jay decided they were separating. How could she get him to understand the flowers and messages were not for her? The voice never identifies her by name. And who goes by Babydoll anyway? Her anger faded to sadness as she saw her best friend near the entrance and thought of the real reason for her return home.

Rachel Taylor MacKenzie was standing just to the left of the entrance in a fitted black dress with her blonde hair pulled back into a tight bun. She turned her head as she felt someone approach and was relieved to see Clara entering the hall alone. Rachel was just not ready to deal with all the questions that no one seemed able to answer. She held out her arms for the greatly needed hug.

"I'm so glad you arrived early. Thank you for being here. I don't think I can do this alone," Rachel whispered.

"Of course, I'm here for anything you need me to do. I wouldn't let you go through this alone. I wish there was something I could do besides stand here," Clara responded, giving her friend a gentle squeeze. "I'm sorry I couldn't get here sooner. Jay hasn't been returning my calls, and I had to get the kids situated at my neighbor's."

"You still haven't heard from him? I thought you two were only taking a break. This is sounding more like a bitter divorce."

"I don't know what is going on. I tried calling his friend's loft and his job. They tell me he has taken a few weeks off and did not leave a forwarding number. I don't want to talk about this right now. Have you talked to Gigi yet?" She was referring to Rachel's grandmother, who was currently residing in the small town's only nursing home.

Rachel quietly nodded her head thinking of her visit. How could she begin to explain the one-sided conversation? Telling Gigi her only daughter was gone was one of the worst moments of her life. It was tied with finding her mother in bed gone as if she were just sleeping. First, she gave her hand a gentle squeeze, and then she told her grandmother her mother was gone, found in her bed earlier in the day. Rachel's mother was the director of nursing. She had to tell her grandmother before she heard everyone talking. Gigi just turned her green eyes out into the hills beyond the town as if it were just another day. Rachel thought maybe she didn't understand, but then she noted a tear falling down her cheek. Mother had always said Gigi understands just fine.

A bad fall had rendered Gigi mute years before. She had been returning from her morning walk in the woods behind the family estate. She must have tripped while climbing the patio steps and hit her head on the corner. The resulting head injury kept Gigi from talking. She tried for months but could only manage sounds that never produced words. She could walk just fine, with no need for a walker or a cane, and she could take care of herself. She was even able to continue to care for the house and cook for the family. Gigi did just about anything, as before the fall, but talk. As long as Gigi didn't need to read or learn something new, she was just as strong and independent as ever. She continued to watch over the girls after school, with Mother's frequent checks to ensure all was well. Gigi had been cooking and baking for years without using a recipe book and did not need to start. But new learning she could not do.

After Rachel left for college, Gigi stopped cooking, cleaning, and taking care of herself. With no one at home during the day, Elizabeth had no choice but to have Gigi placed in the local nursing home. Rachel cried when she heard this and considered returning home to attend a local community college, but her mother would not allow it. The one comfort was that her mother was recently promoted to director of nursing. She was able to keep an eye on Gigi while at work and sit with her on evenings and weekends. Gigi had changed. The doctors were never able to confirm if she had a stroke or what. Mother once said it was more like she gave up, and her will was gone.

Rachel thought the alertness in her eyes was still present. Not many people agreed, and they didn't guard their conversations and behavior around her. During their conversation, Rachel assured Gigi she would be relocating back home again. Rachel felt as if Gigi was trying to communicate with her, almost as if she were warning her. Gigi started to shake her head and got worked up until a nurse came in and requested she leave. She will need to see her again tomorrow before the funeral. Maybe the visit will go better with Clara at her side.

Clara Noelle Hawks Gibson O'Reilly was her best friend since forever. They grew up two houses down from each other on Park Avenue. They were always together, usually staying over at Rachel's house. They shared their clothes, books, and dreams. During the sleepovers, they talked late into the night, discussing the current local gossip and boys. Often, Lila and Shannon would join them. While everyone took turns hosting the overnights, the four frequently stayed at Rachel's because Gigi loved the company.

At one time, four generations were living under the same roof. But, for some reason, it was only the women. All the males in her family never seemed to last. After Clara's mother ran off, Elizabeth and Gigi were in charge of both girls when school was not in session until Clara's father returned home. Even then, Clara rarely remained at home, always spooked in the house built by her ancestors many generations before.

As the evening went on, everyone who was anyone came through for the viewing hours. When Lila Foxwood arrived, Clara felt herself relax, as much as one could at a funeral home. Lila was another close friend. As children, Clara, Rachel, and Lila, with another friend Shannon, were always together, either riding in the woods, swimming in the lake, or just hanging out. Lila, like Clara, was petite. She stood at five feet and two inches. The bright red hair of her childhood darkened to a soft auburn as she grew older. Her skin was fair, with the freckles sprinkled over her face, which seemed to accent her gray-blue eyes. She was usually the quiet one and the peacemaker. But she was also adventurous. She grew up about five miles south of town on her family farm. When the girls were preteens, they would walk through the woods behind Rachel's and Clara's houses to get to Lila's farm. The trips were usually exciting but often led to detours with adventures they never talked about with the adults.

Lila came over to hug both Rachel and Clara. "Shannon says she's sorry she couldn't get here sooner. She'll be arriving tomorrow first thing in the morning. Where are you staying tonight?" She asked both of her friends. She understood the emotions both had with their family homes, though for different reasons. Rachel always had her mother or grandmother at her house. She had previously commented how large it was now that she was on her own. And for the first time, she felt easily spooked by the shadows of the night. But this was not a new feeling for Clara. She always felt this way. During the day, her home was beautiful, calming, and spacious. Yet somehow, during the twilight hours, it turned hideous and haunted with a sense of pure evil. No one else seemed to notice until after the explosion. After that night, all four friends agreed the house was evil.

Clara just shrugged her shoulders. "To be honest, I haven't given it much thought. I can stay only one night. I have to get back tomorrow night."

"I have been staying at my house, but I usually make sure to get up to my room before the late hours. I have to head back to the city after the weekend is over. I need to get my resume in order. Once the school year is over, I'm going to be returning home. I am going to apply to the local elementary schools. My first pick would be here in town, but beggars can't be choosers," Rachel informed her friends.

Clara sighed quietly, "I wish I could move back here. I don't think I can make it in the city on my own with the kids."

"That's a great idea. Why don't you?" Rachel jumped at the thought.

"A small town like this does not have a large demand for a physical therapist," Clara responded.

Just then, they were interrupted by a tall blonde man with friendly blue eyes and an easy smile. He came over to hug Rachel. "Always good to see you, but I am sorry for the circumstances." He turned to look around the group of beautiful women. His eyes stopped on Clara. "Wow! Look what the cat dragged in! Clara Noelle! Is that you? I haven't seen you since what, your graduation? How are you?"

"Hello, Eric! I'm alright," Clara lied as she allowed the hug from her childhood neighbor. It was great to see so many friendly faces. As the two continued with small talk, Rachel mingled with the crowd.

Lila walked over to her brother, Rob. While she remained in the city a few years after graduation, she eventually followed her brother and cousin back home to the family farm.

Rob Foxwood was two years older than his sister. He stood a full foot over her at six feet two inches. He was the first to return home after graduating from college. While he enjoyed the unchaperoned life in the city, he missed the family farm the most. He loved getting up at the crack of dawn to watch the sunrise over the mountains while tending the livestock. He was a true country boy. The farm life gave him a strong solid build with the callous hands of a worker. His blonde head nodded toward their friends as he asked, "How is she holding up?"

"I'm not sure. It's hard to tell. Rachel has the Taylor genes. She knows how to keep it together. But for some reason, it's Clara I'm worried about."

"Why?" He asked, silently agreeing.

"She just looks so distant and jumpy. We haven't had much opportunity to talk yet, but something is going on."

"Did her husband stay back with the kids? I'm surprised he didn't come out here with her. He has to know Elizabeth was like a mother to her," Rob stated as he kept his steel-blue eyes on her.

"They are separated," his sister shrugged.

"What? Why? When did this happen?" Rob was shocked to hear this. Clara Noelle seemed like the married forever type. He was surprised she was the first to get married and have kids, but once they tied the knot, she would do everything to keep it from unraveling. *Hmm, unless Mr. Right was abusive,* he thought to himself.

"He thinks she is having an affair," his sister responded. "Just thinking such thoughts suggests he does NOT know her well."

"Why does he think she's seeing someone?" He wondered. He fully agreed with his sister's assessment as his eyes continued to follow Clara around the room.

"It's stupid and a major misunderstanding," Lila exclaimed. She felt herself getting angry as she defended her close friend to her brother. "Apparently, flowers have been delivered to their place for some time and phone calls late into the night. Hang up calls. He usually answers the phone because she would need to put her hearing aids on first, but the caller always hangs up. Caller ID is blocked. Clara's devastated by this. Her family is the most important thing to her. She cherished him, and he absolutely adored her. You saw how they were in college. Once they met, they were inseparable. It was most likely because they both felt abandoned by their parents while growing up and being raised by non-family. They each understood how the other one felt. No matter what, the rest of us did not understand. As brutally honest as Clara is, she won't admit to how upsetting this is."

"I think Shannon is the brutally honest one. Clara is more deceptively honest."

"Deceptively honest? What is that?" Lila quietly chuckled as she looked at her brother.

"Oh, come on, you know. She always sounds sincere, but she uses a tone that's just dripping with sweetness. You always walk away thinking, is she being sarcastic? Did she just insult me?"

Still chuckling Lila responded, "I don't ever walk away feeling as if I was insulted. It must just be you."

"How long will everyone be here before returning to the city?" Rob asked his little sister, noting his cousin had just arrived.

Chase Foxwood was six feet tall with the shoulders of a swimmer. His light brown hair was prone to blonde streaks in the summer. While he was only eight months younger than Rob, he had been a grade younger. He had gone to college on a swimming scholarship to become an architect. When he returned after graduation, he expanded his father's construction company with his cousin and assisted on the farm. Raised on the farm with Lila and Rob, his relationship was more like a sibling than a cousin.

After entering the room, Chase's gray-blue eyes immediately found Rachel. He walked over behind her to place his hand on her shoulder.

Rachel knew the second Chase arrived. She could feel his presence even before he touched her. At that moment, she realized he was her rock. He was always the one to hold her up in the storm. When she turned, she sighed with relief as she stepped in for a quick hug. She allowed herself a moment to absorb his warmth and strength to assist with getting through the evening. Then, without a word, she stepped back and looked up into his eyes as she smiled sadly.

"Rach, anything you need. And I mean anything, you just name it, and it's done. Alright?" Chase squeezed her hands as she stepped back. Only Rach would worry about being proper at her mother's wake. He wanted to pull her back into his arms to shelter her from the pain but knew she would not allow displays of affection in public.

"Actually, I will need help moving back home when the school year is over. I can't leave Gigi here all alone," Rachel answered.

"No problem. You just let me know when. Rob and I will drive the truck up," Chase answered as he stepped back. He watched as another came over to Rachel. He turned to look around and spotted his cousins across the room. As he joined them, he was not surprised by the topic. Of course, they were discussing Clara.

"It doesn't sound long. Rachel is going back this weekend to finish out the school year. Then she'll be relocating back here. Clara wants to return home but thinks she can't get a job in this wonderful small town," Lila was stating sarcastically. "It would be tough to commute to the surrounding communities once winter sets in."

"Well, if she has any interest at all, she was talking to Eric. Being the administrator at the nursing home, he may be able to work something out for her."

"I hope so, but does his facility need another physical therapist?

Maybe the hospital would have something available." Lila speculated as she turned in his direction. She was a nurse with experience in trauma and emergency care. Against her brother's better judgment, she had chosen to work in the emergency room, usually the evening or night shifts.

"Never know. It wouldn't hurt to ask. There could be something opening up," he answered with a gentle squeeze of her shoulder as he looked over at his cousin.

Throughout the evening, Eric could not keep his eyes off Clara. While he mingled, his mind thought of ways to see her again over the weekend. It wasn't until his cell quietly chimed that he realized he was late for his date. As he quickly texted he was running late, he turned to see his parents entering.

"Eric, how is everyone holding up?" His mother asked as she quickly adjusted his tie.

"Clara is here," he whispered excitedly, gesturing with his head in her direction.

"Really? An unexpected death brings her home?" His father asked as he shifted slightly in Clara's direction.

"Well, she's only home for the weekend. She's a physical therapist. Wouldn't it be great if we could hire her at the nursing home," Eric thought out loud.

"The nursing home doesn't need another one," his mother responded. "The last thing the town needs is another Hawks woman stirring up trouble."

His father chuckled, "That could be exactly what this town needs."

The friends decided they would crash together at Rachel's house. Anticipating the possibility, Lila had packed an overnight bag and rode over with Clara.

As she slowly turned on to Park Ave, Clara could feel her heart rate pick up as her eyes looked ahead to the house where she grew up, and her mother before her. Once she parked the car, she slowly stepped out and stood at the foot of Rachel's driveway gazing toward her house. The sudden heaviness in her heart surprised her as childhood memories flooded her mind. The mixed emotions caused her to pause as she stared.

Her house stood in the shadows of the street light back in the lot. The warming spring season prepared the azaleas to bloom in all their glory of bright pinks and whites. She sighed over the confusion of the whole thing. The house had been in the family for generations. The deed was currently in her mother's name, the only child of Graham and Silvia Hawks to survive to adulthood. It was tradition for the parent to turn the house over to the child after marriage. The house came with a trust fund to be used only for maintenance. They could use it for upkeep as well as any modern updates or even redecorating. However, the current owner was the only one that could authorize any payments or changes. As a result, bills such as the electric, water, and heat were paid automatically from the trust. And continue to be as her mother had initiated the automated billing. Apparently, this also included the yard work as the lawn was neatly trimmed.

Somehow, they set up the trust so that if a marriage were to dissolve, the other party could not touch the house or the trust. The house was to always remain in the family and be turned over to the next generation once married when the previous generation was ready to turn over the responsibilities. The only exception was death. Then the house would immediately go, usually, to the firstborn of the next generation, regardless of marital status.

The rumor was, Clara's mother had run off with her lover. She never returned home, let alone made changes to the estate. This left the house in limbo. No one could step forward to claim the house and responsibilities. Clara was able to live there with her father until completing high school. But the rules were strict. Once she graduated and moved out of town to college, her father was no longer allowed to remain in the house. The day after her graduation, he had already packed up his few things. He quietly relocated a few towns over with his girlfriend. Clara initially planned to spend her last summer living with Rachel, her mother, and Gigi. But at the last minute, she enrolled in summer classes and left for the city. She never returned, until today.

The widely believed story was that Susannah Marie Hawks Gibson took off with another man when Clara was nine years old. She didn't believe the rumors, but how does a child make the world think otherwise? The "proof" that did exist was a missing luggage set and a partially empty closet of clothes. Her purse was gone. Her wedding rings were removed and left on the emptied vanity. Her last phone call was to the airlines. A day later, her checking account had been closed out from the city. What was one to assume? Her father was devastated by his wife's betrayal. Everything was different after that morning.

Clara thought back to that early morning. She woke up excited to spend Saturday with her mother. They had plans to go to the Foxwood Farm for riding. But as soon as she touched the first step of the back staircase, she knew something was off. Her mother was usually an early riser, always had her first cup of coffee before anyone else was up and about. But the coffee pot was empty and cold to the touch.

Something was definitely wrong. Maybe it was the scent. The kitchen smelled of bleach as if mother had been up all night scrubbing it from top to bottom. While it was possible, it was not likely. Susannah kept things clean and organized but not sterile. There was no way she would spend an entire evening cleaning. As Clara continued walking through the kitchen, everything was very much in its place. It looked as if the kitchen chairs were measured and evenly placed around the table. The cornflower blue tablecloth and the vase of lilacs she had arranged the previous evening were gone. Still feeling alarmed, she walked through the hall and glanced into the dining room. Nothing was out of place. Continuing down the hall and up the grand staircase, she ran towards her parent's room. She came to a stop as she noted the closet doors closed and the bed made. She walked further into the sitting area and saw the book her mother was reading on the settee. The bookmark Clara made for her mother when she was six was still in place in the middle of the book. Clara slowly walked into the bathroom. On the vanity were her wedding rings and high school ring. She always took them off when taking a bath after an incident when one of her rings slid off. Luckily she found it before it went down the drain as the water emptied. She continued the search for her mother. When she could not find her, she walked outside and sat on the steps near the driveway.

"Is everything all right?" Lila asked when she realized her friend was no longer beside her.

Clara smiled warily, reached for her bags, and assured her friend she was ok. Then together with their arms linked, they headed into Rachel's house. She tried to ignore the building sensation of being watched. As when she was a child, she could feel the presence of others. She shivered at the memory of once being told it was the spirits of the generations before her.

evil did this

After the funeral the next morning, Rachel returned to her house with Clara, Lila, and Shannon. Relieved the worst part was over, the four friends made their way to the kitchen. Rachel continued to the back yard to sit alone. Her friends understood her need for alone time as they worked together to prepare for the arrival of the town.

They were quickly joined by all the older ladies who were close friends and co-workers of Elizabeth. The younger women were slowly pushed aside as the older ones seemed to have a better grip on the kitchen scene. As they worked together, they shared various memories of their growing up years. Clara smiled as she tried to picture Elizabeth and her friends daring to go skinny dipping in the lake near the caves.

Realizing they did not need her, she wandered around the parts of the house still open for the gathering. She admired pictures of Elizabeth, Gigi, and Rachel from various stages of life. She stopped short when she saw the picture of two young women with toddlers on their laps. She smiled as the picture reminded her how long she'd been friends with the MacKenzie family. Her mother and Elizabeth were raised two houses apart as the best of friends. They not only grew up together, but they also raised their daughters together. How she would love to raise her children with Rachel's, she thought with a sigh. Replacing the picture, she turned and bumped into Eric.

"Oh! Excuse me, I'm sorry. I didn't hear you come up behind me," Clara stated as she stepped back to give more space between them.

"Clara, that's alright," Eric responded as his hands reached out for her arms as if she were falling over. His smile grew wider as he looked into her eyes.

"I am so glad you were able to make it. It's been so long since I've seen you. I know we always talked about keeping in touch when we were away at school, but it just never happens, does it? What kind of work do you do?" He asked as he slid his hand around her waist guiding her towards the open French doors and onto the patio.

Clara allowed him to guide her into the sunshine. She vaguely answered his questions as he shifted the conversation toward his own life. She listened as he talked about his fraternity years at the university, ending with his current life in town. Eric explained he was currently running the nursing home. She found her mind wandering as he continued talking about his achievements, oblivious to the many pairs of eyes watching her every move.

· · · ·

Evil stood back in the shadows watching everyone as the flow of people went from the house to the back patio. Everyone seemed to be sad. He was careful to keep his sunglasses on and his face mournful. He didn't want anyone to suspect his busy night before. He could not believe how gullible people were. His plans seem to be moving right along. After last night's events, he was sure everything else would fall into place. He just needed to complete the turnover and let it flow. Oh, look at her, acting all sad. He walked closer to listen to her tell the boy about her life in the city. He noted she wasn't even talking about her husband. Yup, it's as he suspected. She is ready to make the move back home...

Further down, Rob watched silently from behind his sunglasses as he pretended to listen to a fellow farmer talk about the coming rainstorms. He couldn't seem to take his eyes off Clara as she talked with Eric. It had been years since he last saw her in the city. She hasn't changed, he thought as he kept his feelings for her tucked away. Rob remembered years back in the same spot he was standing, coming around the corner of the house to see Clara kneeling beside blood-covered Gigi.

Rob and Chase had arrived with his uncle after receiving a frantic call from Lila. The older woman had taken a bad fall. She was unconscious while Clara was quietly and calmly assuring Gigi that help was on the way and she would be just fine. Instructed by his uncle, Rob gently pulled her away to make room for the paramedics. He had been impressed she had done everything right: kept Gigi still, applied pressure to her head wound and, he later learned, instructed the others to call for help. Even as the youngest in the group, Clara was able to remain calm and to keep control of the situation until help arrived. He led her toward the front of the house to sit with her on the steps leading to the grand porch. Once Clara realized she was relieved of the responsibility, she lost her composure and cried while he held her tight. When the tears eased up, he looked into her eyes and saw panic and despair. He had never understood her comment, he often wondered if he misheard it.

"Evil did this," Clara had whispered.

And similar to twenty years ago when he first heard the phrase, Rob felt a shiver at the memory.

A pair of brown eyes hidden behind sunglasses also followed Clara's moves. She grew up into an amazing woman. He should have kept better tabs on her, he thought as he watched her accept a hug from Eric before she appeared to excuse herself. To his amusement, he had been well aware of her crush on him while she was growing up. And when she outgrew her infatuation and married young, he found himself disappointed. He did maintain contact with her but less so once he realized she was content and safe. It was easy enough to run into her since they both lived in the city and worked at the same trauma center. But once he moved back home, he felt it was inappropriate to continue the contact. He didn't want to follow the same road as his brother, wasting his better years over something that wasn't meant to be. Besides, it had been easier to date when she was no longer constantly on the horizon.

Connor Emerson was about to intercept her as she walked across the patio towards her friends, but paused when he felt a hand on his arm. The woman beside him was considered beautiful by anyone's standard. Her perfectly made face, highlighted hair, and size six body would be any man's dream, if he could be content with the constant boredom of her limited topics and understanding. While she could adequately meet his physical needs, they were not compatible on an intellectual level. She didn't enjoy any activity that could potentially ruin her manicure or her inch-thick makeup. Despite not growing up with money or household servants, she believed she was entitled to have access to his, for the simple fact she was on his arm.

Last night when he heard her tell others they would soon be engaged, that was the final straw. He wasn't sure how she arrived at that conclusion since they'd only been seeing each other for three months. It didn't have any of the markers of a serious relationship. They never spent the night together, neither had the other one's key nor did they even see each other daily. Hell, they went days without talking or texting. He knew for a fact she went out with other men when he worked the weekends. It was time to cut the noose, he thought.

"I am ready to leave. They have closed up over half the house! I had hoped to see the place so let's just go," she stated in a harsh whisper.

He smiled to himself. How like Rachel to realize most of the "mourners" present were really hoping to get an unescorted tour of the big mansion. The fact that he didn't bring her to his own family home to give her "the tour" was a constant battle since the first date. He sighed as he admitted he wasn't even bothered that it would never work between them.

"Don't be tacky," he responded, knowing she hated it when he said that. She was constantly trying to elevate her status. "I am not ready to leave. I warned you about coming with me. I knew you would be bored."

Her facial expression was torn. He could see, to his annoyance, she debated having a temper tantrum on the spot. However, his brown eyes warned her she was stepping on dangerous ground. If she remembered from the last one, he would not tolerate it and especially not give in to her demands, "Yes, you did, but why would we stay? We don't even know these people."

"I grew up three houses down. I know these people. These are my people. I am going to get a plate of food," he stated, realizing this wasn't the time or the place as he started to walk away.

"Connor, wait," she grabbed his arm, "If you walk away from me, I won't be answering the phone the next time you call."

He paused, removing his sunglasses before turning back, "No worries. I won't call."

Connor replaced his sunglasses as he walked away. Damn that was easy, he thought as he stepped up to the line at the buffet. The person ahead of him immediately turned to greet him. He was easily pulled into the conversation.

Tiffany Krause froze on the spot at the realization of what just happened. Fuck! Did he just break up with me? She quickly debated chasing after him, but he was already talking to another woman. She was fuming inside but remained calm as she remembered, time and place make all the difference in the world. She was confident he would change his mind when she showed up at his door later wearing her newest lingerie. She smiled to herself as she quietly walked towards the side entrance into the house for one last glimpse of the magnificent place.

• • • •

This plan might just work after all. The sooner she gets back here, the better. It's amazing how easy it was to get rid of the one holding her hostage in the city. As for the other, she was just in the way. She was actually talking about getting married and starting a family. As if anyone would want to have children with her. Evil shook his head over her stupidity. His Babydoll has been talking to others about returning. This will be great! I just hope it all stays as it is while she packs everything up. Fortunately, the need to have a physical therapist start immediately will keep her busy so she won't have time to search out the loser. I better start preparing for the return…

Clara reluctantly went into the house to see if she could assist with anything before heading upstairs for her luggage. As she passed into the front foyer, she was surprised to see an unfamiliar face walking around the entrance taking pictures with her cell phone. She shook her head. It takes all kinds, she thought as she started towards the grand staircase.

"Excuse me, I don't think we're allowed to go up there," the woman stated. She shrugged as she continued, "Well, I suppose you could try, but it's all locked up anyway. I don't see the point in having a beautiful home if you aren't going to allow others to see it."

Clara paused on the fourth step, turning around towards the other woman, "Are you a family member of Rachel's?"

"I wish," she chuckled. "No, I'm here with my fiancé. He's friends with the family. He grew up just three houses down. His family and hers go back."

"Connor's getting married?" Clara asked with surprise. She stepped down towards the woman, reaching for her left hand. "I shouldn't be surprised, but it's about time. Congratulations."

"How did you know it was Connor?" She asked with a slight panic. After last night's argument, he made it clear they weren't engaged and almost did not allow her to tag along with him today.

"I'm Clara," she answered as she held out her hand as she explained.

"I grew up two houses down. Matt is already married, so that only leaves Connor."

"Tiffany Krause," she responded as she shook her hand. "We haven't had a chance to look at rings yet."

"Best wishes on your life together. I need to head upstairs. It was a pleasure meeting you. Please extend my wishes to Connor," Clara started to turn but stopped with the next question.

"You have access upstairs? Can I come with you?" Tiffany pleaded. She was not aware her comments were sending off many red flags.

"Oh, I couldn't. I don't have the authority. However, I do recommend you return through that door before security finds you here taking pictures. The last person caught doing that was arrested," Clara warned as she turned to quickly ascend the steps, careful not to chuckle out loud as she lied about security.

About ten minutes later, Clara was closing up her weekender bag when she heard a knock on the door. Initially she was irritated, wrongly assuming Tiffany had called her bluff about security and followed her up the steps. Instead, Rob was standing in the doorway.

"Hi, Rob."

"Need help with that?" He asked as he reached for the bag on the bed. "You aren't preparing to leave, are you? I came to see if you want to go riding tomorrow at the farm."

"Oh, Rob, that would be great, but I need to get back to the city," she answered with a smile.

"Today is Friday. I thought you'd make a weekend of it. Stay and return on Sunday with the others."

"I need to return home to my children. I couldn't leave them for too long."

"I'm surprised you didn't bring them," Rob stated as they both started down the grand staircase.

"The drive is too long for such a short trip. Besides, I came to support Rachel through this. If the children were here, I would be too distracted caring for them. Shannon and Lila are here. Rach will drive back to the city with Shannon. And I will be in the city when she needs me," Clara explained as they stepped out onto the porch and down towards her car parked on the street. "I don't have any child care here to watch them."

"We could have helped with that."

"Possibly, but Reese and Hailey don't know anyone but Shannon and Rachel," she answered as she closed the trunk and returned towards the house to say her goodbyes.

Later that afternoon, Connor pulled into the parking lot of the nursing home. As he reached the door, it was opened by Clara as she was stepping out.

"Clara? I was hoping to see you before you returned. What are you doing here?" He asked as he hugged her.

"Hi Connor, I stopped to see Gigi before I left," she answered. "I understand congratulations are in order. Your mother must be ecstatic!"

Connor stepped back as his eyes narrowed in confusion, "What the hell are you talking about?"

Ha, I was right, she thought with a laugh as she continued to tease, "I ran into your fiancé at Rachel's. I thought you were the romantic type who would purchase the ring and have it all expertly planned out before you proposed. Were you nervous she would refuse you, so you waited until she said yes to purchase the ring?"

Connor's eyes rolled towards the sky as he groaned with annoyance before he muttered under his breath, "That bitch."

Clara laughed at his irritation, "Connor, trouble already?"

"How did you hear this?"

Clara laughed again as she told him of their encounter in the foyer. Within minutes, Connor was also laughing.

"She believed there were security guards there?"

"She must have! Tiffany was out the door before I reached the top of the stairs," she answered. "Connor, I have to get on the road. It was great seeing you."

"It was. We should all meet up for drinks when I'm in the city again," he suggested, not aware of her current marital troubles.

"Absolutely," she responded as they hugged.

3 moving home

Four weeks later, Clara slowly lowered the rag and sighed as she looked around her new home. She was up most of the night cleaning and scrubbing as her three year old son and fifteen month old daughter slept. She sighed to herself, to be able to sleep so innocently at night. Clara could not remember the last time she was able to sleep peacefully, let alone all night long.

Clara quickly rinsed out the rags and bucket in the utility sink in the basement as she mentally prepared herself for the arrival of the moving truck later in the day. She and the kids were camping out in the master bedroom upstairs until then. She quietly debated where each piece of furniture would go to avoid having to move everything around again later. She was relieved to have found the duplex with the extra space and yard within her budget ready to move in so fast.

Looking around again, Clara compared the size of her new home to the size of her previous apartment in the city. All her household goods and furniture could probably fit into the rooms on the first floor alone. When entering the front door, one was welcomed with a large L shaped room. Going straight to the end of the room led to the entry of the kitchen. Turning left after entering the foyer led to a large spacious living area. Through that room was another "small foyer" leading to another door and small porch or, turning right, up the staircase to the bedrooms and bathrooms.

What was I thinking, renting a four bedroom place? Complete with basement, garage and attic! Finishing her task, she rushed up the stairs to her bathroom to shower. Clara would treat the kids to McDonald's before the movers arrived.

It was just a bit after dawn when she placed her purse over her shoulder, picked up her daughter Hailey while her son Reese followed her out onto the porch. As she turned to lock her door, she felt Reese's hand tapping her thigh, "Mommy, who's truck?"

Clara was hearing impaired. She was initially able to make do with hearing aids but did have a cochlear implant in her left ear two years ago. Despite the significant improvement, she was still impaired. Both her children had adapted, always touching her to get her attention and waiting until she looked over before speaking. Looking over her shoulder, Clara wondered who could possibly be here this early? She sighed with relief as she recognized Rob in the driver's seat with his cousin Chase riding shotgun.

Rob and Chase were hopping out of the truck and called a greeting to Clara as Rob reached back in to retrieve a basket of sorts. Likewise, Chase reached in to pull out a to-go tray of coffee cups.

"What's all this?" She asked as she was greeted with a hug from each of the guys.

"Lila says you just have the bare essentials until the movers arrive later today. She packed a few things to help the day go smoother. She's just getting off her shift and needs to sleep before she gets here. She also said something about painting?"

Clara grinned back at the guys and peeked into the basket. She was rewarded with the smell of fresh baked banana muffins and bacon cheddar biscuits. Her favorite treats from the Foxwood residents when she was a child, "The famous Foxwood bacon and cheddar biscuits!"

Her smile lit up her face as her bright green eyes met his steel blue, Rob felt his heart skip a beat as he smiled back.

The quick moment was over when she heard Reese ask what was in the basket. Remembering her manners, she introduced her children to Rob and Chase. Each bent down to high five Reese and then waved to Hailey. Big sky-blue eyes turned away as she pushed her face into her mother's shoulder. Clara turned back to the door to lead the way into the house.

"I'm surprised to see you guys are up and about this early in the day," she commented.

She was greeted with a snort from Rob as he stepped into the house, "You are gone for what, twelve years and already forgetting this is farm country? We've been up for a couple of hours already dealing with the animals."

Nodding, Chase stepped into the front door and looked around the clean, empty rooms. "I don't get why you need to rent this place when you have the big house over on Park Ave. Is this temporary until you have the other place all spruced up?"

Shaking her head, Clara responded, "You know how the trust works. I have not been handed over the keys yet. My mother is still the rightful owner of the Hawks House. I can't even plant annuals outside, let alone move in."

"Right. The good old trust. I'm glad our family land is operated differently. My parents decided to move away seasonally to be closer to my mother's family and farm. They were able to do so without so much as making sure I knew where the keys were." Seeing the distress in Clara's eyes, he quickly changed the subject. Eyeing the multiple paint swatches on the wall he asked, "What would you like painted?"

"You guys have a lot on your plate with the family farm and construction company. I don't want to burden you with my moving," she responded. Opening the basket, she noticed the table cloth from Lila. Taking it out, she spread it out on the floor and assisted her kids with a juice box and muffin.

"As owners of said farms and construction companies, we can pretty much decide our hours and delegate as needed. Besides, it doesn't look too bad here. A little fresh paint, some furniture and curtains and you're good," replied Chase.

Clara smiled and thought back to the closeness of her friends and their families. This was just like them! She instructed the kids to stay put and walked the guys around to explain what she had in mind for colors for each room. Rob and Chase quickly measured up the sizes of the rooms. Taking the swatches they headed out to the store to get the necessary items.

An hour later, the guys returned with the supplies and extra hands. They quickly instructed what needed to be done and set out to work. At the sound of the doorbell, Clara thought the movers had arrived early. She was surprised to see Eric, her new boss, standing on her front porch. He was holding a fruit basket and had a tall houseplant on the porch next to him.

"Good morning, Eric," Clara greeted as she opened the screen porch to invite him in. He stepped inside, handed her the basket and stepped back out for the plant.

"I wasn't sure if you'd be up this early. Just stopping in to welcome you back! I wanted to check in to see if you need anything to help ease the transition. I see you already arranged painters. When will your furniture be arriving?" Eric turned at the sound of someone calling her name and was disgruntled to see Rob jogging down the steps in his work clothes.

"Hey Clara, come on up to see if this is how you want the colors," he called out before he noticed Eric standing beside her. "Hey Eric, how's it going?"

"Great, just swinging by on the way to work to see if Clara needed any help setting up. I see she's already been arranging everything." He gave Clara a quick hug before heading back out the door, "I'll see you

Monday morning at work."

Clara quietly closed the door behind him and turned to Rob. Pausing when she glanced at his face, "What are you smirking about?"

"Am I?" He responded. He knew better than to comment about Eric's infatuation with her. It apparently hadn't faded over the years. "I just have some questions about the colors in your son's bedroom."

Clara grabbed her daughter and followed him up with Reese close behind. At the top of the stairs, the first bedroom was to the left, over the garage. She turned around the railing, passing the bathroom on her left, the second bedroom was straight ahead. She noticed Chase and a friend already completed half of the room in pink. She entered the next room behind Rob.

"Am I understanding you correctly? You want one green wall, one blue, one yellow and one red?"

Clara smiled as Reese followed behind her, "Yup! Mommy says I can have any color I want. I want this one blue, that one red, this one green and yellow there," pointing to each wall as he walked around the room.

Rob slowly nodded his head and looked down at the little boy with his mother's bright green eyes. "Sounds like you have this all planned out. Do you want to help me?"

Reese jumped up excitedly as he turned to his mother. She raised her eyebrows questionably at Rob, "That can complicate the task."

"Wouldn't hurt to start his training for household chores now. Besides, it'll be fun for him to help create this masterpiece that will soon be his room." He reached down on the plastic covered floor for an extra paint brush and began to work as he patiently instructed the young boy.

Clara looked around the room and thought, this might actually keep him occupied while the movers are in and out. She headed back down the hall and stopped again in the pink bedroom. Hailey clapped her hands and wanted to get down. Instead, Clara quickly moved out of the room to keep her daughter from making a mess. As she headed down the stairs, the doorbell rang again. She was relieved to see it was the movers this time. By earlier agreement, the bedroom furniture and boxes were kept downstairs off to the side while everything else was set up in the kitchen and living room.

Once the movers were finished, Clara closed the doors behind them and started to give serious thought to lunch. She turned around as she heard her son coming down the stairs. He was following Rob while he explained his favorite game. She laughed when he reached the bottom step, he was covered in paint! Streaks of blue, red, yellow and green covered his blue jeans and t-shirt with red on the top of his head.

"How is the painting going?" She asked her son.

"It's all done! My room is finished!" He exclaimed with a clap of his hands.

Clara looked over at Rob, noticed he didn't have as much paint on his clothes. Rob met her eyes, smiled and shrugged, "I hope they weren't his good clothes. But mission accomplished. You don't have much, do you?"

Rob looked around at the limited furniture and boxes placed to one side of the living room. There was still enough room for the living room furniture to be properly arranged.

Clara shrugged. She didn't want to admit she had hoped to get permission to retrieve some pieces from the family house. "Our place in the city was a quarter of the size of this townhouse. We just had two bedrooms with a main room for the kitchen, dining area and living room."

"Who could that be now?" Clara wondered as the doorbell rang again.

She was surprised to see a teenager standing on her porch with bags in each hand. He smiled and looked over her shoulder at Rob. Rob pulled out his wallet to pay the delivery boy and reached for the bags.

As Clara closed the door, Rob whistled loudly and the others came down from upstairs. He walked into the kitchen and started to pull out the various items while he explained. "We arranged to have lunch delivered thinking it would be less distracting than to stop and go get it. Hope you don't mind."

Chase came into the kitchen with a cooler full of various juice boxes, water bottles and sodas. He handed Clara a water bottle and assisted each of the kids with juice boxes. He grabbed a can of soda for himself and tossed one to his cousin as the others waited before helping themselves.

"Not a problem. I'm surprised the kids haven't been complaining of being hungry before this," she replied as she assisted with their lunches.

She enjoyed getting reacquainted with people she knew before she moved away. When Lila arrived in the late afternoon, the children were sound asleep on sleeping bags in the dining room while the friends brought each other up on the latest while organizing the kitchen.

While Clara listened to her friend tell a funny story from work, she found herself relaxing. The tension of the move was slowly easing. Being surrounded by her friends assured her moving home was the right decision.

it's so great to have you back

A week later, Clara stepped out onto the front porch holding Hailey's hand as her son ran ahead and jumped off the last step. Both were surprised when he landed in a pool of mud which splattered up and all over his body. He turned around and smiled at his mother.

Clara sighed to herself. Of course there will be mud with all the rain from last night! Momentarily forgetting she was back in the valley. Spring time rain storms always brought the flow of rain downhill, often flooding the streets. More often than not, the water would be drained away by the next morning with mud left behind on the streets and sidewalks. She assisted her daughter down the steps and allowed her to join her brother. May as well let them have fun in the mud before she drags them back upstairs for a bath!

A couple of hours later, each child was scrubbed, dressed in clean clothes and in their carseats as Clara backed from the driveway. She almost regretted agreeing to go to lunch at Lila's today. She could have used the extra time over the weekend. Mentally thinking of all the chores still to do: finish unpacking, grocery shopping, laundry and review her finances again.

Seems like not enough time in the day. But Lila was right. She needed the relaxation, thinking back to when she went over her bank statements last night. She was pleasantly surprised to note Jay had not touched any of their savings. Clara felt it would be an invasion of his privacy to check his checking account as they always kept their own checking but each put into the savings every month. She noted he had not contributed any in the months since he moved out. Maybe he's just using his checking for his own needs, knowing she has most of the expenses with the kids. She thought for sure she would need to separate her savings or at the very least, start over.

But, she thought, Jay's not a malicious petty person out for his own gains. He always put her and the kids first. It really made no sense for him to not contact her, if for no other reason but to see the kids. With his upbringing in the system, moving around from foster home to foster home, Jay preferred to stay at one place and be surrounded by her and the kids.

A tear slid down her face as she thought over the last few months with frustration. Clara drove quietly over the hills past the green fields, noting the sun shining and clouds all but a distant memory of last night's storm. She missed all the green! The trees, grass, open space! As she wiped her tears away, she slowed down for the sharp turn as the road continued on up the hill, leading towards the Foxwood Farm. Clara became aware of the silence in the back. Peeking into the rearview mirror she noted her children looking out the windows in fascination. True, they really have never seen so much open land before, she smiled to herself. This was definitely the right thing to do.

She turned onto the long drive leading to the big old white house which had been in the Foxwood family for generations. Lila came out onto the porch and waved. Clara parked the car and reviewed manners to the kids as she stepped out and unbuckled each child.

Lila came down the steps with a big smile. She was relieved to see Clara made it. She was worried the previous night's storm would cause some major delays.

"I'm glad you made it! How did you make out with all the rain last night?" Lila said, hugging Clara then reaching for the little one.

"It really wasn't too bad. I think the worst of it started after we were all asleep. Everyone was so tired from the busy week. But this morning, there was mud all over! I forgot how bad the mud can be! Reese stepped outside and was immediately covered!" Clara laughed.

"Horses, Mommy!" Reese exclaimed as he started to pull her arm into a run. "I want to see!"

Lila laughed and took his hand to lead him and his sister towards the barn. Clara paused for a moment, turning to look around at the farm she had not seen since high school. Not much has really changed, she thought. Then she saw Rob jump down off the tractor. He waved at her just as Reese arrived at his feet.

Later after lunch, Clara assisted Lila with the cleanup. It was so relaxing to eat out on the porch overlooking the hillside which led to the forest. She smiled as she remembered the horse trails, riding and hiking while they were growing up.

"Want to go for a ride on the trails?" Rob asked, as if reading her mind.

"I can't leave the kids," Clara responded as she looked down and saw both had fallen asleep on the couch.

"Nonsense, I can watch them. You two go ahead. Clara, I can be on a horse any time. They need exercise and I know you miss riding. I'll look after the kids," Lila said, gently pushing her friend towards the back steps leading to the stables.

Rob led the way onto the trail, up the hills and into the forest. Clara smelled the lilacs mixed in with the wet from the rain. She was surrounded by the deep green of the grass and trees. She sighed. She really did miss this.

"How's everything working out with your new place and new job?" Rob asked, looking over his shoulder, pleased to see Clara was relaxing.

"I'm getting there. I owe you and Chase for all the help with the painting and unpacking. I was expecting to be up late each night just painting for the first month," Clara responded. "The week has been tiring but no complaints. Just learning the ropes and adjusting to a slower pace. I was so tired last night after a busy week, I fell asleep after putting the kids down. I didn't even know how much rain we had until I woke up and saw the mud! I'm surprised we aren't sliding down the hill now."

As they continued in silence, Clara closed her eyes and listened to the sounds surrounding her. Amazed she could distinguish between different birds, not that she knew which was which, she admitted to herself. Wait, is that the water from the river? She wondered as she turned her head.

Rob looked over and smiled when he saw Clara's face light up in wonderment, the only word that could describe it. Her green eyes met his steel blue as her face seemed to shine even more.

"This is amazing! I can hear the birds, the water flowing in the river and even the leaves as the wind blows through them," she declared.

"I don't think I ever heard you talk so excitedly about birds before," Rob commented.

"Yeah, likely because I couldn't hear it all before," she admitted.

"Really?" He should have known better. Rob was well aware of her hearing loss when they were younger. Clara would often wait for others to explain what was going on, especially if she removed her hearing aids when they went swimming. She was much quieter without them.

"Yeah, I never really knew what I was missing until I had a cochlear implanted in my left ear," Clara explained as she held up her hair. She pulled a small circular item from her head. "This is a kanso. It acts as a receiver. The magnet attaches onto the piece inside, just below the skin. The inside piece has a tail that gets very small. So small that it is able to weave into my cochlear. That is the inner ear, it's shaped like a snail. There are twenty-two electrodes that send signals to my brain.

When it was first turned on, there was a delay in the time from when I would read someone's lips to when I would actually hear the words in my brain. You know I've always read lips," she saw Rob nod his head.

"Now, I don't actually have to rely so heavily on lip reading. I can hear and understand speech. As I grew older, the hearing loss and the ability to understand speech worsened. I went from literally hearing nothing in this ear to about sixty percent. With the hearing aid in my right, that brings me up to about seventy-five percent," Clara patiently explained.

She paused with a smile, looking up as she heard what she assumed was a woodpecker, tapping on a nearby tree. She looked back over at Rob, "The hearing didn't magically return overnight. I met with my audiologist, Dr. Nada Hanna, every two to four weeks as she gradually increased the parameters of the sounds so I was not overwhelmed at once. I was apprehensive at first but it has been a great experience."

"Do you sleep with it on?" Rob asked.

"No, I also remove them when I shower. I can put the kanso in a waterproof case when I swim," she stated excitedly.

Rob remembered how he or Rachel would explain to Clara what was going on when they went swimming. Even though he always knew she was hearing impaired, he never really understood how much she missed.

"When I first had it turned on, I needed someone to explain what I was hearing until my brain could understand it. It was crazy! I never knew the swishing sound your hands make on a steering wheel, the footsteps on pavement or tile. I am amazed I was able to distinguish a co-worker walking behind me because of a limp in his gait. And thunder! Boy is thunder loud!"

"You couldn't hear thunder?"

"No, I might feel it if it was close but I didn't hear it," Clara confirmed. "I am so pleased with the progress I am hoping to have my right ear done."

Rob was quiet as he thought about all this. How did he not know about Clara getting a cochlear implant? That seems like such a big deal, Lila would have mentioned it. Most likely, he tuned out as he learned to do when anyone talked about Clara. While he also went to the city for college, he was in a different school than Clara. When he learned she was seeing someone, he stopped asking Lila about her. And when her marriage was announced, he stopped listening when his sister talked of her.

"I'm glad we convinced you to go for this ride. You know you're welcome to come riding anytime you want," he told her.

As they left the darkness of the trees, the horses stepped out into the sunshine and onto the meadow. Clara looked around and smiled at the blanket of wild flowers covering the ground. This is definitely worth the ride, she thought as they continued towards a small stream flowing back into the woods.

In the distance, a shade of blue material flapping in the wind caught her attention. Clara gently nudged her horse from the trail where it started a gentle decline into the valley towards her childhood home. When she was closer to the material, she eased off the horse, slowly advancing forward. Suddenly, she let out a loud gasp as her brain clicked in recognition of the material. It was the tablecloth she put on the kitchen table, on the last evening she ever saw her mother!

• • • •

Evil was relieved to be able to sneak into the home without any complications. Believing his Babydoll chose the duplex with a common wall connecting the basements and attics gave him all the permission he needed. He thought the idea of leaving a window unlocked in the empty place next door was brilliant. It allowed him to enter through the basement and up the stairs he went. Evil was cautious to touch as little as possible but still wore gloves. As he ascended the second flight of stairs, he quickly passed the smaller three bedrooms but stopped at the doorway of the master bedroom.

Slowly stepping into the room, his eyes were everywhere. Inside the closet he allowed a hand to linger over the hanging clothes. As he made his way to the dresser drawers, his hand paused before lifting her panties and bras. The smooth silky materials felt so good against his skin. He sighed before he went to sit on the side of the bed. Bringing a pillow from under the sham up to his face, he inhaled the sweet scent. He could feel himself responding as he quickly readjusted the pillows in perfection.

"Oh hello, Babydoll! Oh hello, Babydoll, it's so great to have you back where you belong," he sang softly as he slowly smoothed out the wrinkles from where he sat. "It will be swell Babydoll, it will be..."

the cornflower blue tablecloth

Rob heard Clara's horse turn off the trail behind him. He quietly followed as he noticed the blue material in the ground. He jumped from the horse with an uncomfortable feeling. The material was saturated in mud and appeared to be covering something. The discomfort intensified when he heard Clara gasp in surprise, as he reached her side. He lifted his arm up to motion for Clara to stop.

A female slipper was lying next to the material. And a piece of bone was sticking out of the blue covering! He stepped over to block her view but noted the recognition in her eyes as he pulled out his cell phone.

An hour later, Clara sat on a fallen log quietly hugging her legs towards her chest, shivering in the damp air. She replayed in her mind the evening she last saw her mother. They had just cleared the table of the dinner dishes. While her mother rinsed and placed the dishes into the dishwasher, she wiped the table clean. She had pulled a clean cornflower blue table cloth from the drawer to place on the table. Her mother had assisted with arranging the flowers she picked from the garden out back into the clear glass vase…

Rob had been standing with Anthony and Adam, the two deputies. He was providing the details of their ride while they waited for the county medical examiner to arrive. He looked over at Clara sitting on the damp log covered in moss. Her face was pale, her eyes remained on the blue material.

Clara glanced up as Rob stepped from the group and joined her on the log. "How are you holding up?"

He felt her shivering beside him. Believing she was cold from the dampness in the air, Rob removed his denim jacket to place over her shoulders. "We can head back to the farm. We don't need to be here right now. Anthony knows where to find us if he has any questions."

"No, I need to be here for this. I don't want her to be alone anymore," Clara shook her head as she put her arms through the sleeves, striving for comfort in the warmth of his jacket. It was a poor attempt at masking the overwhelming feeling of despair settling deep in her bones. She did not leave me, she thought. She was taken from me! Who would have taken her? When? How? Why? Many thoughts went through her mind as she continued replaying their last night together, searching for clues. Each time, it seemed a shadow hung over her memory.

Anthony Mancuso's eyes followed Rob back to Clara. He was born and raised in the area with the family business of law enforcement. His father and grandfather had each remained local but his uncle and cousin had ventured out federally. His relief was evident when Dr. McDuffy finally arrived on his ATV with his assistant. He spoke briefly with the deputies before beginning his exam. Adam was taking pictures as the medical examiner slowly opened the material, fully exposing the skeletal remains. Based on the size and clothing, he silently guessed it was a young female. Due to the extensive decomposing of the body, he further guessed she was here for some time and unlikely to be any of the recent missing persons. He shook his head at the impossible task of identifying her.

Anthony's eyes returned to Clara sitting silently on the log. Newly separated from her husband, she relocated back to town with her young family just last week. As far as he knew, she had not been back since graduation and unlikely would be able to help further with the investigation. She did not need to be here for this. He walked over towards them, "You guys can head back to the farm. We'll be here for a bit. It'll take us some time to get an ID and move ahead with this."

"I know who it is," Clara whispered.

"Excuse me?" Anthony asked.

"What?" Rob responded at the same time.

"I recognize the cornflower blue cloth. She said it was her favorite." Her voice was soft as she stared toward the skeletal remains.

"Clara, what are you talking about?" Anthony squatted down in front of her.

"It's my mother. I put that cornflower blue tablecloth on the kitchen table myself. It was the last night I saw her. If you head straight down that hill, you will eventually be in the gardens of the Hawks House. She didn't leave me after all. All this time, everyone said she left me." Standing up, Clara tried to take a step forward but Anthony stood up with her. He stepped in front of her while Rob grabbed her arm to turn her around. Looking into her eyes, he saw she truly believed the remains they found were her mothers. Rob glanced up at his friend with raised eyebrows.

"It gives us a place to start," Anthony shrugged. Not properly preserved, a body would be fully decomposed down to the bones in twenty years, he thought to himself. "You two head back to the farm. We'll just need to get a DNA swab for testing. I know where to find you two. OK?" He asked as he glanced from Clara to Rob.

The guys each nodded in agreement. Rob gently pulled Clara in close for a hug. Closing her eyes, she tried to absorb some of his strength but when she felt the tears threatening to fall, she pulled away.

"I'm fine," Clara lied as she turned towards the horses.

"Are you going to be able to ride back or do you want to ride with me?" Rob asked as he eyed her closely. Just finding a full skeletal body was freaking him out. He couldn't imagine what she was feeling if she believed it was her mother.

"I rode her up here. I will ride her back. How else will the mare get home?" Clara strained to keep her tone controlled.

Rob nodded as he assisted her onto the horse. Riding beside her, it was the longest ride of his life.

. . . .

"It's so great to have you back where you belong," Evil sang as he slowly entered the kitchen. Already familiar with her kitchen set up, he opened the drawer storing her tea bags as he smiled. She still drinks the tea at night before bed, he thought with a smile. He pulled from his pocket the doctored tea, replacing hers. He continued looking into the refrigerator, helping himself to a water bottle. His eyes caught the time on the clock as he drank from the bottle. "Damn, Babydoll, time slows when we are apart. You should be back home soon."

He melted into the shadows to await her return home...

When they returned to the farm, Lila and the kids were sitting at the kitchen table coloring as Rob opened the back door for Clara. Lila watched as the children ran towards their mother. Clara kneeled down to hug each child close, eyes closed in attempts to keep the tears from falling. She wanted to be alone with them. She needed to call Jay to tell him her mother did not leave her... she took a deep breath and pulled away from Reese and Hailey as her son began a monologue of their adventures during the afternoon. She asked them if they were ready to head home. They each nodded.

"Do you want me to come with you?" Lila asked quietly as she stepped around from the table.

"I need to get them back and settle in for the evening. I need to get home," Clara shook her head as she declined the offer. *I need to get home before I totally lose it,* she thought to herself. *I need to keep myself together,* she repeated. *Need to keep it together.*

Lila raised her eyebrows in question as she looked over to her brother. Rob nodded his head as they both followed Clara and the kids out to her car. He stood in front of the driver's door as she buckled each child into their carseat. When she stood before him, she didn't say a word. He placed a hand gently under her chin to lift her face up towards him. Still, she didn't say a word. Her green eyes were wet but the tears didn't fall.

"Let me drive you home. Chase can pick me up. I just want to make sure you and the kids get home safe, alright?" When she nodded her head slightly in agreement, Rob gently brought his arm up to her shoulder to escort her around to the passenger side. As he walked back towards the driver's side, he paused a moment beside his sister. She nodded her head in agreement as she watched them drive away.

Dr. Connor Emerson was exhausted. After his evening shift in the emergency room, he was pulled into an emergency surgery. He was relieved it was successful but there were a few moments when it was touch and go. Already showered at the hospital, he just wanted to return home to sleep the rest of the day. Instead, he paused halfway up the back staircase leading to his loft on the second floor.

Camped outside his door was Tiffany Krause. Shit, so much for an easy breakup, Connor thought as he slowly ascended the rest of the stairs. Since he hadn't heard from her since Beth's funeral, it had been over a month, he thought he was officially in the clear.

Bored with the unexpected wait, she quickly posed into a suggestive position when she saw him climbing the stairs. Connor realized his younger version would have been amused and highly entertained to find a beautiful woman at his door wearing a sheer nightgown, leaving nothing to anyone's imagination.

"What the hell are you doing here?" Connor's voice was soft but the tone left a chill. The landing was shared with his brother's law firm. While it was a Saturday afternoon, he knew both his brother and nephew were likely inside. He saw their vehicles in the lot on his way in.

Tiffany slowly stood awkwardly, leaning back into the door, she shifted her hip out while she posed before him, speaking in her pouty voice, "You never called me."

"Seemed counterproductive, you said you would not answer if I did," he shrugged.

"I've missed you," she stated, still using her pouty voice as she advanced towards him.

At that moment, Connor realized the tone she used grated on his nerves and turned him off completely. It was why, when she attempted to win him over with this approach, he always lost interest. It had been fortunate that she didn't use it often. He held up his hands as he stated in a tired voice, "Tiffany, it's been a long night and an even longer day. I am not interested. Please cover yourself up and go."

The words were barely out of his mouth when the door opened behind him. While he would have preferred no one to witness this embarrassing moment, Connor silently prayed it was only his brother. As he looked over his shoulder, he saw the praying gods were not listening. His twenty-four-year-old nephew stood frozen at the doorway, obviously embarrassed to be walking into something.

"Uhh," Joshua Emerson attempted to clear his throat as he tried to sound worldly as he spoke, "Sorry to interrupt, Uncle Connor."

Connor simply sighed as he realized the kid couldn't seem to take his eyes off the woman standing, more or less, naked in front of them.

"Not a problem, Josh. I'm just going to steal your uncle away inside," Tiffany cooed as she attempted to reach for Connor's hand.

"Tiffany, I told you I'm not interested. Go home!" He jabbed his thumb over his shoulder toward the opened door as he continued, "That's Matt's place of work. This is a public area. If he sees you, he could have you arrested for indecent exposure. If one of his other sons comes out, the charges would include exposure to a minor. You could be labeled as a sex offender."

"But Connor," she attempted to sway his decision but he interrupted.

"Seriously, Tiffany. Put your jacket on and go home. Don't do this again. You're only accomplishing entertainment for the security company," Connor's voice expressed his annoyance as he nodded towards the cameras.

Both uncle and nephew watched as the woman grabbed her jacket from the rail and hurried towards the stairs as she yelled over her shoulders, "Don't expect me to answer the next time you call."

"As if I would even consider it," Connor softly stated, blocking his nephew from heading down the stairs. "I suggest you give her some time to leave the parking lot. You don't want her to get her tendrils in you."

"How do you get women to do that?" Josh asked in awe as he watched the woman turn at the bottom of the steps to don her coat. He remained staring as he silently appreciated the view. "And you just send her on her way?"

"You want women showing up at your doorstep scantily covered? What would your mother say?" Connor asked as he went over to close the door behind his nephew before going to his own. One would think this was a frequent occurrence the way the kid talked.

"Talia isn't my mother," Josh started.

"Yes, you keep saying that. I do mean your actual mother. She would hear of the scandal before you closed your bedroom door," Connor clarified as he went to unlock and enter his loft. Josh followed, closing the door behind them.

"You want a beer?" Connor asked from the refrigerator, pulling out two bottles. "What's going on?"

"Did you hear that new girl found a body, an actual dead body, today?"

"What new girl?"

"You know, the one that works at the nursing home."

"Clara?" He paused the bottle in midair to confirm.

His nephew, obviously relieved with the change in topics, gave what he already knew. While Josh talked, Connor wondered how much of the details provided were correct. He was sure he'd hear many versions. Being a small town, he was confident he would hear them all before the weekend was through. The fact it was Clara, gave the story more fuel. He didn't doubt the part where she and her old boyfriend Foxwood were riding on the trails, "You do realize she's not really new here."

"Yeah, I know. She grew up in the house next to ours. Dad says you are close to her," Josh commented.

Connor nodded absently as he checked a text message.

"Maybe you could introduce us," the younger man started.

Connor heard the interest in his voice and looked up to meet his nephew's eyes, "You'll likely meet her soon enough but I don't think she's your type."

"How can she not be my type?"

"Not only is she married but she's probably one of the last women in this town that would ever pull a stupid stunt like that," he gestured towards his back door. "Isn't she too old for you?"

"Hell no! She's only a few years older than me. If anyone's too old, it's you," Josh threw back.

Connor drank from his beer as he realized for the first time, Clara was actually closer to his nephew's age than his own. He wondered how his brother would react to his oldest son's infatuation with the daughter of a previous lover. "I guess too old isn't right. She's too mature for you. She has two children!"

Later that night, Clara sighed loudly in frustration as she hung up the phone. Jay was still not answering her calls. She left a message as she always did and hoped he would return her call after hearing her voice, knowing she needed him right now.

Expecting sleep to be very unlikely, Clara headed down the stairs to double check all the locks on the doors and windows. She closed the blinds. She thought a hot bath with a relaxing tea would be more calming but did not want to be alone in her thoughts. Instead, she pulled out the floor cloth to cover the floor and set up to paint the dining room…

. . . .

Watching as she moved around, Evil was surprised to see Clara was not turning in for the night. His girl never sleeps, he thought. She did look tired yesterday after work. She's fitting perfectly into his plans. He did leave recommendations for a divorce lawyer on her desk to help her get the process started. It was a shame she was the one to find the body, but now she'll have closure. Plus, the keys will be handed down and she'll finally be allowed to move back into her family home. Close to me, he thought. Disappointed she was not turning in for the night, he faded into the shadows and out of the house. As he returned home, he thought of the previous night when he was able to watch her sleep. The best way to ride out a storm, for now anyway, he chuckled. Her hair was spread out around her beautiful angelic face, rolled onto her side with a pillow, just as she did as a child. She had slept soundly through the night, hardly moving. Soon, everything will be as it was meant, Evil was sure of it.

she stole my watch

Monday morning, after dropping her children off at daycare, Clara stepped into the therapy room. She was surprised to see coffee brewing in the pot and Kim and Marie already at their desks working. They each stood to wish her good morning.

"Hey, girl! Quite the weekend you had. How are you holding up?" Kim asked. The word had spread about her finding a body up on the hillside but not who it might be. She was especially excited to hear about Clara's adventures while alone with one of the town's hottest bachelors.

Kim was the occupational therapist, recently separated from her husband in an on-off situation. She had moved out into her own home with her children but they continued to meet up. She was born and raised in the next town to the east. She was a few years older than Clara, and knew of her during high school. More accurately, she knew of the girl living in the big house with her father as her mother was rumored to have run off with her lover. But in the last week, she was quick to discover Clara was a good clinician and a fair boss.

Marie was a rehab tech. She did whatever needed to be done, processing the paperwork, transporting patients, or even helping out on the unit if needed. As a widow close to retirement, she didn't drool over the town gossip. It was always the same story but different details. Like most everyone else in the facility, she was local, born and raised in the rural area south of town. She lived alone in her old farm house on many acres of land with her adult children nearby with their own families. Clara's mother had been friends with one of her daughters. Marie was well aware of the few times Susannah Hawks had left town as a teenager for months at a time, but she didn't share the details with anyone else in the department.

Before Clara could give details about the weekend, there was a knock on the door. Eric stepped in, holding the door open as he eyed the others. He initially followed her into the therapy room to provide comfort but was suddenly feeling awkward. "Are you sure you want to be here? I can give you the day off."

"Don't be ridiculous! The patients are here for therapy, and therapy is what they will get," Clara responded. She needed to keep busy and work was guaranteed to deliver.

Later in the day, Kim was looking for her watch all over the therapy gym and office area.

"Has anyone seen my watch?" She asked the others. "I took it off to wash my hands. I swear I placed it on the counter next to the sink. But as I was drying my hands, one of the nurses asked me to assist with feeding Mr. Jones." She continued to look around all the items on the counter.

"We'll all keep an eye out for it," Clara absently answered.

Three days later, Clara and Marie were reviewing paperwork at her desk when Kim suddenly came into the gym, closed the door behind her and announced, "That bitch is wearing my watch!"

"What?"

"That bitch Lauren, the CNA with blond hair and too much makeup. I can just kill her right now! She was on this floor the other day when I lost my watch. She is now wearing it. Come with me down to Eric's office. I am so angry right now!" She exclaimed, shaking her fists in frustration.

Before she could enter the hall, Clara grabbed Kim's arm. "Wait. Don't go barging into his office like this. You need to take a deep breath and keep it together. I agree, we need to report her. But don't go around saying you'll kill her. With your luck, she'll end up dead in a week and everyone will look at you!"

Marie chuckled, "She's right, Kim. The last thing you need is bad karma."

Kim nodded her head as she closed her eyes and breathed. After breathing deeply for a few minutes, she appeared calmer. "You're right," she agreed. "He's likely to fire me for going after someone he's sleeping with."

Clara paused in mid stride at the door, "Do you know that for a fact or are you purely speculating?"

"Oh, come on, Clara! How can you be so naïve?" Kim responded with a slight snort. "Everyone knows it. His SUV has been at her place in the evening for the last few weeks."

"I wasn't aware he was dating anyone," Clara responded as she looked over at Marie who simply shrugged, not really caring either way.

"I didn't say they were dating," Kim answered back. When she saw the confused look, she further explained. "They are never out together in public. It started after his girlfriend broke up with him and returned to her hometown. Rumor had it he was about to propose to her."

"Really? When was that?" Clara asked.

"Last month, she was the PT you replaced," Kim explained as she grinned at her friend. "I think he has a thing for physical therapists."

"Kim, stop the gossiping," Marie advised.

"There's nothing going on between us. He grew up in the house next door," Clara was quick to explain. The idea of something between her and Eric was down right ridiculous if not nauseating.

"Well, I have to admit I believe you. Though the boy next door has a nicer ring to it, the other guy after you is much hotter," she stated, pausing to clarify, "You have the farmer hot on your trail anyway. He's a much better catch."

Clara was going to remind her she was married and not looking for anyone but Kim was already out the door and halfway down the hall before she could get her wits about her. Best to not bring it up again, she thought as she headed down the hall to Eric's office.

The nursing home was an outdated three story building built into a hill. If entering from the parking lot in the back, her therapy gym appeared to be on the first floor. But if one entered from the front entrance, it was in the basement. The top two floors hosted the residents and each had nurses' stations at the center. The basement held her gym, the kitchen, and the administrative offices. It also had the laundry room across the hall, activities room/dining room for the residents. The end of the hall was storage and central supply. An old elevator was in the middle of the hall, and a staircase on either end of the building. Since the front rooms had minimal windows, the lighting was poor, giving the hall a gloomy presence.

With Kim at her side, Clara knocked softly on Eric's office door. He was sitting at his desk reading over papers. He glanced up and smiled when he saw Clara standing at the door. He felt a slight irritation as his eyes moved to Kim standing beside her.

"Come in. What can I do for you, ladies?" He asked, keeping his eye on Clara.

They both stepped into the office. Kim sat down on one of the chairs facing the desk while Clara closed the office door. Eric raised an eyebrow in silent question as Clara sat beside her co-worker. She looked over and nodded.

Taking a deep breath and letting it out, Kim explained how she recently lost her watch, and had now observed it on Lauren's wrist just a few minutes ago. Eric sighed as he lifted his phone to call the nurse supervisor. He requested she come down to his office and to bring

Lauren with her.

"Come in," he called out to the knock on his door a few moments later.

It was opened by Susan, the day shift nurse supervisor. Clara liked Susan. She was twenty years older and had short brown hair worn to her chin. She was dressed in the required uniform of blue scrubs with a blue lab coat over. Her eyes often sparkled as she spoke of events from her life. Like others, she was raised in the area and had relatives not only working here she also had family that lived at the facility long term. She stepped into the office, closed the door after them.

Lauren was dressed in deep forest green scrubs, making her skin appear pale yellow. Her sparse blond hair was down but brushed away from her face. She was very thin without any curves causing her face to be angular and her green eyes to appear concave. Without a word, she scanned the room as she entered.

Eric stepped around his desk and greeted the women, gesturing to them to sit on the couch. Once seated, he began, "That's a lovely watch there, Lauren. Where did you get it?"

"I bought it at Walmart," she replied.

"Do you still have the receipt?" He casually asked.

"What's this about?" Lauren asked as she protectively covered her wrist with her other hand.

"Kim has reported that her watch went missing from the therapy gym on Monday. Now you are wearing it." Eric explained quietly as he gestured towards her.

Clara was pleasantly surprised by his professionalism.

"She's lying. This is my watch," Lauren responded in an offensive tone.

"That watch was my last birthday gift from my mother before she died. It was purchased at Zellner's Jewelry Store in the next town over. If you don't believe me, look at the serial number on the back. I have it written down here." She handed the paper to Eric. She previously called the jeweler to confirm the serial number in preparation for reporting it missing to her insurance company.

He accepted the paper while gesturing for Lauren to hand him the watch in question. In fine print, he read Zellner's Jewelry with the serial number on the back of the watch. "Zellner's Jewelry" Eric read out loud, "And it's a match."

Everyone looked over to Lauren, simply shrugging her shoulders.

"Can I hold on to this until the police arrive?" he asked. Kim nodded as both Clara and Kim stood. Eric nodded in dismissal as he reached for the phone, gesturing for the others to remain sitting.

Kim and Clara returned to the gym and closed the door behind them.

"I can't believe the nerve! To say she bought that at Walmart. I mean really. I forgot the jeweler's name was right there on the watch!" exclaimed Kim.

"She really isn't too smart," agreed Clara. "She was pretty shocked about having to turn the watch over, almost like she thought she could win the argument. But keep in mind, we cannot be gossiping about this here with everyone. The police are going to have to do a full investigation. If she is willing to take a watch when you look away for a moment, what would she be willing to take from the residents upstairs that cannot speak up?"

Nodding in agreement, Kim returned to her desk to complete her morning paperwork and plan for her afternoon.

Later that day, Connor was answering a text while walking beside his nephew when Josh suddenly stopped with a gasp. Connor came to a full stop as he looked over, expecting something terrible had happened.

"She's here!" Josh announced as he brought his hands up in an attempt to quickly comb over his hair and then patted his chest. "Do I look alright?"

"What?" Connor asked distractedly. Josh simply nodded his head in the direction of the nurse's station. Sitting behind the counter, Clara was writing in a patient's chart. "Yes, she certainly is here. She should be here, she works here."

He glanced back at Josh, still trying to improve his appearance, and he chuckled. Man, he has it bad for her. Connor was surprised to see his nephew's behavior revert back to an insecure teenager. He hated to be the one to burst the poor guy's bubble but he just didn't see anything happening between them. The Clara he knew would never have a casual relationship with someone like his nephew, he was a bit too self-absorbed. But so are you, he thought to himself, especially at that age.

"You have to introduce me, Uncle Connor," he pleaded.

"What are you, fifteen?" Connor chuckled as he continued ahead with the besotted following in his wake. "Hello Clara, it's about time we ran into each other while working, just like the good old days."

She uttered a distracted hello as she belatedly looked up to see the medical director, Dr. Connor Emerson, smiling down as he leaned onto the counter. Beside him was a young man also dressed in a white lab coat. He simply smiled as she looked back and forth between the two men. Clara was surprised by the sudden intense feeling she had when her eyes met Connor's. In an attempt to not make it awkward, she finally opened her mouth, "Hello, Dr. Emerson."

Connor chuckled again and his eyes narrowed a bit as he wondered what was going through her mind. He gestured between the two, "Clara, have you met Josh? He's my new resident and will be my sidekick for a while. Josh, Clara."

"Hello Josh," she greeted politely. "How is it going, being his sidekick? Learning a lot?"

"Hi Clara, it's great to finally meet you," The words slowly stumbled out as the younger man felt his heart beat faster.

"What is all the excitement going on? I saw the police escorting an aide out of the building when I came in," Connor wondered out loud as his brown eyes seemed to ask more questions than he actually stated.

"You'll need to talk to Eric," Clara replied dismissively. Standing up, she replaced the chart before turning to head back to her desk in the gym downstairs.

"Wait here, I'll be right back," Connor instructed Josh as he walked beside Clara, adjusting his gait to match hers. "I had hoped to run into you before this. How are you transitioning back to the slow pace?"

Clara paused just before she reached the door leading to the stairwell, "Fine."

"Yeah? I heard what happened this weekend. That had to be difficult, finding a body," he commented as he studied her, again wondering what she was thinking.

Clara was momentarily startled by the hidden question. Pausing a moment before answering, reminding herself it was Connor Emerson, not someone she barely knew, "It was not the brightest moment of my day. How did you hear about it?"

"My nephew told me," he answered honestly with a gesture back towards the nurses' station.

"Your nephew?" Her green eyes moved down the hall for a moment as she studied the younger man. She remembered when Connor announced he was an uncle, showing her pictures of a baby and occasionally pictures of a young child over the years. She turned back, "He's your nephew? Really? I can remember the first time you told me about him. How old is he?"

"Yes, he's Matt's oldest and he's twenty-four," Connor confirmed. "He decided to go against his parents' wishes and went to med school instead of law school. Proudest moment in his life was when he asked me how to tell his dad. You were only five years old when he was born, do you really remember that?"

"Yeah, you just came home with your parents after he was born. I remember coming over when you were sitting out on the porch. It was in the spring, right? I don't think I ever met him until now. I thought he was much younger than me."

"Clara, you were only five years old, I'm impressed you remember at all," he answered.

"I remember a lot of things. Matt and his wife are both lawyers?" She asked stupidly as she searched her brain for any previous talk about Matt and his family. "Do I know her?"

"Well, she's his ex-wife. His current wife isn't a lawyer," Connor confirmed.

"How many times has he been married?"

"Three, none are from here." He explained before asking, "Was the body partially buried?"

"No, she wasn't buried when we found her but she had been. All the rain from last week must have washed the dirt away. She was wrapped in a tablecloth except," she paused a moment as she heard her voice crack. Clara took a deep breath before continuing. "She wasn't partially decayed. Listen, I'd love to hang out and talk but I need to get back to work."

"Clara, I would like to take you out to dinner. How does this Friday sound?" Connor quickly asked, side stepping in front of her.

Caught by surprise, Clara came to a sudden stop just before she opened the door and looked up at him. They were raised in houses next door to each other. He was older than her, already away to college before she started middle school. She had enjoyed watching him play basketball from her bedroom window when he was home on summer breaks. When her green eyes met his amused brown, she felt the familiar butterflies in her stomach. But the rise in her heart rate was something new. While they had run into each other over the years, she was still caught off guard by the invitation. It felt like more than a casual dinner between lifelong friends.

"I am flattered, really, but no thank you, I am married," she informed him quietly.

Connor smiled as he noticed her blush in embarrassment, "I don't see him around town. He didn't move back here with you. But if you need more time, I understand. Think about it. We can go a few towns over to keep the gossip minimal. Let me know." He winked at her as he started to walk away but stopped and turned just as she opened the door to the stairwell. Placing his hand on her arm he asked, "Clara, what do you mean the body wasn't partially decayed."

"Her skeletal remains," she whispered sadly before she descended down the stairs, leaving Connor behind, immobile and totally astounded. It wasn't what she said but the way she said it that caused the hair on his neck to raise as his eyes followed her until she was gone.

When Connor returned to Josh, his nephew was eager with questions, "Well, what did she say?"

"About what?" Connor asked confused as he reached for a chart.

"About me!"

"Why do you think we were talking about you?"

"She kept looking at me while you two were talking."

"Yeah, she can't believe how big you've gotten. She remembers when you were a baby," Connor teased.

"She remembers me as a baby?" Josh asked, disappointment evident in his voice.

"Says you two never actually met. She just remembers you from pictures," he patted his shoulders in mocking sympathy. "How are you so head over heels about her if you don't even know her?"

"I remember watching her from the window once when we came to visit," Josh explained as he followed his uncle down the hall. "She's even more beautiful close up."

Connor nodded agreement.

The night started out peacefully. Clara dreamed of a young local girl raised with a poor background and hard upbringing. She always went for the easier way. She stepped out of her house and walked in the shadows towards the park. He was waiting for her when she arrived.

He didn't say a word as she stepped into the vehicle. The car quickly pulled away as soon as the door was shut. She chanced a look over at him but noted his mood. He was pissed. She figured she would be able to work her magic when they arrived at their spot. Once he parked, she stepped out and followed behind him on the narrow trail. She chuckled to herself as she glanced down and noticed the shoe covers worn by those in surgery. He always worried about the mud. Can't risk getting his $400 dollar shoes dirty now, can he? Suddenly, he turned around, one arm around her neck and the other hand reached around to cover her mouth, softening any scream that could escape. Within seconds, she was seeing black...

Clara sat up in her bed, her eyes wide open as she breathed heavily. She brought one hand up to her neck and the other to push her hair from her eyes. It was just a dream, just a dream, she tried to reassure herself. She thought she saw a shadow pass by her bed into the opened bedroom door as she slowly sat to the edge of bed. She leaned over to turn on the bedside lamp. Standing, she hesitantly walked out into the hall. Before she went across the hall into Reese's room, she stopped when she smelled a familiar fragrance. She closed her eyes and sniffed again, attempting to place it but she could no longer smell it.

Clara quickly peeked into each child's room before heading down the hall. Since she didn't put her hearing aids on, there was no chance she would hear the main front door slowly open and close. Nor did she hear the chain quietly clattering when it was quickly undone. The chain was still and hanging noiselessly when Clara walked by on her way into the kitchen to start the coffee.

It never dawned on her that the front door was not as she left it the night before.

late night visit

The following Monday, Clara was looking over her schedule for the day. She looked up to see Kim entering the gym, "Good morning, Kim. How was your weekend?"

"What's wrong," Clara asked, noticing her friend's pale look.

"Marie just called me. Have you talked to her yet?" Noticing Clara shake her head, Kim continued. "She was out for her morning walk and found a body floating in the pond behind her house!"

"What? Does she know who it is?" Clara asked in total shock.

Kim just shook her head, "She didn't go into details. She just said the police were at her place and that she would be late getting in, if at all. She tried calling you but assumed you were either dropping the kids off or in the shower. She didn't want to leave a message so she called me instead."

Trying to focus on the patients during the day, Clara's mind kept returning to the recent events since she moved back to town. It hadn't even been a month yet. In that time, she found skeletal remains in the woods behind her family home and a co-worker found a body in her pond. What the hell? Did she do the right thing, returning home? This did not seem to be a safer community to raise her children in.

That night, after the children were in bed, Clara was debating a hot bath or a cup of tea when the doorbell rang. She paused for a moment as she stepped into the dining room, looking at the front door. While it was still fairly early in the night, it was on the late side for her to be receiving visitors. She felt her heart beat faster as her anxiety played reasons for the late visitor.

Don't borrow trouble, she reminded herself. Focus on the present and what you know, don't dwell on what may not even happen. She slowly advanced toward the front door, peeking out of the window. She recognized Anthony Mancuso and his father, the sheriff. Both were still dressed in work uniforms. Clara stepped back a moment as she closed her eyes to take a deep breath before turning on the porch light as she opened the door, "Good evening, Anthony, Mr. Mancuso".

They both nodded politely as she opened the screen door, suddenly nervous. The gentlemen both removed their hats as they stepped inside. Clara quietly closed the door as she gestured towards the family room, sensing the uneasiness as each watched her sit down in the chair opposite them. The younger Mancuso began.

"Clara, we are sorry to stop in so late in the evening. We are here to inform you that the ID was completed today. It was your mother that you found in the woods. I am so sorry." Anthony broke off when he noted a tear sliding down her cheek.

His father took over, speaking quietly, "We are investigating the disappearance of your mother. Apparently, foul play was never suspected when she disappeared twenty years ago. What do you remember?"

Sitting on the chair with her feet up on the seat, her arms around her legs, Clara wiped the tears from her cheek with her knees. With clarity as if it were only yesterday, she talked of her last evening with her mother. She talked of helping her mother finish the laundry, folding the white bathroom towels, placing them in the laundry basket, and leaving it on the dryer; eating her favorite dinner of beef on Weck sandwiches; making plans for the next day; helping her mother clear the dishes from the table, cleaning off the table; placing the cornflower blue tablecloth onto the table, rearranging the flowers in the vase; and reading Little Women together as they both sat on her bed. "The next morning, my mom wasn't there. As soon as I entered the kitchen, I knew something was wrong."

"Why?" Mr. Mancuso asked.

"Because the kitchen smelled of bleach, the tablecloth was different; the flowers were gone. I never saw the glass vase again. In the laundry room, the laundry basket was empty and the towels were in the washing machine, still wet and waiting to be put into the dryer. I helped her with the laundry that day. I swear I had folded them. There was no reason for them to be back in the washer. And if there was, she would not have allowed them to sit wet in the washer all night. Never."

Clara had paused for a moment as she lifted her green eyes up to the sheriff, "But mostly, I knew something was wrong because she was not there. My mother would never have left me alone."

Nodding, the sheriff looked over at his son. "Clara, do you want me to call someone for you?"

"No, that's ok," she answered with a shake of her head. "I knew it was her when I saw the blue tablecloth."

Clara followed the sheriff and deputy to the door. She decided to leave the porch light on but locked the door, turned the bolt and replaced the chain. She turned around and walked throughout the downstairs, checking and double checking the locks before heading upstairs to peek in on her kids. Hailey was sprawled out in her toddler bed with her baby doll tight in her arms. Clara quietly reached down for the blanket to cover her. When she looked in on Reese, he was lying prone with his arms hanging over the sides of the bed. Clara headed across the hall to her room. She sat on the bed. Without thinking, she reached for the phone to call her husband.

"Hey Jason, it's me. The sheriff just left. It's been confirmed. It really was my mother that I found. Can you call me? I really need you right now, Jay. Please call me." She hung up the phone, slid down from her bed to sit on the floor and allowed herself to cry.

It was after midnight when Connor arrived home from a long shift at the hospital. When he had stepped out from surgery, he had been surprised to find the Sheriff with his son Anthony waiting for him. They had questions regarding the disappearance of Susannah Gibson from over twenty years ago. He felt it was a bit late to be initiating a murder investigation. Connor had debated on the drive home to stop over at Clara's but decided he would check in on her in the morning. Just as he placed his cell on the charger, he heard footsteps on the back stairs. He sighed in frustration. He wasn't expecting company. He glanced over at the security monitor and sighed. It was going to be an even longer night...

Exhausted from the emotional strain, Clara collapsed into bed. Not expecting to sleep, her mind drifted. And she was once again a young girl, turning restlessly in her bed but paused when she realized the room was cold as her body shivered in the chilly air. The sudden chill was always her first warning. The second was the smell, which she later learned was stale alcohol weeping from one's pores. That was when the shadow would emerge into her room from the wall. She kept her eyes closed as she focused on her breathing, pretending to be sleeping. Sometimes she would feel the mattress sag, as if the shadow had weight as it sat beside her. But she always felt the cold touch to her forehead as a curl was moved away from her face. Her body would, more or less, sag to the side closer to the shadow as it seemed to lean towards her. This is when her heart paused as she held her breath. She could feel the dried sandpapery lips touch her skin as it kissed her forehead. She could feel a soft breeze onto her face, but the whispering words were lost on her deaf ears. For this, she was always grateful. Who would want to hear the damning words of the Evil shadow? Occasionally, she felt the covers pulling up but never, ever, did she open her eyes as she patiently waited for the shadow to fade. Not able to fall back asleep, she burrowed deeper under her covers as she waited for the light of dawn to melt the Evil shadow…

Clara sat up suddenly, looking around her room in the dim light. It's alright, she told herself. It was just a dream from her childhood. A damn realistic nightmare, she corrected, as her mind replayed the common scene over again. It never failed to amaze her how this one dream always felt so real. There were a few differences over the years. Her mind refused to entertain the idea it was something more. It started when she was young and continued until she left for college. Then the dreams stopped, until now. Great, my stupid childhood nightmares are anchored to this stupid town, she thought as she pushed back the covers.

She didn't hear the soft footsteps in the hall or the slight squeak of the fourteenth step as the shadow faded into the darkness downstairs…

don't need to be alone

Clara was up and about early the next morning as if it was just another day. She had not even bothered to return to her bed in the wee hours of the night, choosing instead to sit in Hailey's room, rocking as she watched her daughter sleep.

Clara struggled to keep herself together as she assisted her children with getting ready. After she dropped them off at daycare, she stopped in the funeral home at the edge of town. She wasn't sure when they would release her mother. They had her for over a week but Clara felt she should just deal with this now. She arranged for a small memorial service as everyone was so sure she ran off. No one but me believed that she was actually missing. They don't get to come and mourn her passing from twenty years ago, Clara thought as she decided to wait until after work to contact her friends. She wasn't ready to be comforted nor could she talk about it.

Once she parked her car at work, Clara sat a few minutes, trying to assure she could keep herself together before she slowly walked into the building, down the hall, and into her therapy gym. She was surprised to find she was the first one in.

"What are you doing here?"

Startled by the voice behind her, she turned around. Eric had followed her into the room.

"I work here. Where else would I be?" Clara wondered. "Do you know where everyone else is? My department seems to not be here."

"Kim is down at the sheriff's office giving her statement. Marie is still at home, keeping an eye on her property since it's a crime scene, I guess. I mean, why are you here? You should take time off. You just found out your mother is gone," he patiently explained as he awkwardly squeezed her shoulder.

"Eric, I appreciate the offer," Clara unconsciously stepped back as she spoke. "But I need to work. First of all, I don't have PTO time yet. I just started. Secondly, my mother has been gone for twenty years, more than enough time to adjust."

"What about your dad? How is he taking this?" Eric changed the subject as his hand dropped down, unaware of the discomfort his touch caused.

"I honestly don't know. I haven't called him. He believed she left us. Looking back, he was devastated but he didn't seem surprised, just disappointed," she shrugged her shoulders and sighed. "I'm sure his girlfriend will be happy he can now get married but she has to know, there is no money. He has no rights to the house."

"You didn't call him?" Eric asked, surprised.

"We aren't close," Clara shrugged. "I was a hindrance, a means of providing shelter, a mighty good shelter with all expenses paid but I was also an anchor that impeded his ability to move on and have a family with his girlfriend," she explained, feeling the agitation rise in her that she was trying to forgive but would never forget.

"Besides, I suspect he may be a person of interest. The sheriff said he would inform him in person. Probably to gauge his reaction." Clara pulled her desk chair out as she felt a sudden need to sit, weighed down by her grief.

Eric had followed her. Leaning back onto the desk facing her, he reached for her hand, "No one knows better than I the craziness of the trust with regards to the house. I get it. I grew up next to you. But if there is anything I can do, just let me know. Take time off if you need it. I can call Jerry," referring to a retired physical therapist that would cover as needed for short durations.

"He would be able to cover for you. Let me know if you need anything," he said quietly as he squeezed her hand. Once Clara quietly nodded her head, he left.

Clara remained deep in thought, too distracted to focus on her work. When she suddenly felt a hand on her shoulder, she jumped with a startled scream as she quickly turned around.

Standing before her was Connor, her childhood neighbor and, though she would never admit it out loud, her lifelong crush. Her mind quickly put a lid on the last thought when her green eyes met his always amused brown.

"Clara, I'm so sorry. I didn't mean to startle you," Connor paused as he stepped back to give her a moment to collect herself. He noted the red puffy eyes with the dark circles underneath. "I just wanted to stop in to offer my condolences. Is there anything I can do for you? Go with you to make arrangements?"

Clara, feeling the tears close to surfacing again, could only shake her head. She took a moment to pull herself together before she could allow herself to speak. When she did, her voice was very soft and cautious, "I already went this morning. I haven't told anyone yet. How has the word spread already?"

"The sheriff and Anthony stopped in to see me last night. They had a few questions about the morning your mother went missing," Connor answered. He was not aware she wrongly assumed he told his cousin. He slowly stepped forward as Clara remained silent, too focused on maintaining her composure. When she did not retreat, he pulled her in for a hug.

Without any warning, Clara felt herself enveloped into strong warm arms. She lost all attempts to control her grief and sobbed into his shirt.

Connor remained quiet as he held her. He had questions but wasn't sure if he dared ask. After a few minutes he broached the uncomfortable topic, "Will your husband be coming into town?"

"Doubtful, he has been avoiding direct contact with me," she hiccupped into his shirt.

Without a word, Connor reached for her bag and grabbed her hand as he pulled her out of the room, down the hall and out to the parking lot to his SUV. He opened the passenger door to assist her in. He even snapped her seatbelt in place. As he stepped around towards the driver's side, Connor paused for a moment to make a call before getting into his seat. Once he pulled out of the lot, he noted in the rearview mirror a blue pickup truck pulling into the lot.

Connor smiled to himself as he quickly navigated the side streets to a parking lot in the back of the stores and restaurants on Main Street. He walked back around, reached for her hand to guide her up a flight of stairs to his loft. Once the door was unlocked, he turned off the alarm and closed the door. He stopped when they arrived in the kitchen. He gently guided Clara onto a stool at the island of the kitchen before he stepped around to make coffee.

As he waited for the coffee to brew, Connor watched Clara once again attempt to pull herself together. Once the pot was full, he poured a mug half full with cream before adding the coffee, and a second mug he kept black. He placed the one with cream in front of her and waited.

Clara suddenly looked around, as if not aware how she got there, "Why did you bring me here? I can't be here. I need to get back. I have things I need to do."

Connor reached across the counter for her hand, "Clara, I called Eric and told him you need to take some time. Your children are at daycare and you already made the arrangements. You need to take some time for yourself right now."

He was relieved when he saw her green eyes flash with anger as she pulled her hand back, "Who are you to pull me out of work and tell me what I need right now. You don't get to say where I need to be or what I should be doing!"

"Clara, you don't need to deal with work right now. I know you have always suspected something sinister happened to your mother. I can't even imagine what you're going through. No one, especially you, should have to go through it alone."

Clara felt the emotions of the last couple of months finally reach their peak. She was preparing to give him a piece of her mind when her cell vibrated on the counter next to her. She only looked to assure it wasn't the daycare before letting it go to her voicemail.

Connor leaned over to read the caller ID then watched her debate picking it up. "It's your boyfriend. You better answer or he'll worry and keep calling."

Her green eyes glared at him as she reached for the phone. As she did when she was a teenager, she became defensive when Connor used the nickname. "He's not my boyfriend. Hello."

"Clara, I just heard they confirmed it was your mother. I am so sorry," Rob's voice came over the line. He paused a moment before continuing. When Clara did not respond, he continued, "I stopped by your place and then work but Eric said he gave you the rest of the week off."

"Yeah, I guess I just need some time. I'm fine," she answered with irritation in her voice.

Rob couldn't quite read the tone. He was sitting in the lot behind the facility looking at her car. Where could she be? Clara had always been a private person, opening up to very few people. Lila hadn't yet returned from work, and Rachel and Shannon were still in the city. He wasn't even sure if they had heard the news. "Do you need a ride or anything? Anything I can do for you?"

"Nothing to do right now, but thanks," Clara was not quite able to pull in her irritation as she answered.

"No? How about I stop over with dinner later," he suggested, correctly reading the tone in her voice.

"That will be fine. I will see you then," she hung up the phone before he could say anything more. Clara tossed the phone back onto the counter and raised her eyes back up to Connor's.

He was leaning back against the opposite counter with his arms folded across his chest as he watched her interaction with Rob. Some things never change, he thought.

"I can't stay here, I need to leave," Clara stood up and began to pace restlessly as she ranted. Connor came around the counter to sit, allowing her to vent her emotions as she appeared to switch from anger to grief and back again. "Why is the sheriff's department now conducting an investigation? Why not when my mother went missing twenty years ago? All these years I had to endure people believing my mother left me for a lover? My mother chose her lover over me? But why would people believe that? Why did she have to be the one to leave? It had been my mother's family home, not my father's!"

"And where is he now?" Clara turned around to face Connor as she yelled the last question. He wasn't sure if she was still talking about her father, the killer or even the lover. "Where the hell is he? We don't even know. It's been twenty years! Will they even care enough to catch him? He was so heartless, he just dragged her out into the hills while she was breathing her last breaths and left her alone all this time wrapped up in her favorite cornflower blue tablecloth. The terror and pain she felt as she laid there dying!"

Clara's hand came over her mouth as a sob escaped and she could not stop seeing the image of her mother's skeletal remains. Her over active mind played out her mother's final moments before she was laid to unrest. She was freaked out at the vivid details of her mother lying, bleeding as she was placed on the blue cornflower table cloth...

Knowing the woman before him all her life, Connor was very aware of Clara's overactive imagination. He believed her comments were reactive and did not pause to consider she was speaking of a memory. Connor inwardly cringed as he thought of her seeing her mother's remains lying in the mud. Even though she hinted at it the week before, he still went to Anthony to confirm the details. No one should ever see that. She must be having nightmares again. He slowly advanced towards her and wrapped his arms around her.

But the touch seemed to bring Clara back to her ranting as she stepped back from him with a puny push into his chest as she yelled, "What do you care? Who are you to care?"

When she couldn't back up any further due to the wall, her knees gave out and she started to slide down towards the floor.

Connor sat beside her, holding her as she cried. It was a moment before he heard her whisper softly, "I am so scared, Connor."

It was a bit of time before he was able to coax her from the floor and back into her seat at the counter. Connor was going to dump her coffee and refresh it but she stated it was alright. She preferred it cooler than too hot anyway.

They sat in silence as she stared into her mug. Clara didn't know what to do with her hands so she cradled her mug and slowly sipped.

"What's going on with your husband?" Connor calmly asked, partly to change the subject but mostly because he was curious. When he first learned she was returning home, he expected Jason would come as well. He was not yet acknowledging his reasons for wondering.

"I don't know. Jay doesn't answer any of my calls," Clara started with a shrug. And because talking of her husband diminished the mental images of her mother, she fully opened up about the marriage. She told him of the flower deliveries, the hang up calls and the arguments. Clara spoke of the last argument before he grabbed his wallet, cell and keys and left. The last time she ever saw him. She talked about all the phone calls and text messages she's left, how she calls daily to give him an update on the lives of her and their children. And how he usually responds with only a simple text message about once a week. Without realizing it, she shared more details with Connor than she had with anyone else, as she did when she was a child.

Connor heard the sadness as she talked about being abandoned again for the second time in her life.

When Clara looked back down into her mug, she realized it was empty. He grabbed it without a word and refilled it. Connor had a shift at the hospital later in the evening so he switched to water in case he had emergency surgeries.

When he placed the mug back in front of her, Clara smiled softly in thanks. She felt the familiar flutter as she did when she was younger. But now, she didn't know how to respond to it so she chose to ignore it. She closed her eyes and breathed in slowly before exhaling. She opened her eyes again to see his soft brown eyes gently smile into her green.

"Feel any better?" He asked.

"Not really," she answered as she leaned forward to prop an elbow on the counter, resting her chin in her hand as she played with her mug. Just as she did when she was younger, Connor thought.

"Sounds to me like you have a stalker," he began as Clara stood up.

"No, I don't. Who would be interested in me? I lead a boring life and that's probably what happened. Jason got tired of me and left," she stated firmly. Clara couldn't even allow her mind to entertain any other possibilities. She looked around her.

"Through the doors on the right," he gestured towards the bathroom. "Clara, you want something else to drink?"

While he mixed her drink, Connor thought about all the things she said. He had met Jason O'Reilly. He had always made it a point to check in on Clara when she was at college. He had been relieved to find her transition was smooth and she was making friends while maintaining the closeness with her childhood friends. He had been confident she would never return.

When he learned she was returning home without her spouse, Connor was shocked. In the city he would often meet up with her for coffee or occasional lunch when both of their schedules allowed it. Jason was a good guy, exactly what she needed. His personality complemented hers. When he saw them together, Connor could see how they felt about each other. Clara was relaxed and comfortable with him. And Jason absolutely adored her. That was when he knew it was time to step back. But he also knew a guy like that would never just up and leave his family. Maybe he'd want to divorce his wife but Jason would be the kind of guy with one of the most civil divorces in history. And no way in hell would he just up and leave his kids. No way in hell. He'd talk to his cousin.

As the day progressed, Connor had relocated Clara to the living room as she just rambled on, as she did as a young child. It always amused him how she was reserved but once he asked a key question, the lid came off and she would talk for hours. Granted, the key question usually varied but once he asked it, he learned a lot about those in her life, school and the town. Or college when she was older. There were always two exceptions, the father and the boyfriend. Those were the only two topics she wouldn't openly talk about, at least not with him. Connor understood her issues with her father, to a point. But he wasn't sure exactly about Rob Foxwood. He was fairly confident Foxwood and Clara were never actually intimate but he knew they were always close.

When the topic turned to shadows, Connor realized it was a sure sign Clara needed food. He called downstairs to Memories, a locally owned restaurant specializing in sandwiches during the day and home cooked meals in the evening with a full bar as the night progressed. It was one of the more popular hangouts.

When the food arrived, Clara followed him towards the breakfast nook off the kitchen. He set up the sandwiches on plates as she checked her sandwich.

"Is something wrong with your sandwich? You didn't go vegan, did you?"

"No, I was going to take out the tomatoes but there aren't any," she answered as she put it back together before taking a bite.

"I ordered it without the tomatoes," Connor explained as he gestured to her to continue with her story.

"I am telling you Connor, the shadow would just appear out of nowhere. I would be awakened by this sudden coldness and I knew it was there in my room with me. I would feel a gentle tap on the bed and knew it was right next to me, staring. I would keep my eyes closed so I wouldn't have to see the violent blue eyes. It would always lean down and touch my hair before going down the hall," Clara stated before she lifted her sandwich for another bite.

Connor had been eating his sandwich quietly but paused for a moment. She used to tell him about the shadow as if it were a dream but now, it presented as more of a memory, "How do you know the color of the eyes if your eyes were closed?"

"Not really sure," Clara answered thoughtfully. "But you know how in dreams, you know things but don't know how? It's like that, I guess. I just know his eyes are violent and evil."

"Clara, did this shadow hurt you in any way, ever?"

"Not me, no," she dismissed with a shake of her head.

"Did it ever talk to you? Did you hear anything?"

"No. Hello! Hearing impaired! You know I don't hear anything without my hearing aids," she commented sarcastically.

Connor decided against reminding her she told him many times she wasn't hearing impaired in her dreams. Clara loved dreaming at night because she could always hear and never missed out on conversations.

"But it did have a smell. I would occasionally be out somewhere and smell the same odor and I would immediately think of this dream," she stated thoughtfully. She dismissed with a wave of her hand before she continued. "I tried to follow it a few times when I wasn't so frozen in fear, you know how dreams are."

"Yeah? Where did it go?" Connor asked intrigued, as when she was a child. The details and his questions had not changed over the years as she talked about the frequent recurrent dream. He used to wonder if it were simply her father, checking in on her before he went to bed at night. She was as young as six when she first started reporting the dream. Occasionally she followed it and other times, she would burrow deeper into her bed.

"I don't know. I usually lost it to the light," Clara answered with a shrug. "Once, I thought it went into my parents' room and another time I followed it down the back stairs…"

Connor's eyes squinted when she paused mid sentence. He thought she had a moment of panic but it was quickly gone. And he wondered, did she see something? Is she remembering something about her mother? When she did not finish her sentence, he raised his eyebrow in question.

Clara simply shrugged dismissively, "I don't know but the dream was so frequent back then. And I had it again last night. I couldn't go back to sleep. I didn't even try."

"What did you do?"

"I rocked while Hailey slept," she responded.

"Why didn't you call me? I could have kept you company, especially if you don't want to sleep alone," Connor asked.

"Connor, why would I call you in the middle of the night? First, I don't have your number," she paused as he motioned for her cell. He turned it on, then held it in front of her face to unlock it by facial recognition. Then he pulled up her contact information. Connor inputted his private cell, work cell, loft number and office numbers. He also added his email address. Then he called himself from her cell so he also had her number.

He placed the phone back down next to her glass. Connor noted it was empty as he reached over and held it up in question. When she nodded her head in agreement, he went to refill her glass.

When the afternoon grew late, Connor had Clara call the daycare to inform them he would be picking up her kids. Before they headed out, he pulled her in for a hug. As he held her close, "Remember, you don't need to be alone. I am here. I am whoever you want me to be."

When Clara stepped back, she had tears in her eyes again. He wiped a tear with his thumb as he kissed her forehead.

Feeling the familiar sense of comfort as when she was a child, she simply nodded, "Connor, you're right. I shouldn't be going into the daycare. I must look a mess!"

"You are still Beautiful," he stated as he grabbed her hand to kiss it before reaching for her bag to lead her down the stairs and out to his SUV.

Clara smiled softly at the nickname he used when she was younger. She was barely in elementary school when she started to complain about her ugly green eyes and plain brown curly hair. Danny Thompson, a playground bully, would frequently tease her. Later when Clara told him about the incidents, Connor would ask her why she cared what the bully thought. Danny wasn't anyone important, was he? When Clara agreed he wasn't, she would sigh and state she wasn't pretty, like Rachel, Lila and Shannon were. Connor quickly agreed, "You're right, you're Beautiful."

Looking back, Clara realized he always used the name when her self-confidence was low. Nothing could elevate her self-esteem more than being told by Connor Emerson she was beautiful. In college during a particularly difficult semester, she was panicking and stressing out prior to a test. He had calmly reminded her she was beautiful and smart. He asked her a few questions and learned, due to her hearing impairment, she couldn't remember the big medical terms because she couldn't pronounce them. He would make it a point to meet with her while he, more or less, gave her speech lessons. Once she learned how to say the words, she could spell them out. Connor later learned she would write the words over and over, and then she was able to remember them. Everything fell into place. It took her a while to learn how to study. She never really needed to during high school as long as she attended class and did her assignments. But as he pointed out, college was a whole different ball game. Clara was annoyed when Connor stated he simply needed to read something once and he would remember it. But Connor thought she was beautiful so Clara forgave him.

First, they drove to the nursing facility to switch to her car for the car seats. Then they pulled into the parking lot behind the hospital, where the daycare was located on the lower level in the northeastern wing. Clara remained in the car while Connor went in to get the kids. She made the mistake of pulling back the visor to view herself and cringed. Her eyes were all red and puffy and the dark circles underneath seemed to get bigger. She pushed the visor back up in disgust and donned her sunglasses.

When Connor returned with her children, she twisted back as she watched him buckle each into their car seat. Reese, happy to see his mother, began his usual monologue of his day as Hailey listened and added her comments with words no one but Reese seemed to understand. He would occasionally ask his sister questions and respond as if he understood her. Connor sat behind the steering wheel, then handed her the daily report from the school before he started the car. He noted the sunglasses but didn't comment during the short ride home as he listened to the chatter in the back with amusement.

As they pulled into her driveway, Rob's blue pickup pulled up in front of the house, actually more the neighbors than hers. Clara sighed loudly as she remembered she had accepted his offer to bring over dinner. She slowly stepped out and assisted her son from the back as Connor came around with Hailey in his arms.

Without a word, Clara walked up the porch steps and attempted to unlock the door as Connor patiently waited, holding open the screen door. When she couldn't get it unlocked, he gently took over the task. After he opened the door and allowed them through, he stepped in, causing the screen door to close just as Foxwood stepped up with a couple of bags.

Clara walked back into the kitchen as the children distractedly went into the family room. Connor followed her, placing each of the kid's backpacks on a kitchen chair. Then he stepped over towards her.

Clara had filled a glass with water and was drinking it as she leaned into the counter. She watched as Connor stepped closer to her.

Rob followed, placing the bags on the table while silently watching both Clara and Emerson together.

"I am going to head out. Looks like he has it from here," Connor nodded towards Foxwood. He brought his hands up to cradle her head as he leaned down to whisper, "You have all my numbers now. Don't hesitate to use them."

He kissed her forehead and commented, "Play nice."

Connor winked before he turned around. He stopped next to the obviously irritated Foxwood and stated, "Keep an eye on her."

Then he let himself out.

Rob was annoyed, he wouldn't deny it as he stepped closer to Clara with his steel blue eyes locked on her green.

"Have you been hanging out with him all day?" Rob accused.

Clara remained silent as she placed the empty glass on the counter before attempting to walk away.

Rob, without touching her, stepped in front of her. He had noted the sunglasses still on her face and now smelled the alcohol, "You have been drinking this early in the day with him? Clara, what's going on? Talk to me."

"What do you want me to say?" Her voice was low but the irritation was clear.

"I want to know why you have been hanging out with Emerson all day! I heard this morning from someone else they confirmed it was your mother and when I get here, I can't find you. I call you and you won't tell me who you are with or where you are! I was worried about you! And now, I learn you were with the good doctor? What the hell, Clara!"

"Connor is a friend. He has always been a good friend of mine. He was the one that found me alone on one of the worst days of my life. The sheriff talked with him last night after he notified me. Knowing my fear was validated, he came to see me at work. He thought I wasn't fit to be working so he got Eric to get someone to cover for me," while Clara continued to keep her voice low, the annoyance was obvious.

"Yes, I hung out with him. I can hang out with whoever I want to! You are not my boyfriend. You don't get to dictate who I see and who I talk to. If I want to have a drink or five, I can and I will. You got that?" Clara had stepped forward and was poking him in the chest with her last comment. Then she stepped around him and walked out of the kitchen.

Rob had inwardly cringed as he realized, once again, he had overstepped his bounds in his relationship with Clara. Same old song, just another decade, he thought miserably but he followed her anyway. Again, without touching her, he stepped in front of her. Looking down, he removed her sunglasses and noted her eyes were red and swollen from crying. He felt bad about stressing her out more.

"Clara, I am sorry. I realized the news of your mother's death could not have been easy and I wanted to be here for you. I didn't mean to sound controlling or try to dictate who you can talk to and hang out with. I guess I'm hurt it wasn't me that you called. I'm surprised you would be hanging out with him. I didn't know you guys were friends," he stated as he placed a hand on her shoulder. "I guess I was a little jealous."

Clara sighed in frustration, "Rob, I grew up in the house next to his. We were friends when I was growing up. We are friends now. We have always kept in touch. Because he lived next door, he was the one that found me the day my mother disappeared. He was the one that called the sheriff." Connor was the only one that believed me all these years, she thought sadly.

Clara further continued as her fists tightened at her side, "I am a married woman. I am not looking for a relationship. You have no business being jealous or controlling in my life. You need to know and understand this. If you don't, there's the door because I cannot continue these arguments with you. We aren't in high school anymore. It's so exhausting!"

"Wait a minute, you said he knew your fears were validated? I thought it was determined back then that your mother ran off. I didn't know there was an investigation," Rob asked.

"When Connor saw me sitting alone early in the morning, he came over to see me. I told him she was taken," she quietly answered.

"Why did you think she was taken?"

"Why would she leave me?" Clara asked back.

Before Rob could even comprehend what she was implying, they were interrupted by Reese declaring his hunger.

Keeping his steel blue eyes on her green he answered, "No problem, Buddy. I think I have something you'll like."

When he looked down at the young boy with his mother's green eyes, he smiled.

Clara took the opportunity to step away and went up the stairs. Alone in her room, she called Jay to leave a message. She filled him in on the grim events of the day and finished with a declaration of her love and a request that he please call her back. She needed to hear his voice. After she hung up, she slid down onto the floor. She pulled her feet in and rested her cheek on her knees. Why won't he call me back, she pondered.

The room darkened as she lifted her head up again. Clara felt his presence at the doorway.

Rob hesitated when he saw her sitting on the floor. When she lifted her head up, he slowly entered the room and sat down beside her. They remained in silence for a moment. He placed his arm around her shoulders companionly and felt it was a good sign when she leaned into him.

"Clara, I am sorry I hurt you. The last thing you need is me arguing with you and trying to dictate who you can and cannot talk to. I am sorry. Old habits die hard." Rob winced at the unintended pun. "I want to be here for you as a friend. We have always been friends and I don't want to do anything that could change that. Please just tell me what you would like me to do and I will do it, alright?"

When he felt her head nod, he continued, "Alright. First thing, do you want me to stay or go?"

"I want you to stay. I don't want to be alone right now," Clara quietly answered.

Rob nodded his understanding, "Alright, I can stay on the couch tonight, no problem. Are you hungry? There's plenty of food left which is really surprising since those kids eat more than I do!"

Clara smiled in agreement. Rob stood before reaching down to assist her up. Once she was on her feet, she gave him a hug, "Thanks, Rob. It means a lot to have you here right now. I really appreciate it."

"No problem. It's what friends are for, right?" He answered as he led her down the stairs.

Hours later during the night, Rob was startled awake. He glanced around, remembering where he was and why. Rob thought he heard footsteps, but wasn't sure. It could have simply been the house settling, he wasn't familiar with its various sounds. The place was over a hundred years old.

Wide awake, he stood up and patrolled the downstairs for anything off. This place has so many damn doors, he thought to himself. The garage door and the French doors leading out to the back deck and don't forget the door leading to the basement. That was just the kitchen! The living room had two front doors! Then he remembered, the house is a duplex. Clara's home was attached to a mirror image of the home to the left facing out into the street, sharing the dining room wall but at the moment it was vacant. The sheriff's family owned the home as rentals.

Glancing around the kitchen one last time, Rob headed down into the basement. He did not know if there was an old-fashioned entry out into the yard. In the dark damp area, he noted the washer and dryer, an empty laundry basket and a few paint supplies on shelves next to the utility sink. The front wall held a small room with a step to enter through the doorway. This was the old coal room. Back in the day, the coal truck would back up to the window and pour the coal into this room. That explained the extra driveway both homes seemed to share.

Stepping into the room, Rob was surprised at how big it was. Then he noticed another door. The coal room was shared by the neighboring home! He stepped further into the room, after assuring the window was locked and assessed the door. Noticing the locks in place, he tried the door. It was also locked on the other side. Good, he thought as he relocked the first one. He stepped back out of the coal room, closed the door and headed back up the steps.

As he entered the kitchen, Rob's heart stopped as he heard a scream coming from upstairs.

early morning visit

The cold draft pulled her out of her pleasant dreams and without thinking, she opened her eyes. Clara could see the shadow coming closer to the bed. Frozen with fear, she closed her eyes and focused on her breathing as she pretended to be asleep. She smelled the familiar stench as the shadow stepped closer. Evil was in the room. Her thoughts were yelling in her head, where is Daddy? As the shadow reached her bed, she could smell the bleach. She held her breath as she felt a hand, surprisingly gentle, move a curl from her face. She could feel the stale hot breath touch her cheek as he whispered into her ear, although she could never hear the words. She felt the covers come up higher, to be tucked under her chin. She felt the harsh lips as Evil kissed her forehead before the shadow slowly faded into the wall...

Clara sat up suddenly, covered in sweat. Her heart was pounding into her chest as she gasped for air. She looked around the dim room and realized it was all a dream. She was not at the Hawks House. She is at her place on Prospect Avenue with her children across the hall. She is alright. Clara brought her legs in close as she rested her face on her knees. Then she saw a shadow entering from the hall as her heart skipped a beat.

Rob was standing in the doorway. He stopped when he realized Clara was likely just recovering from a bad dream. He paused with his hands out to his sides as he slowly entered her room. "Clara, are you alright?"

She can't hear me, he thought as he closed the door and turned the bedside lamp up from the low dim light. Rob saw her hearing aids on the bedside table and handed them over. When Clara leaned back into the headboard, he tried to not notice the low neckline of the green nightie with thin straps. He sat on the edge of the bed, placing a hand on her cheek, "Clara? You want to talk about it?"

Now able to hear, she looked up into his eyes and tried to smile but her eyes were wide with panic as she shook her head, unable to speak.

"Hey, come here," Rob pulled her in towards his chest as a tear fell down her cheek. "You're safe. Both Reese and Hailey are safe."

Without a word, Clara simply nodded as she focused on her breathing. After a few minutes she pulled back, "I am so sorry. I didn't realize I screamed out loud, didn't mean to wake you up."

"No worries. It's why I'm here, to keep you company. You want to talk about it?"

She shook her head again as she leaned back, still unable to speak of it. Rob remained quiet as he watched her struggle to pull herself together.

"Do you want me to sit here with you so you can get some more rest? It's pretty early. You still have a few hours before sunrise," Rob asked quietly, as he reached over to brush a curl out of her eyes.

"I won't be able to sleep anymore," Clara pushed the covers away and scooted over to the other side of the bed. Once she was standing, she removed her hearing aids, placing them onto the bedside table before she walked towards the bathroom. She stopped at the doorway and turned before she spoke, "I'm going to take a shower. You're welcome to use the bed and get a few hours. That bed is much more comfortable than the couch."

Rob silently admired the way the nightie fell over her body, barely covering her bottom, showing her strong legs. He leaned back into the bed as he debated taking a short nap but the pillow smelled of her. When he heard the shower running, he started to visualize her removing the short nightie. Rob groaned out loud, telling himself he needed to be out of the bedroom when she came out. He looked at his watch and realized it wasn't that much earlier than his normal time getting up. He stopped in the children's bathroom before heading down into the kitchen.

Once downstairs, Rob opened the fridge and a few cabinets before a few ideas formed in his head for breakfast. But first, coffee needed to get started. A half hour later, Clara walked into the kitchen wearing an old pair of faded jeans and a flannel shirt, her hair was still wet and her feet were bare. Rob glanced down, noticed her toe nails were painted a deep rose color. He leaned into the counter as he watched her pour herself coffee. Without a word, she went to the fridge for the creamer.

As he continued to watch, he couldn't resist teasing, "I see some things never change. You still like to put some coffee in with your cream."

Rob was rewarded with a smile as she brought the mug up for a sip. Her green eyes met his steel blue over the rim of the mug.

"What is baking in the oven?"

"What does it smell like?" Rob asked. He was always fascinated by how well she could pinpoint something based on the smell.

Up for the challenge, definitely needing the distraction, Clara closed her eyes as she sniffed the air, "I smell banana, cinnamon and bacon." With her eyes still closed, she sniffed again to confirm as she gasped excitedly, "Did you make banana bread and bacon cheddar muffins?"

"You got it! You still have the nose of a bloodhound," Rob chuckled as he leaned down to accept Clara's hug.

"Rob, thank you so much. I really appreciate it. You're the best!"

"No problem. Clara, I mean it. I'm here to help with anything you need," he answered as he followed her towards the table, each carrying their coffee. He checked the timer, still a bit of time until everything was ready. He sat down after she did.

"I am really sorry I woke you up," Clara repeated.

"You didn't wake me up. I was already awake. I thought I heard something. Don't know what it was," he shrugged. "I walked around the first floor and the basement to make sure the windows and doors were all locked. They were. You have A LOT of doors and windows in this place. How do you keep track?"

"I don't use half of them. It's therapeutic for me to walk around in the morning opening the blinds but I have been keeping the windows locked and locking the doors as I make my way through. I must have too much of a big city girl in me to leave the doors and windows all wide open throughout the day, even when I'm home."

"Have you spent a lot of time down in the basement?"

"Not a whole lot. Just enough to get the laundry going. I don't like the kids on those stairs and it's so dark and damp. I need to get a humidifier. I also need to stop in the hardware store to get locks and bolts for those doors down there. At first, it gave me the creeps having the connecting door but the place is currently empty. Apparently back in the day, it was cheaper to have one shared delivery of coal. Since the original owners were brothers, it made sense to have the one room, hence the connecting door. And the second driveway to the large window." She had brought a small pad of paper and pen with her and began writing a list of things to do for the day.

"That's probably a good idea. I can help you change the locks on the doors and the windows. After we eat, I'll go see what you need."

After sunrise, Rob was preparing to head out with Clara. They would first drop the kids off at daycare and complete her errands before returning to fix the locks and few other chores around the house. As he opened the front door, Rob was surprised to see Eric heading up the steps with coffee and a box of donuts.

Eric looked up as the door opened. He stopped in mid-step when he noticed the person standing in the doorway was Rob Foxwood. What the hell is he doing here this early? It is not even seven in the morning!

"Good morning, Eric. What brings you over this early?" Rob inquired, with a grin as he casually leaned into the doorway. He had been a year ahead of Eric in school. They were never actually friends but friendly enough. They didn't hang with the same crowds, well except maybe for Clara and Rachel, he grudgingly admitted. But that was because Eric lived in the house between them. Rob was also well aware of Eric's infatuation with Clara back then, and pleased to note it hadn't been mutual. It appears he's still holding the torch, he thought.

"I just thought I'd drop these off on the way into work," he explained, trying hard to contain his annoyance at finding Foxwood at Clara's door so early in the day.

Clara came to the door with a bag over her shoulder and her daughter in her arms as the boy followed. She stopped when she saw Eric standing on her porch, equally surprised by the early morning visit.

"Good morning, Clara. I wasn't expecting to see you heading out so soon. Where are you going?" Eric asked as he handed the box of donuts first and then the coffee.

"Hi, Eric. Thanks, this is very sweet of you," Clara stated as she accepted the gifts, after handing Hailey over to Rob. "I need to take care of a few things this morning. Are you sure it's alright for me to be off the rest of the week?"

"Absolutely. Take as much time as you need. I have Jerry already lined up through the week. Just keep me posted about when you are ready to come back. And, please let me know if there's anything I can do for you," Eric answered as he reached over to give her shoulder a squeeze. He would have given her a hug and kiss if Foxwood hadn't been standing there. Instead, Eric nodded at Clara as he said his goodbye.

Rob grinned inwardly at being ignored as he watched Eric make the mistake of also ignoring what was important to Clara, her children.

Both Clara and Rob remained on the porch as Eric pulled out.

"I wonder what that's all about," Clara wondered out loud as she brought the donuts and coffee into the kitchen.

Rob just shook his head when she returned to the door. He didn't think she was ready to hear she was the number one most interesting girl in town. She was definitely going to be getting attention from many interested parties. I'll need to keep close, he thought annoyingly. First the good doctor and now the dipshit.

"Maybe he's trying to be a good supportive boss. Do you have everything you need?" Rob asked before he closed and locked the door.

"Are you sure you're able to help me with all this? I really do appreciate it."

"Not a problem," Rob responded as Clara opened the door and assisted each child into their seat.

"I want to help," Reese declared from his seat.

"You will be helping later," Clara responded as she handed the keys over to let Rob drive. She was just not into it today.

Eric pulled into the parking lot at work, fuming at finding Rob at Clara's house this morning. He had not noticed Foxwood's truck there until after he returned to his own vehicle. That prick must have spent the night! Clara doesn't need this, he thought in frustration. It had been his intention to catch her early while she was still in her pajamas and mourning her mother. Eric wanted to be the one to hold her close while she cried on his shoulders. If she brought him upstairs to her room so he could appropriately comfort her, what was the harm? He honestly forgot all about her children until he saw them beside her. Eric sighed heavily.

His annoyance increased as he noted the sheriff pulling in behind him. Oh great! What now? He stepped out, pulling his briefcase and coffee.

"Good morning, Sheriff. What brings you here?" Eric inquired pleasantly.

"Sorry to bother you so early in the day. Just wanted to ask you a few questions, if you can spare the time." He followed Eric into the building and down the hall. Tony noticed the ease of entering the building early in the day without so much as a locked door or anyone around. He did hear the kitchen staff down the hall. He waited as Eric stopped to unlock his office door and went inside.

Placing his briefcase on a small table beside his desk, Eric invited Sheriff Mancuso to take a seat. He contained his irritation as the good sheriff closed the door prior to sitting down across the desk from him.

"I came to ask you a few questions regarding Lauren McDonald," Tony began.

"I can't really tell you much about her. She was fired last week after being caught stealing from a coworker. I had to open up an internal investigation to see if there were other incidents of stealing, especially from any of the residents," Eric explained. "I placed her on the banned list."

"So, you are not aware that she was found Monday morning, dead?" He looked closely at Eric. "She was found in the pond of one of your employees, Marie James?"

"What? Are you serious?" Leaning forward, his face displayed total shock. Then he leaned back into his chair and sighed, "I knew Marie had called off because there was a body on her property, but I didn't know it was Lauren. Is Marie being charged?" The week was heading even lower. Last thing he needed was another scandal!

Sheriff Mancuso shook his head. "Just getting some background information regarding Miss McDonald's relationships with her coworkers and all."

A few blocks over, Connor was standing at his large front window looking out onto Main Street watching the town version of early morning rush hour. The children were riding along on bikes or walking in small groups towards school. He chuckled when he saw Toby Sinclair pull off a girl's hat and run. She ran after him and tackled him with such force that Connor winced as she grabbed her hat back. Hmm, she should go out for the football team, he thought. He watched Toby laughing on the sidewalk as his friends caught up, he didn't seem to be hurt.

As he sipped his coffee, Connor mentally planned his day. He would meet his nephew first at the nursing home and then do rounds at the hospital. The previous evening had been quiet. He had debated checking in with Clara but noted Foxwood's truck was still at her place when he drove past her street on his way home.

Speak of the devil, he thought as his eye caught her car parked just a bit across. Looks like they're doing some shopping. Hardware store just opened. Connor continued sipping until they returned to the car, focusing on the body language. He watched as Foxwood opened her car door and they both paused looking at each other. He wasn't able to read the discussion, lip reading was Clara's thing. Clara said something which made Foxwood laugh before getting into the car. He's still in love with her, Connor thought as he watched the car drive away.

Feeling a little mischievous, he pulled out his cell to place a text. Connor smiled when she immediately responded that all was well. He turned to head out, thinking he'd text her again later in the day.

As the day neared dinner time, Clara stopped at the local grocery store to get a few items. She planned to stop next at The Lantern, another locally owned restaurant that served soups, salads, and burgers during the day, then becomes the evening hang out for the younger drinking crowd. Her plan was to pick up take out before swinging by to get the kids. She was in no mood to be dealing with people or making dinner. Cooking was so not her thing even on the best of days.

As she walked around the store, Clara could not shake the feeling of being watched. She wrote it off as being in a small town where everyone knows your name and business. She was certainly upping her gossip value! Back a few weeks, and she was the constant talk of the town! Why did she think it was such a great idea to return home? Clara quickly checked out and carried her bags to her car. After placing her items in the trunk, she felt a tap on her shoulder and jumped. She turned with a startled scream but relaxed when she realized it was Rob.

"Hi Rob. Long time, no see eh?" Clara quietly asked, attempting to be funny.

"I didn't mean to scare you. Sorry, you didn't hear me call your name. Are you alright?" Rob noted the early morning was showing in the dark circles under her eyes. But he sensed something else. Clara seemed restless and jumpy. He watched her closely as she momentarily closed her eyes to take in a breath, as if to center herself before she could answer him. He was pleased she did not lie.

"I don't know what I am," she quietly responded. Trying hard to not let the tears start, she looked up into his eyes. They were somehow calming and reassuring. Why do I suddenly feel safe when I'm around him, she asked herself.

Clara looked so fragile, Rob didn't think she was ready to be alone just yet. Nor did he think she would admit it. Nodding, he looked over at the trunk. "How about I stop over again with dinner? We can hang out for a bit."

"I already have dinner cooking, I just need to swing by The Lantern and pick it up," Clara answered. But still looking at him, asked "Why don't you join us? Let me know what you want so I can add it to the order."

"I can pick up dinner while you get the kids," Rob suggested. For some reason, he felt relieved. He held his hand up when she motioned towards her purse. "I got this, ok."

Nodding in agreement, Clara allowed Rob to take the keys from her hands and click to unlock her car as he walked over to open the driver's door. He handed her the keys, quietly closed the door as he winked at her. Rob watched her drive off before he continued towards his truck.

Neither seemed aware of being watched from across the street.

Within the hour, Clara was home with the kids. They had already unloaded their bags for the day and were washed up for dinner. The kids were playing quietly in the fourth bedroom, destined to be a playroom. She had just changed her clothes when the front doorbell rang. The kids came running out behind her as she descended the stairs. Expecting to see Rob with their dinner, Clara was startled to see Dallas standing on her porch.

Dallas Thompson was a tall quiet figure. He had light brown hair that appeared to give to curls when it grew long. He had a light in his blueish green eyes that made Clara think he was more intelligent than his parents ever seemed to give him credit for. He graduated two years ahead of Clara. His parents divorced when he began middle school. Dallas spent most of his teen years back and forth between this town and the next, as his parent's social, or more correctly, romantic lives seemed to control where he stayed and when. His mother was the newly divorced Mrs. Thompson that was always around after Clara's mother disappeared.

And yet, thinking back, Clara didn't recall her visits including Dallas very much. Despite their parents dating and now living together, they never really hung out or got to know each other. Dallas seemed to live elsewhere and came around the house on the rare occasion. As she thought about it, she never actually went to his mother's house either.

"Hi, Clara. I'm sorry to be stopping in unannounced like this." Dallas glanced down as he saw a young boy and girl standing next to her. He smiled, "Your children are beautiful."

He smiled as he waved to them, pleased they both smiled and waved back.

Dallas glanced over his shoulder as a blue pick-up truck pulled in behind her car, "I can see this is a bad time but I just wanted to stop in and tell you I'm really sorry about your mother. I do need to talk with you when you have a chance. Here are my numbers. Call me when you can. Good seeing you."

Clara had remained speechless to see Dallas at her door. She had not given him a thought in a long time. He initially seemed embarrassed but there looked to be some irritation when Rob pulled up next to her car in the driveway. When she looked back at Dallas, he handed her a card.

"Call me when you have a moment or if you need anything. Anytime for any reason." Dallas quickly stepped back and nodded when Rob stepped up onto the porch. His irritation showed again when each of her kids let out a squeal of delight as they saw Rob.

They both eyed each other but no words were exchanged. Rob stood at the front door, handing the food to Clara as he watched Dallas step into his SUV. He felt an unexpected but familiar emotion pass through him. He turned towards Clara once the vehicle was out of sight.

"What the hell did he want?" Rob asked, hoping to keep the irritation out of his voice as he stepped away from the door and closed it.

"Not sure. He said he had something we needed to discuss but you arrived. Then he left," Clara gave him a soft smile. She turned around to head towards the kitchen as she wondered what he could possibly have to tell her. As far as she knew, her father and his mother were still living together. She often sent a note to update her father during her college years and an announcement when she married but he never responded or acknowledged any of her achievements.

A part of her felt guilty she was the one that moved away. But couldn't he have arranged for a visit or two? Or maybe they could have met up somewhere halfway in between. The short notes became less frequent as the children arrived and he still displayed no interest in her or her family. Not even a card of congratulations or a gift when either child was born. Since she had been back, she still hadn't heard a word from him. Clara had already decided she wouldn't be the one to call him. She made the attempt many times. Maybe he isn't doing well, she thought. Then Dallas should just say that.

After dinner was cleaned up, Rob settled on the couch as Clara was upstairs getting the kids ready for bed. He could hear the laughter and running and then the quiet as she read to them in Hailey's room. Then Clara returned down the stairs. He looked up and their eyes met.

She gave him a slow smile but stopped suddenly when the house phone rang. Clara turned to look at it as if she were debating answering before reaching for it. Picking up the cordless phone, Clara turned away from Rob as she answered. She closed her eyes and held her breath as she heard the familiar silence. She said hello again before she hung up and replaced it in the charger.

Rob watched her face change from calm and relaxed, to irritated. She turned away when she answered the phone but he sensed fear when she hung up. He stood up and walked towards her.

"Who was that?" Rob asked, keeping his eyes on hers.

"I don't know. I have been getting hang up calls all day," she answered with annoyance. Clara closed her eyes as she willed herself to control her emotions.

"Care to share?"

"No, it's just not been one of my better weeks. Can I get you a beer?" Without waiting for a response, she headed into the kitchen.

"Is there something else going on?" He asked as he followed, thinking of her jumpiness earlier. Rob watched her shrug. This was like pulling teeth, he thought to himself. He leaned into the doorway of the kitchen as she busied herself with the drinks.

"I just feel like I'm being watched. I keep telling myself it's a small town and everyone is just fixated on watching Graham Hawk's granddaughter return. It's like when my mom first disappeared. I always felt as if I was being watched and never really alone," Clara struggled to explain.

"When did you start to feel this way," Rob wondered. "Was it when you first came back or after that day riding?"

"I'm not sure when it started. Those dates were only a week apart." She responded as they returned to the family room. Handing him his beer, she sat quietly on the sofa. When Rob sat beside her, Clara remained quiet, attempting to absorb his strength.

Rob watched her as he sipped. He thought over what he knew about her parents, about her father after her mother disappeared. Clara was his sister's age, a couple of years behind him. He always felt a closeness with her. Rob felt the need to protect her. From what, he did not know but it was the same as when they were kids. Right now, he felt her hesitance to share.

"Do you want me to stay the night again on the couch?" He asked. He did not want her to know where his thoughts often go, it would probably scare her. Rob further clarified, "Would you be more comfortable with someone here tonight? Lila is working another night shift."

"Rob, I can't." Clara stopped and thought, why not? Who would care? It's not as if Jason has even called her in the last how many months? She's not doing anything that's breaking her marriage vows. "Actually, if you don't mind, I would like that. I'll sleep better, thanks."

Carl Gibson kept his pace leisurely as he strolled down the sidewalk, barely pausing as he once again noted the blue truck. She doesn't waste time, does she? Barely back and she's already sleeping with the guy. He had heard from others Clara was separated from her husband. Since he never met him, or even made an attempt, he was willing to admit, he couldn't judge. Seemed as if the apple didn't fall far from the tree. Clara was just like her mother, couldn't seem to sleep alone, he thought as he continued on his walk.

everyone is a liar!

The next evening, Clara had just finished a warm bath and was applying her lavender vanilla lotion when her cell phone rang. Staring at it for a moment, she was torn between answering or not. A quick glance at the caller ID showed it was Shannon. She picked up by the third ring.

"Hey Shan," she answered, placing the call on speaker as she finished applying lotion to her legs.

"Clara, I am so sorry to be calling so late. I just need someone to talk to. Is it alright if I stop by?" Shannon asked.

"Where are you?" She asked, standing up and heading towards her closet to get clothes out.

"I'm parked right outside in your driveway. Actually, I hope it's your driveway."

Clara suddenly turned around, headed out her bedroom door and ran down the stairs. She paused at the side front door at the bottom of the staircase to unlock the door and flipped on the smaller porch light as she stepped out. Sure enough, Shannon was sitting in her car.

Upon seeing Clara on the smaller of the two porches, Shannon stepped out of the car. She reached over to the passenger seat to retrieve her purse, small overnight bag, and computer bag. Quietly closing the car door, she walked over to her friend. As she climbed the few steps up, she realized this was probably not the best idea she had all day. Clara is having a worse week! What am I doing, coming to her with my stupid problems?

"I'm sorry to barge in on you like this so late in the night! I just needed to get away! Lila is working the night shift and Rachel is finishing up the week at work and heading home tomorrow," sighing as she looked into Clara's concerned eyes.

"No need to apologize. Come in! Let's go to the kitchen." Clara reached over for the weekend bag as she closed and locked the door. She placed the bag on the couch as she led the way through the living room and dining room, into the kitchen. Turning on the light, Clara motioned for her friend to have a seat while she filled the water kettle for tea.

Slowly turning around, Clara studied her friend. While she, Rachel, Lila, and Shannon were all close and inseparable while growing up, she and Shannon had the most distant relationship. Clara thought she would be the last person Shannon would call late in the evening in a crisis, let alone drive hours to see. Looking closely, she noted her green eyes were swollen from crying, her eye makeup was more under her eyes than around them, and she had tear streaks down her face. Shannon's normally short sophisticated chestnut hair was overdue for trim. It looked spiked as if her fingers were constantly raked through.

Shannon Kathleen Doyle was the most A personality of the group. She graduated with honors in accounting, and worked in a large firm in the city. She was usually dressed in power suits which fit just right to show off her feminine figure. She never lacked for male company. Shannon not only loved the fast-paced life of the city, she thrived on it. Currently dressed in sweatpants and a hoodie, Shannon was fidgeting with the strings of the hood. She slowly raised her eyes to look up at Clara and immediately began to cry.

Clara went over and hugged her friend tightly as the tears flowed faster. Neither said a word for a few minutes. Pulling over a chair, Clara scooted over but held onto her hands and patiently waited.

"Everyone is a liar! My parents, my boss, my boyfriend..." Shannon stopped as she began to hiccup. "I don't even know where to begin."

Clara stood up when the kettle began to whistle. Without a word, she prepared the tea and carried it over to the table. She walked over to the pantry, pulled out cookies, and held them up to her friend. Seeing a slight smile and nod, she brought them over. Clara sat down and patiently waited for her friend to explain.

"Last weekend, I decided to go through the boxes of papers from my grandmother. It's been six months! I should be able to deal with it! And those boxes were beginning to annoy me. I was constantly stepping around them. I don't know why I waited so long." Sighing again, Shannon lifted the neckline of her sweatshirt up over her face to wipe her tears.

Picking up an Oreo, she opened it up and ate the white center. Sighing again, "My grandmother kept a journal. Three of those boxes were filled with composite notebooks, each and every one a journal throughout her life. She started writing when she was in high school. At first, reading them was relaxing. It took my mind off the stress from work. My grandmother grew up in the city as a child of an immigrant. She met my grandfather when he was at college. She moved here in town when they married. Together, they raised my mother and kept a good home. I knew all this growing up, but it was soothing reading her thoughts, I could hear her voice while I read. How she loved my grandfather and he must have loved her! I really want that someday."

She stopped for a moment to bite her cookie and sip her tea. "My grandmother wrote about the joys of raising my mother and uncle. Then, she talks about the stress of my mother's fertility treatments and the joy when she became pregnant. Then about the sadness of my mother's miscarriages. I knew about those as well. I was always called their miracle baby. I just figured it was because my mom was finally able to carry to full term. But my grandmother wrote about the day my parents brought me home after adopting me! I was adopted!" The tears began again. Remaining silent, Clara simply squeezed her hand.

"I was so upset! No one ever said a word and now everyone is gone. I called my boyfriend and he was too busy at work. You've met Joel. Hell, we've all hung out together. You remember how we met about a year ago at the gym. We were surprised to find he works for the same company but in a different department. A month ago, he started talking about us living together. He had been, more or less, staying at my place without any actual agreement or discussion." She paused again to finish off her cookie and tea. Clara remained silent, knowing this was all connected somehow.

"It was more like he would take me out to dinner, take me home and end up spending the night. I didn't think too much of it. We were dating for a while and it seemed we were exclusive. It never dawned on me until today, that we never went to his place. Always mine. There might have been an evening here or there when we weren't together. I just figured he still had his place. I don't even know if he gave me his real address. Then, this morning at work, my boss called me in and fired me! Can you believe that?" Shannon exclaimed.

Suddenly, Shannon stood up and began pacing the kitchen with a restless energy as she continued. "He accused me of turning over confidential material to the police! He said my boyfriend was an undercover cop and accused me of knowingly giving him information about an account I don't even have anything to do with, let alone know of its existence." Shannon ran her fingers through her hair and turned to look out the back window.

"I was shocked. I said a few things, but he already had security ready to escort me out of the building after I retrieved my purse from my office. I was told my personal items would be shipped to me after everything was searched through for EVIDENCE. Can you believe the nerve? I worked for years at this company and this is how I'm treated! As I am escorted through the lobby, a swarm of policemen come in! They are serving a warrant and seizing all accounts and property! Leading the damn group is Detective Joel Montgomery! Also known as Joel Adams, that bastard!" she said quietly.

Turning around from the window, Shannon further explained, "Everyone was detained and separated. He must have researched me, followed me around for the best angle. He even came to the gym to watch me from afar and determined I was the best way in for his undercover assignment. My password would allow him access to all of the accounts. But I never bothered with anything but my own assignments. That bastard used me to take down my employer! And my employer accused ME of disloyalty!"

Wiping a tear, she quietly turned back towards the window and continued in a whisper. "My employer was arrested for laundering money for local sweat shops, including child labor. I never knew. I never knew any of this," she slowly repeated. "I was already planning to come tomorrow for the memorial service on Saturday and thought, why wait until morning? I don't want to talk to the bastard!"

"Wow, you certainly had a day. I'm glad you came here. I have plenty of room. To be honest, I am kind of spooked about staying here alone with the kids." Clara stood up and gave her friend another hug. She felt her cell phone vibrate. She glanced down to read a text from Rob. He was checking to make sure she was alright. She texted him back that Shannon had arrived early and was keeping her company. He wished her a good night.

Later, with her unexpected guest settled in for the night on the other side of her bed, Clara turned off the light. For the first time since finding her mother, she fell immediately to sleep without any unpleasant nightmares of her past.

· · · ·

Outside, an SUV remained parked for an hour after the last light went out. Evil was again frustrated at not being able to return inside Clara's home. He thought about chancing it but sighed quietly as he remembered the last time he went inside while she had company. He had quietly entered through the connecting basement door. He climbed the basement stairs into the kitchen. He had slowly made his way to the living room when someone had suddenly sat up on the couch. Not moving for a moment, he slowly faded into the woodwork before sneaking out. It made no sense. There wasn't an extra vehicle in the driveway. And now tonight her friend arrives. When will they all leave Clara alone?

SHADOWS OF THE NIGHT

11 evil is here

Late Saturday morning, Clara and her close friends walked into Memories. It was a local family restaurant by day with a bar almost the length of the place. In the later evenings, it turned into one of three local bars. It specialized in warm sandwiches during lunch hours and home cooked food in the evening hours. The bartenders were able to make almost any cocktail asked for. The atmosphere often depended on the current town, wild and rowdy during football season or quiet and mellow due to recent death.

Really, it was stupid, Clara thought, to expect the town to respect her wishes. She had received just about every salad and casserole known to these parts, and cakes and pies from people acting as if her mother had just died. The memorial service was meant to be private as her mother had been gone 20 years. Most of the people in town had disapproved of Clara's marriage to an outsider and her moving away from town. Forget the fact that she had already moved away when she left for college. But Clara guessed she was an equivalent to a town Nobleman, being born and raised in one of the big houses on Park Avenue. People had high hopes for her. She shook her head and tried to focus on the conversation among her friends.

"Do we want to sit at the bar or table?" Rachel inquired.

"Looks like Ted's training a new guy. Let's go check him out," the newly available Shannon replied. The others all shared a look and shrugged as they followed her to the bar.

"Good afternoon, ladies. This is Devan. He's going to be covering while Carrie is out on maternity leave," Ted gestured toward the man beside him. "He's also known as Sheriff Mancuso's nephew from the city. He'll take good care of you. If not, then let me know," he winked as his attention was pulled to the other end of the bar.

"Hello. What can I get each of you?" Devan smiled as he stepped closer. Silently, he looked the four friends in the eye, taking a measure of each. Lovely looking bunch of ladies, totally unexpected to find in such a small town he thought to himself, trying to place them from his many visits as a child.

"What are we drinking today, Clara?" Shannon asked as she sat on the stool and eyed the new candy in town. This town certainly needs some new guys if it's going to continue to grow, albeit distant relations of those already here.

"Can you make margaritas?" Clara inquired.

Pretending insult, Devan replied with an easy smile as his hazel eyes sparkled, "Of course. Frozen or on the rocks?"

"Frozen with the salt," she responded as each of her friends nodded in agreement.

"Are you staying with your family?" Lila inquired.

"For now. I am moving this weekend into a duplex," Devan answered as he poured the tequila into the blender.

"My duplex is next door to an empty one. Is your place on Prospect?" Clara asked, relaxing with the simplicity of the discussion.

Devan nodded yes as he turned on the blender. When he served the drinks, each of the girls nodded a thanks. Shannon attempted to open a tab but was informed one was already done. He stepped away before she could ask about it.

Devan had been surprised by the recent calls from his uncle. They had always been close enough, as any family. But his uncle had called again on Monday with further distressing news regarding another dead body. Even more surprising was the number of missing women in such a small town. He had just finished up a previous assignment which allowed Devan to render assistance to his uncle and cousins. The bartender job was just a bonus for extra cash and a way to meet the fine citizens of such a small rural town without them knowing they were being monitored. To his amusement, people always opened up to the bartender or lacked attempts to keep a private discussion from being overheard in such a crowded setting. It was the perfect cover job.

He watched the four friends interacting. Devan had already been provided the general details from his cousin Anthony. Looking at the woman with the curly hair, he remembered her the most as a young girl. Clara Noelle Gibson, now O'Reilly, had just returned to town after being newly separated from her husband. It was her mother's memorial service and the reason the place was packed more than usual for this time of day on a Saturday. Devon shook his head at her bad luck of being the one to find her remains. The blonde next to her currently lives in the city but had buried her mother almost two months ago. The current talk was she would be returning home after the school year was completed. The one with the auburn hair had already moved back home. She lived on the family farm and worked as an emergency room nurse. And the last one, certainly not the least, he thought with a smile, still lived in the city. Per his cousin, she was the "wild one" in the group back in high school. Devan wasn't sure exactly what that meant.

While Clara found herself being pulled into conversations with those around her, Shannon sat on the end in silence as she drank and checked her phone. She appeared to be denying many calls and finally turned it off before placing it into her purse.

"Everything alright?" Devan inquired as he replaced her drink with a fresh one.

"No, nothing is right," Shannon answered with a dramatic sigh. "I am currently loveless, jobless and familyless. Why do people feel the need to lie about important things in life? Why can't anyone be honest?"

When she later looked back on the conversation, Shannon would cringe thinking how uncharacteristic she was at that moment. Why did she say so much to a total stranger? Naturally, she blamed the tequila.

Devan simply allowed her to vent for a bit as he watched her green eyes flare up. She really is something to look at. He wondered if it was a guy problem, family or work. Not realizing he hit on all three, he gave his two cents, "Well, any guy not able to treat you right, doesn't deserve you. I say don't waste any more time or thoughts on him."

Shannon chuckled before she sipped from her drink, licking a little of the salt first, "You are right! I don't deserve to be treated like crap. I am going to move back here. I just made the decision. I should be able to find something here in town, well, hopefully."

"What kind of work do you do?"

"I'm an accountant and financial planner," Shannon answered.

"Oh yeah? You could tell me where to put my money?"

"I could, do you have a lot of it?" She flirted with a smile.

Devan laughed as he stepped away to check in with other customers.

When Rob and Chase arrived, the four friends had already been drinking for a couple of hours and the place was packed. They had to return to the farm after the service to deal with some issues before leaving it in the hands of the workers.

When Rob spotted Clara, his first thought was she needed food. He was sure none of the girls had eaten anything all day. His eyes met hers in the mirror behind the bar before he reached her side. He leaned down for a hug as he asked her if she was hungry. She simply shrugged. A moment later, a menu was placed in front of her as the seat next to her became vacant. He sat beside her and ordered a late lunch for them both. He figured the others would follow.

Clara suddenly felt a cold shiver as her heart started pounding in her chest. The intensity of being watched was magnified as she looked to the mirror at the various faces throughout the bar. Many were looking in her direction but no one really stuck out. People had stopped over to express their sympathy. Some only stayed for a drink while more seemed to make a day of it. Clara wasn't really able to place most people without Lila's help.

Oh, this can't be happening! Not here, Clara thought as the voice in her head told her Evil is here. Looking in the mirror, her panic increased as she searched the room. When her green eyes met familiar warm brown eyes, her scanning stopped as she instructed herself to simply breathe. At the far end of the bar, Connor was sitting with a glass in front of him. He nodded his head as he lifted his glass in her direction.

Clara smiled and nodded back as she sipped from her drink. Evil has never harmed me in public, she reminded herself. She is safe and surrounded by good loving people that care. As she slowly breathed in again, she felt herself relax.

Rob had noticed Clara's green eyes move in panic as her face paled. He leaned over, "Clara, everything alright?"

"I'm just a little cold, I guess. Kind of stupid with all these people in here," she shrugged.

Rob removed his jean jacket and placed it over her shoulders. He kept his arm on her shoulders as she thanked him.

When Clara looked back into the mirror, Connor winked. She smiled back before excusing herself to use the restroom.

When she came out, Clara was stopped by many people. As she stepped back, she bumped into someone and almost lost her balance. She felt strong arms grab her, preventing a fall. When she turned around, Clara's eyes met with Connor's.

"You alright? Did someone just shove you?" He asked in an irritated tone, keeping his arm around her waist.

"I'm fine. I don't know what just happened. Probably too much drinking," Clara tried to brush it off.

Connor sensed something was off and had been earlier as he studied her pale face. He was slightly annoyed that she was wearing Foxwood's jean jacket but he realized Clara would be safe and have company when he left for his shift at the hospital. He had just signed off on the open tab for Clara and her friends, the girls anyway, he thought with a smirk. He left strict instructions for Devan to keep an eye on Clara and those around her. He had no doubt the Foxwood cousins would assure the girls returned home safe.

Clara was talking with others around her while Connor had remained at her side with a hand on the low of her back. She leaned into him and sighed with his warmth surrounding her. She felt him lean towards her ear to whisper.

"Looks like your food has arrived," Connor stated as he escorted her back to her seat next to Foxwood. Before she sat, he leaned down to hug her as he stated in her ear, "I need to get to the hospital. Are you going to be alright tonight? Want me to stop in after my shift?"

"I'll be alright. We are all staying at Lila's tonight before Rachel and Shan head back to the city tomorrow," she answered.

"Ok, that will be good for you. Call me, alright?" Connor knew how important her friends were.

When Clara nodded, he realized Foxwood was watching them through the mirror. His hand came up her back and onto her neck as he leaned down to kiss her forehead, "Stay safe."

Without thinking too much of it, Clara sat down next to Rob and began to remove the tomatoes from her club sandwich. Rob looked over to watch as she removed every last one before she started eating. He leaned over, placing his arm possessively around her shoulders as he asked, "Everything alright?"

"About alright as it can be," she shrugged, unaware of the silent battle around her.

the hawks house

Monday afternoon at work, Clara found herself getting anxious. Unable to say why nor would she admit, Clara was dreading the meeting with Chase and Rob at the Hawks House, her family home. For the first time, Clara would be entering inside since her graduation. With her mother's death certificate, she had been supplied with the official keys and a fat file to review various bills to initiate and sign off. They were going to discuss potential options and changes. She had some ideas but didn't know if it would get approved.

When Clara pulled up in front of the house, she debated getting out or waiting for the guys.

"It's just a house. Simply an object with walls, floors and ceilings," she told herself. "An object that does not have any actual evil. It can't hurt you and if it does, it's because it's old. You are a strong independent woman. You already made the choice of not living here. Besides, the guys will be here soon. You don't want them to think you're a puny dependent girl, do you?"

Leaving her purse in the car, Clara grabbed her cell and keys. As she slowly walked the pathway leading to the steps, she surveyed the front yard. It actually looks pretty good and well maintained. She had to decide if she wanted to keep the same gardener. Maybe she should find out who it is first, she thought as she looked up towards the house. It was white with black shutters and a wrap-around porch. The front door was a glass panel with a wood frame enclosed by more glass panels on either side. Her mother had blinds put up to provide privacy.

Before she reached the steps, Clara looked up to the second and third story windows and stopped. Her heart skipped a beat as she was sure she saw movement. Was someone up there, currently looking down at her? Should she wait until the guys get here?

After a quick debate, Clara decided to continue up the steps. Using her key to unlock the door, she was surprised the door moved smoothly and without effort. Keeping the door open, she stepped inside, pausing to look around. With the exception of the layer of dust, everything seemed to be as she left it twelve years ago. It smelled musty and stale. She sighed again as she hesitated but continued inside. Straight ahead was the grand staircase. There were seventeen steps to the landing which allowed one to go either right or left, both with another eight steps to the second floor.

Instead of climbing the stairs, Clara turned to the right. The closed French doors opened to what her mother called the formal parlor. It was where the guests were entertained back in her grandfather's day. If you walked through it, it led to the library, then the study and finally, the back room. Her grandparents had it changed to open up to the kitchen with a more casual sitting area. Across the foyer was another set of French doors leading to the family parlor. While it was more casual, it was still what her mother called an adult room. No place for toys. That room led to the music room, then the formal dining room, the casual dining room and finally the kitchen.

Still in the foyer, Clara continued straight along the hallway past the staircase, passing the doors for direct access to each of the rooms until she finally made it to the kitchen. She was surprised she could hear her feet echoing in the large open space. At the doorway, she paused as she pictured her mother standing at the sink debating with her the various colors to plant the next day. Clara was clearing the table as her mother rinsed off the dishes.

Clara felt her eyes water as she realized her mother was the same age then as she is now, twenty-nine. Her eyes moved to the back stairs and without warning, she felt a chill as her breaths became shallow. She thought she heard footsteps above her. A part of her wanted to go up to investigate but her feet wouldn't go any further. Another part thought her mind was simply misinterpreting the sounds. She had never been able to hear this well inside the house so how could she possibly properly place the sounds?

There is no one in the house, she told herself, just you.

Clara slowly backed into the wall as she looked up towards the ceiling. She thought she heard something else overhead. She braced herself against the wall as her mind saw violent blue eyes through the smell of bleach, while her face felt a cold embrace on her cheek. She heard whistling...

· · · ·

She is back! So exciting to have her looking the place over. Evil had debated going down the steps but realized she was likely going to be meeting with contractors to bring this place into the twenty-first century. Oh, this place will be very grand again, Babydoll! You will look beautiful lying naked once again in the antique bed, he thought as he smiled at the memories of years ago. She was so willing and so beautiful as her long straight hair framed her face as she slept. He remained standing in the shadows at the top of the back staircase. Seeing the curls, his mind wondered again why she curled it. He preferred it straight, just as she kept it in her teens when they first started seeing each other. He could feel himself responding to her closeness as he fought the internal debate of descending the steps to have her right here and now. It had been so long but the wait was almost over. But for now, he would be the gentleman, waiting for the proper time. He sighed as he blew her a kiss before he slowly made his way towards the back bedroom, whistling "Oh Susannah..."

It seemed forever had passed but it was only a few moments before she found herself squatting down on the floor with her legs hugged close to her chest and her chin on her knees. Clara stood up and leaned into the wall as she focused on her breathing. Her mind was simply overreacting. No one is upstairs, no one is out to get her, she is safe. There isn't any whistling. She quickly returned to the foyer and out the front door as she realized she would never be able to convince herself. There was whistling.

A few minutes later, Rob and Chase pulled up behind Clara's car. They were a bit later than expected due to some minor issues at the last job. As they both climbed the steps to the porch, they saw Clara sitting on the old porch swing.

"Hey Clara! Sorry we're late," Rob stated as he sat down beside her. "Were you waiting long?"

"Not too much," Clara answered as she opened her eyes and smiled, relieved she was no longer alone.

"Have you been through the house already?" Chase asked when he realized the front door had already been opened.

"I saw enough," she answered quietly.

"And you know what you want to do?" Chase asked.

"I have some ideas but I don't know if it can be done. I want to turn the house into apartments."

"Hmm. That sounds like a major overhaul. It certainly has the space. Do you mind if I head in and get a feel for the place? I don't think I've been inside since I was a kid," Chase stated. He was thrilled with the potential job.

"Have at it. You guys don't really need me, do you? I made a copy of the key. You can go ahead and do your thing. I'll need a written proposal and I have some paperwork that would need to be filled out for payments and what not." Clara stood up. She could see the delight on Chase's face at the idea of going through the house.

"You sure? I guess you don't really need to be here. I need to take some measurements, get some ideas and pictures before we apply for a permit. It needs to be approved for apartments first," Chase said as he accepted the key. "Do you have a preference on how many apartments?"

"No. I will leave it all in your hands. I trust you guys. Thanks, Chase. I'll leave these papers here for you to file. I already signed them," Clara went over to give him a hug and kiss on the cheek.

Chase smiled over her shoulders at Rob, knowing his cousin was irritated with her hugging any other man. Without a word, he went inside.

"Everything alright, Clara?" Rob asked as she turned to him.

"Yeah, I'm fine. I need to get the kids before the daycare closes and I have no idea how long this will take. He's like a kid on Christmas morning," Clara stated as they both headed down the steps towards her car.

"Yeah, I think you made his week, just asking his opinion about this. If you were to accept the proposal, he might actually propose to you," Rob teased as he placed an arm around her shoulders.

"I don't know, I think he would have more fun with the Taylor House," Clara stated thoughtfully.

"Yeah, you're probably right."

Shannon was surprised to be enjoying the change of scenery with the transition back to her hometown. She was able to easily find a position at the bank on Main street and found the banking hours refreshingly light with occasional Saturdays. When the weather allowed, she would walk to work. But most of all, she loved being in the same town with her friends again. Granted Rachel wasn't back yet, but she had already made arrangements to move when the school year was over.

After dinner, Shannon went for a stroll. Naturally, she stopped at Memories to check in with Devan. She thought he was absolutely sweet! He was such a refreshing change from her usual A type previous boyfriends. Devan always seemed to be genuinely pleased to see her and always had the patience to listen to her about whatever frustrated her that day. Tonight was no exception.

"Good evening, Shan," Devan greeted her once she was sitting at her normal spot at the bar. He immediately set her up with her favorite wine.

"Hi Devan. How's the evening going?" She smiled back.

"Can't complain," he answered as he stepped towards the other end to assist another customer.

"Hello Shannon."

Shannon turned around, total shock on her face when her green eyes met up with Joel Montgomery's brown eyes. She was speechless.

"I have to say, I was surprised to learn you moved back home. You always made it pretty clear you would never return," Joel stated quietly. He was very aware of the bartender following his every move with an easy change in position in front of the bar.

"What are you doing here?" Shannon softly demanded. She never wanted to have both Devan and Joel in the same room.

"Shan, I need to talk with you. It's very important. You can't keep hiding from me. Please just give me five minutes of your time," he pleaded.

"I don't have anything to say to you. You made it clear you weren't interested in me, remember. I was having one of the worst weeks of my life and you not only ignored me but you were using me all this time," she turned back towards her drink and made eye contact with him through the mirror behind the bar. "You can go to hell."

"Shannon, please just come back to my table and listen to what I have to say. I promise, it's important."

"Everything alright here, Shannon?" Devan asked from behind them.

Joel turned around, standing between the bartender and Shannon when he spoke, "This is a private conversation that doesn't involve you."

Joel was annoyed when Devan didn't back down. There was something about his stance that suggested a cop, hmm. A cop undercover in this small town? What the hell for, he wondered distractedly.

Shannon, in an attempt to keep things civil, finally agreed when Joel turned back around, questioning her with a silent look. After a long moment, she sighed, "Alright, five minutes Joel and then I will be right back here in this spot. Devan, you can have another drink ready for me when I return in five minutes."

Her sweet smile melted before she looked over at her old boyfriend, standing as she grabbed her wine glass.

Joel, on high alert at the idea of an undercover cop working in the bar, gestured towards his table in the back. He pulled out a chair which allowed him to remain sitting across from her with his back facing the wall. When he looked into her green eyes, he lost his thought and original purpose for being here. He really made the mistake of allowing his personal life to cross into his professional one. No one was more surprised than he when he fell hard for her. She was one of the best things that ever happened to him and he treated her horribly.

Unable to focus on keeping her temper, she drank her wine to calm her nerves. Putting the glass down on the table while she stated, "You have four minutes left before I return to my seat."

Joel was jarred back to the present, "Shan, I am sorry for the way everything happened. It should never have ended the way it did. I meant everything I said to you when it was just us at home. You were the best thing that's ever happened to me, I love you."

He attempted to reach for her hand that was fidgeting with her glass. She immediately pulled her hands into her lap. Unable to maintain eye contact, she looked down into her wine.

"But Shannon, I didn't use you. I already had a way in, I just couldn't keep myself away from you," Joel continued. He looked over her shoulder to assure their privacy before he continued, "I had meant to pull you out before we raided the place but someone tipped him off. He has someone on the inside. When we discovered this, we went into lock down and had to move in quickly. I wasn't ignoring your calls. I was literally not getting them."

Joel paused a moment as she lifted her eyes, "Someone on the inside was feeding him false information about you. That someone knew I was a cop. He believes you have more information. You are in danger. You need to come with me into hiding so we can protect you."

"Joel, I never knew anything about all this! All my accounts and clients were legitimate. I never knew there was anything illegal going on. I can't report what I don't know! He has nothing to fear from me," Shannon stated in frustration.

"I know you didn't know anything. You know you didn't know anything, but he doesn't believe that for a minute. We have reason to believe he has hired someone to take you out, you are not safe."

"You have been lying to me since day one, how can you expect me to believe anything you say now? I really loved you but I will not go anywhere with you. And, your five minutes are up," she lifted her glass and finished off her wine before dismissing him and returning to her spot at the bar. She was pleased there was another glass waiting and Devan was busy with another customer. This gave her a chance to pull herself together. Nothing puts a damper on a fun carefree moment with a new crush like an awkward moment with an ex present, she thought miserably.

Devan had been watching Shannon and the ex-boyfriend cop closely. He had also been keeping an eye on the quiet lone unknown guy in the back drinking only coffee. If he were reading this right, and he was confident that he was, this was not some useless attempt to win her back romantically. No, this had professional concern. Knowing where Shannon had worked previously, he was well aware of the scandal involving her prior boss. When he did his own investigation, he learned the bad guy had some advance warning and was able to destroy key evidence prior to the raid and arrest. With the visit from this cop, he wondered how involved she really was.

"Hey Devan, what time are you getting off tonight?" Shannon asked as she drank heavily from her glass.

"Shannon, have you eaten dinner yet?" Devan asked. The last thing he needed was the ex-boyfriend cop assuming she was trying to pick him up. He was not in the mood for a fight.

"Yeah. Devan, I would really love a refill before I get back," she smiled sweetly as she jumped from her stool to go to the ladies' room.

Once she was out of sight, Joel stepped up to the bar to close his tab. Without a word, Devan retrieved his check. When he returned, Joel already had his cash out with a business card in the pile, "I have no idea why a small town this size would need an undercover working here but be aware of potential danger from the city. I don't think the cops in this town would recognize the trouble until it's too late. If anything, or anyone looks off, please contact me. Whatever you do, keep her safe. She's a good person and totally innocent."

Without waiting for a response, Joel Montgomery left before Shannon returned.

13 apple pie

Four weeks later, Clara had easily settled into the slower pace of life in a small town. The very short commute gave her extra time with her kids. The kids adjusted well to the new daycare and were making friends. Shannon, to her surprise and pleasure, had taken over the guest room with her own furniture and made the house feel more occupied. While she continued to have nightmares, she wasn't as uncomfortable sleeping alone at night with her good friend down the hall.

But Clara still could not shake the feeling of constantly being watched. She tried to dismiss it as being back in town with most everyone stopping to acknowledge her by name. It didn't matter if she was at work or out around town. Everyone acknowledging her by name took some getting used to: the mail person, grocery cashier, bank teller or even the high school kid serving the happy meals. It had taken her a moment to realize, most were simply reading her debit card. Some were polite enough to explain their past connection, "you sat in front of my little brother in English class." Who actually remembers something like that?

When Clara was at work, running into Connor became a frequent occurrence, making her wonder if he was doing it on purpose. Her tongue was often tied, keeping her from saying something intelligent, usually falling back on something stupid, amusing him, she never doubted. While her young girl crush appeared to grow into an adult version of attraction, Clara frequently reminded herself he wasn't the type for a serious relationship. More importantly, she wasn't his type. His reputation for a different girl every week was well known. After her poor attempt to appear professional and sophisticated, she found ignoring him worked best.

However, his nephew, Joshua was another matter. His encounters were less intense, as well as more amusing. He acted as Connor's assistant: scheduling of patients to be seen, organizing the lab work and prioritizing his appointments. Josh even asked to shadow her a few times when his uncle was busy in surgery. Initially very shy and hesitant around her, he quickly relaxed after a few therapy sessions. It never occured to Clara, Josh felt the same awkwardness she had with Connor. He had the same easy-going personality. And he knew the patients' families and histories, like everyone in town.

But he was also smart and asked appropriate questions, "Why are you ace wrapping Mr. Fischer's stump? He still has staples."

"It's important to start shaping it by controlling the swelling, preparing him for a prosthesis," Clara answered.

"Can I try wrapping it?"

"Sure," Clara handed over the ace wraps.

Josh looked down at the ace wraps in his hand and over to the amputated limb before him. When his blue eyes met Clara's, she simply smiled as she provided instructions.

"First you want to anchor it distally, then keeping a firm grip, wrap in figure eights, just like I showed you," Clara instructed as his hands slowly moved around. When he was completed, she turned towards the patient, "What do you think, Mr. Fischer? Did he pass?"

"Honestly, not as good of a job as you, Clara. It feels like it'll fall off if I move my leg," the older man announced. "You have nicer hands, too."

Josh nodded in agreement as he watched her rewrap effortlessly into figure eights.

"Is Josh causing trouble?" A voice asked from behind them. Everyone looked to see Eric standing at the doorway.

Clara knew he was attempting to be funny and tried to insert himself into various conversations at work, struggling to pull off the role as the boss. But she thought Eric's sincerity fell short. She finished up with her patient, assured he had his call light and other needs in his reach before she and Josh left the room.

"No trouble, Josh is following me around to help understand my role to the patients. It'll help him transition from a great doctor to a brilliant one," Clara informed Eric as he followed them to the nurse's station.

"Brilliant? Don't you think that's a bit far fetched?" Eric asked with dramatic disbelief.

"Not at all," Clara answered. "He's smart and knows the terminology, he's approachable with a good bedside manner. His skills will continue to grow as he navigates his training."

To Josh's amusement, Clara appeared to dismiss Eric while she informed him where they were heading to next.

Growing up next door to Eric, Clara had learned to tread lightly around his tantrums and eccentric behavior. As children, he was often a playmate and pleasant enough when he was alone. She learned early to avoid him when his friends were around, especially Danny Thompson. While Eric had been annoyingly immature during high school, she couldn't say what it was that he did now, as adults, that bothered her. Maybe he was trying too hard. But she wasn't sure what it was Eric was trying to accomplish. Was he trying to please her? Keep her happy since he was the one to convince her to relocate back home? Was he trying to ask her out? Clara had no idea. Eric was always bringing her coffee in the morning and often in the afternoon. He was always agreeing with her, finding awkward reasons to visit with her at her desk when she was alone and inviting her out for a drink. Clara couldn't get a read on him. It just felt, not wrong, but off. While he didn't necessarily have a reputation as a lady's man, she heard whispers of his extravagant appetites with women. She reminded herself she was back home and simple small talk was often exaggerated. And since it always made her uneasy, she declined his invitations.

However, she had no issues with meeting out for a quick drink with other co-workers such as her department or nursing staff upstairs. As time went on, she was able to recall many of the people from her life when she previously lived here. Clara often sat with Rachel's grandmother during her lunch break. She would stop in with Reese and Hailey about twice a week so they could also visit with her. They were both so good with her, especially Reese. He would simply provide his whole life story, as if it was the most exciting ever. No need for her to participate as he kept the conversation going all on his own. Clara would bring Gigi down to the therapy room, set everyone up at the table to color while she caught up on paperwork.

Connor had stopped in at the nursing home to check in on a patient before heading to the hospital one Saturday afternoon. Surprised to see the therapy door open with the light on, he stopped in the doorway to watch the scene before him. Clara was sitting at her desk typing while both Reese and Hailey sat at the table with Ms. Taylor, Rachel's grandmother. The three at the table seemed to be enjoying themselves and each other's company while Clara worked. She occasionally looked up and smiled before returning to her screen.

When she looked up again, her eye caught his. To his amusement, Clara blushed before turning away. With a quick glance at his watch, Connor could spare a few minutes.

"Dr. Emerson, how are you?" Clara asked quietly as he entered the room.

"Doing alright, Clara. You know you don't need to call me that. Do you work every Saturday?"

"Not really. I usually bring the children a couple of times a week to visit with Gigi. They all seem to enjoy it and Rachel feels better knowing she's around family," Clara shrugged as she looked over towards the group, unable to make eye contact.

"She certainly seems to be enjoying the company. Your moving back and working here has had a great impact on her mental health, especially after losing Elizabeth so suddenly." Connor placed a hand on her shoulder. As he hoped, Clara looked up at him. "You are looking great. Sleeping better?"

Clara nodded, "Yeah, more or less. I'm sure you heard Shannon moved in so there's someone else there which makes the house feel less big. I don't know what I was thinking, moving into such a big place. When you get a chance, I need to meet with you about some stuff."

"Music to my ears but I can't now. Can it wait? I need to head upstairs to see Mr. Bryce before heading to the hospital."

"Yeah, no problem Dr. Emerson. Let me know on Monday when it'll be a good time for you," Clara dismissed.

Connor touched her shoulder as he leaned down to whisper, "Clara, you don't need to wait until you have a problem before you use any of my numbers. I could even just come over one evening because you miss me."

He kissed her forehead before heading out, chuckling softly when she blushed. When he reached his office, he was surprised to see the administrator's office open. More surprising was seeing Eric and Matt together looking over some paperwork.

"Wow, I am surprised with all the extra work everyone is putting in today, a Saturday, of all days," Connor announced from the doorway.

Matthew Emerson was the facility's lawyer and CEO. He oversaw the nursing home's big picture. He and his father together approved of the major costs and change in policies and assured new health care guidelines were being followed, from a legal standpoint. He was also Connor's older half-brother by many years. Matt was almost a teenager when his father remarried and welcomed a new baby boy. Despite having different mother's they were, more or less, raised in the same household. The Emerson House was next door to the Hawks House. The Emerson family owned the nursing home.

Their father's much younger sister Kathleen, was married to Leander Howell, Eric's parents. While she never wanted anything to do with any of the family's extensive businesses, Kathleen thrived on the lifestyle it provided. She secretly begged her older brother to let her only son have a role. Eric was encouraged to get a degree in health administration and after an extensive training period, he was provided with the position of administrator. As Connor was the medical director overseeing the medical aspects, Matt oversaw the financial and legal aspects. Eric was responsible for the everyday running of the facility and the marketing in the community. Still, Connor was surprised to see both working here. Not really surprised to see Matt working on a Saturday, he was the definition of a workaholic, but he usually worked from his office right next door to his loft. It always surprised him to see Eric working, regardless of the day.

"There are some concerns that need to be addressed," Matt stated as he looked up from a file. He was standing to the side of Eric's desk. Eric was looking through various files in front of him. His annoyance at being pulled into the office over the weekend was obvious.

"Oh? Anything I need to be aware of?" Connor wondered.

"Maybe. We are missing numerous pre-hire paperwork," Matt stated as he looked knowingly at his brother. It was no secret he was against Eric's place in the family business. He felt his younger cousin's high school and college years focused too much on partying with rumors of his father bailing him out of many unsavory situations. Connor, too busy getting his medical degree and training as a surgeon before he returned home, never really gave Eric much thought. It was more his brother's department. Unless, of course, it affected the care of his patients.

"When you say pre-hire paperwork, are we talking about not enough references?" Connor asked as he stepped further into the room.

"It depends on the person, I guess. Someone as apple pie as Clara O'Reilly has a complete background check: fingerprints returned clear, no outstanding warrants or arrests, not a convicted felon; drug test was negative; her license and CPR certification are to date and she has many well written letters of recommendation, professional and personal. But someone like Lauren McDonald is another story. She was arrested after a fellow co-worker accused her of stealing here at this facility. Not only does she not have a background check in her personnel file, she's also missing her fingerprints and a drug test," Matt's voice was soft but his tone was harsh, as he closed the file. He looked up when he announced, "And I was recently informed she had been arrested previously within the last five years for shoplifting. Oh, and let us not forget there doesn't seem to be any proof of certification of CNA training either."

"I don't see what difference it makes now, she's dead. How did you get this information anyway?" Eric demanded from his desk.

"Does it matter how? The point is she should have never been working here in the first place. How many others are currently working upstairs that have no business being in this setting? Our priority has been and always will be the residents' safety. We are responsible for their care, legally, medically, ethically, need I continue? Can you honestly tell me we don't have a sexual predator or convicted felon working here?" Matt demanded.

"Oh please, really? We never needed this kind of background check back when my mother worked here. We know all our employees. Hell, most of them have actual blood relatives living here as residents and are related to other employees. We all look out for our residents," Eric justified.

"Your mother worked here?" Matt let out a harsh chuckle. "Eric, your mother stopping in every few years for photo shots is not working."

"Eric, laws have changed in recent years. We are required by law to show proof that anyone working here is drug free with an appropriate background. We cannot have felons working here. That includes any contractors hired by an outside company, like an electrician or painter. If we are ever found in violation, we would be fined, lose admitting privileges, and not be allowed to bill insurance companies," Connor lectured.

"So what if we get fined. Everyone gets a fine. You pay it and move on," Eric dismissed.

"Yeah, state surveyors often fine facilities for minor deficiencies but if you have too many certain major deficiencies, the state can revoke your license and shut down the facility. A whole different matter than simply paying a few thousand dollars in fines. Hell, if they discovered we have a convicted felon, someone with assault background or even a sex offender working here, there could be criminal charges brought up," Connor stated.

Eric simply shrugged, "If someone were to get caught and arrested, they need to be held accountable for their actions. I agree."

"No Eric. The person arrested is the one they can prove agreed to the hiring of the individual without the appropriate background check and educational credentials. In our case, the administrator would be arrested," Connor tried to maintain his patience as he explained. "That is part of the administrator's job."

"And if we are buried deeply in fines that could have, hell, should have been avoided, there won't be any money left for your defense. You'd be on your own," Matt harshly threatened. "Now, I am saying this one more time, here is the list of every person you signed off on hiring since I cut the umbilical cord last summer. I want to see the original paperwork required for each position myself. If you cannot find it, you will personally pull each person with an incomplete file off the schedule until we get the required paperwork. Is that understood?"

"Why does it have to be me? It's Saturday. This could take all day. I have plans you know," Eric whined.

"Yeah, it certainly is Saturday. I am missing my sons' baseball games. If I have to be here cleaning up your mess, so will you. I don't care if it takes us until Monday morning, we don't leave. This is your responsibility, your job. If I have to hang over your shoulder or do your job for you, then what the hell is the point of having you here? For your sake, I hope the list is short. You don't want us to be fined because we don't have the appropriate ratio of nursing staff to residents," Matt's authority rang loud and clear. "Get those personnel files in here and get started. You decide if you need to cancel your evening plans now unless you're confident all the necessary paperwork is already accounted for."

Connor and Matt remained silent while Eric stomped from his office to the HR office with the list.

"I almost wish I could stay and help but I have a shift starting at the hospital. Are you going to be alright here with all this?" Connor asked his brother.

"It's partly my fault for not actually looking over his shoulder longer. I will be installing some safety measures this week. He is right about this being a small town with everyone knowing each other's business. Most likely he was just lazy. I'm confident Beth, when she was alive, would have ensured the nursing staff had appropriate paperwork before getting started. I'm going to have a talk with Judy in HR about the check list with added signatures before the starting date so this doesn't happen again," Matt was looking out the window as he spoke, suddenly distracted.

"What is Clara doing here with her children on a Saturday?" Matt asked as he watched her assist her children into the car.

"She brings the kids in to visit with Ms. Taylor," Connor explained as he walked over towards the window.

"Yeah? Clara really is Apple Pie. Ms. Taylor's probably the only grandparent in those kids' lives." Matt looked away once she pulled out.

"Did you hear she's hired the Foxwoods to complete the renovations of her house? A permit was approved yesterday to turn the house from a single family home to apartments."

family jewels

Clara had arrived early to work Monday morning. She was planning to work through her lunch and finish early so she could stop in at the Hawks House to check on the progress. She realized there wouldn't be much as it was just the first day. But still, she wanted to check it out. Or at least she did on Saturday when she came in to get a head start on paperwork and payroll.

She closed down her computer, put what she needed in her briefcase, and grabbed her purse to head out. Just as she reached the door, Connor opened it. Clara paused in surprise.

"Clara, just the person I came to see. Can I take you to lunch?" Connor asked as he stepped back to allow her into the hall. Without waiting for an answer, he started down the hall.

"Dr. Emerson, what's this about?"

Connor raised an eyebrow as he looked down at her, "I told you before to call me Connor. Aren't you the one that requested we have this meeting? I figured we could hit two birds with one stone. Or did you already eat lunch?"

Clara hesitated before answering. She was the one that requested a meeting to discuss legitimate work-related issues. He probably figured she was heading out to lunch anyway. "No, I haven't eaten yet."

"Perfect, I am starving," he smiled as he opened the first door to the back exit. After she stepped through, he saw Eric coming out of his office.

"Hey, where are you two going in the middle of the workday?" Eric demanded, trying to sound authoritative.

"Just a business lunch, we all have to eat, don't we?" Connor answered pleasantly. He had learned from his brother there were a total of sixteen current employees with missing paperwork in their files. Apparently, Matt had already done the research in half the time it took Eric to complete it due to his constant whining. He had listened to an earful during Sunday brunch regarding the cousin's lack of work ethic and poor time management. He also showed a new check list for all new hires to be signed off ultimately by either himself, Matt, or their father before the start date.

When Connor opened the passenger door for Clara, she hesitated. Looking up as she finally admitted, "Dr. Emerson, I wasn't stepping out to go to lunch. I was actually going to the Hawks House to check out the first day of work."

Connor smiled when she again called him doctor. He nodded, already aware of where she had planned to go, but was not willing to admit. He replied with a question, "So you already ate?"

Hell no, Clara thought. Who could eat with all this anxiety? But aloud she admitted, "No. I worked through lunch so I could leave early without getting into trouble."

Connor chuckled with a nod towards the car. Matt was right, Apple Pie. She's a salary employee who probably actually works over forty hours but worries about an hour or two. Once they were on their way he asked, "Is Memories alright?"

"Yeah, sure," she answered distractedly. "How come your sidekick isn't with you today?"

"He's at my office coordinating my schedule. I can't really have him at the nursing home, emergency room and the operating room. It's too overwhelming right now. I'm going to have him at the ER later in the week and take it from there. He had his hands full doing his homework before that," he answered cheerfully as he looked over at her. Was she hoping to have him as a buffer, he wondered?

Connor was lucky to have a spot directly in front of the restaurant. Clara was already up and out of the car when he came around to her side. Without a comment, he grabbed her hand as he went inside. They were immediately seated and drinks were already ordered.

Once they were alone again, Clara took a deep breath before she began, "Dr. Emerson," Connor raised an eyebrow in question and she sighed. "All right, Connor, are you happy?"

"Clara, we have known each other for twenty-nine years! You have always called me Connor. There's no reason for you to call me doctor, especially when it's just the two of us. And if you keep this up, I will believe you want to keep this formal and professional," he gestured between the two of them. "And if that's the case, please continue Mrs. O'Reilly."

Connor leaned back with amusement as her green eyes flared up, "I wasn't being formal, just respectful."

Jill, the young server, returned with the drinks and to take their orders. Alone once again, he looked over to Clara and waited for her to begin.

"Connor, there, are you happy now?"

"Clara, I am always happy to be in your presence," Connor stated with a wink and he laughed out loud when she blushed.

Clara sighed in frustration as she started again, "We need to figure out how to get all the therapy evaluations signed within a timely manner. Currently, the original evals are left in a file in your box at the nurse's stations. You only sign them about once a month. We can't bill the insurance companies until after your signature is received or we aren't in compliance."

Connor nodded understanding, yeah that is certainly an issue. He was surprised the previous manager didn't address the issue earlier. After he sipped from his drink he responded, "Alright. How about when the papers need to be signed, you contact me and we schedule a time you can bring the papers to my office for me to sign."

"That's it? Marie just needs to contact you about a time and she can bring the evals for you to sign?" She clarified.

"No, you contact me and we discuss a time and place to meet."

"Why does it have to be me? Why can't it be Marie?" Clara impatiently asked.

"Because I, as medical director, may have questions you, the rehab director, could answer. For example, why is Lettie Mae getting only speech and occupational therapy and not physical therapy?" Connor wondered out loud.

"That's because her insurance only pays for an hour a day, that's only two disciplines for thirty minutes each. Speech therapy believes she has potential to have her liquid thickness and food texture upgraded with some training. Occupational therapy has been focusing on her self-feeding to increase her calorie intake with adaptive equipment. Physical and occupational therapy have agreed she's going to be contact guard to stand by assist for transfers and ambulation due to her impaired cognition. That's not going to change soon but once she is safely able to eat regular textured foods and thin liquids, speech will pull out and physical therapy can step in to improve her balance and endurance for safer ambulation," Clara easily explained.

"Alright, that makes sense, especially since she had been refusing the pureed food and honey thick liquids. Knowing her family, they would have been sneaking her food. Lettie Mae would have been back in the hospital with aspiration pneumonia," Connor paused when their food arrived. "See? I have questions and you have the answers. It saves time if it's the two of us meeting."

Clara remained silent as her green eyes met his soft brown. He was right, he would often have questions or even she would. She reluctantly agreed it did make more sense.

"Clara, prior to you, we averaged five but usually less new admissions a week. Since you started, we have doubled the admissions with a shorter length of stay. The faster turn over has resulted in more urgency in getting the paperwork processed quicker and correctly. We can schedule two meetings a week, like this," when her green eyes narrowed with suspicion, he chuckled. "We can adjust the meeting as needed as well as the frequency. We both have other things going on. I can always stop in your place or you can bring them to my office at the hospital before or after the kids are in daycare. I'm flexible. Just text before to assure I'm not in surgery."

Clara sighed as she completed removing the tomatoes from her club sandwich and began to eat.

"Why don't you order without them?"

"I usually do but I have been so flustered about stopping at the house I forgot," she stated absently.

Connor was surprised she said out loud what he already knew. To avoid embarrassing her, he did not comment. Instead he changed the subject, "Now that I'm doing something for you, I need you to do something for me."

Clara had just taken a bite and groaned inwardly. Her green eyes looked up at him in silent question.

"I need an escort to a fundraiser this Friday evening," Connor announced.

"You want me to suggest some ladies you can ask?" Clara asked hopefully.

"No, I don't need you to give me recommendations. I want you to go with me. It's a black-tie affair just a few towns over. I'll pick you up at seven."

"Connor, this Friday is too soon, there's no way I'd be able to get everything ready in time! I would need to get a babysitter. I don't have a dress! It would never work!" She quickly concluded.

He noted she never stated she didn't want to go.

"Why would you want me to go with you? You have plenty of admirers you can ask, all are much better options," she stated quietly. "And I am married."

"True, there are many others I could ask and you are married but I would enjoy your company the most. It'll be great networking for you as the rehab director. I know you have something that would fit the bill in your closet. It'll be fun. Besides, don't you want to hang out with your favorite neighbor?" Connor purposefully used her phrase from when she was younger and tried to get him to do something she wanted. Usually it was minor, like a cookie from his cook or a piggyback ride home from the park. Once, she even asked him to assist her in running away from home.

Connor ate all his food and started to eat her fries. When she pushed her plate towards him, he finished off her club sandwich as well.

Neither seemed aware of being watched by the others in the restaurant. However, a pair of blue eyes and blueish green eyes sat at a table in the back corner, both monitoring the two sitting up front. One was surprised by the apparent level of intimacy and comfort the couple seemed to display in public. The other was horrified at the idea she would want to be present in his company. Still, neither discussed with the other their thoughts, not even aware they were each watching the same couple.

After Connor paid the bill, he opened the passenger door again for Clara. Once they were moving, Clara gave it a minute to determine they were indeed not returning to work.

"Connor, I thought we were going back to work. Why are you going this way?" Clara anxiously asked.

Connor looked over, "I thought you were going to the house to check on the progress during the first day. Did you change your mind?"

"No, not at all," she answered.

"I want to go with you. I am curious to see how it'll be done. Brilliant move, making the house into apartments! I love how you're sticking it to the Trust and making money doing it!" Connor exclaimed excitedly.

"Really? You are alright with this?"

"Sure, why not? I don't live in my family home anymore. Matt lives there with his family, rent free with all household expenses covered. One of his sons will inherit the house later. Honestly, I don't really care either way. It doesn't affect me," Connor answered. "My father and grandfather have established trust funds. I was provided with an education through medical school. Granted, the degrees were not simply handed to me. I worked my ass off. There was a list of expectations, and still is, for me to continue to receive money from the family trust. Not all the families had the foresight to plan for their children's futures."

Clara inwardly cringed, thinking of her family. While she did receive an elaborate house, she had no desire to live there. She was also fortunate to not have excessive student loans as many of her peers did. Like Connor, she studied hard and worked a few jobs throughout her college years but she received grants not money from a family trust. She had been under the impression her father didn't have any significant money. Clara wouldn't have been surprised if he and his girlfriend lived paycheck to paycheck.

"Look at Eric, he's a perfect example. His family lives the most lavish lifestyle of all the families but neither he, his father, nor grandfather really work for it. They have been living off the Howell trust without ever adding to it for many years now, as well as making many poor investments. He can't even do his job correctly as an administrator because he's too damn lazy," Connor stated with disgust.

"Really? I thought his father is a lawyer and his grandfather is a pharmacist," Clara commented.

"Yeah, his father did go to law school. Lee graduated in the bottom of his class but somehow became a prosecutor and now the town mayor. May sound impressive but he would never be able to do those jobs anywhere else, certainly not in the city with real cases and problems. He would have to work a minimum of sixty hours a week to be half decent. How many leading prosecutors do you think work banker's hours? As for the grandfather, he was never able to adjust to modern technologies with computers and keep up with the current laws. Required too much work," Connor stated as he parked in front of the Hawks House. He saw his attempts to keep her distracted had worked. She looked surprised to see the house when she looked out her window.

Connor walked around to her side and opened the door. When she continued to hesitate, he stated, "You don't have to do this today. We can come back another day."

"No, I need to do this," Clara stated as she slowly stood up but found herself leaning back into the vehicle, frozen as she stared up at the house. It really was a beautiful house. The azaleas were in full bloom and if she closed her eyes, she could smell the fragrance of the flowers from the gardens. The furnishings inside were antiques collected from various family members over the generations. Clara was once again second guessing herself. Did she really want to have her family home destroyed? Sell or auction off all her family history?

Clara shook her head as she felt herself torn. She wasn't sure what the right thing to do was, but she had to at least do this, walk into her family home.

"Come on, Beautiful, Evil won't get you today," Connor grabbed her hand to lead her up the path to the porch.

Clara paused as her feet landed on the first step, her chest tightened and her heart was pounding. She thought for sure Connor would hear it but she quickly became distracted by trying to catch her breath. Her vision was beginning to narrow. It seemed inevitable she would pass out.

Connor paused on the second step when Clara remained still. When he turned to her, he noted she was on her way to a full panic attack. He placed both hands on her neck as his thumbs rubbed her cheeks. He looked directly into her eyes as he instructed her on breathing. When she blinked and her eyes met his, he knew she was back. He leaned in to kiss her forehead before giving her a hug.

When he pulled back, she was taking one last deep breath before she finished climbing the steps to the porch. With his hand in hers, she reached out to open the front door.

Instead, Rob beat her to it. He had anticipated Clara would make an appearance, however he was more annoyed than surprised to see the good doctor at her side, holding hands, no less. Minding his thoughts, he greeted them as he stepped back.

"Hi Clara. As we discussed the other night, we haven't started any of the demolition yet. We have been packing the furniture in preparation for storage. We can drop off the dining room set tonight if you like."

"Yeah, that should be alright. Just text when you're on your way to make sure I'm home." Clara was distracted by a painting leaning against a box, waiting for proper wrapping. It was a landscape of the lake further back in the hills behind her house.

"I was able to inventory all of the items but I don't think we should just leave this box lying around. She needs to get a safety deposit box," Chase was descending the grand staircase case with a medium size box. He paused when he saw Clara and Connor at the base of the stairs. "Clara! You made it!"

Chase continued down, paused to unload the box to Connor. He gave her a hug, partly because he was so excited to be starting the project and also to annoy his cousin. Keeping an arm around her shoulders, he guided her towards the boxes along the wall. "We have a few boxes that are photo albums and framed pictures you may want to look through before storing. We have been inventorying everything by room and numbering the boxes as such. The box I just brought down is what was in the safe. You should seriously stop at the bank when you leave here.

It really needs to be in a safety deposit box. Shannon can help you with that."

"I want this painting brought over when you guys drop off the dining room set, alright? And the phone booth." Clara gestured towards an old bench made of dark wood with a desk built into the side where her mother used to keep the telephone. It had a shelf underneath for the phone book and calendar. She had many memories as a child sitting at the booth.

"No problem. Do you want the tea cart too? It was in the dining room," Chase inquired.

"Yeah, I do. Was the silver tea set still on it?" Clara looked over her shoulder as she continued to study the painting. The artist simply signed it, "Shelby." Who was that?

Rob remained quiet as he studied Clara. He didn't believe she wanted to have her family home gutted and split into apartments for strangers to live but he shared his opinions only with his cousin.

"No worries, we'll bring it all to you later." Chase was reaching for her hand to bring her into the parlor as he began to show her what the plan was once everything was removed.

"Chase, what's in this box?" Connor asked as he followed the group.

"Oh yeah, that has the family jewels," he stopped and turned around. Lowering his voice, very aware of the tendency for voices to echo in the large house. "The envelope on the top is the inventory list with insurance numbers. You probably want to store that in a separate box and confirm everything with the insurance company. Normally, I would just say put the box down until you're ready to leave but I strongly encourage you to hold on tight."

"Family jewels? Where did you find them?" Clara asked. She had no knowledge of family jewels. The only jewelry she remembered was what her mother referred to as party jewelry. Her father called it cheap but her mother said it was fun. She loved to sit at the vanity in her grandmother's room and play with it.

"In the safe in the upstairs front bedroom," Chase gestured towards the ceiling to the room above.

"I want to look," she whispered as she gestured towards an antique sofa table.

Connor placed the box down and stepped back.

Clara slowly opened the box and placed the envelope beside it. She reached in for a green velvet square box. She gasped when she opened it. Inside was a triple strand choker of pearls with what appeared to be an emerald in the center. The next was a smaller matching box, it held matching earrings, three pearls dangling from smaller emeralds. When she opened a tennis bracelet, Clara was too overwhelmed to look any further. She quickly returned everything back to the larger box, almost as if looking too long would damage them.

"Looks like you have everything under control. Any problems I should be concerned about?" Clara asked, suddenly realizing all the guys were watching her closely. "What? Why are you all looking at me?"

"Have you seen these before?" Connor asked.

"Never," Clara confirmed with a shake of the head. "I think I am ready to head out with a stop at the bank before work."

"Ah, Clara, before you head out, just more of an FYI. There were some calls over the weekend from the security company. Apparently, the new alarm was triggered a couple of times on Saturday night. We met here with the company to assure no one did get in. Not really sure if it was just a glitch or what but just wanted to mention it," Chase reported.

Clara gave each Chase and Rob a hug before leading Connor with the box outside onto the porch. Rob assured he would text her later in the evening.

Once they were back on the road, Connor looked over at Clara looking back at the box, "Do you want to stop at my place and review the items before heading to the bank?"

"I don't know. I just can't believe my mother had all this jewelry. The room Chase was referring to was my grandparents' suite, not my parents'. I don't think my father was ever aware of it. If he was, he would have either pawned it all off or given it to his girlfriend," Clara answered before she became quiet.

Connor silently agreed with her assessment. He wondered if her mother ever had knowledge about the safes in the house. The late Mr. Hawks was very old fashioned and private about his personal life, or as private as one could be in a large household with servants in a small town. Without any further discussion, he pulled into his parking space and carried the box up the flight of stairs to his loft with Clara. For safety, he actually locked and bolted the door before turning on the security system. He was not taking any chances. After seeing the few pieces, he was confident they were all real and very old. Some pieces were easily over a century old.

An hour later, Clara sat on the stool looking at all the jewelry spread out on the island. She and Connor had both confirmed the information on the inventory list. She had made a point of putting the insurance information into her phone with the client number. Without asking, Connor had stepped out to use his brother's copier machine. He made two copies. He was relieved no one was in the office. He returned to see Clara in the same spot.

"I just don't know what to do about this. I am speechless. Clueless," she opened her mouth but could not think of anything else to say.

"It's a seriously nice collection. Are you going to try on the choker or not?" Connor wondered.

"What? Why would I?"

"Why wouldn't you? They are yours. And I know you want to." Without a word he grabbed the choker and then her hand to lead her into his bedroom, stopping her in front of the mirror. Connor slowly placed the choker around her neck as he worked on the latch.

Clara watched his brown eyes as she felt his fingers gently on her neck. When he was finished, he brought his chin down towards her shoulder as he whispered, "Looks good on you."

The warm air from his breath blew into her ear and she suddenly shivered as her stomach tightened. Clara turned her head slightly, very aware his lips were close to hers. Without thinking, she leaned in and kissed him on the lips. It was quick and over with before he had a chance to register what she was doing. "Thank you, Connor."

He remained quiet standing behind her as he watched her through the mirror. She silently modeled, turning a little with a slight smile on her face until she saw the clock.

"Shit, dammit! I need to get going if I'm going to stop at the bank. It's close to closing." Clara lifted her hair in silent request to have him remove the necklace.

Connor's fingers gently brushed against her neck as he slowly removed the choker. He remained standing there as she slowly turned around to face him. He reached for her hand to cradle the choker with one hand while his other hand gently used his knuckles to caress her cheek. His brown eyes were on her green as they remained standing there looking at each other. His hand was soft and so gentle. When she did not back away, he leaned down to kiss her forehead. Slowly he moved down to kiss her cheek and then he slowly moved to her other cheek. He slowly leaned in. When she still did not move away, Connor slowly moved towards her lips. He paused for a moment as his lips remained on hers.

It was everything he could do to keep the kiss from progressing deeper. He was confident she was interested and attracted to him but Connor also knew she wasn't ready. He pulled back and whispered in her left ear, "Let's go, Beautiful."

It took Clara a moment to pull herself together. When he walked away, her eyes immediately went to his king sized bed and she lost control of where her thoughts went. She snapped back to reality when he called her name.

It was late when Connor parked next to her car. She winced when she realized the daycare would be closing in less than fifteen minutes.

"Connor, thanks for lunch and going with me to the house," Clara paused for a moment. "And thanks for being with me this afternoon. Can you stop in sometime tomorrow to sign those evals?"

"I have time now if you like," he answered.

"No, I need to get the kids before the daycare closes."

"How about I get the file, is it on your desk?"

Clara nodded her head, "It's in the out box labeled "Evaluations" to the right if sitting at the desk."

"I'll run in and grab it while you go pick up Reese and Hailey. I'll swing by and pick up a couple of pizzas. Meet you at your place." When her eyebrows furrowed, Connor further explained, "Aren't the Foxwoods stopping over to drop off the furniture and boxes? They have to be getting hungry. Any weird food issues I need to know with pizza?"

"No, the guys like the meat lovers but Reese prefers pepperoni," Clara hesitated before she opened her door. "Thanks, Connor. I'll see you in a bit."

He nodded his head as he reached for his cell. Connor placed the order for the pizzas as he waited for Clara to pull out of the lot. Then he went inside to retrieve the file.

When Clara arrived home, she sat the children at the kitchen table to eat fruit and steamed veggies. She texted Rob to let him know she was home for the evening and Connor was bringing over pizzas.

Rob groaned as he read the message.

Chase stopped in mid-step as he was about to step into the van, "What's wrong?"

"Clara said she's home for the evening and pizza will be available," he grumbled out.

"Alright, nice," his cousin stated as he opened his door. He knew what Rob was going to say before he said it.

"Not nice at all. Try annoying and ridiculous. The good doctor is picking up the pizzas," he stated with obvious frustration.

"At least she had the foresight to warn you. I'll meet you there," Chase chuckled as he slapped his cousin's shoulder before getting behind the wheel.

Connor arrived just after Chase and Rob. He brought the pizzas in before he assisted with bringing in the furniture and boxes. Shannon was already home. She had planned to meet with Lila for a drink but sat with the children in the kitchen while everything was being moved into the dining room.

When everyone was in the kitchen eating, Shannon invited everyone to go with her to Memories. Chase and Rob both agreed but Clara declined, "I need to get these guys to bed. It's already past their bedtime."

She picked up Hailey as she instructed Reese to say good night to everyone. She informed Connor she would be down in a few minutes. When she returned, Clara was surprised to find the kitchen was already cleaned up and Connor was sitting at the table reading and signing the evaluations.

Clara had opened a bottle of wine and poured a glass for each of them before sitting down with him at the table. She was impressed he was reading before he signed them.

Connor looked up at the glass of wine when she sat down beside him, "Thanks. How did you get Winnie to walk so far?"

Clara just shrugged after she sipped from her glass, "She wanted to find her mother, so we went on a walk looking for her."

Connor looked up at Clara in confusion. She was able to answer the unasked question, "Yeah, I know. Her mother probably died over twenty years ago. But she was very determined and slightly agitated that her mother might not know where she was. Marie distracted her with milk and cookies after she returned to her wheelchair."

Connor chuckled as he signed and dated the note. Since the pile had accumulated longer than she should have allowed, they sat at the table drinking wine while he read and asked questions. It was an overall pleasant evening. When he was finished, Clara returned the file to her work bag and placed it by the door. Connor followed her with both glasses refilled. He continued past her and into the family room. Placing the glasses on the end table, he sat before tapping the sofa beside him.

When she sat down, he handed over her wine glass before he pulled her feet up into his lap. Without a word, he gently massaged her feet.

Clara leaned back while she sipped her wine and relaxed. He was pretty good at this, she thought as she continued to internally debate the appropriateness of the situation.

When she opened her eyes, Connor was studying her face. Her green met his brown as her stomach continued to flutter, "You have nice hands."

"Hands of a surgeon. There's a lot I can do with these hands," he said softly as he reached for his glass. He could feel her tense up and immediately changed the subject. "Your place is pretty nice. I didn't realize it was so big inside. How many bedrooms upstairs?"

Clara eyed him closely at the sudden turn in topic, "Four with two full bathrooms. Another half down here."

Connor placed his glass on the table and shifted with one arm on the back of the sofa while the other rested across her legs on his lap. He could have been content to watch her all night. But he also knew this wasn't the right time.

Clara silently studied him as she sipped her wine and he retrieved his cell to read a message. His other hand continued to gently caress her calves. He answered the text and returned the cell back to his pocket.

"Everything alright?"

"Yeah, except I need to get going so you can get some rest. You have been able to sleep, right?"

Clara nodded, "Yeah, I usually get in a few hours before I get restless. That one week was the worst but Rob stayed down here on the couch until Shannon arrived."

As Connor continued to watch her, he leaned in but she pulled her legs back, placing her feet on the floor to stand up. He followed her lead, reached for the wine glasses but she said to leave them. When he followed her to the door, she turned and he continued forward until she was up against the wall. Without touching her, he leaned in to kiss her gently on the lips, "Have a good night. I'm sure I'll see you soon at work."

"Connor, I'm sorry. I can't do this. I'm married. It's not fair to you or Jason," Clara found herself whispering.

"Clara, you have nothing to apologize for. I'm not expecting anything. I just don't want the evening to end. I enjoy hanging out with you." Connor was again caressing her cheek with his knuckles as he softly spoke. He leaned in for another kiss on the lips. When she didn't move, he continued, "I just want you to know, I am here whenever you're ready."

"Ready? Ready for what?" Clara whispered back. She was not able to focus when he touched her.

"The next step," he sealed the deal with a slow kiss on her lips. He started to pull back but leaned in again, faster, for another kiss. He smiled and winked when he fully stood up again.

Clara had placed her hand on his chest. She wasn't sure if she was going to try to stop him or caress his chest. She just looked up into his warm brown eyes and sighed in frustration, "Connor?"

"Yeah, I know. You're married. Clara, I'm working the next three evenings at the hospital. I'll pick you up on Friday at seven." He winked at her when her green eyes flared up again. He leaned down and kissed her forehead.

"Good night, Beautiful, sweet dreams," he said as he opened the door and stepped out.

Clara remained standing against the wall a few minutes more as she wondered how he could make her so ready with the minimal touching. Her mind began to wander. She slowly tapped her head against the wall and told herself she needed to get her act together.

She washed out the wine glasses and dimmed the lights in the family room for when Shannon returned home before she went upstairs to call her husband.

"Jay, please call me. I get that you apparently don't want me anymore but don't ignore the children. They love you and need you. Also, if you are so sure it's over between us, then please get the nerve to tell me so we can both move on with our lives. I love you, Jason."

the fundraiser

Friday evening arrived sooner than Clara wanted. Of course, she would have admitted skipping the day altogether would have been better. As it turned out, Connor was right. She was able to find a babysitter and she did have dress options in her closet. One of the daycare teachers was looking to make extra money and was more than happy to watch the children two evenings a week. She requested only one weekend night and the other be during the week. For now, Clara just booked her for Friday evenings.

As for the closet, she did have a few evening dresses to pick from. Clara chose a simple black dress. It was a sleeveless fitted dress with a high neckline, low back and came just past her knees. It had a slit on the left side. She debated the jewelry but decided to keep it simple: a long pearl necklace that was her mother's, which she wore knotted at the center of her chest and matching pearl earrings. She wore no rings or bracelets. She had her hair pulled back in a loose French twist with a few loose curls left down to frame her face. With her makeup done, Clara was completing the switch of necessary items to a small clutch purse. She carried her shoes and purse down the stairs to model for Michelle and the kids as both her cell and doorbell each rang at the same time.

As Michelle was teaching both Reese and Hailey how to give a thumbs up approval, she answered the cell just as she opened the door.

"Hello?" Clara said into her phone as she lost her thought.

Standing before her was Connor dressed in a black suit with a black shirt and tie. While he may have shaved that morning, he looked to be in need of another shave but the five o'clock shadow looked good on him. Clara admired him slowly down to his feet and back up to his face. When she realized he was doing the same to her, she blushed. She stepped back and smiled, "Come in. I'm just going to say goodbye to the kids."

"Hello?" Clara heard Rob's voice over the phone. Shit, she thought as she held up a finger and excused herself to the kitchen.

"Hey Rob, sorry I was distracted for a minute. What's going on?" Clara asked.

"I was just calling to suggest I stop over with a movie," Rob suggested.

"Oh, no I can't. I already have plans and I'm just stepping out now. Can I take a raincheck?"

"Yeah, sure. Who is with the kids?"

"I have a sitter," she answered, about to get annoyed. It wasn't so much the question, but the tone, suggesting she didn't clear her arrangement with him first, just like in high school. Without even thinking, she found herself explaining, "It's one of Hailey's teachers."

"Alright, I guess maybe we can try something tomorrow," Rob stated slowly. He was trying to read her tone. He wanted to ask where she was going and with whom, but he knew that wouldn't go over well. He knew it wasn't Lila, she was working. Maybe it was Shannon, but he doubted it. "Everything alright?"

"Yes, everything is fine. We'll talk tomorrow," Clara stated, hopefully not too irritatingly. She had been looking out of the window to the backyard during the conversation. She groaned in frustration as she hung up and turned around.

Connor was standing at the doorway, leaning into the frame with his arms crossed looking highly amused. "You did it again, didn't you?"

"What did I do again?" Clara asked in confusion.

"You didn't tell the boyfriend where you are going with who again. And he is not happy," Connor chuckled as he slowly advanced towards her. Once he was close enough, he gave her a quick kiss. "You look great. I had thought of bringing flowers but figured you would think this was a date. Now, I really wish I did."

"Well, you clean up pretty good yourself," she responded, reaching out to adjust his tie. Just as she was finished, she looked up into his eyes and realized her mistake. It was a bit too intimate of a gesture and he seemed to be enjoying it too much.

Connor brought his hands up to hers as she attempted to pull her hands back. He brought them each up to his lips and kissed them while their eyes remained locked.

"I'll wait by the door while you say good-bye to the kids and check in with the sitter," he stated as he followed her from the kitchen. At the door, he watched as Clara reviewed everything with Michelle. She kissed both Reese and Hailey, instructing them to behave.

As Connor opened the door, he was surprised to see a man dressed in jeans and a t-shirt step up onto the porch. He had been about to ring the bell when the door opened. He was familiar but Connor couldn't place him.

"Can I help you?" Connor asked in a not friendly tone as he blocked the doorway until he knew who the visitor was.

"Uh, yeah, hi. Is, uh, Clara home?"

Connor was about to answer when he felt Clara's hands on his hips as she navigated him to the side, stepped up to the screen door and out onto the porch, "Hi Dallas. How is it going?"

"Hi Clara. Sorry to be just dropping in on you again. It looks like I got you at a bad time. Again. Can I come back tomorrow, about two? I really need to talk with you."

Dallas was embarrassed. He had always been on the shy side until he got to know someone and the doctor was not helping to ease his discomfort.

Clara looked to be debating about the meeting but realized, what harm would it do to just have a conversation with the guy? He had never been anything but polite and friendly. "Can I ask what this is about? You know what, don't worry. I'll be here tomorrow at two. The kids should be napping."

"Great! Tomorrow at two. I'll see you then. You both have yourselves a lovely evening," he smiled and made eye contact with each of them as he nodded and turned back towards his SUV.

Connor watched Clara, trying to read her reaction. Who was this guy?

Clara turned to lock the door and placed the key in her small purse. When she looked up, Connor was already standing on the ground with a hand reached up to assist her down the steps. He walked her to the passenger door of a low sports car and opened it. Once she was in, Devan stepped out of his place. Connor paused for a moment to talk with the bartender before getting behind the wheel.

Clara waved as they drove off. Then she looked around the car. "Is this a Porsche?"

"Yes, it is," he answered proudly. "It's a Porsche 911."

Clara leaned forward to place her hand on the dashboard, "This is nice. How come you weren't driving it the other day?"

"She's been in storage. I had her washed today. I figured a beautiful ride for my Beautiful Girl," Connor looked over as he shifted the gear. When he looked down towards his hand resting on the stick, he realized his hand was mere inches from her legs. He groaned to himself as he watched her shift in her seat, crossing her right leg over the left, causing her split in her dress to expose her toned legs. Alright, just focus on the driving and not her gorgeous legs, she's not ready for this yet.

"Connor," Clara started.

But he cut her off with a wave of her hand, "I know, I know. You are married, Beautiful."

They drove in a comfortable silence for a few minutes before Connor finally asked, "Are you going to tell me who that guy is or do I have to ask?"

Clara laughed, "You don't know who that was?"

"No, I don't know. If I did, I would not have to ask, now would I?"

"No, I guess not. I just figured you knew or I would have introduced you guys. He seemed to know who you were," she chuckled again. "I thought you had a photographic memory. It was Dallas Thompson."

Connor just looked at her as he raised his eyebrows in question, waiting for her to further explain.

"Clara?" Connor asked when he realized she wasn't continuing, "And?"

"Sorry, you really don't know?" Clara laughed again. She tried to control her giggles when he just gave her a look. "Sorry, I can't help it. I just think it's funny you don't know who Dallas Thompson is."

"Even with the name you can't place him?" She teased as she laughed again. "Sorry, I just realized that I don't know why you would know him nor why it's funny. It really isn't. Dallas' mother is my father's girlfriend."

"Oh. Ok. Yeah, I guess I should have guessed from his name. I should have known that." Connor looked over at her before he asked. "Are you two close?"

"Hardly, we only know of each other. We have always been friendly enough but our parents never really brought us together for dinner or anything. At the beginning, I wanted nothing to do with her. She was always hanging out at the house, offering to watch me while my dad was working. I think she was trying to move in. I probably would have gotten to know Dallas better if they had moved in. Instead, someone stepped in, no idea who it was or how it happened. Apparently, the trust became involved and told my dad under no circumstances would he be living in my mother's house with another woman. I was allowed as the current heir's daughter. He was allowed to live in the house with me as my legal guardian. It was made very clear he would no longer be allowed to live there once I turned eighteen unless my mother returned and invited him to stay." Clara became quiet as she looked out her window.

"I remember hearing about that," Connor stated softly. He would not have admitted he was eavesdropping on the conversation. During that time, there were many conversations among his parents and brother, as well as among the Trust regarding Clara and the rights to the house. "There were a lot of discussions about your dad's girlfriend. There was a suggestion of having a housekeeper placed in your home to assist with maintaining the house and watching you. And knowing the Trust, probably spy and report back. But your dad wouldn't agree to the housekeeper and he lived by the rules set.

"There was also another discussion about releasing the house to you. Again, there were concerns you wouldn't be able to keep the control, as a minor it would be your dad. And when you did become an adult, they didn't think your dad would allow you to take over control. Some thought nothing but a death certificate would allow the house to be turned over to you. Others were in favor of your receiving the house when you turned eighteen. Instead, you moved to the city."

"Wow. You know more than I did. My dad never told me what was going on. I just heard them arguing downstairs. She was demanding to move in and to allow the servants, but he would only shrug her off. It was a frequent argument between them. I am surprised they are still together."

"I am surprised they aren't married. What has it been, almost twenty years?" Connor commented.

"Yeah, twenty years but he never had the paperwork necessary to get married. You need to prove the previous marriage has dissolved. Honestly, it surprised me she stayed with him. The two are such high maintenance. I have no idea how they make their money." Clara was quiet a moment. Wanting to change the subject, "What's this evening about? You said it's a fundraiser."

Connor glanced over at Clara, very aware of the stress the topic caused. He explained about the purpose of the fundraiser and the beneficiaries.

· · · ·

Evil was pleasantly surprised to see her at the event. She looks wonderful! The simple dress and jewelry absolutely accented her beauty. The doctor beside her, while a fool, was certainly one lucky fellow. It always annoyed him how that family always had good luck. They have the sexiest and most willing women, fancy cars, and the money for traveling. It never occurred to him that the family in question actually worked multiple jobs as their career paths allowed. He had taken his chances with his current wife. While she did bring in some money from her trust fund, it was a headache every time to withdraw more than her monthly allowance. As if such a pathetic sum could provide with just his immediate needs.

His blue eyes continued to follow her around the room. She was so elegant and held her shoulders high like the princess that she was born to be. He sighed as he thought back to the last time when she slept beside him, her beautiful hair fanned out on the pillow like a royal crown. The soft touch of her skin. Her sweet soft floral scent always made him respond to her. As he felt himself start to respond, he realized he needed to control his thoughts or at least sit at a table. He retrieved a glass of champagne before heading to his assigned seat.

Once he sat, his frustrations seemed to take over. It had been some time since he was able to see her. She was so kind and giving, she allowed a friend in need to stay with her in the extra room. He simply could not chance his visits right now, he sighed. He wanted to be the one to pull the hairpins out and watch as her hair fell around her shoulders and rip the dress off as he had his way with her while she wore nothing but the black heels and white pearls...

Clara enjoyed the evening. When they arrived, both she and Connor were handed an envelope with tickets to place in the drawing for various baskets. Some baskets were simple, such as a cheese and wine theme, while others were more for the makings of a romantic get away with all expenses paid at various bed and breakfast places or dining out. She walked around the tables to place her tickets in interesting baskets. Connor was behind her and watched with amusement as she appeared to debate a romantic night.

"Why are you debating?" He whispered as he placed one in.

"Who would I take to a romantic evening at The Meadows Bed and Breakfast?" Clara demanded.

Connor chuckled, "I'm sure you'd find someone. You have up to a year to use it. Live dangerously." He made a point of dropping in another ticket and then he opened her hand that was hovering over the basket, releasing her ticket.

Clara shrugged and moved on, "It probably won't make much difference anyway. What are my chances of even winning? When do they announce the winners?"

"At the end of the evening we hand over our card to the attendants. They will hand us any baskets we win. We have assigned seating for dinner in case they have any questions. They'll likely find you if arrangements need to be made for delivery. The more exciting part is the silent auction." Connor grabbed her hand to lead her over to another set of tables. "Have you been to a silent auction before?"

Connor explained the rules after she shook her head, "Each item has a picture with a description. The sheet before it states the valued price and minimal starting bid. I put my assigned number down and my bidding price."

Clara watched as Connor bid on a boat and again for a pair of jet-skis. "Connor, you want a boat and jet-skis?"

Connor grinned like a boy on Christmas Eve, "Why not? I have a lake house. I could use a new boat. This is a fundraiser. The money goes towards research for certain cancers and treatments. There's a table over there if anyone wants to simply write a check. But this is more fun."

"You have a lake house?" Clara asked in wonder. Knowing him all her life, it surprised her she didn't know everything about him. She shouldn't have been surprised.

"I do," he stated absently as he debated placing a bid on a pair of ATVs.

"What do you do there?"

"Depends, fish, water ski or just relax. It's where I go when I have a day or two off. I'll bring you and the kids my next weekend off," He grabbed her hand to move her along. "See anything here you want?"

Clara laughed, "Yeah, the weekend in Paris and the Disneyworld package."

"Alright, sounds good," he went over to place a bid on each.

"Connor, I can't afford those," she stated as she realized he was using her number.

"Clara, it's a fundraiser for a good cause. If you win either of them, I will cover the cost. And I get to go with you. So, it's a win-win," He stated as he raised his eyebrows and grinned. "Are you ready for another drink?"

Grabbing her hand once again, he led her over to the bar. After she had her drink, he was approached by an orthopedic doctor he often worked closely with in the emergency room. Connor introduced Clara as the new rehab director at the rehab facility. The doctor was pleased to meet with her as each had several questions regarding various protocols for post-op care. The conversation was concluded as they each exchanged professional numbers and emails. He promised to have the information sent before the end of the weekend.

After Connor had made the first introduction, he had been pulled into other conversations. He kept an eye on Clara as she continued to mingle.

"She looks to be having a good time," Matt stated as he came up behind his brother. She looks like her mother, he thought as he felt his heart squeeze.

"Yeah, I think so. She's going to get us many new admissions. The acute care kind with shorter lengths of stay and a return home in better shape. Clara wants to increase her department size and has already made comments about more updated equipment," Connor stated.

"If the referrals are coming and the returns happen, no reason not to give it to her. I'll need some estimates so I can start crunching numbers for the budget this fall," Matt answered as he sipped from his glass.

Connor looked around, "Didn't bring your wife?"

"No, Hunter has a stomach bug and was very clingy. I offered to be the one to stay because she lives for this stuff, but the little guy prefers his mother," Matt shrugged. "She was specific about where to put the bids and on which baskets. Joshua came in her place, though he won't be able to place any bids."

"No?" Connor's eyes roamed the room, finding his nephew. He also saw Eric's parents but decided to keep his distance for the evening before turning back to Clara. "You won't let him access his trust for a good cause? Are you still upset that he went to medical school instead of law?"

"No," Matt denied with a shake of the head. "I'm over it. As Dad pointed out, I can be equally proud of a son that's a doctor as a son that's a lawyer. It's important for him to enjoy his work, heaven knows he'll be enduring long hours. I don't think his mother is over it. Josh will have a nice enough time, enjoying dinner and drinks. He still has chances with the baskets. He's already exceeded his allowance for the quarter. Besides, it's his first time attending. Once he sees what it's about, maybe he'll budget better for next time."

"I'm surprised Talia didn't instruct him on the baskets she wants to win."

"She knows better than to make any suggestions to him. He'll only do the opposite anyway." Matt sipped from his drink as he reviewed the items up for auction. "Check out the lovely sailboat. Maybe I'll surprise her with the Paris weekend."

"No, Clara wants that one," Connor claimed with a shake of the head.

Matt turned to look at his brother, and noticed his eyes were following Clara's movements as various men approached her.

"Isn't she married?"

"Yeah but they're separated. He doesn't seem to be interested in working on their marriage," Connor answered defensively, hearing the tone in his brother's voice.

"I advise you to wait until her marriage has legally dissolved before you touch her," Matt's voice was soft but harsh as he sipped from his drink.

"Matt, it's not like that," Connor's defensive tone suggested otherwise.

"No, of course it's not," he agreed sarcastically. "You both have known each other a long time, seen each other on your worst days, know what makes the other tick. What happens if the husband wakes up one morning to realize he's been an ass and wants his beautiful young wife back. Think she will choose you?"

Connor glanced at his older brother before looking back towards Clara. His expression suggested he believed she would, but Matt continued. "You don't want to put her in a position to have to choose between the man she's literally known all her life, who has seen her at her worst and makes her happy," his brother was arguing his case until he made the final point, "Or the man that's the father of her young children."

Connor's brown eyes flashed onto his brother's blue eyes. Matt knew he hit the mark. Clara was her mother's child and she would do what she needed to keep her family intact. He whispered, "Who do you think she would choose?"

"Matt, there's nothing going on. We aren't sleeping together," he attempted to protest.

"No? I saw you bringing her up to your loft in the middle of a workday," Matt challenged. He didn't mention the time after the notification of her mother's death.

"True. We were looking over the family jewels," Connor stated absently. He didn't catch the unintended pun until his brother laughed.

"Is that what you kids are calling it these days?"

"Will you stop. Seriously, we were looking over her family jewelry. The Foxwoods have been supervising the packing up of her furniture and household goods to place into storage until she decides what to do with everything. They somehow opened the house safe. Clara was comparing the original inventory list to what was present. Then we went to the bank to open a safety deposit box," Connor explained.

"Was everything accounted for? It's been a long time since I heard about the Hawks jewelry. Her mother never had it out. I wondered if she was keeping everything locked up away from the bastard husband of hers," Matt commented. He had decided his point was made but he would continue to monitor.

"Yeah, I think Clara was thinking the same thing, not the bastard part," he clarified.

"Give her time to come around, she's smart. A leopard doesn't change its spots." Matt couldn't hide his dislike for the father.

Ignoring the last comment, "I think she also believes her mother wasn't aware of the safe combination."

"Very likely to be true," Matt agreed. "The old man lived in a man's world. He was training his son for the roles to head the house and family business. His daughter was never even allowed in his home office. I don't see him ever giving her the combination, nor his wife. They both passed so suddenly."

Clara was surprised to be enjoying herself during the evening. Conor was right, it was an excellent opportunity for her to be networking. She met many of the doctors in the local community who would be referring their patients to the nursing home. Clara was working to change the reputation to a rehab facility where one can go to recover and get stronger before returning home. Not the old-fashioned idea of going to a nursing home to die. Clara would have many policies to be reviewing during the next week. She followed Connor to the assigned table in preparation for dinner to be served.

"Clara, you remember my brother Matt," Connor reminded Clara. He wasn't sure when they saw each other last. He was confident it was before her mother's disappearance.

Clara turned to the man beside her and she felt like a young child again. He didn't look any different from the last time she saw him, except a few wrinkles around the eyes and some white hairs sprinkled in, "Yes, hello, Mr. Emerson."

"Clara, a pleasure seeing you again. Please, call me Matt," he chuckled as he instructed. Yes, she is definitely her mother's child. "My wife was not able to attend. Our youngest is sick. My oldest son came instead. I believe you already met Joshua?"

Clara looked over to see the familiar face and smiled, "Yes I have. Hello Josh. Are you enjoying the evening?"

Josh's blue eyes met hers as he nodded, "Yes."

Matt squinted in question at his son's inability to converse. An unusual thing, he was well aware of his son's many female acquaintances. He noted the amused look on his brother's face, remembering the pair likely have already met at the nursing home. Ahh, he must have a school boy crush on her. He shook his head as he thought of the effect the Hawks women seemed to have on the Emerson men. To prevent further discomfort for his son, he turned to pull out her chair. Matt sat to her right while Connor was on her left, giving his son the seat on his other side.

"Connor tells me you are interested in increasing your department size."

Connor noted with amusement his nephew still could not maintain his usual cool with Clara. He had thought his shadowing her would allow him to become more comfortable as he learned the purpose of why a doctor prescribed therapy.

Clara was pleased Matt was open to possibly expanding her department as she talked about her ideas for the therapy gym. She understood while Eric was the facility administrator and her immediate supervisor, Matt was the CEO. He was the man behind the curtain silently running the facility.

Clara was not aware of the many eyes following her around during the evening. Some were simply men appreciating an attractive woman while others were trying to identify the woman sitting with the Emerson men.

When Clara excused herself to use the restroom, Matt watched his brother's eyes continue to follow her. He debated with himself the likelihood of Connor walking the line, not likely. Then he also noted his son's eyes were following her. Now he's likely to keep his distance. Joshua's apparent infatuation seemed to prevent his participating in a simple conversation, he thought.

When Clara came out of the stall to wash her hands, the woman beside her was touching up her lips as she studied through the mirror the woman that arrived on Dr. Connor Emerson's arm. She had immediately set out to learn her name as well as the true nature of their relationship. She learned only she had a hearing impairment, so obvious with her hair up, and she was a physical therapist at his nursing home.

"Jenna Hudson," she turned to Clara to introduce herself, believing the best strategy was to be direct.

"Hello, Clara O'Reilly," she answered as she shook the woman's hand. An acquaintance recently suggested she should provide her maiden name, to allow others to better place her. But her maiden name was Gibson, not Hawks. It would never help to clarify her family or her home. Just as well since she had no wish to be "properly placed."

"Are you Connor's flavor of the week?" Jenna asked, attempting to be fun.

Clara read the envious tone as she reapplied her lip gloss, but she chuckled when she answered, "Not at all. I am simply an old friend escorting him tonight. Last week's flavor wasn't available."

She dropped her tube into her purse and walked out while the other women chuckled.

When Clara stepped out of the restroom, the smell of lingering cologne triggered a memory. She felt a sudden chill as her heart started to beat faster and her throat narrowed, causing her breathing to be labored. She took a few steps, using her hand to balance herself along the wall as she heard in her head, Evil is here. She looked around the room to assess the danger, but her eyes spotted the safe zone and she quickly returned to her seat.

Connor had returned to the table with another round of drinks. Wine for Josh and Clara, and club soda for himself and his brother. Neither had seen her moment of panic but Josh did. Or rather, he saw her confidence wane for a quick moment as she scanned the room before her eyes found his uncle. What is going on with them, he wondered.

Once Connor sat beside Clara, she felt a sense of calm and security as his arm stretched out on the back of her chair. Looking for comfort, she pulled out her cell. They were each checking text messages when she heard Matt ask, "Who is that and why is she looking so furiously at you?"

They both looked up and Clara answered while looking back at her text, "Oh, that's just Connor's flavor from last month."

Matt and Josh both laughed out loud while Connor gave her an annoyed look, "Why the hell would you say that?"

She shrugged when she answered, "She introduced herself in the ladies' room."

"She actually said that?" Connor challenged.

"No, that was just my interpretation. She asked if I was your flavor of the week. Did I read it wrong?" She turned in question to Matt and

Josh. "Because I told her last week's flavor was unavailable. Was she last week's?"

"More like four weeks ago, I believe," Josh answered with a chuckle as Matt realized why she looked familiar. He looked over her head to see his brother roll his eyes. He wasn't reading any annoyance or jealousy on her part.

"Why were you even talking to her?" Connor demanded. The last thing he needed was Clara mingling with his previous dates.

"She introduced herself to me. I just thought she was networking. How was I to know she was one of your previous girlfriends? What did you do to make her so bitter?" Clara wondered out loud.

"Clara, we only went out a couple of times. I didn't do anything to her." He gave his brother a dirty look when he heard him laughing. "I didn't feel any chemistry between us."

"Really? She seems your type," she answered thoughtfully.

"My type? How the hell would you know what my type is?" Connor asked, flabbergasted, and further annoyed by his brother's continued laughter.

Clara laughed, "You have a type. It's very obvious. You are with the same high maintenance type every time I see you, even in high school."

Matt decided to not comment, despite agreeing. Josh found he was thinking back to all his uncle's previous girlfriends and was confused. "How can you tell?"

Clara turned her green eyes on his blue as she answered with a shrug, "That a woman's high maintenance? It's very obvious."

Matt was quiet as he listened to the conversation around him. Her voice was similar to her mother's but her articulations and expressions were different. Her mother usually kept up a properness while Clara seemed more carefree. As he watched his son's interaction, he wondered if he needed to monitor Josh as well. The last thing the family needed was another major family riff over a married woman.

As the evening ended, Connor did not comment on Clara's sudden quietness as she appeared to remain close to his side, linking her arm around his as they exited down the steps. While they waited in the cool air for the valet to bring his car around, he realized she was shivering. Without a thought, Connor removed his jacket, placing it around her shoulders before pulling her close to him, not aware of the eyes watching from afar.

more lies and secrets

The next day, Clara was folding the laundry on the dining room table as she thought of the previous evening. She was pleasantly surprised to win two baskets. One was a wine basket filled with a corkscrew, two wine glasses, and three bottles of wine. The other was the Backyard Oasis complete with a gas grill, outdoor dining table for six, and three half wheelbarrow planters. She had arranged for delivery the following Saturday.

Connor won the boat and the jet-skis, so he promised his old boat to his nephew. His brother won the Paris trip. Matt wasn't too upset about losing the water stuff as he explained to Clara. "I'm his brother, he has no choice but to let me take them out for a ride. Sorry you lost the Paris trip, but my wife will be pleased. You are definitely getting a ticket to the next fundraiser. You are the good luck charm."

When they reached town, Clara had agreed to stop in at Memories for a drink before Connor brought her home. He had explained Matt bought the tickets in the facility's name. She was shocked at the price of each ticket.

"But it included dinner, unlimited drinks and tickets for the basket auction," he reasoned. "And you won two baskets!"

"True. Why were you and Matt competing for the same things? It would have been cheaper to simply go out and purchase them," Clara commented. "Competing against each other is what brought up the price."

"True, but it's a fundraiser. The competition is more exciting. If he really wanted those things, he would have placed a higher bid. His focus was on the Paris trip. He's smart enough to keep his focus and not over bid. Besides, I can claim the cost on my taxes," Connor grinned.

Clara enjoyed the evening and looked forward to her new outdoor deck. She would need to figure out what flowers to plant. Glancing at the clock, she realized it was almost two. She sighed as she speculated on Dallas' reason for a visit. And then it happened again, her doorbell and cell both rang at the same time. Clara opened the door as she answered the phone.

"Hi, come in," Clara said as she opened the screen door and gestured towards the phone and then the family room.

"Clara?" Rob asked over the line. "I was calling to see if we are on for today, but I guess I got you at a bad time again."

Clara sighed with annoyance at Rob's jealous streak showing. It was one of the reasons they never actually dated in high school. The incident at the prom didn't help either. He would have blown a gasket if he knew Dallas was inside her house right now. She chuckled mischievously but decided to play nice.

"Rob, I was just thinking about calling you. We are still on for today. Any time after three works for me," she stated.

"Good. Is everything alright?" Rob detected something in her tone. Chase often accused him of reading into everything when it involved Clara.

"Rob, I promise you, all is well. See you in a bit." Clara hung up before he had an opportunity to ask more questions.

She stepped into the family room to see Dallas looking over all her pictures. "Dallas, can I get you something to drink?"

Dallas turned and followed her into the kitchen. She gave him a list of options before pulling out two water bottles.

They both sat silently at the kitchen table for a few minutes before Dallas started the conversation. While he was shy by nature, Dallas could hold his own when the situation called for it. He wasn't a pushover by any means but tended to sit back and watch his surroundings instead of trying to be the center of attention, like his parents.

"Are you adjusting to being back home?"

"I am. I'm enjoying the slower pace. You never realize the tranquility of it until you spend years elsewhere," Clara answered.

"Very true. I heard you plan to have your house changed into apartments. Very impressive. I haven't told my mother yet. She still has the misguided belief your dad will marry her and they will both live with you at the house." Dallas shrugged as if to say, what can you do?

"Do they plan to get married?" Clara wondered.

"I don't know. I don't really talk with them," he said while rolling the water bottle between his hands.

Clara felt he was working towards the real reason for his visit. To say she was surprised was an understatement. She focused on the present moment, to avoid thinking of the many reasons he could be here.

"I felt you should know, well actually, I wanted you to know," Dallas paused again. He wanted to be tactful and not disrespectful. "I don't know if you're aware that our parents dated before they married their spouses."

He paused as he looked into her green eyes. Clara looked into his familiar blueish green eyes. It hit her instantly why his eyes were so familiar to her, shit!

Dallas knew the instant it clicked. Her eyes were big with shock but he kept quiet as she processed the information.

"You are telling me that you and I are..." she trailed off, her hand gesturing between them. When he nodded, she continued, "Wow. Really? How did you find out?"

He sighed, "I always suspected but it was confirmed when I was, I don't know about eleven or twelve. My mother and father were arguing over child support and alimony. She wanted him to pay more each month and he told her she would need to go through the lawyers. The argument grew louder and she said, well, I'm sure you are aware she has never been tactful. She made a few comments that didn't sit well with him, leading him to do a little research. Stupid on her part, as it made him second guess her. He somehow convinced me to get something of your dad's, then he had a DNA test performed on me. After he got the results he disowned me, and his lawyer was able to dissolve the alimony and child support. She had to repay him."

"Wow, I am so sorry you had to go through that. My dad had never said a word to me," Clara stated as she reached over to squeeze his hand.

"Yeah, well she hasn't said a word to me either. Zachariah, my non-father, told me," Dallas shrugged. "They didn't have another epic argument. His lawyer simply delivered a letter to her lawyer. She was forced to get a job and support herself. This is not common knowledge around town. I was initially embarrassed but now, I look at you and see a sibling I am proud of and would like to get to know you."

Clara was still reeling in the shock of having a brother all these years on the periphery of her life. Her father never said anything, damn. "Does he know?"

"I'm confident he does," Dallas answered without explaining.

Clara simply nodded her head, more lies and secrets. She shouldn't have been surprised, but she was. She couldn't get beyond that.

"Look, I have given you a lot to think about. I haven't come here to ask you for anything. I don't want money or your house, I just want it in the open that you're my little sister. Here are my numbers. When you're ready to talk or hangout, please call. I've heard nothing but good things about you over the years," he stated with a smile as he pushed a card over towards her. "I'll be around."

He stood up and left the house.

Twenty minutes later, Clara was still sitting in the chair in shock. She glanced at the clock before reaching for her cell to make a call.

"Hello Clara. I was just about to call. Should I bring dinner?" Rob asked.

"Rob, I am so sorry to be doing this at the last minute, but can we reschedule for another time?" Clara asked.

"Yeah, sure. Is everything alright?" He wondered as he tried to read her tone. What happened in the last hour to cause her to change plans? He heard a male voice in the background both earlier and last night.

"Everything's fine," she quickly answered in frustration, unaware her tone caused Rob to cringe. But before he could comment, Clara continued, "I'll call you later." She hung up before he could argue.

Rob was already in town when he received the call. Instead of turning around, he parked on Main Street across from Memories. As he entered, he was surprised to see the good doctor sitting at the bar. Rob was so sure he was the reason for Clara's sudden change in plans. He grudgingly sat on the only empty bar stool, next to Connor.

"Foxwood," Connor nodded after sipping from his beer.

Rob ordered a beer and nodded his greeting.

Amused at his neighbor's forlorn mood, Connor looked at his watch. "Don't you have plans with Clara this afternoon?"

"She cancelled," Rob sighed as he drank from his beer.

"Oh yeah, that's right. That guy was stopping over today at two," Connor stated as he looked at his watch. It was just after three now.

"Who was stopping over?" Rob demanded, obviously annoyed that the good doctor knew more about what was going on with Clara than he did.

"Dallas Thompson," Connor answered with a shrug.

Rob felt his temper rising at the thought of Clara hanging out with his nemesis.

Connor was always aware of Clara's issues with Rob while she was in high school. He was a bit possessive and didn't approve of male friends. She didn't like Rob's controlling side. Since Connor never hung out with the guy until recently, he wasn't aware of his reasons for the obvious dislike of Dallas Thompson. But he thought it would be fun to poke at it. Connor had nothing better to do for the moment, "Why wouldn't Dallas and Clara be friends? Their parents have been dating for a while."

"I don't like him," Rob simply stated with a shrug as he lifted his drink up for a sip. He never really considered Clara would have a legitimate reason for a relationship with him. "I especially don't like him hanging out with her."

"She seemed comfortable with him," Connor stated as he watched the man beside him struggle to not let his temper get the better of him.

"And how do you know this?" Rob demanded.

"Dallas was at her place last night when I picked her up," Connor shared, trying hard to not sound as if he were bragging.

Rob felt his heart sink as the rumors he heard were confirmed. Clara and the good doctor were indeed all dressed up for a romantic evening out on the town with a nightcap at Memories before stopping at her place. He should have kept quiet. Instead Rob asked, "What's the deal with you two anyway?"

"Oh, you know, friends, colleagues, neighbors from the same side of the tracks. She's always saying she's a married woman," Connor nonchalantly explained before he sipped from his beer.

"Speak of the angel," Connor announced a moment later as his cell's caller ID popped up with Clara's picture from the evening before. He picked up the phone with a smile and showed Rob before answering.

"Hello Clara," he greeted before being interrupted by a small voice.

"Mommy is down on the floor," Reese announced.

"Reese? Is everything alright?" Connor asked. His eyes met Rob's. "Can you put Mommy on the phone?"

"Mommy is on the floor. She won't wake up," the young boy stated, fear was obvious in his tone.

"Did Mommy fall?" He asked as both he and Rob stood up. He instructed Devan to have an ambulance sent to her house.

"The man pushed her down the stairs," the boy answered.

What the hell? Connor thought, what man, he wondered as the blood drained from his face. "Reese, buddy, I am on my way. Ok. Help is on the way. Is the man still there?" He followed Rob across the street as he pointed towards his truck.

"No, he ran out the door. He is gone," the boy confirmed.

"Where is your sister?" He asked as Rob sped down the two blocks, arriving at Clara's in under a minute.

"She's right here," Connor was able to visualize the young boy gesturing beside him as if he could see them.

Connor and Rob both jumped out of the truck and ran to the opened front door. He placed his cell in his pocket as he stepped through the door.

When he looked over, he saw Clara sprawled out on the floor at the bottom of the stairs. Reese was sitting on the bottom step with his arm protectively around his little sister's shoulders.

Rob picked up the crying toddler and grabbed the boy's hand to lead him away from the steps to give Connor room. He watched as they sat on the sofa together.

Connor was relieved Clara was breathing. Her heart rate was elevated, and he noted the blood on the back of her head. Concerned about a possible neck injury, he kept her neck still until the paramedics arrived. Connor requested a cervical collar to keep her stabilized as they moved her onto the backboard and then the stretcher. He gave instructions before announcing he would ride with them.

As they headed out, Connor squatted down by the children, "Are you hurt? Did the man hurt either of you?" He gave them each a quick assessment, not seeing any obvious bruising or swelling.

"No, he did not hurt us. We were playing in Hailey's room when the man came down the hall and jumped over the railing onto Mommy,"

Reese explained.

Hailey made some comments that neither Connor nor Rob could understand. But Reese understood, he nodded his head as if agreeing with her.

"I'll take them to the farm with me," Rob stated.

"Sounds good. I'll stay with Clara. Reese, you did a great job keeping Mommy and your sister safe until we got here. Mommy will be very proud of you," he messed his hair as he stood up.

As Connor was walking out the door, the Sheriff and both of his sons had arrived. He gave a quick explanation of what happened before getting into the ambulance.

Lila was working at the emergency room when the ambulance arrived. She was waiting in the bay as the paramedics pulled the stretcher out. Initially she was surprised to see Connor assisting until she realized the patient was Clara, "Oh my God! What happened? Where are her kids?"

"Someone was in the house and pushed her down the steps. Your brother is taking the kids back to the farm for now," Connor stated as he grabbed the stethoscope from Lila's shoulders. Once they entered a room, he began a more formal assessment and yelled out orders.

It was close to seven in the evening when Clara started to stir. She had the worst headache ever and wondered if she had been out drinking the night before and was currently suffering the consequences. When she shifted slightly, her back ached and a pain shot through her shoulder. Clara groaned softly as she opened her eyes.

She was shocked to find herself in a hospital bed with Connor sitting beside her in a chair. He was leaning forward on his elbows holding her left hand. He smiled as he reached into his chest pocket, and pulled out her hearing aids.

Once she could hear, Clara demanded answers from Connor.

Instead of answering her questions, Connor stood up and sat on the edge of the bed. He pulled out a pen light and flashed it into her eyes. He gave her instructions and waited until she followed them as he completed a quick neuro assessment.

Then he grabbed her hand and asked her what she remembered.

"Connor, if I knew what happened I wouldn't be asking, dammit. Tell me what the hell happened!"

"Reese used your phone to call me. He said a man was in the house and pushed you down the stairs," he watched as Clara seemed to process the information and search her memory. Before she asked, Connor continued, "Both Reese and Hailey are alright. They say they were both in her room when it happened. Neither one was touched. I checked, no bruising or swelling. They're scared but alright. Foxwood took them home to the farm."

"There was a man in my house?" She repeated. "A man was in my house with me and my children? Why?"

Connor hesitated to give the details so soon, but he knew she would eventually hear about it. They had known each other her whole life, he wasn't about to start lying now. "What do you remember?"

"I was going upstairs to see if the kids were up from their naps. I was probably halfway up when I saw a shadow over the banister. It was too wrong to be either of the kids but when I turned," she stopped and shrugged. "That's all I remember."

Clara was moving her shoulder, to assess her injuries. That's when she realized she was wearing a hard collar, "Why am I wearing a cervical collar? Did I break my neck?" Horrified at the thought.

"It was placed as a precaution when the paramedics arrived until it could be confirmed you don't have a cervical injury. Clara, the scan was clear of skull fracture and bleeding. No obvious injury to your neck but you do have a concussion. They are keeping you here overnight with a repeat scan in the morning to assure you don't have a slow bleed. Let's take this off and see how your neck feels," Connor decided as he reached over to remove it. He watched as she moved her head around.

"Any pain?"

"Yeah, my head is killing me, my shoulder is sore, and my back is achy," Clara commented. She reached for his hand as she asked the next question, "Connor seriously, are Reese and Hailey really alright?"

Connor was already reaching for his phone. He pulled up a contact and waited for the other end to answer.

"Yeah, she's awake." He shook his head as he answered, "Nothing different than before. Here she is," he held the phone out towards her.

"Hello?"

"Clara!" Clara heard Rob's voice, "I'm glad you are awake. You gave us all a scare! I have someone here that wants to talk to you." She could hear him talking to someone and then she heard her son's voice. She closed her eyes to prevent tears from falling.

"Mommy? Are you going to be ok? I miss you! Hailey misses you too. When are you coming back home? Rob let us help him and Chase feed the animals. We might get to go for a ride tomorrow! Is it alright if we stay the night? Can you come over too?"

"Reese, I am fine. Connor says you called for help. That was very smart of you and very brave to look after your sister. I am so proud of you! I love you. Tell Hailey I love her too, alright?"

After Reese promised to be good, she heard Rob's voice again, "Clara, you rest up and we'll see you tomorrow."

"Thanks, Rob."

"Anytime"

Clara handed the phone back to Connor, "Do I really need to stay all night?"

"Yeah, doctor's orders," he confirmed.

Just then there was a knock on the door. When it opened, a good looking guy wearing scrubs entered. He introduced himself as Brad, her nurse for the night shift. He had dark hair with blue eyes, accented by his scrubs, and broad shoulders. Definitely someone that spent a lot of time keeping in shape. Clara noted his dimples when he smiled, asking if she needed anything.

He had been about to initiate a neuro check, when Connor informed him he had just completed one.

"You are a doctor. Can't you simply come home with me?" She pleaded as the nurse left. "I don't want to stay here all night by myself."

Connor reached for her hand to hold as he talked, "Clara it wasn't my order. The neurosurgeon ordered you to stay to assure you only have a concussion, no bleeding. You were out for a significant amount of time. After he repeats the scan tomorrow with good results and you don't show any neurological symptoms, you'll be released. I will stay with you tonight."

He paused as he debated how much to share. "Clara, the sheriff and his deputies are doing an investigation at your place. Since he's the landlord, he was pretty angry at someone not only breaking into your place but monitoring your activities. They found surveillance equipment. He has posted a deputy at your place, with the kids on the farm, and outside your room here."

"Surveillance equipment? Videos and audio? Live recordings?" Clara repeated as the horror sank in, "Where?"

"I don't know all the details yet, only what Anthony told me a bit ago. I guess there's audio with recording in the kitchen and bedroom," he answered softly. Connor felt his anger renew as her face went pale.

"Just my room and the kitchen? Not the children's?" Her eyes were wide with horror. Someone was listening to her private conversations with her husband. "Someone was listening to me while I live my life? They could hear everything I was doing and saying? Oh my God! Why? Why would anyone be interested in my life? You know me, I lead a boring life! What's to monitor?"

Connor remained silent as he thought about the millions of dollars worth of antique jewelry. He was relieved she had it secured at the bank. But was that what this was about? Or was it unrelated? He had been walking around the room with restlessness as he debated what to tell the sheriff. He thought it best the fewer who knew about the jewelry, the better. When he turned back around, Clara was removing the covers, "What do you think you are doing?"

"I need to use the bathroom," Clara stated as she started to scoot towards the edge of the bed. Before her feet reached the floor, she felt a sudden wave of dizziness. She stopped moving as she placed her hands out to support her. "Shit."

Connor was at her side as he debated how to assist. He offered to carry her, but she yelled at him instead.

"Connor, why would you carry me to the bathroom? I have a concussion not a spinal cord injury. Don't touch that button. I don't need a nurse or a bedpan. Just give me a minute for the dizziness to go away," she knew better than to close her eyes, but it was the only way to slow the spin of the room. Clara kept them closed until she was sitting on the edge and felt the floor under her feet. Then she slowly opened them. She let out a slow breath and looked up at him, "We can do this, Connor."

"Clara, I want to believe you, I really do but I have no idea how to help you right now. This is more your area than mine," Connor confessed. He should have been embarrassed but he was more concerned about her falling. "Should I put one of those belts around your waist?"

"Do you know how to use it?"

"Not really. Are you sure you don't want your nurse to assist with this?" His concern was evident in his voice.

She smiled mischievously as she tilted her head to think, "You know, he was pretty cute. I wouldn't mind his strong arms around me."

"Oh, you must have a worse injury than we thought because you don't remember you're married," Connor teased back. "The neurologist may want to keep you here for a week."

"That is so not funny. Just stand there in case I lose my balance. The dizziness is likely to start up again," Clara instructed as she stood.

"Oh shit!" She reached for his hand and felt his arm around her low back. She closed her eyes again as she focused on her breathing. Then, she opened them. The room was no longer spinning but she felt she was swaying, as if she were on a boat as she whispered, "Don't let me go."

"Never, I have you," he whispered back. I am never letting you go, he thought.

Clara was looking down when it finally dawned on her she was wearing a hospital gown, "What the hell am I wearing?"

"A hospital gown," Connor casually answered, knowing where this was leading.

"Yes, a hospital gown. Who put this on me?" She demanded. Her green eyes glared up at him. He was pleased to see she could move her head around while walking without any further complaints of dizziness.

"Clara, Lila is working down in the emergency room. She removed your clothes and put on the gown. But I have to say, I did like the green matching panties and bra," he cheerfully commented.

"What? Why couldn't you have been a gentleman and stepped out?"

"I did! I saw the clothes through the bag," Connor laughed as she groaned with embarrassment.

"I don't think anyone really paid attention to your choice of underwear, Sweetheart. In the ER, you'd be surprised by what people are wearing or not wearing. It's not like everyone wakes up and says, 'I need to put on my best underwear in case I go to the emergency room today.' Most visits are not planned."

Seemed to take forever but Clara finally arrived in the bathroom. Her bladder was so full she was worried she would not make it, much more horrifying than Connor and Sheriff Mancuso seeing her underwear, she thought. Once she was sitting, she assured him she was alright.

He instructed her to hold onto the grab bar before he closed the door to give her privacy. While he waited, he pulled out his cell to check messages and answered a few. He heard the toilet flush and was standing at the doorway when she opened the door with her green eyes flaring as she stepped out.

"Why didn't you tell me my butt was hanging out?" She demanded as she paused with one hand reaching for the sink and the other was holding the gown closed.

Connor chuckled as he looked over her covered backside. When he looked up appreciatively and his eyes met hers in the mirror, he started tying her gown, "Clara, you are black and blue with stitches. Very lucky you weren't injured worse. I'm not going to be concerned with your lovely bottom showing. Happy? It's tied."

Clara had been washing her hands and made the mistake of looking at the mirror, "I look horrible! I have never looked so bad in my life!"

"I don't know, I think you looked worse after the time you fell from your bicycle," Connor stated as he tried to distract her. He gently brushed her hair over her shoulder as he re-tied the top of the gown. When he finished, he impulsively kissed her sore shoulder as he brushed her hair back again.

Clara became defensive about the incident from when she was eight, "I did not fall from my bike! Stupid Danny Thompson! He should never have been allowed to have that slingshot. He ruined my favorite purple shirt and matching flower shorts. My mother couldn't get the blood out and threw them away."

"Your mother almost had a stroke when she answered the door and you were in my arms with blood and dirt all over. You even had a few leaves in your hair," Connor remembered as he assisted her back to the bed.

"I didn't have leaves in my hair," Clara declared as she scooted over to make room for him to sit beside her. She thought back to the incident. "Wasn't your brother at the house with her?"

Connor sighed, figures she would remember such a detail. He didn't think she put it together yet. "I am amazed your mother allowed you to go to the park at all. I think I had to carry you back more times than you change the batteries on your hearing aids."

"You exaggerate more than Mrs. Dyer," she said dismissively.

"Are you hungry? I haven't had dinner yet and Devan is asking," Connor asked after reading a text.

"Yeah, I haven't eaten anything since breakfast," she answered as she gave her request.

Connor texted back the order and then placed the cell on the table beside him. He removed his shoes before he scooted beside her. He placed his arm around her shoulders as she leaned into him.

"Connor, thanks for spending your Saturday evening with me. Will you apologize to your date for me?" she asked.

"My date? What date?" He asked, confused.

"Oh please, Connor Emerson not have a date on Saturday Night? Never! I do appreciate you cancelling to hang out with me. You should get her some pretty flowers," she stated expertly.

"Clara, I'm not seeing anyone," Connor felt the need to clarify.

"No? No one wants you, hmm? Well, that's ok. You can hang out with me," she leaned over to kiss his cheek before she snuggled up next to him.

Connor watched as she slept. She looked like a little angel. He closed his eyes as he made a mental list of people who would want to spy on her. His one thought was the person that sent the flowers while she lived in the city. Then he wondered who knew about her jewelry…

Connor sat up suddenly when someone knocked on the door. He was surprised to discover he had fallen asleep. Beside him, Clara was still sleeping. When he looked up again, his cousin Eric was standing in the doorway holding a tray of drinks and a bag of food. Connor had been expecting his nephew.

Eric was so surprised to see Connor snuggled up beside Clara on her bed, he paused with the door open. The obvious bruising and stitches on her face angered him, the bastard that did this, he thought. He would make him pay!

Connor had already stood up and reached for the food as he greeted his cousin.

"I was at the bar when Devan placed the order. I offered to bring the food. How is she doing?" Eric whispered.

"She seems to be doing alright but I don't know when she'll be able to return to work," Connor answered. "Thanks for dropping off the food. I appreciate it."

"No worries. Let her know I'll get someone to cover for her at least for Monday. We can figure out if she needs more time then. She fell down the stairs and didn't break anything?"

"Surprising, isn't it?"

"Yeah, pretty lucky. Ok man, let me know if there's anything else I can do." Eric glanced one last time towards Clara before heading out. He had debated suggesting he stay the night so Connor could leave, but he was already dismissed.

Clara opened her eyes when she smelled the food. She did not realize how hungry she was until she started to eat her burger. She smiled when she realized he ordered it without tomatoes, and again when he handed her a chocolate milkshake.

When she was finished eating, Clara lifted the covers off as she scooted to the other side of the bed.

"What are you doing?" Connor asked.

"I need to use the bathroom," Clara explained.

Connor stood up. "You can ask me to move."

"Connor, I'm not an invalid. A few extra steps aren't a big deal." She paused once her feet were on the floor. Taking a deep breath, she slowly stood. The dizziness wasn't too bad this time, she thought before heading towards the bathroom.

Connor remained close by to ensure she didn't lose her balance.

Clara stopped when she felt his hand on the low of her back. "Can you see my butt?"

Connor looked back and nodded as he teased, "Yup, I see it. It's just as lovely as it was before."

She let out a gasp as she reached back only to discover it was already covered. Then she tried to shove him but lost her balance instead.

"Clara, easy. You don't want to be falling over."

Once she was in the bathroom, he stepped back to give her privacy. He was cleaning up the food and washing his hands as Clara came out. He was standing by her side when there was a knock on the door. Connor stepped out to see who was entering the room.

Clara was surprised to hear Connor growl, "What the hell are you doing in here?"

Connor felt her hands on his hips as she gently shifted him aside. He remained standing between Clara and her visitor. He was pleased Anthony, the deputy, remained standing at the door, prepared to arrest him if necessary.

"Dallas! How are you? Come on in. Anthony, it's alright. He's welcome," Clara said as she waved him in. She should have been annoyed when the deputy first looked at Connor before nodding his head and stepping back. She could hear him sigh in frustration. She tried to keep the peace by keeping close to him.

"Clara, are you alright? The sheriff stopped in to see me because Rob Foxwood told him I was stalking you. I swear, I have not been following you around." Dallas stayed near the door as he spoke.

"Dallas don't be ridiculous," she said as she waved the thought aside. "I know you didn't do this. I'm ok. I just have some bruises and this cut." She pointed to her forehead. "No broken bones, just a concussion."

"I was told you were pushed down a whole flight of stairs. You could have broken your neck!"

"I guess but I didn't. I promise you, I'm ok," she reassured him again. She would have considered inviting him to sit, but realized he wouldn't be comfortable with Connor standing on alert.

"Where are the kids?" Dallas asked as he looked around, "Were they hurt?"

"Not at all. They're at the Foxwood Farm. They're safe." Clara smiled, thinking it was sweet and brotherly that he was here.

He decided to be brave and stepped a little closer so he could grab her hand and give her a gentle squeeze. "I'll give you a call in a couple of days. Let me know if you need anything in the meantime."

"I will." She watched as he first nodded to her and then Connor before turning towards the door.

"Dallas?" Clara waited until he turned back. "Maybe you can stop over on Monday for lunch?"

He smiled back, looking very relieved. "I will do that, thanks. Get some rest."

Connor watched the exchange with puzzlement as Clara smiled and waved good-bye.

Once the door was closed, she climbed into bed. She scooted over and then looked up at him when he remained staring down at her. "What?" she asked.

"Last night you were suspicious of his visit on your doorstep and now you two are all chummy. What's happened since?" Connor demanded.

Clara shrugged while she sighed. She hadn't had time to think about it and wasn't sure she was ready to talk about it. She patted the bed and waited until he sat down beside her. "He stopped by this afternoon. We debated if my dad and his mother were ever going to marry. He was surprised I'm turning the house into apartments, but he's amused by it and can't wait to see his mother's reaction."

Connor waited a moment. He felt like she was leaving out the important part. "And?" he asked.

She paused again and then shrugged. "He's my older half-brother."

"Oh, wow. Of all the things I was thinking, that was not one of them." He looked at her closely, "How do you feel about that?"

"I don't really know. He told me and minutes later I'm pushed down the stairs." She squeezed his hand when she felt him tense next to her. "I know it wasn't him. My point is, I literally have not had time to process it. It's weird. Like you, I wasn't expecting him to tell me that. I was preparing myself for all kinds of crazy stupid things. Like maybe he needed money, his mother sent him to convince me to invite her to live at the house, my dad was sick or needed money."

"I can continue with the list, I had a lot to drink last night and my mind is very active," Clara stated after a moment. She watched Connor stand up to remove his belt and empty his pockets, placing everything on the bedside table.

Connor paused before returning to the bed. "What?"

"Nothing," she stated as she lifted the covers up. "I was just waiting to see if you were going to take more off."

"You can watch me strip all my clothes off another time, Beautiful. This isn't the appropriate time and especially not the place." He climbed into the bed and scooted towards her. Connor laughed at her wicked smile. "Clara Noelle, I am shocked by your thoughts right now."

Clara giggled as she removed her hearing aids before turning over onto her side. Without thinking about it, Connor placed his arm around her waist. Her hand grabbed his and she squeezed it as she said, "Connor?"

"Hmm?" Not able to hear, Clara could feel the vibration of his answer.

"Thanks for being here and not leaving me alone. It means a lot. I really appreciate it." She kissed his hand. "I love you, Connor."

"I love you too, Clara." He kissed the side of her head, knowing she could not hear him. He closed his eyes and felt her body relax as she leaned back into him. He knew by her breathing she was asleep minutes later.

A few moments later, there was a quiet knock on the door as Brad, her nurse, entered the room.

Connor lifted his head in question.

"She's sleeping? I came to see if she needed anything. She hasn't had any pain meds since she arrived on the floor," he explained. Brad was surprised to see the doctor curled up beside his patient. He hadn't been aware they were seeing each other. His friend Jenna was going to be disappointed.

"She's good. She's reporting a headache but not complaining enough for medicine. She's been walking around the room and talking. I'll complete the neuro checks every two hours so you don't have to return unless the call light is on," Connor instructed the nurse.

Brad nodded his understanding. "Of course, doctor. Have you two been together long?"

"A short time," Connor answered. Once the nurse left, he remained up on his elbow as he watched Clara in the dim light. He gently brushed the hair from her face as she slept. He leaned down to kiss her before snuggling back up.

Billy Kingsly was nervous about the meet. He knew the boss was not happy with him right now. He had received the call and instructions to meet him here. He was going to be giving him money so he could leave town for a while. At least until everything calmed down.

He tensed when he heard a car approach. It stopped and the lights flashed. He stepped from the shadows, looking over his shoulders to assure no one was around. When he sat down in the passenger seat, he could tell the boss was pissed, but he didn't say a word as he pulled from the curb.

He was getting nervous as they drove higher up the hills and further from civilization.

As if sensing the younger man's fears, the older man explained, "I have a cabin up here in the mountains. It's small and out of the way. You can stay there as long as you need. There's plenty of food and drinks. Just don't use the phone or start any fires.

"Really, Boss? I won't be in the way? I really appreciate it. It was an accident. I didn't mean to hurt her!" The young man, barely old enough to legally drink, tried to explain.

The boss turned and looked at him, "Your instructions were very clear! You were to only monitor and report back. You were never to engage!"

"I understand that, but I never meant to hurt her. This one guy had been visiting. He had this big announcement, I thought you should know. I thought she was still in the kitchen, she was so quiet, never heard her moving around. I was trying to sneak out without her knowing I was even there. I was too surprised to see her on the stairs when I leaped over the banister."

"You never meant to push her down the stairs?" When the other man shook his head, he asked "What is this important news?"

"Dallas Thompson is her half-brother."

"Really? Hmm that's interesting," he wondered about the significance as he parked the car. The other man looked at him in confusion. "I wanted to avoid the main road to the cabin. It's just through here along the path."

They both got out. The older man gestured towards the path to allow the younger man to take the lead. Once they were on the trail, the man in the back pulled gloves out of his pocket and then a guitar string. He rolled the edges around his gloved hands and quickly wrapped it around the stupid one's neck and pulled…

Clara sat up in the bed as she tried to catch her breath. When she felt a hand on her back, she screamed…

a guitar string

L ila was reading over her text messages as she hurried down
the hall. Her shift had ended hours ago. When she turned the
corner, she ran right into Dallas Thompson.

"Dallas!"

"Lila, I'm sorry," he apologized as he steadied her before he looked
down at their feet.

The bump caused her bag to fall off of her arm and onto the floor,
spilling everywhere. Dallas was quick to retrieve her items from the
floor. When he stood back up, he placed the strap back on her shoulder.
His hand remained on her shoulder a moment before it slowly caressed
her arm. He was looking around them and as his hand reached hers, he
pulled her in for a kiss.

Lila allowed the kiss but pulled away first. Dallas smiled down at
her with a wink, he continued to walk beside her towards the door.

"What are you doing here?" Lila asked.

"I stopped in to see Clara. Did you hear what happened?" Dallas
asked as he scanned the parking lot.

"Yes. I was her nurse when she came through the emergency room.
I can't believe someone was in her house! She could have broken her

neck when she fell down the stairs," Lila stated. "How did the visit go? How is she feeling?"

"She seemed alright, she had some bruises and that cut on her forehead." He shook his head as his temper seemed to rise. "I couldn't really stay long, there were too many bodyguards."

"Yeah, I bet. The sheriff has a deputy posted at the farm as well to assure the kids remain safe. Rob's not too thrilled right now."

"I can imagine." Dallas stopped looking around when they reached her car. Looking down into Lila's gray blue eyes, he slowly leaned down and kissed her. He pulled back just enough to whisper, "Are you coming home with me?"

Dallas kissed her again, deeper. He smiled when she leaned back into her car and sighed.

"Dal, I shouldn't! Rob and Chase are watching Clara's kids tonight. I told him I'd be home to help," Lila stated.

Dallas kissed her again. He left a trail of kisses towards her neck. "I didn't ask you what you should do. I am asking you what you want to do." He kissed her neck in between the words as he softly whispered, "Come home with me for just a few hours. I miss you."

"Yeah, OK, just for a couple of hours but then I have to get back to the farm." She smiled when Dallas kissed her on the lips.

"Good deal." He reached around her to open the door. "I'm parked by the exit, wait for me and I'll follow you."

Connor was suddenly awake when Clara sat up. He touched her back attempting to reassure her, but the simple physical contact startled her, causing her to scream.

The door to the hall flew open and the bright light poured into the room, showing the silhouette of the deputy standing just outside.

Connor turned on the light first before waving him away, "She's fine, Anthony. She had a bad dream."

Once the door was closed, Connor grabbed her and held her as she shivered in his arms. He assured her she was safe, even though he knew she could not hear him.

A moment later, Clara's breathing was under control and she whispered, "I'm sorry, I didn't mean to wake you up."

"Clara, don't apologize, you didn't do anything wrong. You've had a rough day," Connor stated after she pulled back to reach for her hearing aids and stood up. He watched her walk around the bed. "Do you want to talk about it?"

She stood at the end of the bed and simply shook her head. He walked over towards her and placed his arms around her, saying it was alright to cry. He could feel her fight it as she tried to pull away. He kept her close as he held her tight.

After a few minutes, he asked her what her dream was about. He held her head in his hands, and used his thumbs to wipe the tears. She closed her eyes and shook her head.

"I don't really remember it. It just seemed so real. You know how dreams are, you know who the people are and what they are thinking and then scenery changes and the people change. I..." she sighed at the absurdness of it.

"What? What were you going to say?"

"I think the guy killed him," she whispered.

Connor's thumbs stopped moving as he looked into her green eyes. Keeping his voice low he asked, "Who was killed?"

"Like I said, it was a dream. I have no idea. It was just horrible." Clara shuddered as she walked into the bathroom.

Connor watched as she walked, her balance was steadier.

After using the toilet, she was washing her hands at the sink. She made the mistake of looking in the mirror again and groaned out loud.

Connor was immediately at her side, "What's wrong? Are you in a lot of pain?"

"I look horrible! Why didn't you tell me I look this bad? It's even worse than before! My face is all swollen and black and blue! There are stitches? How many stitches?" Clara leaned in and started to count.

"Fourteen," he informed her quietly as he reached for her hand and led her away from the mirror. "It's all temporary. The swelling will be down in a few days, the coloring will be gone, and the stitches will be removed."

"How can you be looking at me right now without laughing? This is terrible. All my patients will be too scared to work with me!" She turned her face away from Connor, suddenly embarrassed. How could she be sleeping next to him looking this horrible?

Connor reached for her hand as she tried to walk away, he gently turned her around and tilted her chin up to face him. "Clara, you are still Beautiful. You look as if you had it out with someone and came out the winner."

"Yeah, right. You should see the other guy. He definitely looks worse, he had a guitar string to his neck," she responded without thinking.

Connor's eyes squinted in question as he looked into her eyes, "What?"

Clara was already walking away with a wave of her hand. "I have no idea where that came from."

He watched as she walked around the room, restless and anxious. Clara found a basin on the shelf with personal supplies and carried it back to the sink. She brushed her teeth and tried to wash up as much as possible. When she was back in the room, Connor completed another neuro exam. Aside from the headache, she had no other symptoms.

"Do you want anything for the pain?"

"No."

"Hungry?"

"Not really."

"What do you want?"

"Tiramisu."

"That's specific. And not something I can get right now. I was thinking maybe a candy bar or some chips." He held up the bag that was dropped off to the deputy by Lila after her shift ended.

"That works." She took the bag and looked inside. "Thanks."

"The bag is from Lila," Connor explained as she looked up at him. She leaned up onto her toes and kissed his cheek.

A few hours later, Lila was lying beside Dallas in the dark. She was afraid to fall asleep. She propped up on her elbow as she looked down at him with his eyes closed. Her hand was playing with the hair on his chest. "Are you sleeping?"

He placed a hand over hers before he spoke. "I can't sleep with you doing that."

"Sorry, I should be heading out."

Dallas looked over at the clock. "It's only two, you can stay a few more hours."

"If I fall asleep, I won't wake up until noon. I promised my brother I would help with Reese and Hailey." She leaned down to kiss him with the intention of getting up immediately afterwards. Instead, he pulled her in to deepen the kiss. Pulling her down on top of him, he rolled her over onto her back. He was propped up on his elbows as he kissed her neck and whispered in her ear.

Lila sighed, "I can stay a bit longer…"

When she opened her eyes again, the room was more dim than dark. The sun was already on the horizon, "Shit! Dallas, it's morning! I am going to be late."

She threw the covers off and ran naked into the adjoining bathroom. Dallas, never one to rush if it wasn't necessary, simply remained in the bed with his hands stacked up behind his head. He smiled as Lila ran back in and turned on the light. She was looking around the room for her clothes. She found her panties and then her bra. She spotted her cell on the bedside table on the other side. She crawled across the bed, her chest on his as she reached for it.

Dallas couldn't help himself. He grabbed her and started to kiss her. She initially allowed the kiss but pulled back. "Dal, I need to get back to the farm. The guys are up by five if not earlier. I promised."

He reluctantly released her as he sighed in frustration at the continued secrecy of their relationship. As he watched her dress he commented, "I thought we had a deal. I would talk to my sister and you would talk to your brother."

Dallas pushed back the covers to sit up on the edge of the bed. He reached for his boxers and jeans. When he turned around, Lila was walking around the bed holding her scrub top, suddenly distracted from her immediate mission.

"You talked to Clara? What did she say? Did you tell her about us? Why didn't you tell me?" Lila pushed him.

He brought his arms around her to pull her in closer. "I was distracted. I'll go make you some coffee."

"Dal, I don't want to be a bother," Lila said as he pulled the top out of her hands and tossed it onto the bed.

"Baby, you are never a bother." He leaned down to kiss her.

An hour later, Dallas was escorting Lila to her car while she drank from a mug of coffee. He was telling her about the conversation with Clara. "We never talked about anything else, so you weren't mentioned. I don't think she'd have a problem. And when I stopped in last night, we made tentative plans for lunch tomorrow. I'll text her in the morning to confirm the details."

He had her keys and opened the door for her while she sipped from her mug. Lila was about to get in but paused when he asked the next question. "How is it Rob is watching the kids? Why not Shannon?"

"You know Rob and Clara have always been close, until the prom," she clarified. "Shannon was at work when it happened. She didn't know anything about it until she returned home. She stayed with the neighbor next door. She wasn't comfortable staying at home by herself and especially with the kids."

"Yeah, ok. But how does the doctor play into all this?"

"Doctor? What doctor?" Lila looked closely at Dallas in question. Then her mind replayed the scene in her head of Connor Emerson assisting Clara out of the ambulance the day before. "Do you mean Connor? Dallas, what do you know?"

Dallas was never one to gossip, as he hated being the subject of it. Lila always tried to squeeze information out of him by explaining they were a couple without secrets. His argument was always that it wasn't his story to tell. He usually compromised by telling her only what he knew as fact and made clear his opinion. He rarely speculated, leaving that to Lila.

"All I know is Clara and the doctor were all dressed up on Friday evening. She was wearing a dress and heels while he wore a suit. He was escorting her out onto the porch for an evening out. Last night in her hospital room, she was wearing a hospital gown and he was standing protectively between us. He was not wearing shoes and his shirt was untucked. He was obviously settling in for the night. That is all I know."

Lila leaned back into her car as she processed the information. She sipped her coffee as she wondered aloud, "Wow, Clara and Connor? I wonder why she didn't say anything."

"Could be the same reason you haven't told her about us," Dallas commented.

"We are keeping our relationship a secret so my brother or father don't try to kill you. She doesn't have a brother." She paused when he looked at her with his eyebrows raised in question. "All right, she does have a brother, but would you kill someone she's dating simply because you don't like him?"

"Are you giving me permission to kill your brother?" Dallas teased, his eyes twinkling with amusement.

"Well, according to you, he's not dating your sister. Connor is so my brother's life is not in danger."

"I think this is the craziest conversation we have ever had. No one is going to kill anyone. I say we simply wait it out and see. They used to live next door to each other, right?" When Lila nodded in agreement, he continued. "With everything going on in her life, the doctor is someone she knows and trusts. She's comfortable with him."

"You don't think she's comfortable with Rob?"

"Not as much after that incident at the prom," Dallas speculated.

"Yeah, true. That would be difficult to bounce back from."

Dallas leaned in for a quick kiss before he asked, "Don't you have to be heading back to the farm?"

Lila immediately pushed him back and got into her car, "Damn it! Yes."

"Call me later," he instructed as she handed him the empty mug and he closed the door. He remained on the driveway as he watched her drive off.

Rob sighed with relief as he received the text from his sister stating she was delayed and on her way home. Lila was alright, just running late. He read the next text from Clara. She was waiting for the results from the repeat CT scan before the neurosurgeon would release her. He texted back asking if she needed a ride. She declined, stating she already had one lined up. Rob sighed with annoyance, realizing the good doctor was still at her side.

At noon, Connor pulled into Clara's driveway. He opened the door to assist her out and then up onto the porch. While she didn't complain, he knew she was sore. Just as he was opening the screen door, Shannon opened the front door.

Shannon felt bad about not being home when the incident occured. She had been busy at work, catching up on paperwork and filing. When she returned home, the place was filled with deputies. The Sheriff had explained what happened. Before he allowed her to prepare a small overnight bag, she assessed to see if anything was missing. Devan had been present and offered to let her stay at his place. She was thrilled at first when he offered her his bed, it was the only one he had. But then she was silently disappointed when he was a complete gentleman and slept on the couch downstairs. She had worried it would be awkward in the morning, but it wasn't. He even made her breakfast and came back to Clara's with her later in the morning.

"Clara! How are you feeling? You look horrible!" Shannon declared, the brutally honest one in the group.

"Yeah, I know. I had a mirror at the hospital. Connor keeps lying to me, but he's assured me it's temporary," she sighed as she stepped inside. "Hi Devan."

"Hi Clara, Connor," he greeted as he observed the two together.

Connor escorted Clara down onto the sofa. He would have propped pillows under her or even lifted her feet up, but she shooed him away. He just nodded and leaned down to kiss her forehead before he turned to give Shannon instructions.

"She has a moderate concussion, but the repeated CT scan confirmed no fracture or bleeding. She may be more tired but that's normal. Wake her up every two hours. If she becomes too lethargic, starts slurring her words, throwing up, or has trouble walking, you call me immediately. My numbers are in her phone. You can transfer them into yours." He paused for a moment, looking down at Clara with her arms folded, glaring up at him. "And don't let her get the stitches wet."

"Yeah, no problem. We'll be fine," Shannon stated. She found his actions very interesting.

"Any questions?"

Devan had been leaning into the doorway watching, but he remained quiet until Shannon's next comment, then he chuckled.

"I have it, Connor. It's not like this is our first concussion." Connor had been preparing to step out but turned to give her a look. "Seriously, we'll be alright. Lila is heading over with the kids. She plans to stay the night. If you don't feel we can handle this, you are more than welcome to stay."

Connor glanced over at Devan and simply shrugged. He stayed only until the children arrived with Lila. He hadn't been forewarned about Rob and Chase also coming over. The place was getting too crowded so he took his leave, following Devan to his place.

SHADOWS OF THE NIGHT

we don't go to the movies

The next morning, Clara was starting to feel better, but the mirror informed her she looked worse. Shannon was not able to call off from work, but Lila stayed until late morning before leaving. She was scheduled to work later in the day. Plus, she knew Dallas was planning to come over for lunch. She was slightly disappointed when Clara didn't say anything but realized he was probably right. She had a lot going on lately and it would take her time to adjust.

The children remained home with Clara and were napping in the family room when Dallas arrived with lunch. They talked quietly in the kitchen.

"I want to say you are looking better but I have a thing about lying," he teased.

"Oh, don't even bother. I have mirrors. Connor is the only one that's been lying," Clara answered with a chuckle.

"Yeah? What does he say?" Dallas wondered.

"He says the swelling and bruising are only temporary and that I am still beautiful," she said as she rolled her eyes.

"Well that is a good sign. He sees past the superficial. How is he doing?" He watched her green eyes light up as she talked about him.

The conversation was kept light, neither brought up the parents. Clara already knew Dallas had joined the army out of high school. She learned he had been medically discharged four years ago. He didn't mention what the injury was, and she didn't ask. He currently worked at the nearby federal park as a ranger. He had saved his money and bought land out in the country adjacent to the park, where he built a log cabin with assistance from his friends.

Clara told him about her life in the city, and explained why she returned home with her children. Dallas noted she kept the details about her husband minimal.

The children were still napping as Clara walked him to the front door. She had paused to check her cell. There was a message from Connor informing her he was on his way over.

"Connor is on his way. Did you all stagger your time to make sure I was never alone?" She accused Dallas as he opened the door.

He laughed and denied it, then leaned in to kiss her forehead as he hugged her. "Take care of yourself and let me know if you need anything."

By the time he stepped out, Connor had arrived. He stopped a moment to talk with Dallas. She couldn't hear the discussion but was pleased when they shook hands before each walked away.

Dallas heard Connor greet Clara, "Hey Beautiful, how's the headache?" He looked over while he opened his car door and paused as he watched Connor kiss her on the lips. Yeah, there's definitely something going on, he thought with a smile. He was secretly pleased Connor acknowledged him as Clara's older brother and was surprised when he apologized for being rude over the weekend. Personally, he preferred his little sister with the doctor over the farmer. Though, he would never admit that to Lila.

Clara returned to work on Wednesday. Connor would have preferred she take the whole week off, but she was getting too restless at home.

On Friday afternoon, she was gait training with a patient down the hall. Halfway, she assisted Miss Maggie with a U-turn. She noted Connor was standing at the doorway of his office while his brother handed him a file. Clara wasn't sure why she suddenly felt uncomfortable. Once she and her patient were back in the therapy gym, Miss Maggie was settled in her wheelchair and transported back upstairs by Marie.

With the last therapy session finished, Clara sat down at her desk to complete her paperwork. She shouldn't have been surprised by the knock on the door or to see both Connor and Matt enter the room.

"Clara, how are you enjoying the new outdoor furniture?" Matt asked. He tried not to cringe when he saw her face up close. He had heard about the incident at her house and had been warned by Connor about her sensitivity to her looks. The bruising was fading to a dull yellow and a bandage was covering her stitches.

"It's not being delivered until tomorrow," she answered.

"Why so long?"

"It was the first time I'd be available. I didn't know I would be home this week. Was your wife pleased with the Paris trip?" She inquired.

Matt smiled, "Yes, she was. We are planning to go in the spring."

"Nice. What do you have there?" Clara motioned to the file he was holding out.

"Capital budget. I want you to write down your wish list of equipment with expected cost and increase in personnel with anticipated raises. Also, if you want to start interviewing therapists, here's a form to fill out so we can post the positions. If you have any questions, my number is in there. Good seeing you again, Kiddo" he said as he turned to say good-bye to his brother.

Connor had been quietly leaning against a desk watching the interaction between Matt and Clara. They seemed to have a level of familiarity he wasn't expecting. After closing the door, he went over to Clara, standing next to her desk. He kissed her before he explained he was removing the dressing from her forehead.

"This is healing up well. I can remove the stitches if you want," he stated. When she nodded, he gestured her to sit while he placed a suture removal kit on her desk before washing his hands.

"You can do that here and now?"

"Yes I can, and I am," he answered as he donned gloves.

"But Connor, shouldn't the doctor that did them take them out?" Clara asked. When he just stood there staring at her she asked, "You put the stitches in? You were in the emergency room?"

"Yes I was, and I did. Now sit still," he firmly instructed.

She leaned back as she saw the instruments coming closer. "Shouldn't you give me something for the pain first?"

"You told me you haven't been taking anything for pain."

"I'm not."

"Does your head hurt?"

"Not unless I accidently touch the bump."

"And your face?"

"What about it?"

"Does it hurt?"

She sighed as she answered, "Not yet."

"Clara, why are you being so difficult?"

"I'm not! I just don't like seeing the scissors close to my eyes!" She finally admitted.

"Reese wouldn't be this difficult. Close your eyes and tell me what you have planned for this evening."

"Why?" Clara opened her eyes suspiciously and leaned back again.

"I am trying to distract you so I can do this. Clara, I could have finished by now if you weren't being so difficult." He gestured for her to close her eyes before he continued, "You told me you have Michelle set up to babysit every Friday evening. Can I take you to dinner?"

"Oh Connor, I don't think that would be appropriate," she commented. "When are you going to start?"

"In a second. Keep your eyes closed." He continued talking as he snipped, "Why can't we eat dinner together? We slept together last Saturday night. I would think dinner would be more benign than us sleeping together in a public place," he chuckled when her face turned red.

"It's not like anyone saw us," she defended. "If we went to a restaurant, half of the town would see us, and the other half would know by breakfast."

"Probably but I know for a fact at least six people saw us last week at the hospital. So, if you won't let me take you to dinner, you must already have plans." Connor said as he made the last snip and gently pulled.

"I'm meeting up with Shannon and Lila for a girls' night out," Clara finally admitted.

"Yeah? Staying in town or going elsewhere?" He stepped away, properly disposed of the sharps, and tossed the dressing. He looked again and admired his work. She would barely have a scar. He leaned back onto the desk with his arms folded as she answered.

"What do you mean staying in town? Where else would we go but down Main Street for a few drinks?" She asked.

"You could drive up the hill to the bowling alley. They often have karaoke later in the evening. You could go to the movies." He paused when Clara shook her head.

"We don't go to the movies," she whispered as she opened her eyes.

"Sorry, Clara. I don't know what I was thinking," he stated quietly. During high school, Clara and Lila had been in the theater when it exploded. He had been a resident, working in the emergency room when it happened. Connor would never forget the shock and horror of watching an unconscious Clara being pulled from the pile, covered in blood and dust.

He was stepping closer when she brought her hand up to her forehead, distracted again, "You finished? I didn't feel a thing!"

"I didn't think you would. I never expected you would be such a baby about this! But I did forget how you screamed when your mother was trying to remove the splinter from your foot," Connor teased. He had rushed over from his backyard when he heard her screaming. The shrilling sounds had him convinced she was about to be axed to death.

Back in the city, Detective Andrew Sanders had sixteen years on the force with the last five as a homicide detective. He had hoped for a quiet day to jump start the weekend but instead, he and his partner received a call to the basement of an old abandoned building before he even finished his first cup of coffee. The body was severely decomposed leaving dental records as the only means of identification. Andy had spent most of the afternoon reviewing missing persons reports for the last three to six months. He was looking for a male Caucasian, six feet tall, blonde hair and blue eyes, but none seemed to match his latest victim. The medical examiner should be able to narrow the time of death by tomorrow, he thought.

Then his partner, Jim Walters, came in. "Found him. His name is Jason Michael O'Reilly, friends call him Jay. He was thirty years old, an accountant, married with two young children. I have his address right here."

Detective Sanders reached back for his jacket as he stood up and followed his partner out of the office and down the steps. They finally had a lead.

SHADOWS OF THE NIGHT

the seabreeze

L ater that evening, Clara was all dressed up with nowhere to go. Her sitter had already arrived and was hanging out with the children while they debated which movie to watch. Then she received a text first from Shannon saying she had a project that needed her attention before she left work. A minute later, Lila stated her shift was lasting longer than she anticipated.

Clara decided to walk down to Memories and get on with her evening. She was confident if she were to sit down, she would fall asleep and not be interested in going out later.

It was a beautiful evening for a stroll. When she arrived on Main Street, she ran into a nurse from work who was walking with her boyfriend. They invited her to join them at the biker bar in the alley. She figured, why not? She had time. It would be at least an hour before her friends caught up.

The Joint was the least attractive bar in town. It was strictly a drinking establishment with a few pool tables. It looked as if it was last remodeled around the time Clara was born and possibly cleaned when she graduated from high school. She had never been inside. Despite the bad reputation, she was enjoying herself. Her friend's boyfriend bought her a drink while she mingled with the many people she knew. When her drink was finished, Clara said good-bye. Another co-worker decided to join her, showing her the back exit into the alley which was also attached to the back entrance of The Lantern. Looking at her cell, she estimated she had at least thirty minutes before Shannon and Lila would be arriving.

Clara remained standing at the back entrance, slowly surveying the scene before her. Compared to the previous place, the crowd was much younger. When she approached the bar, Clara turned to the touch on her shoulder.

"Hello Clara, what are you drinking?"

"Joshua, how are you? I'll stick with the Seabreeze," she answered as the young bartender approached. After he placed the order, she thanked him.

"I'm taking a break from a crazy week. I heard what happened last weekend. I'm surprised to see you out drinking alone," Josh commented as the drinks arrived.

"I'm not really. My friends are late getting off from work. I was ready and came out ahead of them. I should be meeting up with them soon. As it turns out, this is the second place I've been to tonight and I know half of these people. I forget how small this town is sometimes," she stated as she sipped her drink.

"Yeah, this town seems to be smaller every time I return home," Josh commented as he sipped his beer.

Clara looked over at him, surprised at her comfort with him. While he wasn't drunk, his drink had obviously relaxed him. When their eyes met, he smiled instead of looking away. "It's not a bad thing to be surrounded by people you know and trust."

"I guess not. There's just less pressure here at my dad's than at my mom's," he commented. He had been raised hearing the rumors of his father's infidelity with her mother. Looking at the woman before him, he could hardly fault his father.

"What kind of pressure?"

"Oh, you know, to be a lawyer, be the best student, have the perfect 4.0. My mother doesn't want me to stay here in town. She wants me to move back to the city but hell, she's not even there half the time anyway. She travels a lot for work. Her company is international. She's worried my father and uncle are a bad influence and will lead me down the wrong path," Josh chuckled.

"Your dad and uncle are some of the most hard-working men I know. You are lucky to have such strong role models, definitely better than me," Clara stated softly.

Josh's blue eyes studied her a moment before he commented, "You obviously had someone in your corner, from what I hear about you, you're not doing too bad yourself."

Clara's eyes narrowed, "What exactly have you heard? You know what, don't answer that. You likely know my father though I doubt you would remember my mother."

"I know our parents used to date and my father never got over your mother," he impulsively commented before he sipped his drink.

"What? They used to date? When? How do you know?" Clara asked with total shock.

"You never heard the talk?" The younger man wondered out loud. "My mother likes to blame your mother for the marriage not lasting but I don't agree. I think she used it as an excuse to not even try."

Without saying a word, he signaled to the bartender and ordered a round of shots.

"Clara, I'm sorry. I should not have said anything. I don't know why I did, probably too much alcohol." Josh gently pushed a shot glass towards her. "Forgive me."

Clara raised her glass in a silent toast as they clinked together before both drinking. When she lowered her glass, she studied the young man beside her. She placed her hand on his as she commented, "You have never done anything that warrants forgiveness. We make enough mistakes on our own, we can't carry the weight of our parents. Hell, if that were the case, I'd be too weak to stand."

She motioned for another round, laying a twenty on the bar. "This next one's on me. My mother and your father were together? All this time, I thought they were just friends. And if we remain sitting here too long, people here will start thinking the same about us."

Joshua laughed as he propped an elbow on the bar, leaning his head onto his hand. "I like you and how you think. I can certainly understand my uncle's interest in you, it's a shame."

When the next round was delivered, they both repeated the silent toast. Once her shot glass was down on the bar, she asked, "What's a shame?"

"I won't ever be in the running. Just as well, you are way out of my league," he chuckled.

"I'd say I have too much baggage to weigh you down, not something you want to get involved with at this time of your life. But being friends would definitely be best," Clara agreed.

"Clara! You are finally out! Come on over and join us for a drink," Nic stated as he stepped between the two. "Josh, you can't keep the best looking girl in the bar all to yourself."

Without a word, Nic grabbed her hand to lead her towards a table in the corner. Clara quickly found herself surrounded by a few coworkers while others introduced themselves. As she settled beside Nic, she looked back apologetically towards Josh. He grinned at her as he held up his beer in a silent toast.

Later, Clara would not be able to recall what exactly she was drinking or how the drink came to be in her hand. But as soon as she sipped from it, she felt relaxed and free. She was very much enjoying herself. When she turned to talk with someone, she was not aware of her drink being replaced with another. She was simply sipping and talking, not really thinking when she felt her cell vibrate in her pocket. Thinking it could be either of her friends letting her know they arrived at Memories, she checked the message:

> "'Nothing' to work out. It's over. I have moved on, you should
> too. I have started the divorce process"

Clara simply laughed as she returned the phone to her pocket. Of course you have you bastard, she thought as she decided to head across the street. Once she was at the door of Memories, she stepped inside and looked around, sipping from the drink that seemed to once again magically appear in her hand.

Diners were still finishing up, but people out for the evening were already gathered three deep from the bar. Needless to say, it was packed. When Clara later thought about the moment, she could have sworn she heard Madonna singing "Crazy for You." It may have been in her head, but she would never know for sure.

While she would always remember what she did next, she would never, ever be able to explain why. With a quick scan of the place, Clara's eyes immediately locked on Connor's. He was sitting at his usual spot at the far end of the bar.

Connor noted the moment Clara entered the bar. He would later think there was something different in the air. He was drinking from his beer when his eyes hooked with hers.

Clara slowly advanced towards him, it was as if the crowd parted to allow her an easier path. Their eyes were locked, neither looking away. Connor rotated his stool as she came closer. She stepped so close she was standing between his legs as she placed her glass on the bar. Without a word, she placed her hands on his knees and slowly rubbed up his thighs, to his chest, onto his shoulders, and into his hair. She pulled him closer as she leaned in, and their lips met.

Connor was caught off guard. He was always the one initiating something with Clara. He never tried anything more than a peck of a kiss or holding her hand. He was always able to control himself. But when her tongue touched his lips and then met his, he lost all ability to think. His hands came around to the low of her back as he pulled her in closer, and then he heard someone cheer, "Hot damn, Connor!"

He quickly returned to reality, immediately pulling back. Clara smiled up at him as she brought her hands down onto his thighs, softly caressing.

"How's the girls' night going?" Connor asked. When he looked into her green eyes, he realized her pupils were pinpoint. Shit, he thought. Was she drugged? He gently tilted her chin to look into her eyes to assure she was indeed drugged. Connor was suddenly pissed as he grabbed her hand to keep her from wandering off.

He looked around the room to see if anyone was following Clara. She was reaching for her drink, but he pushed it away. Connor pulled out his cell to text Devan. He was quick and to the point:

"Clara has been drugged, save her glass; going upstairs."

Devan had watched the whole incident from the other end of the bar. Immediately after reading the text, he nodded understanding as he went to retrieve the glass.

Connor pulled Clara out the back door and led her upstairs to his loft. Once inside he turned to lock the door. When he turned back around, Clara was standing right in front of him. She pulled on his shirt as she stepped back into the wall, pulling him closer. Before he had a moment to think, his shirt was unbuttoned with her hands on his chest. She had somehow pulled his face down towards hers as her tongue was once again mating with his.

Connor was suddenly gasping for air as his heart beat faster. He quickly realized he was not in control of the situation. He reminded himself she was drugged. He pulled back and looked down at her beautiful face. Her lips were swollen, her face was flushed, and her pupils were still pinpoint. She was not in control nor would she be agreeing to this right now. Connor pulled back and walked into the kitchen.

As he expected, she followed him, still holding onto his shirt. Connor gently assisted Clara down onto the stool at the island and went in search of water. He needed to get her rehydrated to help her body metabolize the drug.

But what drug is it, he thought as he went to retrieve his medical kit. When he returned, he took a sample of her blood. He was explaining everything to her as she played with his hair. He sent a text to Devan with a request to have his dinner delivered.

Downstairs at Memories, Rob and Chase were finishing up with dinner, sitting at a table along the wall opposite the bar. Facing towards the door, Rob had spotted Clara as soon as she entered the restaurant. His steel blue eyes followed her as she made her way through the crowd and started making out with the good doctor. Damn it! The guy sat on that same stool not even a week ago and told me there was nothing going on. He lied! There is no way Clara would be kissing him like that if they weren't already together. Damn it.

Chase saw the change in his cousin's face and turned to see what it was. He should have known Clara had arrived. He was equally surprised when she started kissing the doctor in public. Wow, Rob's chances are going downhill fast, this is almost as bad as the prom. Well, she didn't have plans with Rob tonight, so not quite the same, he thought.

Both cousins watched as Connor pulled back, looked around the room. He sent a text before he grabbed her hand to lead her out back. Rob waved over the waitress to order a round of shots. Chase immediately understood he was the designated driver.

If Connor had timed how long it took Devan to arrive upstairs, he would have been surprised to discover it was less than thirty minutes. It seemed like the longest evening of his life, keeping out of Clara's reach. He kept the kitchen island between them. When Connor finally received the text that Devan was on his way up, he went to the door.

Devan was shocked at Connor's appearance when he opened the door. His shirt was out and unbuttoned, his hair was sticking out all over. He handed over the bag of food as he stepped through the door.

"I took a sample of her blood. Can you get this and the glass to a lab? I am curious to see what the drug is. I have never seen Clara this disinhibited in all her life! She is always telling me she's married. We've never had more than a peck on the lips or a casual hug," Connor declared.

"Uncle Tony is meeting me in a few minutes. He'll initiate the chain of custody and get it to a lab. Connor, you two were sleeping together in a bed last week," Devan reminded him. When Connor gave him a questioning look, he admitted Anthony told him.

"Devan, she was hurt and scared. She didn't want to be alone. Nothing happened. You have to agree, that kiss downstairs was out of character for her. I looked around to see if anyone was following her, but no one seemed to pop out. She must have started across the street at The Lantern. Whoever spiked her drink wasn't closely following. Foxwood was shooting lasers at me."

Before Devan could say anything, Clara appeared. Her blouse was almost fully unbuttoned, exposing her purple bra underneath. She slowly advanced as she greeted Devan. Connor, worried she would try to kiss him, intercepted by anchoring his arm around her waist.

Devan was shocked by Clara's loose behavior. While he did not know her very well, he was confident this was not normal. He tried to ask a few questions, but should have known he wouldn't be successful. "Clara, where were you tonight?"

"I went bar hopping. I have never gone bar hopping here before! I made all the rounds before I came over to meet Lila and Shannon," she answered as her hand started to rub Connor's chest.

Connor handed the bag of food to Clara in an attempt to distract her hands.

"Clara, where is Shannon? Is she still over at The Lantern?"

"No, she had to work late. So did Lila. Tell them I'll be down to see them when we are finished up here," she said, smiling wickedly. She handed the bag of food back to Connor as she slowly stepped backwards, allowing her blouse to fall from her shoulder as she slowly unbuttoned the last two. Her blouse fell onto the floor as she waved to Devan and called Connor's name as she disappeared around the corner.

Devan was speechless.

Connor groaned.

"Well, I think that's my cue to leave. Are you going to be alright?" Devan asked.

"I'm hoping the food will sober her up. I don't know how much she's had to drink. Maybe she'll pass out once she eats. Thanks for everything."

Eric's excitement put a bounce in his step as he crossed Main Street. He was finally going to be with his love! After everything he's done to get her, the moment has arrived. Eric smiled with the anticipation of touching her, watching those sexy green eyes as he removed her clothes, and hearing her groans of pleasure.

Eric learned his lessons from his attempts before. While the explosion at the theater was unexpected, he missed his opportunity by not immediately following her into the bathroom. And the prom, all the planning he did. Eric arranged a simple accident involving his love's original date. Nothing major, just snipped his break line causing the idiot to crash into a tree. With a broken leg, he wasn't able to go to his prom. But when Eric offered to take her, Clara already had the stupid fool to escort her. Eric had to go with plan B. His plan had been flawless. Enlisting Isabella's assistance, Eric conned her into ditching her original date, allowing him to go instead. And she did her part by distracting the fool, not only for the evening but for the whole summer. And yet, it backfired once again. His damn cousin intercepted her on his way home.

This time, he kept his plan simple. Eric gave her the drink himself and watched her drink it. And most importantly, he stayed close. He mentally kicked himself for letting her leave without him. When she started to say goodbye, he had to quickly close out his tab, a stupid delay. But he quickly followed her across the street.

As he stepped into Memories, his mood was immediately crushed. His love was already being led out of the back door by none other than his cousin, damn it.

Lila and Shannon had already arrived when Devan returned to work behind the bar. He had spent ten minutes with his uncle discussing some theories. Were there other women getting their drinks spiked? Was the situation with Clara random or was she targeted? They were determined to get to the bottom of it. Devan had requested his uncle keep a lid on who was involved in the investigation. He narrowed the task force to his cousins, Joe and Anthony, within the sheriff's department, and Devan was already reaching out to his supervisor in the FBI.

Devan spotted Shannon. When their eyes met, she smiled and waved. He didn't realize until that moment when he felt relief, how much he was starting to care for her. "Ladies, I am sorry to keep you waiting. What can I get you? The kitchen will be closing soon if you want to order any dinner."

Shannon and Lila each placed an order. When he returned a moment later with their drinks, Shannon grabbed his hand. "Devan, have you seen Clara? She should be here."

"Yeah, she was here but she left. Were you planning to meet her here?"

"Yes, but we both were tied up at work. She decided to head out on her own. She was worried she'd fall asleep and not want to go later. Said she was stopping in at The Joint. She ran into some co-workers and had a drink. Did she head home?" She started to pull out her cell to call her.

"She left with Connor," Devan stated quietly. He didn't want her worrying.

"Ahh, she left with Connor. Those two are certainly doing the slow dance. It must be killing him," she commented.

"What do you mean?"

"He's in love with her. He's always over at her place but doesn't stay long. He seems to know how close he can get before she pulls back. She's not ready for the kind of relationship he wants. I think she still believes Jay will come back," Shannon shrugged.

"So, what happened between them? Did someone cheat?" Devan speculated.

"No! Clara is the most honest person I know. Well, maybe Rachel is but that's because she's the most naïve in the group. But Clara and Jason complemented each other well. He is the introverted geek and she's the extroverted socialite. His jealousy surfaced too much for her liking. She does not tolerate being controlled by a jealous man. That was her issue with Rob in high school," Shannon said as she gestured towards the back of the room.

"Clara and Rob dated in high school?" Devan's attention was captured.

"Not really. They were just pretty close. With the way things were at her house, she didn't like being home much. She was usually at Rachel's or Lila's. When they were younger he was big brotherly, but by high school, he started getting jealous of the attention other guys gave her," Shannon shrugged. "I have no idea if anything went on between them, or if they even ever kissed. He lost any chance after the prom."

Shannon sipped from her drink while Devan looked at her expectantly. "Shan, you can't just leave me hanging. What happened at the prom?"

Shannon just smiled as she stood up on the bar step and motioned him to meet her over the bar. Expecting a kiss, he complied. She whispered, "Not my story to tell."

She leaned in to give him a quick kiss before stepping back with her drink to mingle.

Lila had seen her brother and cousin sitting in the back. After she ate her dinner she began mingling her way towards them. The multiple empty shot glasses on the table alerted her to his negative drunk state. She did not like Rob when he was drunk. As he grew older, he matured enough to know he was better off sticking to beer.

"Hey Chase, what's going on?" Lila gestured towards the empty glasses on the table, just as Jill came by to clear it up.

Rob was flirting with her and placed another order, then he turned to flirt with the women at the next table. While Rob's back was turned, Chase called Jill back over to cancel the order, then handed her his card to close out the tab. She nodded and turned away with her tray of empties.

In response to Lila's question, Chase rolled his eyes as he summed it up in one word, "Clara."

"Oh," she immediately understood.

"Sorry to have to end your evening short if you want to ride home with us. I need to get him to the truck before he starts a fight," he sighed. Jill was back with his card and tab. Chase stood up as he returned his wallet to his pocket.

"I'll be staying out tonight, Shannon and I just arrived. Don't worry about me. I'll help you get him to the truck," she stood up to give him a hug.

"Nah, I can handle it. I've learned to get him out while he's still in the flirty mode before he falls into the asshole mode. Have fun and keep safe," Chase kissed her forehead before he grabbed his other cousin's arm.

Lila followed them as they made their way to the door. Rob was stopped by many people while Chase redirected him out. She chuckled when he hugged his recently retired third grade teacher. Once she was back at the bar, she sat on a stool with her drink.

She was looking over the crowd when she heard a voice whisper in her ear, "Hey pretty lady. Want to go make out with me in my truck out back?"

Lila turned to see Dallas leaning on the bar next to her. He had motioned for his tab.

"Dallas! How long have you been here? I thought you were going out with the guys."

"I am. I did. We had dinner and a drink. And now I see a pretty lady I'd like to hang out with." His smile was mischievous as his blueish green eyes sparkled.

"Have you seen Clara tonight?" Lila was ignoring the flirty suggestion. They were in public.

"Hell, yeah. After that entrance she made, everyone here saw her," he answered, not wanting to go into details.

"What happened? Did she fall or something?"

"Or something," Dallas answered as he signed his tab. "Are you sure you don't want to make out in the parking lot before I head home?"

"Dallas, I am not going to make out with you in the parking lot like a couple of horny teenagers. Tell me what happened with Clara," Lila asked firmly.

Dallas sighed. He really didn't like to gossip, and he especially didn't want to talk about his little sister's inappropriate behavior in the bar. He looked over before he answered, "She walked into the place and made a beeline straight for the doctor with a greeting that made half the town blush."

Lila was shocked, "What? You mean she kissed him?"

"Oh, there was kissing, tongue, and touching. Didn't leave much imagination to what is probably going on upstairs at his place right now. I don't want to talk about it anymore. It's an image I may never forget. I would rather not see that side of my sister. Why don't you want to come out back with me?"

Lila giggled, "Spoken like a true big brother. Dal, what would you rather have, me making out with you for a few minutes in your truck or all night in your bed?"

The giggle captured Devan's attention. He saw a guy he'd seen around Clara's place a few times. He didn't really know the guy. He knew his uncle had questioned him as the last person to talk with Clara before the incident at her house last week. Is he trying to pick Lila up? He appeared to be smooth talking while she was shaking her head. Devan filled another round of drinks while he continued to monitor.

Dallas was thoughtful for a moment before he asked, "I only get one? Not both? We can't make out in the truck before we spend the night in my bed? I was actually thinking of hanging out in the hot tub when I get home."

"The hot tub is here? I don't have my bathing suit," Lila announced.

"What do you need a bathing suit for?"

She giggled again, "Dallas, is the tub outside on the deck? You want me outside without a bathing suit for all the world to see?"

"It's dark out and it's overlooking the woods. The only ones watching will be the wildlife," Dallas answered with a mischievous grin. He fought the urge to kiss her when she nodded her head slightly in agreement. "Is your car parked out back?"

"No, it's at Clara's," she confirmed. "Shannon and I each parked there and walked since we planned to drink."

"I'll head out as you close out your tab," he winked before he turned around.

Devan watched how the guy appeared to smoothly talk to Lila. First, she was shaking her head and then she finally nodded in agreement before he left. Why would they need to hide the fact they were obviously leaving together? It seemed suspicious. He brought Lila's tab over as she paid. Before she could step away, he reached for her hand. She looked down in surprise as she brought her blue eyes up to meet his hazel.

"Lila, do you think it's a good idea to leave with this guy? Do you even know him?" Devan asked in his federal agent tone.

"Yeah, I know Dallas. We went to high school together. He's a good guy, I trust him," Lila defended him.

"Yeah? If he's such a good guy, why are you hiding it?" He demanded.

"I have loved him since high school, since the night the movie theater blew up. He saved my life. He loves me despite everything that's wrong. But my family won't ever approve of him," she said sadly.

Devan watched the emotions play across her face. He made a mental note to look at Dallas Thompson's background before he made his own conclusions. He squeezed her hand, "Just checking to make sure you're safe."

"Please don't tell anyone," Lila pleaded.

"I won't as long as he doesn't hurt you."

"You would have to get in line if he did, but he won't. Thanks, Devan," she smiled as she slowly followed Dallas out the back door.

When Clara opened her eyes, the room was dark. She felt a moment of panic as she looked around the unfamiliar room, where the hell am I?

Then she saw Connor sitting in a chair in the corner with his legs elevated on a matching ottoman, balancing a tablet in his lap. When he sensed her moving, he glanced up and placed his tablet on the table. As he approached her, he picked up her hearing aids on the bedside table and placed them in her hand. Connor wanted to sit down beside her, but he decided to play it safe. He turned the light on the dimmest level.

"Connor, what happened? Why am I here?" Clara asked with panic.

"Clara, you're alright. You had a bit too much to drink and I brought you up here," he answered vaguely. Connor continued to keep his distance, not sure if she was still under the influence. It had been a struggling couple of hours avoiding her advancements. "I called your place and informed the sitter you were out for the night."

"Oh man, my head is killing me. That last drink really hit me. I swear I only had two," she stated as she sat to the edge of the bed. "Well, two before the shots then maybe another drink."

Connor handed her some Tylenol and water as he continued to monitor her. "What do you remember?"

She shrugged. "I was walking down towards Memories. Both Lila and Shannon were running late. I met up with a nurse from work during the walk. We stopped at The Joint in the alley before heading over to The Lantern. Talked with a bunch of people, did shots with Josh and then I walked across the street to Memories. I saw you sitting at the bar."

Connor was taken aback when she mentioned doing shots with his nephew, but when she blushed, he knew she was back to her usual self. He was relieved she seemed to be remembering the details and that he was the one who caught her attention. If it had been Foxwood, he would have treated the evening as a wrapped gift on Christmas morning, no questions asked. But why was she drinking with Joshua?

"Oh my God, Connor! I am so sorry. I kissed you in front of half the town. I never should have done that!" Clara whispered.

Connor chuckled, only she would make an apology sound like an insult. "Well, I still think us eating dinner together in a restaurant would have been less scandalous than that greeting."

As Clara stood up, she looked down at her clothes, "Connor, what am I wearing?"

"My old college t-shirt," he answered with a grin. He thought she looked beautiful. It was big and came down past her bottom, showing off her toned legs. "And before you ask, I didn't do it. You did."

She eyed him suspiciously before stepping into the bathroom. When she returned, she headed back into the bed for a few more hours of sleep, "Connor, why are you sitting over there? This is your bed you should be sleeping in it."

He chuckled, "Clara, I don't think that's a good idea. You can't seem to keep your hands off me."

"Connor! Why would you think that?" She asked but then remembered another kiss once they were up at his place. Did she really unbutton his shirt, oh my God! What was in that drink?

Connor watched her blush again and wondered which part she was remembering, the kissing, touching, or the stripping. He laughed again when she stated, "I promise, I won't take advantage of you. I'll keep my hands to myself."

"Clara, it's not just your hands I'm worried about. You are a wild woman!"

"Not really but seriously, come over here," Clara pulled the covers back and scooted over.

He saw a glimpse of her purple thong as the shirt creeped up. Definitely not a good idea, Connor thought as he stood up to walk towards the bed. He pulled the covers down to lay on top, thinking to play it safer. Lying in bed next to Clara Noelle after the level of intimacy they had earlier was not smart. She leaned up to kiss his cheek before rolling over onto her side away from him. Once he was lying beside her, she leaned back into him and his arm came around her as if it were the most natural thing, the two of them sleeping together in bed. Connor felt content as he finally closed his eyes for the night.

20 drugged

Clara woke up just as the sun peeked up over the hillside. She rolled over, surprised to be alone in the bed. She pulled his pillow in to breathe in his scent and smiled. After using the bathroom, she followed the scent of coffee. Connor was sitting on a stool in the kitchen, still in his lounger pants and t-shirt. He had a day old beard and his hair was ruffled. When he looked up with a smile, she felt her heart melt. She motioned for him to stay as she walked around him to get her own coffee.

Connor watched as Clara moved around the kitchen with ease. He admired her legs and grinned when she reached into the refrigerator, causing the shirt to shift up and expose part of her lovely derriere. After her coffee was prepared, she stepped back around the counter, letting her hand trail onto his back. Connor was slightly disappointed when the hand didn't slide lower down or when she didn't step in close between his legs. She's definitely back to herself, he thought with mixed emotions.

"Connor, I am sorry to have been so much trouble last night. Thank you for once again taking care of me," Clara apologized as she sipped her coffee.

Connor couldn't resist teasing her, "Clara, last night was my pleasure. Being kissed and touched by you is never any trouble."

Clara put down her mug and stared at him, "I still can't believe two or three drinks would make me act like a slut."

Before she could say anything else, Connor felt it was time to explain his theory. "Clara, I don't think it was just the drinks that caused your behavior. I think you were drugged last night."

Clara's smile faded as she looked into his brown eyes. "What? Why do you think that?"

"Last Friday evening, you had more than three drinks and didn't come near me the way you did last night. You haven't been taking anything for the injuries from last Saturday, have you?" When Clara shook her head, Connor continued, "So we can rule out mixing alcohol with prescription meds. That leaves us with the option of someone spiking your drink. The sheriff has the blood sample I took last night as well as the glass you were drinking from to confirm all of this. Do you have any idea who it was?"

Clara simply shook her head as she had some images from the night before. She groaned and lowered her face into her hands as she remembered her behavior once they were upstairs. "Oh God, Connor, I have never been so loose with anyone except my husband. It was like any thought that went into my mind immediately came out in my actions. Devan must think I'm a dollop!"

Connor placed his hand on her back in an attempt to reassure her. "Hey, he was aware of the situation. I'm sure he will never think of you the same way after that strip tease. But I am more than willing to watch it again."

He laughed when she groaned again, "I really did strip in front of both of you, didn't I? How can either of you ever respect me again?"

He reached for her hand and kissed it, "Don't worry, Devan left after you removed your top. He missed all the good stuff."

Connor pulled her over. As she stepped between his legs, she let her hands slowly caress his thighs as he brought his arms around her. This time, he allowed the kiss.

Later in the morning, Matt was surprised to see Devan standing on his front porch. He was immediately suspicious as he opened the screen door, "Devan, what's going on?"

Devan nodded in greeting, "Is Josh home?"

"Why? Is there a problem?"

Devan simply stared at him. He knew the lawyer in Matt would act as a barrier but the sheriff gave him permission to allow him to be present in the questioning. As of right now, Joshua Emerson was only being questioned as a witness. Someone present when Clara was likely drugged.

"I have some questions for him."

Matt's eyes narrowed as he asked, "As a law enforcement officer?"

"Does it matter?"

"Hell, yes it does!"

"Look Matt, I just have a few questions for him. You are more than welcome to hear them. Is he here or not? Is he at a girlfriend's?"

"I'm right here," Josh stated as he came down the grand staircase. Without saying anything, he led them both into the parlor.

"Were you at The Lantern last night?" Devan started without preamble.

"Yes. I was there for a few hours and then I walked home," Josh answered as his eyes darted between the two men.

"Anything unusual happen last night?"

"Unusual? As in fights?" Josh asked.

"Anything that's never happened before or was suspicious," Devan answered. He didn't want to be too leading.

"Well, Clara was out by herself last night. We had a couple of shots together, that's never happened before," he answered.

"Did she stay with you the whole time?"

"No, she sat beside me at the bar and I bought her a drink. We talked and did a couple of shots together. She was pulled away by Nic, one of the nurses from work. He brought her over to her work crowd in the corner. I wasn't really paying attention when she joined them. I don't think she stayed longer than a half hour before she left."

"Devan, what's going on?" Matt quietly asked. He wasn't sure how he felt about his son drinking with Suzi's daughter. He realized it wasn't a crime and they were actually closer in age than she was with his brother.

"Clara arrived immediately after to Memories. Her drink she brought with her was spiked," Devan announced as he monitored their reactions. He was relieved when both looked surprised.

"What? Is she alright?" Matt's face paled.

"Did something happen to her?" Josh asked, equally pale.

"She's alright, nothing happened. Connor realized once he saw her eyes were pinpoint. He pulled her out of there. He had her blood drawn," Devan explained. "When she sobered up, she was a bit hazy on the details but it appears she remembers drinking with you, Josh. After she left you, she can't account for what happened. Not even who she was with. Any details you can give me will be a great help."

When Devan was finished with the questioning, Matt walked him to the door, "Were you initially looking at Joshua for this?"

"No, he was mentioned as a witness. Uncle Tony sent me over to question him. I asked him an open ended question, didn't lead him, and you are the witness or lawyer. The defense won't be able to throw suspicion on him."

• • • •

Evil was initially surprised to hear about the drugging. His initial reaction was not pretty. The thought of anyone bringing harm to his Babydoll! And messing with his plans!. He wanted to kill someone! But after he calmed, a thought occurred. Hmm, maybe this can all be pinned on the kid. He's not too smart and he's always ruining the moment. But if he doesn't do something soon, everything he's planned for will fade from his reach. Questions are being asked because others are screwing up…he almost giggled as he thought it over. It could work…

21

visit from the city

When Monday arrived, Clara was up early. She was pleased the bruising on her face was fading. She and the children were up and out earlier than usual. She smiled as she walked toward her desk, thinking about the weekend. Her actions from Friday night still embarrassed her, but it did seem to jump-start her into something with Connor. He dropped her off early on Saturday before he began his rounds at the hospital. Her outdoor deck furniture was delivered with a large grill. After she sent Connor a picture, he suggested he stop over with steaks to grill. Shannon and Devan joined them for dinner out on the deck. It was a lovely evening.

On Sunday, they bumped into each other while they were visiting with Gigi. Connor joined them for ice cream before he went to the hospital for his shift. And this morning when she was dropping off the children at daycare, she saw him in the parking lot. He just had time to wish her a good morning and steal a quick kiss before getting pulled into the ER.

Clara sighed with happiness. She was enjoying the simplicity of having Connor in her life and was very aware of the complications that could occur. She would start looking into divorce lawyers later that evening. She turned at the knock on her door.

Eric was standing at the door with a tray of coffees. "Good morning, Clara. How was your weekend?"

He smiled when her face turned towards his and lit up the room. "It was a great weekend, Eric. It was very relaxing and fun. How about yours?"

He had stepped towards her desk to hand her a coffee. Once he was closer, Eric studied her face. The bruises were fading, but it still pissed him off just thinking about the attack, and the bastard who did it. "It was alright. It didn't work out as I had hoped but, you know, it is what it is." He shrugged.

"What is all this?" Eric gestured towards the files on her desk as he stepped closer to her, closing his eyes as he sniffed her wonderful scent.

"Oh, I printed out some of the protocols from various ortho surgeons to familiarize myself and staff to help optimize the patients' rehab process. I have also been researching equipment in preparation for the capital budget," Clara explained. "And I've talked with Judy in HR about potential positions opening up in my department."

Eric, not aware that Matt had already informed her of the process, said, "I have the forms in my office, I'll bring them down to assist you with your requests. How about we work on it over lunch?"

Clara decided not to correct him. "Eric, thanks for the coffee. It's really sweet of you."

"Not a problem. I was already getting myself one," he answered as his heart skipped a beat when her green eyes met with his blue.

After the late morning meeting, Eric had called Clara into his office. He had the files they had discussed earlier. He was standing at the door when the sheriff and two other men came down the hall.

"Sheriff Mancuso, what can I do for you today?" Eric asked, attempting to shield Clara, but she had already moved to the side. She eyed the men in front of her, spotting the big city policemen right away.

"Eric, I was wondering if you could excuse us to talk privately with Clara," the sheriff asked.

Eric glanced over at Clara, noting recognition in her eyes. She nodded to him and he quietly excused himself as the sheriff closed the door behind him.

"Mrs. O'Reilly, I am Detective Jim Walter, this is my partner Detective Andy Sanders. How are you doing today?" The older gentleman asked.

"Honestly, I have had better weeks. What is this about? Do you have information about my mother's death?" Clara asked, attempting to ignore the panic growing inside of her.

"I don't have anything new on your mother. Clara, when was the last time you saw your husband?" Sheriff Mancuso asked.

"Three months ago, it was the third Tuesday in January, why?" She glanced over each of the men standing before her as she tried harder to suppress the panic.

"That date came pretty quick. Are you sure?" The younger detective asked.

"Yes, it was the worst argument we ever had. Jason stormed out, he said he was going to walk it off."

"And when was the next time you heard from him?" Sanders inquired.

"The next morning I received a text saying he was going to stay with a friend. He gave me the impression he was house sitting. He said he needed time to think things over. He's an accountant, and this was a busy time for him. He did not want the distractions. When I came home later that day, his clothes, his laptop, and a few other things were gone," Clara answered confidently.

"What was the argument about?"

Sighing loudly, Clara turned to sit on the couch along the wall. The others joined her.

"Flowers kept coming to our place with the cards reading something like 'I had a wonderful time last night' or 'You were beautiful in the green dress last night but I prefer you in the purple.' 'I can't wait to see you again.' I told him they weren't for me. They had the address wrong. He initially agreed with me, but this was going on for a while. Then we started to get hang up calls, usually Jay would answer. The person would simply hang up after a few minutes. Then, that last night, it was still early in the evening. The kids were already in bed. I answered the phone in the kitchen, but he also answered in the bedroom . The caller said, 'Hello Babydoll, meet me at our normal spot. I need to see you.'"

"I slammed down the phone, then looked up and saw Jay standing in the doorway. He just had this look on his face, like he was totally defeated. I tried to explain it was not me, but someone playing a sick joke," she said as a tear slid down her cheek.

"And when was the last time you talked with him?"

"We never actually talked again. I call him every day, leaving a voicemail, either to ask how he is doing or to give him an update on the kids. Sometimes, I just say we miss him and want him to come home. He never answers my calls but he'll send a text."

"When did you last hear from him?" Detective Sanders asked.

"Last Friday night," Clara answered as she pulled out her cell to read the message. "He wrote, 'Nothing to work out, I have filed for a divorce.'"

Both the detectives exchanged looks but neither said anything. His cell phone had not been found, but they did have a warrant for the cell company to release his messages.

"What about his family or friends? Did you reach out to them? Who was he staying with?"

"None of them would talk to me. He doesn't have any family. He grew up in foster care after his parents were killed in an accident when he was young. We met in college. He was more of a loner. His co-workers are his friends." Clara stopped talking and looked each detective in the eye. "What are you not telling me? Is he in trouble?"

"Mrs. O'Reilly, your husband was found in an abandoned building last week," the older detective started to explain.

"What happened?" Clara demanded as she sat straight up, "You wouldn't come all this way to tell me he's in the hospital. He's dead, isn't he? Are you telling me my husband is dead? Oh my God." She closed her eyes, buried her face in her hands, and tried to breathe.

"When did he die? Last week?" She whispered after a few minutes.

"Most likely over the winter," Detective Sanders quietly answered.

"But that doesn't make any sense! He's been texting me all this time, I leave a voicemail every night." She lowered her hands and tried to breathe as she looked the older detective in the eyes. She took a slow deep breath and asked, "What the hell happened?"

"We are not sure at this point. We just began the investigation. Is there anything else you can tell us?" He paused in thought. "Do you remember the name of the florist that delivered the flowers?"

Clara slowly nodded her head as she whispered, "The Westside Florist."

Then a thought crossed her mind. "His voicemail should be full. How am I still able to leave a voicemail every night? Is someone else listening to my messages? Are we in danger? Are my kids in danger?" She looked over at the sheriff and pleaded, "Mr. Mancuso, can you take me to them?"

"I have Anthony out in the hall. He's going to take you home, but you can swing by and pick up the children first," the sheriff answered. He had already informed the detectives prior to this discussion that he did not believe Clara was involved in the disappearance or death of her husband. But he had to agree, things were getting a bit icky.

Detective Walters gave a slight nod to Clara, "Mrs. O'Reilly, we will be in touch. Here is my card. Please contact me if you have any questions or remember anything else."

Clara accepted the two business cards, but simply held them in her hands.

Out in the car, Sanders looked over at his partner as he pulled out of the parking lot, "I agree with the sheriff, I don't think she's involved with her husband's disappearance. She was devastated. No one is that good of an actress."

"She was pretty quick to connect the dots, don't you think," Walters inquired. Being in homicide for too long gave him a dim outlook. It was always someone close. The damage to the body was brutal which suggested something personal, and someone with good strength.

As the city vehicle pulled away from the parking lot, a hand gently separated the blinds while a pair of eyes watched the unknown men drive away. A moment later, the sheriff and his son came out, escorting Clara to her car. He watched her face as she sat in the front passenger seat. He noted the paleness and the panic in her eyes. He debated what to do next as the car pulled out from the lot and he stepped away from the window.

22

sleepless night

Connor was coming out of the operating room when Josh informed him of a visitor waiting in his office. He thanked him before instructing him to head home for the night. When he stepped around the corner, Joe Mancuso, the sheriff's oldest son, stood up. At first Connor thought it was a personal call, because he was not in uniform. But the look on his face suggested otherwise. He opened the door to his office to allow privacy.

Joe graduated high school a year behind Connor. They played on the same soccer, basketball, and baseball teams. While they were close friends, Connor was closer to Devan. The three used to ride their bikes around town, go hiking in the woods and swimming in the lake. Devan grew up in the city with his parents but often spent the school holidays in town with his cousins. Connor grew up in town, went to school and completed his training in the city but returned home a few years back. Joe did go to college at a nearby town and returned home when he graduated to join the sheriff's department. He was the only one in the group married with three children.

"What's going on?" Connor asked.

"Connor, I'm not really sure if I should be telling you this, but

Anthony and I both agree you should know. You have been getting close with Clara since she's been back," he started.

"Joe, you know we've always been good friends," Connor interrupted.

"Yeah but after what I saw last Friday night, I think it's safe to assume you two are a couple," Connor remained silent as he tried to understand where his friend was leading with this. "City cops were in town this afternoon making a notification on Jason O'Reilly."

Connor had been leaning against his desk but stood right up at hearing this. Joe held up a hand, "My dad was present while they talked to her. All we know is his body was found last week in an abandoned building. They estimate he was killed last January. This has been kept quiet, as it's not our investigation. Since Clara and Anthony went to school together, my dad thought she would be more comfortable with him than hanging out with me. It has been several hours and she has yet to call any of her friends."

"Where is she? The kids?" Connor asked as he stepped around his desk to pack his briefcase.

"All three are at her place. I dropped off some food around five. Anthony says the kids ate with him, but Clara hasn't really moved much."

Connor brought his bag onto his shoulder as they started down the hall, "Why didn't you have them pull me out of surgery?"

"Josh said there was a complication." Joe shrugged.

Clara was sitting on the floor in front of the sofa with Reese sitting on her right side while her daughter sat on her left. The tv was on but she had no idea what was playing. She was numb, as if her mind stopped working. She was waiting for Shannon to come home, forgetting Shannon and Lila were off for a couple of days on a hiking trip in the local park. It was just as well as she did not want to talk to anyone right now.

Anthony spent the evening sitting in the chair feeling awkward.

He wanted to help Clara, but he could tell she was not receptive to interaction right now. He used to have a crush on her when they sat next to each other in math class. When his brother found out, he told him she was out of his league. He agreed. He was relieved when his brother reported Connor was finally out of surgery and on his way.

When Connor arrived, the deputy gave a brief update before leaving. After locking up, Connor paused in the doorway of the family room. The look of distraught on Clara's face made him want to pick her up and shield her from the pain and sorrows of the days ahead. What she must be thinking, to learn Jay, like her mother, did not leave her but was killed.

Clara remained sitting on the floor, she didn't even acknowledge him. The little girl was asleep in her mother's lap while the boy clinged to her side. When Connor stepped into the room, his large green eyes, so like his mother's, followed his movements. He didn't say a word.

Connor squatted down in front of Clara and asked if he could take Hailey up to her bed. Clara simply nodded. He carefully picked up the young girl and carried her up the steps. When he returned, he sat quietly on the floor beside her. The boy was soon fast asleep with his head in his mother's lap as she gently stroked his hair. Connor remained silent as they sat for another half hour before he gestured towards the boy. She nodded her head.

When Connor returned, he lifted Clara onto the sofa and sat beside her with his arm around her shoulders. She leaned into him while they remained silent. He thought back to that early morning when he was eighteen years old and found her sitting alone on the porch. She had been quiet then, but eventually she started to talk. He was used to her sometimes not making much sense, but that morning she reported being alone. Evil had taken her mother. That's when he stopped her and asked, "What do you mean evil took your mother? Did something happen to her? Is she hurt?" Clara had nodded her head when she answered, "He did hurt her and now she is gone." She didn't cry at first but when

Connor stood up to go look in the house, she tried to block him. He wanted to see if her mother was hurt, or worse, dead. But Clara started to cry and wouldn't let him into the kitchen as she declared it was evil. He brought her over to his house and called the sheriff.

Connor reached over for her hand and gave it a gentle squeeze. And then he felt her shake as she started to cry. They remained sitting on the sofa in silence.

In the city, Detective Sanders was still at his desk well into the night. When he and his partner had arrived back to the precinct, Jason O'Reilly's cell records were there waiting for them. He initially did a quick scan, noting the date of the last message sent out, and texts and voicemails from the wife just about every day. When he listened to her voice, he could hear the hurt as she provided updates on the children, informed him of her friend's mother's death and the need for a babysitter, giving him the opportunity to come over and stay with the children; she left multiple messages listing the pros and cons of moving or staying. He did respond to a few with simple answers. But of interesting note, his few comments never had anything to do with the children. Not once did he inquire about them or even mention them by name. The messages were simple and agreeable, and seemed to encourage her to get out of the city to some place safer.

According to the medical examiner's preliminary notes, Jason O'Reilly was most likely killed shortly after he left his home. So, who sent the text that said he was staying with a friend? He also noted a text sent out to his supervisor at work with a request for personal time off. This could explain why no one reported him missing. The biggest concern was the last message sent out, "Nothing to work out, I have filed for a divorce."

Not only was the man killed, but someone was using his cell. Was the killer simply using it to hide the man's death. Why? To get away with murder? Was there something else? Where the hell is the cell phone now? Andy knew if they could find the phone, they would find the killer.

Clara and Connor spent a sleepless night on the sofa. No one spoke, but occasionally each would get up. Connor stepped out onto the back deck to talk with Devan. That's when he learned Lila and Shannon were out hiking and camping for the Memorial Day holiday. Devan was going to wait until morning to text Shannon, to inform them what was happening.

Before sunrise, Clara went upstairs to shower. Unable to think straight, she couldn't even decide what to wear. She gave up and went downstairs wearing only her bathrobe. In the kitchen, Connor already had the coffee prepared and brought her mug to the table while they both sat. He asked if she wanted anything to eat, she just shook her head no.

"Do you know what you're doing today?"

"I think I should go into the city. I need to call Eric to let him know I can't work right now. I need to see if Michelle can watch the kids after daycare until I get home." She thought about why she had to go into the city and the tears started again.

Connor grabbed her hand to pull her over onto his lap as she continued to cry. After a few minutes, she apologized and started to hiccup. He remained quiet as she continued to list off again what she needed to do.

"Do you want me to drive you?" He asked.

Clara simply shook her head no. "OK, I have a suggestion. How about Devan drives you into the city. Hear me out, first alright? I am not sure you are aware he is a federal agent and he has connections. He will know where you need to go and help with any of the red tape. Plus, he could be on the lookout in case there's any trouble."

"Connor, I barely know the guy. Why would he want to spend a day babysitting a hysterical girl? I would think he'd have better things to do with his day."

"Clara, you are not hysterical. Really Sweetheart, where do you come up with these ideas? This can't go any further, promise me?" When Clara nodded, he continued, "Devan's been working undercover as a bartender at the request of the sheriff. You know he's the sheriff's nephew. I don't know the details, but you don't need to concern yourself with that anyway, how about it?"

"Do you trust him? Why do you trust him so much?" She questioned.

"He's my cousin," Connor stated as a matter of fact.

"The sheriff is your uncle? How did I not know this?" Clara was clearly puzzled.

"No, Devan's father is the sheriff's brother. His mother is my mother's cousin. They were always close, like sisters, growing up. When his parents married, they moved to the city but they both wanted him to know his roots, so he often spent his school holidays here in town. He usually stayed with the Mancuso's and I often went over there."

Allowing herself to get distracted, she listened quietly. Clara thought through her memories and was vaguely aware of another kid Connor often played with when he was hanging out with Joe Mancuso. Hmm, I wonder if Shannon remembers him?

"If he were to go with me, when would he be ready to leave?"

"Whenever you want. What do you need to do? Take the kids to daycare? I can do that. I can also pick them up after, so they are home when you get here," Connor stated, relieved she was considering this.

"So, you trust him? You think I should trust him?" She clarified.

"Absolutely. I trust him more than my own brother," Connor declared.

"Yeah? What are your issues with your brother?" She asked, absorbing the distraction.

"We don't really have time to get into that now." Connor sighed just as the doorbell rang. The word is now officially out, he thought.

Clara stiffened in his lap. She was not ready to deal with people yet.

"I'll answer the door," Connor said as he lifted her up onto her feet.

He kissed her forehead before he walked out of the kitchen. "Who can I let in and who should I leave out?"

When he peeked out the window he said, "Never mind. Figures he would come running as soon as he heard. It's your boyfriend."

Clara shook her head.

When Connor opened the door, he smiled inwardly at Rob's obvious annoyance seeing him answer the door. He stepped back and gestured him in.

Rob was hurt Clara had once again called the good doctor over him in her time of need. He could not have known Clara didn't call Connor either time, that it was a Mancuso who notified him each time. Regardless, it irked him to see her standing there recently showered and wearing only a bathrobe, while Connor, looking disheveled, was walking around like he owned the place. Rob went over to hug Clara while he explained Lila and Shannon were on the way back from their trip. They sent him to stay with the kids until they arrived.

Connor contained his irritation at Rob hugging her while she was wearing only her bathrobe. He walked past them back into the kitchen. Pouring another mug of coffee, he asked Rob how he wanted it.

"Black is good," Rob answered as he followed Clara into the kitchen, surprised with Connor playing the host. He accepted the mug, leaned back into the counter as he watched the looks between them, I apparently walked into a discussion, he thought.

"What time are you guys heading out?" He asked.

Clara leaned back and sipped from her mug before she turned to him, "Connor is not going with me, but I'll be leaving in the next thirty minutes or so."

Connor nodded his understanding and pulled out his cell as Clara brought her mug to the sink and walked out. As Rob watched her leave the room, Connor was again reminded that Rob was still in love with her. His eyes always give it away.

Rob waited until he heard Clara's feet on the stairs before he turned to the good doctor, "You are going to let her go alone?"

"She's not going alone. She has someone driving her. Right now, she doesn't want you or me at her side. Both Shannon and Lila are not available, so the sheriff has his nephew taking her. Clara made the final decision," Connor explained.

Just then, Reese and Hailey entered the room. Reese immediately went to Rob to discuss what he wanted for breakfast while the little girl came to a complete stop when her sky blue eyes met Connor's. Connor winked at her and was rewarded with a shy smile. When she heard the discussion about breakfast, Hailey wanted to be included.

"Hailey wants French toast, but I want pancakes," Reese declared.

"What did you guys eat for breakfast yesterday?" Rob asked.

"French toast," Reese answered.

"Really? Your mother made French toast?" Rob asked with surprise.

"Yeah, she makes them all the time. She pulls them out of the box and puts them in the toaster," Reese said. Hailey nodded her head.

"Alright, that sounds more accurate," Rob chuckled as he watched Connor stand up and walk out.

Upstairs, Connor found Clara standing fully dressed in jeans and a simple green top. She was looking out the window. Without saying anything, he placed his arms around her. She leaned back into him and asked what was going on downstairs.

Connor rested his chin on her head. "Discussing your lack of culinary skills."

She turned her head and looked at him in question.

"Hey, I didn't say anything. It was your son and Rob talking. I think Hailey was agreeing but I really don't understand her babbles," Connor clarified.

"Reese is the only one that understands her all the time. Sometimes I think he just makes it up and she goes along with him. Yeah, Jay was the one that made breakfast from scratch. When we were kids, the Foxwoods always had elaborate breakfasts every morning. I always preferred cereal, but I enjoyed the big breakfast when I stayed over." Clara sighed as she wrapped her arms over his. "Connor, thanks. I appreciate having you here."

"Clara, I am here for you, no matter what. I told you this a few weeks ago. You need anything, just name it. Even if it's just to sit with you on the sofa during the night or to start up your grill out back, I'm only a phone call away," he kissed the top of her head.

Clara pulled away, and reached for her purse and a sweater as she headed down the stairs.

Connor waited by the front door as she said good-bye to her children, instructing them to behave when either Shannon or Lila picked them up from school. She thanked Rob for coming over early. When she started towards the front door, he opened it to find Devan already leaning against his SUV.

Connor walked with Clara to her door and hugged her one last time, "Call me, alright?"

She nodded before getting inside. He closed the door and tapped the roof.

Devan started up the vehicle and backed away. Once they were on the road he said, "Clara, let me know what I can do and what you prefer. Do you want the music on or off? I'm good either way. I'm going to stop and get some coffee. Just let me know anytime you need to make a stop."

Clara nodded but remained silent during the drive.

Hours later, Devan watched as Clara came out of the ladies' room. She was holding up surprisingly well considering all that she went through. She identified her husband's body, they were able to confirm a scar on his leg from the accident when he was a child. Then the detectives had many questions. It came out during the questioning that his time of death was shortly after she last saw him.

Clara's face had immediately gone pale, "What do you mean he died last January? He could not have been dead all this time!"

Devan was silent as he sat beside her, listening to the discussion. He could feel her fear as her questions went unanswered.

"Why couldn't he be?" The younger detective asked. He already knew the answer but wanted to see her reaction. His job was to find the killer, but he found himself getting pulled into her sharp green eyes. Clara O'Reilly was a beautiful woman. She could easily have a lover on the side that wanted the husband out of the picture.

"Because I have been texting and calling him almost every day. He has even responded. Who the hell has been sending the messages? Who has been reading and listening to us?" She demanded with a voice laced with panic.

"Mrs. O'Reilly, have you been seeing anyone in the last year or so? Someone you tried to end it with, maybe he couldn't let it go?" Detective Walters asked, trying to not sound judgmental.

"Are you kidding me? I was either pregnant or breastfeeding up until January. How could I possibly be seeing another man?" Clara demanded.

"You'd be surprised how often it happens," the younger detective commented while the other two men nodded in agreement. "Alright, so maybe it's not someone while you were married. What about before you married? Give us the names of your previous boyfriends."

Clara looked around at all three men sitting with her at the table, "I don't have any ex-boyfriends. I met my husband during my freshman year of college."

The older detective raised his eyebrows at his partner, "You expect us to believe a beautiful smart young woman such as yourself married the first and only guy she's ever dated? What about high school?"

Clara initially thought of Rob, but they never actually dated. She wondered if he had ever been interested in her, but he always had a girlfriend. Clara sighed with obvious frustration as she tried to maintain her composure, "I may be young and smart, but it does not make me a slut. I was raised to be a lady, considerate of others, and to work hard for what I want!"

Clara had been on the edge of losing her control but instead she stood up and excused herself.

While she was in the restroom, Devan explained to the detectives about the attack on Clara in her home the week before and the discovery of surveillance equipment. "The sheriff is currently investigating but you'll have to call him for details. And honestly, my younger cousin went to high school with her. He always described her and her friends as ladies with high moral standards."

When Clara stepped out, her eyes were bloodshot and she still looked pale. Devan noted her hand was shaking. He opened his arms and she immediately stepped in for a hug. She closed her eyes in an attempt to absorb his strength as she fought to regain her composure. She did not want to once again lose control.

As she pulled back, he could see her temper brewing just below the surface. "Clara, they were never calling you a slut. They are just looking for someone who may have had a grudge against your husband. They have to rule you out and often the questions are difficult, but the reactions and the responses are always telling."

"Oh? Great, so I blew up for nothing? I should have kept my calm as they continued to insult me by suggesting I would cheat on my husband? While I'm breast feeding our baby? Seriously, how could that possibly happen?"

Devan nodded as she vented her frustrations. Yeah, she's definitely vanilla. He assured her they would most likely have her ruled out and would continue to focus elsewhere for the killer.

As they were walking through the lobby, Devan had paused to take a call. He motioned for her to head outside and he would catch up. Clara stopped when someone almost bumped into her. She mumbled an apology but looked up when she heard her name.

"Clara?" A male voice asked.

"Joel?" Clara was equally surprised to see Shannon's ex-boyfriend.

"What are you doing here? I thought you moved back home."

"Yeah, uh some things I had to see to," she vaguely answered. After what he did to Shannon, Clara wasn't giving him her current life story.

But Joel noticed the red puffy eyes and pale complexion. He reached for her hand. "Clara, is everything alright?"

He seemed genuinely concerned but Clara's emotions were too close to the surface. Her struggle to keep her control kept her from answering. Suddenly, Devan was back at her side. With an arm around her, he asked if she was ready to go.

But Joel stepped in front of her. "Clara, did something happen? Tell me." He felt a slight panic at the possibility something could have happened to Shannon. He tried to assure himself he would have been notified if anything had happened to her, but not if no one knew of the connection.

Clara held out her hand as she felt Devan about to get defensive, "Devan, this is Joel. Joel, Devan. He is a friend from home. We had to take care of a family matter and now we have a long ride back. Have a good day."

She grabbed Devan's hand as she walked away. Devan smiled to himself. He knew very well who the guy was, Shannon's cop ex-boyfriend.

Joel watched Clara walk away with the undercover from the small town. Why would Clara be here in the city with Shannon's new boyfriend? He went inside to inquire.

Once they were back on the road, Devan announced they were stopping for dinner. Clara agreed. After they placed their orders and were alone again, Clara looked him over. He was cute. She could see why Shannon was attracted, but Connor had told her that morning he was an undercover agent. She wondered if her friend was aware.

"Devan… Lila, Shannon, Rachel and I are all very close. We trust each other with secrets, but we are also respectful of each other's privacy.

We don't pry in each other's business as we tell each other when we are ready. And we especially don't judge. I like you. You spent your whole day off with me which included some serious driving. I really appreciate it. I hope you don't get offended by the advice I'm about to give you. Please tell Shannon what you do, in the general terms, before you two get too serious." Then she excused herself to wash up before the food arrived.

It was late when Clara arrived home. After locking up the house, she went upstairs to check on her children. First, she stood beside Reese's bed watching him sleep. At one point, he sat up and hugged her before closing his eyes again. She went back into Hailey's room. Feeling the fatigue from the previous sleepless night, she sat in the rocker.

Connor had received Devan's text stating they had returned home. He didn't mention anything else and he wondered if he should text her himself. But after deliberating, Connor figured she'd contact him if she needed him. He turned his attention back to his work.

Clara knew the second he arrived when she shivered under the covers from the icy temperature in the room. She remained frozen in fear as she felt the slight shake of the bed as he sat down beside her. She smelled the stale breath as the shadow leaned over to move a curl from her face with his bleach smelling hand. She could feel his breath in her ear as he whispered. Her heart started to pound faster as his hand lowered down to her shoulder…

Clara sat up suddenly, looking around her. She was in Hailey's room. I'm fine, she thought, trying to calm her nerves as she thought she saw a shadow move past the door and down the stairs.

• • • •

Evil quickly returned to his vehicle. He sat in the darkness for a few minutes as he watched her house. He had seen the lights go out after she was dropped off. Where did she go today? He had not seen her around town. He knew the children went to daycare, but they came home with her friend. He was surprised to not find her in bed or even on the sofa. Why are you hiding from me Babydoll? He felt the usual irritation when she would sneak out of her bed at night. Who are you hiding from, he wondered as he felt himself respond to the memory of her hair sprawled out around her angelic face...

Clara felt restless as she returned to her room. She looked at her bed but hesitated to lie down. She thought about going downstairs to bake. Wouldn't that surprise everyone? But she worried the smells and sounds would wake everyone up. It was barely one in the morning. Her cell charging on the bedside table caught her attention. She shouldn't, she thought, but grabbed her phone anyway.

"R u up?"

There was an immediate reply,

"Leaving the hospital now. Want me to stop in?"

"Y"

Clara sighed in relief as she returned her cell to the charger and headed down the stairs.

Connor was pleasantly surprised to get the text. He figured her friends would be all over it. Not knowing what to expect, he pulled into her driveway. As he turned off the engine, Clara opened the front door. When Connor stepped onto the porch, she simply grabbed his hand and squeezed it before she led him inside.

Connor immediately realized she wasn't wearing her hearing aids, signaling she didn't want to talk. He locked the door before allowing her to lead him upstairs to her room.

Just after six in the morning, Connor's cell went off. As he answered it, Clara went into the bathroom to shower. After the call, he went downstairs to start the coffee. He had two mugs in either hand as he was ascending the stairs. At the top, Shannon was standing in a nightie, startled to see Connor.

"Good morning, Connor. I'm surprised to see you here so early in the day," Shannon greeted suspiciously. She knew he was getting close to Clara but was surprised he would be invited over in the wake of her husband's death.

"Morning, Shannon. I'm getting Clara some coffee while she showers. She had a rough night," he explained awkwardly.

"Yeah, I bet. I told her she could sleep with me, but she was in Hailey's room when I went to bed," she softly answered. "She must have been restless later in the night, I heard her walking around. I wish there was something I could do for her."

Connor vaguely remembered Shannon had introduced Clara to Jason during their freshman year, "Shannon, I am sorry for your loss. Clara had mentioned you and Jason were close friends."

Shannon nodded her head as her eyes watered. She squeezed his shoulder as she stepped past and headed down the steps.

When Clara stepped out of the bathroom wrapped in a towel with a t-shirt around her head, Connor was sitting in a chair in the corner, sipping his coffee while reading an endless medical journal on his tablet. He looked up with concern when he realized her eyes were red and thought maybe she was crying in the shower.

Clara was at her dresser getting clothes when she stopped, "Shit! I forgot to call Eric yesterday. I don't think I'll be able to work this week."

Connor stood up, she wasn't looking in his direction and knew she wouldn't be able to hear him. He gently turned her around so she could read his lips, "I talked with him. He's not expecting you back until you are ready. You have at least the week."

"I'm going to get fired, aren't I?" Clara said sadly.

"No, Sweetheart, you aren't. Can I shower while you get dressed out here or do you need anything in there?"

"Go ahead. There's a shelf with towels," she stated as she watched him walk away.

Once Shannon poured her coffee, she decided to step out onto the deck to watch the sunrise. The morning was cool, but the breeze felt good. She sipped her coffee as she thought back to her college years. She looked over when she heard a door open.

Devan was stepping out from his back door onto his deck with his own cup of coffee. He'd been looking out his window when Shannon came outside to sit by herself. His mind started to wander when he realized she was only wearing a nightie. When she turned, her sad green eyes locked on his hazel.

"Hey, morning. Can I join you?" He sat down beside her after she nodded and gestured to a chair.

They sat quietly together, sipping their coffee while the sun rose, falsely promising a good day ahead. When she reached out, Devan took her hand and squeezed it. He moved his chair closer and placed his arm around her. She leaned into his side while she continued to sip her coffee in silence.

Upstairs, Connor came out of the bathroom to find Clara dressed in comfortable faded jeans and an oversized shirt. He suspected it may have been an old shirt of Jason's. She was sitting in the chair with her eyes closed. She had her hearing aids on so she could hear him as he walked into the room. She opened her eyes and gave him a weak smile.

"If you're tired, you can take a nap. You don't need to be up this early," he said as he sat down facing her on the ottoman.

"I can't sleep. The dream, it's just awful. I don't usually remember it after I wake up, but last night, it was so horrible that when I thought I was awake, I was in another nightmare. Then when I did wake up, for real, I was so paranoid Evil was in the house." She saw his eyes narrow in question. She further clarified, "I thought I was seeing shadows. That's why I texted you. Thanks for coming over," she reached for his hand to squeeze.

"Shannon was heading downstairs when I was coming up. Shall we see if she's making breakfast?" Connor asked hopefully.

Clara chuckled, "Shannon doesn't cook. She especially won't be making a high carb breakfast on a work morning."

Connor grabbed the empty mugs as they headed into the hall. Clara was greeted by Reese, excited to see his mother. While he stopped in the bathroom, Clara went in to check on Hailey. She quickly changed her diaper and got her dressed while she supervised her son. The three were heading downstairs when they met Shannon at the bottom. They hugged before she continued upstairs and Clara took the kids into the kitchen. She paused when she realized Devan and Connor were both in the kitchen sipping their coffee while discussing breakfast ideas.

Reese immediately became involved in the discussion. He grabbed Connor's hand to show him something in the pantry.

Shocked, he looked over at Clara, sitting at the table with the toddler on her lap, drinking from a sippy cup. "You have a waffle iron?"

"Yeah, it was a gift," she answered absently.

"Sweet! What do you think, Reese?" When the boy nodded, he placed it on the counter while Devan pulled up the recipe on his cell. He called out various ingredients while Connor searched. He declared they had everything to make homemade waffles. Devan ran home to grab bacon.

When Shannon returned freshly showered and dressed for work, the dining room table was set for breakfast. The four friends sat with the young children as they planned the day. Shannon wasn't able to take the day off. She offered to drop off the children at daycare. Reese insisted he wanted to go. He was taking a field trip to the local bakery today. He was hoping to get a donut. Connor said he was going to the hospital, and offered to take Clara's car and drop them off. He would leave his SUV in case she needed to go anywhere.

It was before eight in the morning, but Eric felt it was late enough to stop in before work. As he reached out to ring the doorbell, the door opened. It didn't surprise him to see Shannon as he knew she was staying with Clara. But he was not expecting the chaos he stepped into when he entered the foyer area.

The children were running around laughing as Clara remained to the side holding two small backpacks. His cousin Connor was standing in the family room laughing with the children, and Devan, the bartender, was in the dining room. Why was everyone here, he wondered.

Everyone seemed to notice him after Shannon invited him inside. Then, Clara turned and smiled as she said hello. Eric noticed the red puffy eyes and the pale face. He felt bad she had to be going through all this. Then he remembered the box and coffee, "I wanted to stop in to offer my condolences, Clara. I didn't mean to intrude."

"Hello Eric," Clara greeted. Neither she nor Eric noticed the looks exchanged between Connor and Devan as she accepted the box and coffee. She sniffed it and realized it was going to be a treat, her favorite, caramel latte.

Eric's heart skipped a beat as she realized what the coffee was and rewarded him with her bright smile. He watched as she placed the box on the dining room table with the coffee. She squatted down to hug each of the children and wish them a good day. Eric controlled his annoyance as Connor stepped over with the younger child in his arms and kissed her forehead before leading the children out of the house. He patiently waited as Shannon went to kiss the bartender before hugging Clara and stepping out.

While they had been oblivious, Shannon had noticed the looks. She suspected Connor wasn't happy about leaving Clara alone with Eric. If she read their expressions correctly, Devan was staying. Without acknowledging it, she hugged Clara and mentioned Lila would be over in a bit.

Outside, Shannon followed Connor to the car. After he had the children strapped in, she asked him, "Aren't you Eric's cousin?" When he grudgingly nodded, she continued, "Why don't you like him?"

Connor simply shrugged, "Yeah, he is, but he's always been weird and lazy. Clara's usually more tolerant. You know Devan is also my cousin, on my mother's side. He and I have always been pretty tight."

"Yeah, he mentioned that. So, he's a good guy?"

"Devan is the opposite of Eric," he answered.

"Connor, thanks for being here for Clara. I know it means a lot to her." Shannon leaned up to kiss his cheek. "Have a good day at work." She waved to the children as she went to her car.

Inside, Devan started to clear the table. Something in his manner made clear to Eric he wasn't heading out any time soon. It annoyed him that everyone was over so early, disturbing Clara when she needed her rest. He watched as she peeked into the box while she sipped from the coffee. Her eyes lit up and she smiled again as she closed it. She offered him to sit but he declined, stating he needed to get to work. He reminded her to keep him posted about work and let him know if she needed anything. Clara nodded agreement as she walked with him to the door.

Devan was leaning against the counter, sipping from his coffee as he watched the scene in the dining room. He was at the perfect spot without being too obvious. He knew Connor wasn't pleased with Eric. The younger cousin was always trying his patience when they were growing up. His mother had suggested he would eventually outgrow it, but based on what he saw, Devan didn't think it was possible.

After Eric was gone, Clara brought the box and her coffee into the kitchen, "You loaded the dishwasher? And you cook? You are certainly a keeper, Devan. Do you want a donut?"

Devan sat silently as Clara listed what needed to be done. She needed to plan her husband's funeral service. She had her laptop open but couldn't seem to focus. He was relieved when Lila finally arrived. He left the two friends as he returned to his place from the backdoor. He wanted to talk with his uncle regarding the investigations currently open.

"Good morning, Uncle Connor," Connor heard the second he

stepped out of the car. He looked over his shoulder as he opened the back door to reach for his bag. "Josh, you're here early."

"Early bird gets the worm," he said, looking over the car. "Did you get a new car?"

He asked the question just as his uncle disappeared into the car. When he stood up, he had a young girl in his arms. She was babbling away but stopped the moment her sky blue eyes spotted Josh. A young boy with Clara's green eyes immediately followed from the car.

"Why do you have Clara's children? Is she alright?" Josh asked with concern.

Connor paused for a moment as he closed the door, "You've met them before?"

"No, but the little girl looks just like her and the boy has her eyes," he answered, stating the obvious.

"Clara's having a rough week. Since I was heading this way, I offered to drop them off. Her car has the seats," he said.

"Hi, I am Reese. I am three years old. That's my sister, Hailey. She is one. This is Connor, my friend. I have no idea how old he is. How old are you?" Reese looked up to Connor in question as he grabbed his hand for the walk across the parking lot.

"Reese, this is Josh," Connor informed the little boy, ignoring the question about his age as his nephew chuckled.

"Hi Josh. Are you as old as Connor? Connor, are you older than Mommy?" Reese wondered.

"Yes, I am," Connor answered.

"Are you ten?"

"No, he's older," Josh answered for his uncle as he smiled down at the boy. The girl was looking over Connor's shoulder at him with her big blue eyes.

"Is he a hundred?" Reese turned back towards Josh.

Connor came to a stop as he looked down at the boy while Josh opened the door, "Reese, do I look a hundred?"

"I have no idea what a hundred looks like," Reese admitted while Hailey nodded her head.

"I'll meet you in there," Josh called as he watched his uncle effortlessly juggle the kids, their backpacks, and his work bag as he walked towards the daycare entrance. And that's why Connor is the better option, he thought. He can handle an already made family.

23
shan can do better

After Lila left for her shift at the hospital, Clara roamed restlessly around her home. She couldn't decide if she wanted to go for a walk or paint. The painting always seemed to clear her mind and relax her while the walking increased her risk of running into people she knew. Maybe she could put a coat of paint on the dining room wall, go for a run. No one would be able to talk with her if she was running. And when she returns, try sponging a lighter shade over the wall. Decision made, Clara ran up the stairs to change.

Outside, Devan was washing his car as he watched Clara stretch. She waved before taking off towards Main Street, turning towards the hospital and the northern part of town. He reached for his phone to send a text. A few minutes later, to his amusement, a blue pickup pulled up and Rob and Chase stepped out.

Chase, definitely the easier going one, waved cheerfully as Devan called out, "You guys just missed her. She went for a run."

"Yeah? She probably needed it. We were just dropping off some food, but we need to get back to work. Will it be too much to leave with you?" Chase asked.

"No problem. She's not going to try a marathon or anything, is she?" Devan wondered out loud.

"You never know. She did run during college, said it helped to relieve her stress and keep her focused. Thanks, man," Chase answered with a laugh, shaking his hand before returning to the truck with his cousin.

As he backed out, Rob expressed his annoyance, "I don't see what the big deal is with this guy. Shannon seems to have a thing for him, Lila says he's great, and Clara gives him updates on her whereabouts? What the hell? Don't you think that's kind of creepy?"

Chase allowed his cousin to vent. He was used to Rob's dislike of guys in general. He always seemed to get along well enough with the opposite sex, rarely without a date all through high school and even now. But guys, unless Rob played ball with them, he never liked, especially if any guy showed interest in one of the girls. If they were related to the Thompson family, trouble was most likely brewing.

Chase had grown up aware of the family feud with the Thompsons. He wasn't sure of the specifics, and didn't really care as his father had warned him to stay out of it. But his uncle and cousin could not seem to let it go. Rob firmly believed anyone from that clan was fair game. As they grew into adulthood, an unspoken agreement formed, the Foxwood clan would hang at Memories and the Thompson clan would hang at The Lantern. Each ran the risk of initiating a fight if they went into the wrong hangout. Chase was pleasantly surprised when Rob tolerated Dallas Thompson in the same restaurant last Friday evening. He shot him a dirty look, but otherwise didn't let his presence ruin a pleasant evening. Naturally, something else did. Still, he was proud of Rob's maturity. There was hope for him yet.

"Rob, the girls have all been close since they played in the sandbox. If Shannon likes the guy, they would be supportive and let her know if there was an issue. Besides, what's not to like?" Chase asked against his better judgment.

"For starters, he's just a bartender. Don't you think Shan can do better?" Rob demanded as they pulled up in front of the Hawks House.

"What do you have against bartenders? And isn't he the Mancuso cousin that joined the FBI?" Chase asked as they walked up the path. "I think he's also related to the doctor, too."

"Do you know you sound like one of the girls? Why do you think any of this would make me like him better? Don't you think it's suspicious that a guy who was an FBI agent is currently working as a bartender?" Rob asked in a degrading tone.

Chase did think it was suspicious. He had watched Devan interact with the locals. He was extremely attentive, polite, and aware. Made him think the guy was still an active agent working undercover or something. Chase knew if he shared his thoughts with his cousin, he would laugh before dismissing the idea. Rob never thinks positively about any guy, especially one Shannon's currently interested in. Especially if he's connected in any way to the doctor. He's losing Clara again. But, did he ever have her?

As they unlocked the door and continued inside, the conversation switched to the projects of the afternoon. Neither one was aware of the person upstairs watching them from the window on the third floor. He had debated leaving, but decided he would remain. He was too comfortable on the old sofa. He drank from his bottle as he thought of better times, looking at the framed photo lying on his chest...

Clara should not have been surprised by the sudden stitch in her side. What was she thinking? That she could run a couple of miles at a fast pace when she hadn't been running in months! She and Jay used to meet for running dates during their lunch breaks a few times a week as their work schedules would allow. She remembered tearfully as she leaned forward to catch her breath, then tried to stretch it out.

"Clara?"

Clara turned to see Dallas standing beside his SUV. Unable to catch her breath, she waved.

Dallas walked over, eyeing her carefully, "Everything all right?"

She looked up and shook her head no as her eyes threatened to water. Dallas pulled her in for a brotherly hug, surprising himself more than her. He asked if she needed a drink and felt her head nod. Since they were outside a fast food restaurant, he guided her over towards an empty table.

Clara was pleased he chose lemonade. She wasn't a fan of carbonated beverages. She nodded when he offered his condolences. They sat for a little while talking. She told him what happened with her husband, information he already knew from Lila.

Inside a neighboring store, Jenna Hudson was watching the girl in shorts and t-shirt flirting with the guy. She was immediately suspicious and discretely took a few pictures with her cell. She would save them until the time was right. The nerve of the girl, sneaking around behind Connor's back. He was lucky to have her looking out for him. Jenna took it as a good omen to have spontaneously stopped at this store. Pleased with the turn of the day, she continued with her shopping before returning to work.

As the week neared closer to the end, Clara dreaded it. She didn't want to live through Saturday. She wanted to go to sleep Friday night and wake up on Monday morning with the weekend completely over. After all the horrible thoughts she had of him, she felt shameful. Jason was dead. He had not been avoiding her or even messing with her, he was gone.

Like her mother, Jason did not abandon her. He was cruelly taken away from her. Clara felt they would have been able to work things out and could even still be together, if he hadn't been killed. Despite not getting any real answers from the detectives, she knew he was targeted. It scared her to think a second person in her life was murderously taken from her. But why would anyone want to kill her mother or her husband? If the two murders weren't twenty years apart or in different towns, she'd have been suspicious it was the same person. But Susannah

Gibbs and Jason O'Reilly's lives could not have been more different. So the motives behind their deaths had to be different. Pointless, no doubt, but for different reasons by different killers.

Clara wished she could turn off her brain and simply stop speculating about why. She needed to accept that she would never understand why her children would grow up without their father and never have a chance to even meet their grandmother.

During the day, Clara wondered if she was mistreating Connor by allowing him to be close and comfort her during her harsh nights. She could get a few hours of sleep with him at her side. Clara thought he understood as he was different with her. Yes, he would kiss her but only on her hand or forehead. He would come in later in the evening after the children were in bed and lay with her in the dark. She couldn't even think in future tense right now.

Procrastinating enough, Clara needed to begin packing for the weekend. Shannon and Lila were going to ride down with her and the kids Friday afternoon. They were going to stay with Rachel and return on Sunday. She sat on the bed and sighed again as she debated which dress to pack.

• • • •

Saturday night, Evil walked around Clara's bedroom in the dim light, his clothes were already on the floor. He leisurely opened a drawer and let his hands sift through her clothing before moving on to another drawer. He smiled when he opened the lingerie drawer. He pulled out various items, holding his favorite pieces up to his cheek before placing them back in the drawer. He made a mental note to bring her some new pieces during his next visit. He picked up her perfume and sprayed the room. He closed his eyes and smiled as he sang softly. He laid down on her properly made bed and closed his eyes as he pulled her pillow close to his chest and sniffed her scent. He imagined her lying beside him with her hair fanned around her head as she looked over with her bright green eyes and smiled. His other hand lowered to his arousal...

When she returned home Sunday evening, Clara felt numb. She went through the motions of bathing the children and reading. She sat with them longer than usual after they both fell asleep in Reese's room. Her suitcase was sitting on the floor, just outside her bedroom door. When she picked it up and stepped into her room, she thought it smelled odd. Without thinking too much about it, she opened the windows before walking to the linen closet to retrieve a laundry basket. She removed her comforter, blanket, and sheets. Without a pause, she also included the shams before retrieving the towels from the bathroom. She debated spraying her room but thought it would make the smell worse.

Clara brought the basket downstairs to start the washer. As she turned away, her eyes caught the various cans of leftover paint ...

When Shannon returned home from the city, she sensed Clara needed to be alone with her children. It had been a terrible weekend she would never forget. She grabbed her cell and keys and headed out for a walk. She should not have been surprised when she looked up and realized she was standing in front of Memories. Devan saw the sadness in her eyes as she sat down. She tried to smile but instead she felt the tears. In an attempt to hide them, she buried her face in her hands. A moment later, she felt strong arms pull her in for a much needed hug. After a few minutes, he grabbed her hand to lead her out to his car. She was soon sitting on one end of his sofa while he sat on the other. Each had a glass of wine as he listened to Shannon's version of the love story of Clara and Jason.

Lila left a quick note on the kitchen table while her brother was out in the barn. She didn't want to deal with him right now. She had an overnight bag over her shoulder as she walked to her car. She drove silently to Dallas' cabin. She knew he was working, but was planning to head home soon. She went out to sit on the steps of the back deck, watching the sunset over the mountains.

When Dallas returned home, he found Lila sitting quietly as the sky turned marvelous shades of red and orange. He handed her a glass of wine before sitting behind her. She sipped from her wine as she leaned back into his comfortable chest, feeling his strong arms around her. She couldn't imagine what Clara was going through right now, nor did she want to understand. In a short time, Clara had buried her mother and her husband.

"Dallas, it was horrible! I never want to know what she's going through right now. Isn't that terrible?" Lila cried as he held her tighter.

Back at the farm, Rob believed his sister was going to Clara's *to* comfort, as well as *for* comfort. The girls had always been close and rallied together whenever it was necessary. He understood Clara didn't want or need him right now, and decided to keep his distance as he checked the time. He still had enough time before the sunset to take his favorite horse for a ride.

Rachel did something she'd never done before. She broke one of her rules and invited Chase to stay with her for the night. She couldn't be alone. Chase agreed without question or discussion. The two walked together hand in hand around the city. They stopped at a bench overlooking the river and ate ice cream. Sometimes they talked, but other times they allowed the comfortable silence between them. They scheduled a time he would return once the school year was over to help her pack for her move back home. They also talked about their plans for the summer. As the evening grew late, they stopped for dinner before returning to her place. They sat on her sofa, each with a glass of wine while they watched a movie. Rachel fell asleep in his arms and together they slept.

On Prospect Avenue, Clara was sitting on her master bathroom toilet looking at the wall. She had painted a few strokes of various colors and was currently debating which one to use. The yellow was too cheerful for her present mood. The gray was moody, like a storm brewing too close. The pink was too much like bubble gum. The blue, oh the blue, Clara sighed as she looked over at the blue color. The blue was just like Jason's eyes when he smiled and lit up the room, she thought as she started a wall with the blue.

A couple hours later, Clara was frustrated when she ran out of paint. One wall was blue, another was gray, the third was half yellow and half pink. The fourth wall was green around the edges, but she didn't have enough paint to complete the wall. She threw the can and paintbrush into the bathtub in frustration as she sank to the floor and cried.

"Mama?"

Clara peeked up, startled to see little Hailey, her blue eyes so like her father's. She was standing in the doorway holding her little baby doll. She opened her arms and the young girl ran over to sit in her lap. Mother and daughter remained on the bathroom floor as they both cried together.

After a while, Clara stood up with her sleeping daughter in her arms and stepped into her room. She paused for a moment to sniff. Smells better, she thought as she lifted the newly placed sheets and laid down with her daughter, able to sleep a few dreamless hours.

Connor had also gone to the city for the funeral, returning late on Sunday evening after spending the afternoon with his parents. He had debated staying the night but felt he needed to return home, if nothing else but to be closer to Clara. He hadn't been surprised when she didn't text, he wasn't expecting it. Clara had pulled back in the last week and Connor knew she needed space.

Restless in his own place, he went early to his office at the hospital. He had just unpacked his bag when he heard a soft knock on the door. When he looked up, he sighed with annoyance.

"Connor, can I come in? I have something unpleasant to share with you," Jenna Hudson announced as she stepped inside the office without waiting for an invite.

Connor didn't say a word, nor did he move. Jenna seemed a bit too happy for someone about to share unhappy news.

"Connor, I just wanted to let you know your girlfriend is seeing other people behind your back," Jenna started with a condescending tone as she pulled out her cell phone. "I really am sorry to be the one to show you this but Connor, I want you to know I am only doing it because I care about you."

She leaned forward across his desk, allowing her low neckline to fully expose her breasts. Without looking at her or reaching for the phone, he simply looked at the picture. Clara, in her running gear, was standing beside Dallas. He had an arm around her as she looked to be crying. He had a look of brotherly concern. Before he could comment, Jenna swiped the screen, bringing up a picture of Clara sitting at the bar next to Josh. At first glance, he looked a lot like a younger version of Matt at that age. They were both laughing. Connor looked up at her.

"Connor, I am so sorry," Jenna started as she reached for his hand

and squeezed.

"Jenna, what exactly do you think you are showing me?" Connor asked in an attempt to clarify.

"Connor, your girlfriend is first doing shots with this guy on a Friday night and the following week she's all over this other guy. She's clearly not the right girl for you," Jenna stated sympathetically.

Connor leaned back in his chair as he looked up at Jenna with a laugh. He didn't realize until that moment he had been stressed with his concern for Clara. He wondered about the time the picture was taken, if it was from the evening Clara was drugged. Maybe the picture could lead to witnesses to question about that night. But the laughter, likely a bit too much, was exactly what he needed to pull out of his negative mood, "Can you send me those pictures?"

"Absolutely. I will do it right now," she responded as she stood up. Jenna was surprised by his reaction but agreed he would need the proof.

"Do you know who those men are?" Connor asked.

"Well, I know the one is a ranger at the park. I have no idea who the one in the bar is," she stated apologetically. "But I can certainly find out for you."

"Jenna, Clara isn't my girlfriend. Well yes, she's a girl and a very close friend. She grew up in the house next door to me. Our families have been close for generations. Her husband passed away. His service was just this past Saturday. The one guy is her brother comforting her. The other guy is my nephew. Why wouldn't they have a drink together?" Connor asked calmly.

"But why did you want a copy of the picture?"

"It's a good picture of them," he simply answered with a shrug. "But if you don't mind, stop following her around. Stalking is very unattractive."

After she left, he sent the picture from the bar to Devan. They would be able to pull the others from the background, possibly the individual hurting women in this town.

the sun exploded in the bathroom

C lara returned to work the Tuesday after the funeral. She had decided to take it one day at a time, what other option did she have? She ran into Connor at work on her first day back. He was up on the floor doing rounds while she was catching up on progress reports needing her attention. Connor watched as she walked a patient down past the nurse's station and back to his room across the hall. She stayed in his room for a few minutes more before she came out. When her green eyes met his brown, she smiled sadly. Connor walked with her downstairs to her gym asking about her evening plans.

"I have a lot of paperwork to catch up on tonight, but I need to get the kids soon," Clara answered with a quick glance at her watch. She knew he was waiting for her to make the first move. As he followed her to her desk, she handed him a file and a pen. Connor immediately sat in her seat and began to read before signing. She sat on her desk beside him, occasionally asking questions regarding patients.

They both looked up at the knock on the door. Eric was standing there with a file to drop off. Clara told him she would look it over later in the evening. He paused before turning away to ask her if she wanted to join him for dinner. She politely declined.

When they were alone again, Clara asked Connor what he had planned for the evening. He glanced at his watch before answering, "I need to go to the hospital to check on a few people. I'm on call tonight, so it's up in the air right now."

She chuckled, "You want to come over? I can pick something up for dinner."

Connor signed the last form and closed up the file as he stood up, "It'll be a couple of hours still. How about I pick up the food so it's hot."

She nodded her agreement as she turned to place the file in the outbox for Marie to deal with in the morning. When she turned back, Connor was standing right in front of her. Without a word, his knuckle touched her cheek before he kissed her forehead.

When he stepped back, he waited quietly as she grabbed her bag and purse. They walked together out to the parking lot. Connor opened her door and waited until she was settled in before he closed it.

Neither were aware of a pair of eyes watching them from behind the closed blinds.

Connor resumed his evening visits that night. If he had the evening off, he might join her with the children for dinner. He would play catch with Reese or teach him how to kick a ball. Hailey would often simply run around yelling. Occasionally, Connor would sit on the deck and enjoy a beer with Devan. Shannon often joined them when they sat out together.

When he had to work late, Clara would often repaint her master bathroom. Connor was the only one aware of her painting streak. If he thought it was odd, he didn't comment. While he usually slept over each night, their level of intimacy did not progress. He could sense her tense up if he were nearing the line. Clara needed time. And Connor was willing to wait. He never felt about anyone the way he did about her. It wasn't just the physical attraction. He also enjoyed her company. They could talk for hours about their day, the town gossip, or simply hang out in silence if each was occupied with their own thoughts.

One evening, Connor arrived after the children were asleep. They headed up the stairs. He asked if it would be alright if he took a shower. He stepped into her bathroom and turned on the light. "Holy shit!" He exclaimed as he stepped back from the doorway.

Clara was standing behind him, "You don't like this color?"

"Clara, it looks like the sun exploded in your bathroom," he answered honestly. "I may have to turn the lights off while I shower. It's very bright."

"Yeah, I didn't think Smiley Face Yellow would be so bright. I was aiming for something cheerful. I'll go for a soft shade of purple next time. Are you going to be alright in here with the lights off? I could get a flashlight."

"That's alright, I'll keep the door open. You want to join me?" Connor asked with a playful smile.

Clara backed away with a giggle, "In the dark, we would only bump into each other."

"Yeah, you are right. We would have to touch and feel our way around," he answered softly. He had her pinned against the wall with either hand on her hips as he slowly leaned down whispering, "But I'm willing to give it a try if you are."

He was pleasantly surprised when Clara remained still, looking up into his eyes. After a moment, Connor leaned down and kissed her on the lips before slowly working his way to her neck. He smiled when she sighed. Then he stepped back to undress.

"What are you doing?" Clara asked, shocked.

"I told you, I'm taking a shower. You followed me here. You're welcome to join me," he leaned over to kiss her lips before he turned to the shower to start the water. "You never need to wait for an invite to join me."

Clara should have left the bathroom when he kissed her, but she remained watching him undress. While she felt his body up against hers at night, this was the first time she saw him without his clothes.

When she realized Connor was watching her appreciation, she blushed as he winked at her before stepping into the shower. Clara went back into the bedroom and put on her more conservative pajamas.

When Connor stepped out of the shower, he dried off and wrapped a towel around his waist. Every time he saw the paint splattered stains in the tub, he was reminded of Clara's fragile state. Until tonight, he did not mention the new bathroom color every few nights. He understood it was her way of dealing right now and wondered if he should be saying or doing something, but he didn't know what. At least, Connor thought, Clara wasn't drinking herself unconscious every night.

When Connor stepped into the bedroom, one look at Clara made him laugh. She was sitting in the chair with her laptop wearing long flannel pajamas.

"What's so funny?" Clara asked, looking up from the screen.

"Why are you wearing that? I've never seen you sleep in long pj's," Connor answered as he pulled open a drawer to remove a pair of boxers. He let his towel fall as he bent down to don his shorts.

Too late, Clara was already looking up. She tried to keep her eyes on his. The sparkle in his eyes suggested he was enjoying making her blush. Once he retrieved the towel from the floor, he returned it to the bathroom. She answered as he stepped back into the bedroom.

"I don't want to give you any ideas," she explained.

"Beautiful, it doesn't matter what you wear, I only have to look at you and I'm flooded with ideas." He chuckled again when she blushed. Connor figured he better get back over the line before she sent him home. "Are you ready for bed or are you going to work some more?"

"I'm done with the work. I'm just not really sleepy yet. I was thinking of reading for a bit," Clara said as she placed her laptop on the table and reached for her book.

Connor usually only needed about four hours of sleep a night. He often read on his tablet until he was tired. If he were home, he might do chores or start a project. But he hated to read in bed. Which is why he was often in the chair reading either before or after he slept. He always preferred being near Clara and loved watching her sleep. When she stood up to let him have the chair, he grabbed her hand. She looked up at him and he whispered, "Read with me."

He sat down in the chair and scooted over, patting the spot next to him. Clara sat partly beside and on his lap. She scooted a bit with her legs over the arm of the chair while she leaned into his chest. Connor had an arm around her while his tablet rested on her thighs. His hand rested on her knees until he needed to change the screen. She was soon sound asleep with her head on his shoulder. He gently removed her hearing aids, and placed them on her laptop. He should have carried her to bed, but he was comfortable. He waited until he was ready to sleep before he carried her over.

After he lay down beside her, Clara immediately complained about being too hot. She stood up and removed her pajama bottoms, and since the room was dark, she also removed her top while she walked over to her drawer to pull out a light nightie. She pulled it over her head before turning back around. She didn't hear Connor groan as he watched her wearing only a thong. He rolled over away from her as she curled up behind him, her arm around him with her hand on his chest. He lifted her hand and kissed it. In response, she kissed his shoulder, "Good night, Connor."

Shannon was over at Devan's for dinner. They were sitting on the sofa with a glass of wine when he realized their relationship was crossing over into something more serious. As Shannon's hands were around his neck and his were on her low back, they kissed. He heard Clara's voice in his head. "Tell Shannon what you do before it gets too serious." Sound advice, he thought for the hundredth time since it was provided. But how to tell her? While Shannon gave few details, he knew she had an issue with cops, one in particular.

He pulled back and stood up as he debated what to say, "Shan, there's something I need to say." He paused again as he tried to think.

Shannon felt a sudden panic as her insecurity surfaced. Is he about to break up with me? The one time I keep things slow, he wants to break up with me? Trying to remain calm, Shannon stood up and went to Devan as he turned away slightly nervous.

"Are you breaking up with me?" She asked softly.

Devan turned around quickly, a shocked look on his face. "No, absolutely not!" He reached for her hands and stepped in closer, he gave her a quick kiss before he tried to explain.

"I just want to be honest with you. I don't know if you are aware of my background. You know I come from a family of law enforcement, but I'm not sure if you are aware that I'm an FBI agent. I rarely stay in one place long. I go from assignment to assignment and often go undercover," he started as Shannon slowly pulled her hand away as she took a step back.

"You're a cop? After I told you about all my issues with my previous boyfriend, you have the nerve to stand there and tell me you're a freakin' cop? Why are you just now telling me this?" She demanded.

"Because I thought you should know what I do for a living. I am currently working undercover at Memories. My uncle had concerns about people going missing and called me. I had just wrapped up an assignment and talked it over with my supervisor. I'm telling you now because you're important to me and I want us to have an honest relationship. I'm also telling you upfront that I can't talk to you about the current case or future cases."

"I can't believe you're a freakin' cop! Really, Devan? You're a freakin' undercover cop?" Shannon demanded.

"Actually, Shan, it's special agent," he corrected. When she glared at him, he couldn't resist. "There really is a difference."

"But Baby," he said as he stepped closer, attempting to put his arms around her. She held her hands up, silently refusing his touch. He let his arms fall to his side. "I want you to also know I'm not some loser bartender. I want you to know who I really am."

He remained quiet as he watched various emotions across her face. His heart sank when she finally responded.

"I can't do this." She turned to grab her cell and keys before she headed towards the door.

Before she could open it, Devan was standing behind her with his hands on either side of the door. He quietly said, "Shannon, I really like you and I hope you call me after you've thought about this. But please remember, no one else can know about my job here."

He was tempted to kiss her, but he didn't want to anger her more. He stepped back as he opened the door. He followed her out onto the porch to make sure she got inside her place safely, less than twenty feet away.

Connor was called to the hospital early in the morning. He dressed in the dark and leaned onto the bed to kiss Clara before he headed out. He wasn't aware of anyone sitting in the dark kitchen.

A couple of hours later, Clara felt refreshed and energetic. She smiled as she headed down the stairs. She was hoping for a moment with her coffee before the children woke up. Someone would have thought she spent the night having hot sex, she thought. The easy bantering and flirting was starting to heat up. She was afraid to make the first move. A part of her thought she should let Connor, but she knew he was too much of a gentleman. Replaying the scene in the bathroom the previous night, she realized he had already made the first move. He was waiting for her to respond. She stepped into the kitchen, turned on the light, and screamed…

the sun exploded in the bathroom 295

unwelcome early morning visitor

The man walked around the main floor of the Hawks House, assessing the damage. He sighed as he realized he would soon need another place to live. Gradually he ascended the grand staircase and paused at the door of the old master suite. He smiled when he remembered her green sparkling eyes and shy smile, the most beautiful girl in town. He was the happiest guy when she was beside him. He made so many mistakes. He sipped from his bottle as he slowly made his way upstairs to the third floor before the workers arrived...

Chase was up early checking up on the animals, even before the farm workers arrived. He noted his younger cousin was spending less time at home. It was hard to keep track of her work hours as she often went in early or left late, sometimes switching shifts with a coworker. He figured she was usually in town with her friends. He sighed, less than two weeks before he would bring Rachel home. Then all four would be back together again. He couldn't believe how fast time had gone. Clara wasn't even thirty yet, but now a widow with two children. Rachel would be the new owner of the Taylor House. He knew it would only be a matter of time before Shannon would be living with her new guy. Chase was still suspicious about him, in a good way. Was Devan currently undercover? Here in this small town? Was there something sinister going on? Chase wondered when Lila would finally settle down with someone or if she was already seeing someone...

Eric was also up early. He made his usual stop at the bakery and debated over the coffee. He could be the good boss and get the jug so everyone could enjoy the coffee, but he wanted to get Clara her favorite latte. He didn't want everyone to know about them yet, but the smile on her face when she was happy made him grin. Once he returned to his SUV, he debated the route to work. Should he continue down Main Street or take the side roads? He smiled as he knew, there really wasn't much discussion.

Eric knew Clara was usually up and about by this hour. But Connor's SUV was usually out front, keeping him from stopping in for a few minutes. As he slowed, he realized his cousin wasn't there. Did they have a fight? Oh, that would so make his day. He glanced at his watch, debating whether to stop or to continue.

Clara walked into the kitchen expecting it to be empty. She was surprised to find Shannon sitting at a kitchen chair alone in the dark. She was still wearing her clothes from the previous day and had a mug of cold tea in front of her.

Clara walked to the counter to start the coffee. When she turned around, her eyes met Shan's. She slowly went to the table and sat down. "Shan, what's wrong?"

"Clara, I have been such a fool!"

"Oh? Did something happen? The romantic dinner at Devan's did not go well?"

"The dinner was great. He is an impressive cook. Devan would put us to shame! But afterwards, Devan wanted to talk, which caused me to panic. I thought he was going to break up with me, but instead..."

Shannon paused as she thought of what to say.

Clara realized what probably happened. He finally told her. Without a word, she reached for her hand and squeezed. It was all the encouragement Shannon needed.

"He told me he's a freakin' undercover cop! Can you believe that? A freakin' cop?" Shannon finally burst out in anger.

"He said that?" Clara was slightly shocked.

"No, actually he said he is an FBI agent. He often goes undercover and travels. What the hell is going on with this universe? Is Mercury in retrograde or something?" She stood up as she paced the kitchen in agitation.

Clara, despite herself, couldn't help chuckling softly. Shannon would often refer to astrology to explain why she or someone else was doing something back in high school. Clara let her friend vent for a few minutes, pouring each some coffee, hers with a lot of cream while Shannon's was black. Returning to the table, her friend followed. They each lifted her mug in silence.

"I get how you feel about his career choice, but how do you feel about Devan? Are you going to continue seeing him?" Clara wondered out loud.

Shannon shrugged, "I don't know. He's really sweet. He's so good looking! His body is absolutely hot. He listens when I talk. He's never judging me, telling me what I should be doing or instructing me on how to do it. He respects me."

"So, if you really like the guy, what is the problem?" Clara asked.

"He's a freakin' undercover cop, actually working right now. Oh shit! I'm not supposed to tell anyone about that. He said he knew I could do better than a loser bartender," she chuckled slightly at the memory.

"Wait a minute, who said anything about bartenders being losers?"

"He did. Since I am such a strong career woman, everyone would think I could do better than a loser bartender. Rob actually made the comment and I think Devan overheard it." Shannon explained. "And I think Joel made a comment about it when he was here."

"Whoa! Back the truck up! When was Joel here?"

"A week or two after I first started working. He was at Memories, apparently waiting for me," she said as she sipped her coffee. She looked over her mug and sighed when Clara simply kept looking at her.

"He came to warn me about my old loser boss. Said something about him being angry and wanting revenge. The stupid ass seems to think I know something and can testify against him," she stated casually, without concern.

"Shan, what the hell? The guy that was arrested for laundering money for sweatshops? The guy cooking the books? Potentially causing you to lose your reputation and career? Joel thinks you are in danger? Why aren't you more concerned about this?" Clara demanded.

"I never saw anything, heard anything, or did anything illegal! All my cases were legitimate. I had real clients that I met with. I was totally out of the loop," Shannon calmly explained.

"You know that. I believe that, but what does the boss actually believe? Isn't that the real issue? If he thinks you had access to the information you could be in danger! What does Devan say about all this?"

"I didn't tell him. We weren't really together at the time. I don't want him to think I have all this baggage!" Shannon explained.

"I think your safety is the priority here. And you need to discuss this with Devan," Clara stated firmly. "From what I know of him, he'll be able to help you, regardless of the status of your relationship."

The friends were quiet for a moment as Clara sipped from her coffee. "So what are you going to do? Are you ending it or giving the sweet guy another chance?"

"I don't know. At the end of the day, he's still a freakin' cop!" she whined.

Clara looked closely at her friend as she sipped. When she lowered her mug she commented, "I never knew you had a thing against cops. What else did you discover in your grandmother's journals? Was she from a long line of top ten fugitives?"

Shannon laughed, "No! My family was very honest, hard-working people. They were just not honest about telling me I was adopted. I guess I don't have an issue being with a man that's equally honest and hard working."

Clara laughed when she stood up to hug her friend. "Cheer up, Shan. This could be the universe's way of looking out for you. If someone is really out to get you, would you rather have Joel at your side or Devan?"

Shannon glanced at her watch. She had enough time to talk with Devan before she headed to work. She sent a text and slipped out the back door to his place.

As Clara was about to head up the stairs to get the children ready, the doorbell rang. She looked at the clock. Who the hell would be stopping in before seven, she wondered as she carefully peaked out the window. Shit, she thought as she stepped back. What the hell is Eric doing here so early in the morning? She'll be at work within the hour anyway. Clara shook her head and decided against answering it. It would ruin her good mood if she were to start running late. She continued up the stairs.

It was less than two hours later when Clara entered the conference room for the manager's meeting. Eric had stopped her as she entered the room. He touched her arm to get her attention before talking quietly. "Clara, I stopped by your place this morning. You didn't answer. Was everything alright?"

Clara looked surprised at the question and wondered again why he would be stopping in so early on a workday. Or even at all, for that matter. What reason could he possibly have when he would be seeing her at work soon. Instead, she simply answered, "Really? What time? I must have been in the shower."

"Yeah, that's probably it. Sorry, I had been worried," Eric apologized. He had to quickly go sit at the table as he visualized her naked in the shower. If he had known, he could have joined her. If only he were there earlier, he thought.

Clara had accepted the coffee he handed her. That was not awkward at all, she thought sarcastically as she turned to join the group. She was pleasantly surprised to see Connor but only smiled when their eyes met as he entered the room.

Connor had heard the discussion between Clara and Eric. He also thought it inappropriately weird he would stop in so early in the morning. He knew Clara was lying about being in the shower. Why would she lie? Duh, he thought. Give the woman some credit? Why would she want to open the door for Eric? Especially when she was, more or less, alone. He noted Eric was quiet during the meeting and waited until everyone was already out of the room before he left for his office. Damn, he still acts like a teenager around her, awkward and borderline inappropriate. He chuckled at his cousin's expense. Connor would later regret not taking his cousin's actions more seriously.

what happened at the prom?

S hannon and Devan made up that morning. She was often hanging out with him in the evenings, rarely at Clara's place during the nights. Connor continued to stay most nights with Clara unless he worked too late or was called back to the hospital. He would text her when he was about to head out. If she replied, he would stop in. If she didn't, he would assume she was asleep and return to his loft.

As time went on, Clara started to feel anxious. She didn't know why. One Tuesday morning during her drive to work, she thought she saw Rob's truck. It was then she realized she had not seen him in over two weeks. Reminding herself the phone worked both ways, Clara decided to invite him over for dinner with a text. When he didn't respond by lunch time, her anxiety shifted to annoyance. Clara was no longer able to focus on her paperwork. Instead of eating her lunch, she decided to drive over to the Hawks House and give him a piece of her mind.

Clara wasn't aware how irrational her thoughts were until she looked back on it later that afternoon. She was annoyed with Rob for keeping his distance. She was irked by Eric's excessive awkward attention. She felt like she was back in high school! And while she was at it, she should be able to walk into her own childhood home without a man to hold her up. How could that possibly say strong independent woman, she wondered as she pulled up in front of the house.

Shit, Clara admitted, she was overacting. It would be smart to start laying off the coffee. The caffeine was likely causing her anxiety. She should simply drink her two cups of coffee at home and be done with it. And stop drinking the coffees Eric was bringing in throughout the day. She had enough trouble sleeping as it is. Isn't cutting your caffeine usually the first thing they recommend for insomnia?

Clara quickly exited her car and slammed her door shut as she briskly walked up the driveway. She followed the noise towards the back near the garage. Chase and Rob were both present, wearing protective goggles and ear plugs as she approached. Once he was finished with the saw, both removed the googles. Chase smiled as he saw Clara.

"Clara! A great surprise. Are you checking up on us?" Chase asked cheerfully. He didn't say anything more when he saw the green glare aimed at his cousin.

Rob took one look at her then, without a word, he picked up the newly cut wood and walked past her into the house.

Clara was not going to be ignored, damn it! She followed him through the back entrance, into the kitchen, and up the rear staircase. Her temper flared as flashes of her past surfaced, Rob teaching her how to groom a horse. Rob teaching her how to drive the tractor, his steel blue eyes looking over at her with amusement as she stalled the tractor, and the violent blue eyes from the shadow looking over the body lying on the kitchen floor...

Clara's throat was suddenly closing as she tried to catch her breath. She could feel her heart pounding into her chest and her vision started to narrow. Before she blacked out, she heard in her head, "It was Evil." She tried to grab onto a nearby table. Instead she collapsed onto the floor, bringing the table crashing down on her.

"What the hell?" Rob muttered as he heard the crash behind him. Retracing his steps, he yelled to his cousin when he saw Clara lying unconscious on the floor. He immediately checked her heart rate and breathing at the same time.

"What the hell happened?" Chase demanded from the top of the back stairs.

"I have no idea! I didn't even know she was up here! Call 911, her breaths are shallow, her heart is racing. She's not responding to a sternal rub," Rob yelled.

Eric decided to take a walk down the hall. He wanted to check in with Clara to see if she was interested in meeting up for a drink after work. He was annoyed to discover she wasn't at her desk. She's probably upstairs seeing the patients, he thought. It shouldn't have bothered him, but it did. She always seemed to be putting patient care before him. He sighed as he walked back to his office, closing and locking the door. He loosened his pants as he walked over to the couch to take a nap…

Connor was early to his shift. It had been busier than usual for a Tuesday in the emergency room. They had just received word that an unconscious woman was en route by ambulance. The cause was apparently unclear. He arrived at the bay just as the ambulance was backing in.

When the back doors opened and Foxwood jumped out pulling the stretcher, Connor's eyes immediately went to the patient. His heart stopped as he realized it was Clara, unconscious with unknown cause. His eyes met Rob's in question.

"Her breathing is shallow, her heart rate is high, in the 120's. Her blood pressure is slightly elevated but within normal range," he gave off her current vitals. Rob and his cousin worked as volunteer firefighters. In their town, it also involved search and rescue as needed when someone was lost in the federal park nearby. "We placed the collar around her neck because she obviously hit her head."

Connor assisted while Clara was brought into a curtain area. He pulled the curtain closed. He should have instructed Foxwood to remain outside, but instead focused his attention on his patient. As he called out orders, he listened to her heart. It was still racing. Her lungs were clear and exchanging air, but her breathing was shallow. He used his pen light to check her pupils, they were equal and reactive. A good sign, he assured himself as he next checked the red area on her forehead.

He stepped back as a nurse started to cut Clara's shirt and place the electrodes on her chest. She immediately covered her up with a hospital gown. Another nurse started an IV in her arm and prepared to take blood. Connor touched Foxwood's arm and gestured for him to follow.

"Tell me what the hell happened, starting with where was she?" Connor demanded.

"Is she going to be alright?" Rob asked, obviously concerned.

"I don't know yet because I don't have the whole picture. Was she at work?"

"No, she stopped by the house. She followed me inside and up the back staircase. I didn't even know she was in there until I heard a crash. When I went out to the back hall, she was on the floor and a table had fallen on her. After I checked her vitals and Chase called 911, I tried to wake her up. She didn't even respond to a sternal rub," Rob explained.

"She went to the house? She didn't mention it this morning, or I would have gone with her," Connor stated softly, the pieces of the puzzle falling into place.

"Why does she need your permission to go to her own home?" Rob demanded.

"She hates that house. That's why I went with her that first day. Clara was having a small panic attack out on the porch before we went inside," Connor explained.

"She told you this?"

"No, I just know her." Connor shrugged, as if it were the most obvious thing. He turned when the nurse called his name as she came out of the room, handing him a long narrow piece of paper. He studied it for a moment, relieved her heart wasn't the issue. He returned to Clara's side.

Connor contained his annoyance when Foxwood followed, ignoring him as he scanned the monitor and watched her face. "Looks like she's starting to wake up."

"Clara? Hey Sweetheart," Connor said as he gently touched her cheek. He smiled when she opened her eyes.

"Connor? What happened? Why am I here?" Her voice was panicking as she looked around, noting Rob was also there.

Connor glanced at the monitor, and noticed her heart rate spiking again. When he reached for her hand and gently squeezed, it seemed to slow. He talked in a calming voice as he explained, "Clara, you likely had a panic attack. It was pretty bad. It caused you to pass out. When you did, you were probably leaning onto a table which fell over on you. Between the object hitting your head and you collapsing on the floor, you likely have a concussion. You need to get a CT scan to make sure it isn't anything more. Why didn't you tell me you were going to the house? I would have gone with you."

She looked at him and then at Rob before she said, "I wanted to talk to him in private."

Connor looked over at Foxwood, he probably believed their relationship was further along than it really was. He was confident it was going in the direction he wanted, but slowly. He hadn't realized until now how relieved he was not to have Foxwood around all the time. His presence often pulled her away from him. But Connor would never keep her from her friends. He trusted her.

"Alright, stay on the bed and I'll give you two time to talk. It'll be a bit before they are ready to take you down to radiology," Connor stated before stepping away.

Rob remained quiet as he watched the two before him. She always seemed to light up when the good doctor was around. It only confirmed what he already knew, he lost her again.

what happened at the prom?   307

Clara reached out for his hand. When he stepped closer, she took his and squeezed. "Hey Rob."

Rob, not knowing what to say, remained quiet, looking at her.

"Why have you been ignoring me?" Clara quietly demanded.

"I haven't been ignoring you," he tried to deny.

She simply looked at him and then he sighed and admitted he was ignoring her. "I liked it before when the good doctor wasn't always around. You and I would go riding or just hang out together."

"Rob, that was over twelve years ago. We have both grown up and moved on, but I always wanted you as a friend, always," Clara declared.

"I don't know. You were always upset with me back then. Now, I don't seem to piss you off as much," he stated.

She laughed, "See, you have grown up. But Connor has also always been in my life. Our relationships were different. You have always been one of my best friends. You're the one that taught me to drive, ride, swim. You mean a lot to me and I would hate it if you decide I'm not important enough to remain in your life."

Rob kissed her hand as he listened to her talk. After a moment he finally responded, "I don't like seeing you with him. I guess it'll take time for me to get used to seeing you two together. I do want to be in your life."

"Rob, you will be, no matter what." She pulled him in for a hug.

Connor didn't mean to leave a gap in the curtain when he closed it behind him. It just happened that way, but it also gave him the opportunity to observe how Clara and Foxwood interacted when they thought they weren't being watched. He was at the nurse's station filling out paperwork and reading over lab and radiology results for other patients. When he looked up again, Rob was stepping out and Chase was entering the area.

He spotted his cousin and asked, "How is she? What happened?"

Rob simply shrugged as he walked away. He didn't feel like talking as the realization set in that he was officially out of the running. Deep down he had known all along, but there was always a ray of hope until the talk. He hated the talk . It always changed everything. "She's going to be fine. Let's head back to work."

"That's it? You are going to just walk away? Just like the prom, you're going to let her go?" Chase demanded. They had turned a corner as he spoke.

Rob shoved his cousin up against the wall, "Leave it alone! I told you not to bring up the prom!"

He released his cousin and walked off.

Chase decided his cousin needed to cool off before he went anywhere with him in a truck. He returned to the ER to see Clara. His eyes met the doctor's and he walked over to the nurse's station.

The prom again, Connor thought. What the hell happened at the prom? He was never able to get the full story.

"How is Clara? Can I see her?" Chase asked.

"HIPPA laws don't allow me to divulge any information, but I'm sure she'd love to see you," Connor replied with a slight pause in his tone.

Chase paused before turning, sensing the doctor's hesitation. He raised his eyebrows in question.

Connor debated asking, but it's not like Clara would tell him. All these years later, comments were still being made. And Chase might give a more objective answer. "I keep hearing references made about the prom. What the hell happened at the prom?"

Chase was taken aback by the question, "The prom? You know about the prom?"

"No! I know nothing about the prom! I know she went, and she left upset. She's never told me what happened. She still makes references. What the hell happened?"

Chase chuckled a bit and decided, why not? "Clara had a date for the prom. As far as I know, they were going just as friends with the girls' usual group. I wasn't there, I still had exams at college. Rob was already home for the summer. Apparently, Clara's date was in an accident a few days before the prom. He was in the hospital with a broken leg. My aunt suggested Rob take Clara. She probably figured it would be no big deal, they were always close."

"I know they were always close. Did they ever date?" He asked.

"Not in the sense that you're thinking. They hung out, usually within the group, but occasionally alone. As far as I know, they never kissed or anything. But at the prom, Clara was in the bathroom. When she came out, he had his arms around another girl. Rob says she was stumbling and he was keeping her from falling. He said Isabella started kissing him just as Clara stepped out. She turned around and walked out before he could say anything. To this day, Rob has no idea how she got home," Chase shrugged.

Connor thought it must be a very modified version of the story, as Clara was never the jealous type. He did remember seeing her walking along the dark road that night alone. He had been furious with her for walking alone at night on such an isolated road but she would not talk about what happened. Of course, he didn't know at the time she was walking from her prom. That came out later in the weekend.

He chuckled, getting Chase's attention. "It was me. Luckily I happened to be driving home on that road. I was not happy with her, walking alone at night in the middle of nowhere. Needless to say, she was equally pissed, but not at me," he clarified. "She makes references about something being just like the stupid prom. I wouldn't have been so intrigued if I wasn't always hearing about it."

"Well, I only have his version and knowing Clara, I'm sure I'm missing something. Don't tell them I told you. I'm going to stop in before I head back to work," Chase stated.

Connor was relieved Clara suffered only a minor concussion. He was concerned about the severity of the panic attacks. He would be looking into that later. Due to the busy day, the labs were backed up.

Connor would have to review the results of her blood work the next day. For now, he just wanted to get her home.

Connor was able to leave work early. He drove his vehicle to the Hawk's house to swap for Clara's. He needed the car seats. He had thought about getting seats for his SUV but wasn't sure how she would respond. Next, he went across the lot to pick up Reese and Hailey from the daycare before it closed. He left Clara to change into scrubs as the nurse completed the discharge paperwork and removed the IV. When Connor returned, Clara was happy to see the children, but the look she gave him suggested she was irritated with him. It did not take long for him to learn why.

Once he started out of the parking lot, Connor asked what they wanted for dinner. Clara remained quiet while Reese and Hailey both gave suggestions. He still didn't understand the young girl but reminded himself she was only sixteen months old. Like her brother, she was smart and talkative but only Reese could understand her, or so he said.

"Burgers! We want burgers and ice cream," Reese yelled from the backseat.

Connor looked over at Clara in question. She simply shrugged in answer.

"You want to tell me why you are upset?" Connor quietly asked as they headed toward the burger place with the ice cream shop.

Clara glared at him while she answered, "I can't believe you ordered the test! You of all people should know it would be negative."

Ahh, that's what this was about, he chuckled. He didn't know why, but her comment actually touched his heart, "Clara, that's standard procedure for any female in your age group that comes into the ER. I didn't even think about it. Besides, the nurses would have been suspicious if I didn't order it. It's usually just a precaution. Women often deny they could be and that happens to be the reason why they pass out."

"The nurse was so disappointed when she told me the test result

what happened at the prom? 311

was negative, like I have been trying," she stated a little too loud as she expressed her anger.

Connor chuckled as they pulled into the parking lot and asked who wanted to come inside while he ordered the food. Once he had Hailey in his arms, he walked around the car to open Reese's door and then Clara's.

Reese had already unbuckled himself and was standing behind his mother, patting her shoulder, trying to reassure her. "Don't worry, Mommy. The next time you take the test, it won't be negative. I know you always try your best."

Connor laughed out loud. Clara, knowing the boy didn't understand what they were talking about, simply chuckled.

Once inside, they decided to eat in so the children could have the ice cream after they ate. While they waited, Clara sat at the table while Connor and the children played on the video games. When he brought them into the bathroom to wash up, Clara felt a sudden chill as her heart rate started up. She closed her eyes and focused on her breathing.

She didn't see the familiar blue eyes watching her from across the restaurant but she could sense he was near.

When Connor returned with the children, she looked up and tried to smile. He noticed immediately she wasn't right. He thought maybe her head was hurting but she denied it. He assisted Hailey into the highchair as Reese declared he wanted to sit with his mother. They sat together, eating. While this was not Connor's first time eating with the children, it was the first time in public.

"Reese, if I have to tell you to turn around and eat your dinner, you will not be getting any ice cream for dessert," Clara said. The young boy immediately turned to Connor in question.

Connor nodded his head in agreement. "Don't look at me, Buddy. Mommy's the boss."

The boy sighed and stopped talking with his friend in the next booth. They were able to enjoy the time together. After dinner, they ordered ice cream and went outside on the bench to enjoy themselves. Hailey sat on her mother's lap while Reese sat between her and Connor. Connor's arm was across the back of the bench, his hand gently rubbing her neck.

Sensing the tension, Connor looked around but nothing seemed to be the cause of her stress.

Later that night, Chase was finishing his dinner when Lila came into the kitchen. He asked if she had talked to Clara recently.

"Not since this morning. Why? Is everything alright?" She asked as she pulled her plate out of the warming drawer, joining him at the table.

He explained what happened at the house and finished with his conversation with the doctor about the prom. Lila had immediately texted Clara as she ate and listened.

"Interesting that he would ask about the prom after all these years," Lila commented.

"What do you know?" Chase asked. Despite being close, they never really talked about Rob and Clara, not then or now.

"Just what Clara told me. She wasn't feeling good and went to the restroom. She was gone for a while so Rob went to go check up on her. Clara says when she came out, Rob and Isabella Daynee had their hands all over each other and there was kissing," she said with a shrug.

Chase looked at her, "He was making out with her? I heard she stumbled and he caught her. She kissed his neck just as Clara came out."

Lila gave her cousin a look that suggested he was very stupid, "Chase, they weren't just making out that evening. They moved out to his car and were having sex!"

"What? No, Isabella always exaggerates." Chase shook his head in denial as he brought his plate to the sink to rinse and load into the dishwasher.

"Chase, I saw them together. Besides, they continued seeing each other that whole summer," Lila stated.

what happened at the prom?   313

Chase came back to the table, "You saw them? In his car? Really? What did you really see?"

"Something I could have gone my whole life never seeing. I was worried about Clara and went looking for her. She wasn't in the bathroom. Shannon suggested maybe she was sitting in the car. I went to check. Rob and Isabella were in the backseat of the car. Her dress was off, and she was riding him pretty hard. They were both obviously enjoying themselves. Clara was nowhere on his mind. I don't blame her for being upset," Lila concluded as she sipped her drink.

Chase simply looked at her. It explained the severity of Clara's reaction, especially when Rob was so vague on the details. He winced at the idea of his naïve little cousin accidently seeing her older brother having sex, "Are you still in therapy?" Lila laughed as he continued, "So why did you have to tell Clara?"

"I didn't. I just assumed she saw them herself because her dress was in the trash out in the lot near his car. Don't blame her. She had the biggest crush on him and he ditches her for the class slut? And when we returned to school on Monday, I overheard Isabella bragging to Clara. We never talked about it," she shrugged.

"Did you know how she got home that night? Weren't you all supposed to be having a slumber party or something after the prom?"

"Yeah, we were. By the time we got back to Rachel's, Clara had left a message that she was home. All safe and sound. Said she wasn't feeling good." Lila shrugged. "I just assumed she called her father for a ride."

"Really? I guess maybe I did too. But no, it was the doctor. He just happened to be driving down the road and saw her walking by herself. He was rightfully pissed. She wouldn't tell him what happened, so she may have saved your brother's life," Chase chuckled. He couldn't believe he had not heard the whole story before today.

"Clara just texted back, she said she's good. Listen, I'm going to head out. I'll be late or even all night. Tell Rob, alright?" She gave her cousin a hug before he could say otherwise. Chase noted, yet again, she didn't say who she was meeting with. He wondered who she was seeing and why she was keeping it a secret.

time to end this little charade

T he next morning, Clara tried to be in a good mood, but it proved difficult after being woken up every two hours by Connor to assure her concussion wasn't a slow bleed. Her day started out typically. She saw her patients, went to meetings, and had to explain the bump on her head.

Clara was annoyed when Eric called her into his office later that afternoon. She really wasn't in the mood for his stupid juvenile behavior. Her annoyance changed to agitation as he gestured towards the small sofa while closing the door. Eric sat at the other end. He crossed his legs, bringing his body to shift towards her with his arm up on the back of the sofa. Because it was a short sofa, his other hand was close enough to casually rest on her knees.

Clara was immediately on high alert.

Eric offered her a coffee, but she declined, stating she was cutting back on her caffeine intake.

He simply nodded before his hand rubbed her knee. "How are you doing? I heard about the accident at your house yesterday afternoon. I missed you when I went looking for you. Do you want me to take you home? If you need the rest of the week off, just say the word and it's done."

"I will be fine. What did you want to see me about?" She asked as she moved his hand from her lap and placed it into his own.

Eric watched the gesture as he leaned back and chuckled softly, "Don't you think it's time we end this little charade? I know everyone in town has been mesmerized by your returning home. All have been discussing who will win your affection, Connor or Rob? There's even a pool going. Personally, I think you can do better." Eric paused as his hand touched her knee and slid up her thigh. When he winked, Clara immediately snapped out of her shock.

It wasn't specifically what he said or the tone he used. It was the facial expression and the faint cologne she smelled that triggered a memory. Eric was there the night she was drugged. That bastard, she thought in horror at the realization.

Clara stood up, telling herself not to panic when she realized he had her cornered. What to do? As he stepped closer, she stepped back, as if playing a silent dance. Clara felt a table behind her and remembered the heavy figurine. She reached back for it as she tried to speak calmly, "Do not touch me."

"Or what? You think one of your boyfriends will come and save you? It's your word against mine," Eric threatened. He was standing so close she needed to lean back to avoid any contact. Clara became nauseous once she understood his intent. "After we finish, you'll agree, I am the better lover, my Love."

His hand was coming up to touch her face as he leaned in to kiss her. Clara reacted instinctively, pushing him away from her as she shifted her weight forward. He wasn't expecting the resistance, and fell back onto the sofa. Since she didn't need the figurine, she tossed it onto his lap.

Eric laughed at her reaction. He knew she was nervous, but he wasn't prepared for her comments or questions.

Clara should have run straight for the door, but she had to know.

"Did you kill my husband?"

"What? No, I didn't kill him! Wasn't he in the city?"

She read his total shock and confusion as he answered. She believed him. But Clara was still furious as she looked down at him, grinning up at her like an immature high school boy.

"Eric, do not touch me ever again! Is that understood? Just to make sure you understand, I quit!" She kept her voice low, but her tone was firm. Clara went to the door, horrified all over again to discover it was locked. She quickly opened it and stormed down the hall. She went to her desk to retrieve her purse, grabbed her few personal pictures and turned to leave.

Clara was almost to the back entrance when a male nurse called her name. She turned around and stated, she thought calmly, but the nurse later informed Matt she was hysterical and very agitated, "I don't work here anymore."

Once Clara was in her car, she tried to focus on her breathing. The last thing she needed was to pass out again and have Eric find her in the car. I need to get my children, she thought as she started the car. Clara replayed the conversation in her head as she drove.

He acted like I was the town whore! The bastard! No, Clara corrected herself as she pulled into the lot outside of the daycare. Eric acted like I was Connor's whore. When she placed the car in park, Clara looked up. Her eyes immediately locked onto his office window.

Looking back, there were so many things Clara should have done differently that afternoon. It was as if someone else was controlling her actions. She could have sent him a text; text one of the teachers to bring out the children but she had not been thinking rationally. Instead, Clara marched up to his office with a purpose. The confrontation resulted in her making a fool of herself in Connor's workplace.

She didn't knock on the door, she barged right in. But she did have the frame of mind to close the door behind her. Then everything was a blur.

time to end this little charade   319

Connor looked up when his door opened and smiled, pleasantly surprised, as Clara walked in unannounced. He knew instantly she was angry. Since he didn't do anything wrong, he sat back as he watched her temper fully explode.

"You bastard! You were only with me so you could win a bet? You have been in my home, around my children, and in my bed, all so you could win a bet?"

Connor was immediately on his feet and around his desk. He stepped towards her, but Clara backed away from him. He was right in front of her when she softly whispered, "I trusted you."

His heart sank as he heard the defeat in her words. He had her lab results on his desk from the day before and knew she was not herself. There were serious psychotropic drugs in her system. But something else must have set her off. He lifted his hand to gently caress her cheek, a touch that always calmed her.

Clara winced as she stepped back and yelled, "Don't touch me!"

She turned around and paused for a moment, surprised to see Josh standing at the door. "Don't!"

Josh was shocked to see Clara visibly agitated as she whispered, "I don't want to be touched!"

Josh remained frozen on the spot as she stepped around him, storming down the hall. He turned to watch as she disappeared around the corner before he looked into Connor's office, clearly puzzled.

Connor's eyes met his nephew's, confused by the unanswered question. His cell chimed a text. It was from Matt:

"What did you do? Just heard Clara quit. What happened?"

Within the hour, Clara was home with all the doors locked. She had the children playing on the floor as she took a shower in an attempt to cleanse herself. She dressed in an old pair of sweatpants and a baggy flannel as she headed down to the kitchen with her children following. She made them a simple sandwich with fruit and steamed vegetables.

Then she sat on the floor while they watched a movie.

Shannon was late coming home from work. She wasn't surprised to find Clara still up, but she was when she saw the children were. Clara was just staring at the television, not answering any questions. Not sure what to do, she sent a text to Lila.

Lila was supposed to meet her brother and cousin for dinner. She sent them a text saying she would be delayed. There was an issue at Clara's. Without any further prodding, both vehicles pulled up at the same time in front of Clara's house.

Shannon was standing on the porch waiting for Lila. She was slightly annoyed with Rob and Chase also present.

"You didn't give me any indication of what was wrong. I thought we might need the extra help," Lila explained.

Rob was not prepared for what he saw when he entered the family room. Clara was sitting on the floor with her legs curled up and her chin resting on her knees. Both Reese and Hailey ran over to greet everyone. Within a few minutes, Rob was sitting beside her on the floor while everyone else took the children upstairs for bed.

"Clara? Everything alright? Anything you want to talk about?" Rob asked gently as he touched her shoulders.

Clara looked up into his steel blue eyes and sadly shook her head.

Upstairs, Lila had just finished reading to the kids. She and Shannon tucked Haily in while Chase gave Reese a piggyback ride to his bed. When they met back in the hallway, Shannon showed them a text from Devan.

"Well, now we know who upset her," Chase stated. "I say we let him in. If we don't like what he has to say we simply kick him out."

Lila agreed while Shannon answered back.

A moment later, they were back downstairs when they heard the knock on the door. Chase remained near Rob while Shannon opened the door. Devan entered first followed by Connor. His stomach clenched when he saw Clara. Her eyes weren't sad, but defeated. She was on her

time to end this little charade   321

feet with the Foxwoods standing beside her.

Connor calmly stated, "Clara, I would like a moment to talk with you privately."

Clara looked up into his brown eyes. He was someone she could always trust. It broke her heart that he would betray that. But now that she was calmer, she started to think more rationally. It was Eric that pushed her, not Connor.

Without a word, Clara walked past him to the kitchen. Connor followed. He was relieved Devan was present to have his back. Rob tried to follow but Chase held out his arm.

"Let's give them some privacy. If he upsets her more, we can toss him out," Chase suggested. "Do you really think he's the one that upset her?"

Devan agreed, "Something happened between the time they saw each other this morning and when she stormed into his office this afternoon. We just don't know what it was."

"What exactly happened at the office?" Shannon asked.

"Connor just said she stormed in, accused him of things, and stormed out before he had a chance to talk. She was too agitated for him to attempt. The second she was out the door he received a text from his brother wanting to know why she quit her job."

"That is really odd behavior for Clara," Lila commented. "Something significant had to happen for her to walk off the job."

Shannon and Chase both nodded in agreement.

In the kitchen, Clara remained standing with her arms across her chest. She didn't say a word. Connor wanted to talk, she thought, he can talk all he wants. Her eyes remained focused on a button on his shirt.

Connor studied her face. Her pupils were normal, but her eyes were red and puffy. The expression on her face reminded him of her night terrors. The ones that left her shaking and sweating, unable to catch her breath, just as she was when she arrived into his office.

"Clara, we have a history together. We have always been able to tell each other things that we've never told anyone else. We've never judged. We've always been supportive and caring. You have always had a special place in my heart, a place no one else has ever been able to touch. I've always looked forward to seeing you and wondered what kind of silliness you would bring." He chuckled at a memory. "I have treasured every moment we've spent together. And when we are separated, I feel as if a part of me is missing until we are together again. I love you. I always have. And when you returned home, I fell in love with you. I never told you because..." Connor paused a moment as he reached for her hand, but she pulled away as she stepped back.

Not a good sign, he thought as his mind went into overdrive. The ER doctor took over and analyzed how she responded. As if she were abused or assaulted. What the hell happened? Did it happen at work?

Focus, he told himself. Tell her what you came to tell her. He took a deep breath and continued, "Sweetheart?" Clara continued to look down, but he tried again, "Beautiful?" When her green eyes looked up into his brown, he continued, "I love you, but we've never really been able to focus on us because let's face it, when have we had the time? We are just beginning, barely getting started. I would never take part in a bet to capture your affection. I may have competed, but if you were more interested in someone else, I would have stepped aside. I have never gossiped about you or our relationship. Never have I advertised it to be something more than what we have."

"In the few months since you returned, you've hit every major stress factor. You relocated your family, you started a new job, you found your mother's remains, you lost your husband, you've been drugged, and attacked." Connor paused again. Clara had silent tears falling down her cheeks as he listed off each event. When he mentioned the drugging, he caught a glimpse of the anger on her face as her fists tightened. But when he said the word attack, she closed her eyes and the fear was loud and clear. But she claimed to not remember the attack on the stairs.

time to end this little charade   323

And why would it suddenly bother her today? What happened today at work?

"Beautiful?" Connor waited for her to open her eyes before he continued, "Please talk to me. Tell me what happened today."

"I, I can't," Clara was shaking her head as she spoke quietly. "I can't keep living with this fear that's all balled up inside of me. It makes me paranoid and distrustful. I am anxious. Sometimes I can't breathe! My heart starts pounding so hard I think everyone can hear it and that's why everyone is looking at me. I see these violent eyes looking down on me and watching me, everywhere I go. I can't trust people I have known my whole life, I can't even accept a coffee given to me everyday. I..." Clara sighed with a shrug, "I quit. I quit my job that means so much to me because I can't do it anymore. I am leaving. I can't do this anymore because it hurts too much. I hurt so much."

Her voice had grown soft as the tears flowed more forcefully. When she announced she hurt, her knees buckled, Connor stepped forward to catch her. He held her as she quietly sobbed, "It hurts too much and it scares me."

He held her as she cried. He carried her over to the kitchen chair and sat down with her in his lap. Connor had one hand on her hair and the other around her as he held her tight. They remained sitting there together for many minutes, Connor had no awareness of time. His mind reviewed everything she just said.

Someone she knew all her life, coffee, and every day. Was it at work? What the hell did the little bastard do to her, he wondered. When her crying slowed, he tilted her chin up so he could see her eyes while he spoke, "Are you going to tell me who it was?"

As he expected, she shook her head no. Why does she always try to protect the people that hurt her, he wondered. "Clara, I'm going to leave, but you are ok to stay here with your friends, right?"

Clara nodded her head sadly. "I will be back, I promise. I love you." Connor pulled her in again as he kissed the top of her head. He stood up and gave her a moment to get her balance. He looked down at her and was relieved she was looking up. He wiped her tears with his thumbs as he asked, "Are we good?"

She nodded her head. Always like pulling teeth with her, Connor thought as he took her hand and led her out into the family room.

Everyone else had remained near the front entrance. They were trying to listen while also trying to respect their privacy. When they saw Connor lead her out, Lila and Shannon both stepped forward. Connor let go of her hand as he kissed her forehead and headed out the door without a word.

Devan followed Connor. When he caught up to him, it was everything he could do to control his cousin. He literally feared Connor was going to take off and kill someone. He pulled out his phone and called his cousins. He needed backup.

"Connor, wait. What did she tell you?"

"She fears for her life, she's hurting. That stupid son of a bitch has been drugging her. Clara basically listed off every symptom! He's been around her all this time. And he did something to her today, but she won't tell me what," Connor's voice shook with anger.

"Clara told you who drugged her?" Devan demanded.

Connor nodded, as he attempted to go around him, "More or less."

"Connor, stop!" Devan stepped in his path, "You know this is big. We need to do this the right way."

"Oh, don't you worry. I will make it the right way," Connor declared as he tried again to step around him.

"No, you won't feel any better after you beat him close to death. You'll be arrested and ruin your career." Connor attempted to shove past. "And you will lose Clara and the kids forever."

Connor stopped and looked at his cousin, "If we do this your way, will he be behind bars or will his father get him out of this?"

"If we do this the right way, we will have him arrested. We fully investigate the drug charge. Maybe we can get the details of the assault.

time to end this little charade   325

We put him away. If we can link him to multiple cases, it'll be better," Devan assured him as Anthony and Joe pulled up into his driveway.

Connor looked over then back at his cousin, "Did you call them over for reinforcements?"

"Hell yeah. I was not letting you go kill him. Where are we going to do this? My place or yours?"

Chase and Rob remained downstairs as Lila and Shannon went upstairs with Clara. Shannon ran her a warm bath while Lila returned downstairs to make tea. Clara never talked nor cried for the rest of the evening. When she went to bed, she was in the middle between Lila and Shannon. She woke up a few times, as she often did but she remained in bed with her friends.

Chase and Rob remained for the night, one slept on the sofa while the other slept in Shannon's bed.

· · · ·

Evil drove around the block again and cussed. What the hell is going on? Why are there so many cars parked out front? He counted a total of eight vehicles between the two residences. He would have considered chancing it except he saw lights on at the bartender's place. There were too many people keeping him from seeing his Babydoll. But don't worry, it'll be soon, I promise. He continued driving past her house accepting the roadblock for what it was. A simple delay.

each and every time

The next evening, Connor entered Memories from the back entrance. He was slightly surprised at the heavy crowd for a Thursday evening. He noted Devan sitting with his uncle and cousins eating dinner. Eric was sitting at a table beside them with a friend.

Connor casually made his way through the restaurant, greeting people as was common in a small town. When he looked up, his cousin was gesturing him over. When he approached the table, Eric tilted his head, instructing his friend to go to the bar to get another round of drinks while he invited Connor to sit.

"I'm surprised your girlfriend isn't out here with you," Eric commented after putting a chunk of meatloaf into his mouth.

"We broke up. She's moving away," Connor lied, playing with the silverware at his seat. He silently debated which would do more damage to his cousin's neck, the fork or the knife.

Eric chuckled but held his comment as Jill, the young server, came by to ask Connor if he was ready to order or if he wanted a menu to look over.

Connor requested the menu and a glass of water. When she left, he shrugged as he explained, "I'm on call tonight."

Eric nodded in understanding as he sipped from his beer. He couldn't understand the concept of working so hard. Connor was a surgeon with scheduled shifts at the hospital which included time in the emergency room. If that wasn't enough, he was also medical director at the nursing home. He seemed to be constantly back and forth. Sure, the money had to be great but at what price? Eric was content working at their nursing home. It was only a few hours and not really much work. He was able to live his life as he chose.

Well, that wasn't accurate, although Eric would only admit to himself. His first choice would have been to live freely in the house, without his annoying parents and grandfather constantly looking over his shoulder. Even if his grandfather died today, his father was next to inherit the house. And the trust fund from his mother's side was only in her name. It provided a measly monthly allowance. If she needed more, she had to request it. Eric sighed at the injustice of it all.

"I'm sorry to hear about your breakup. It's a shame, really. A young attractive woman like her has a lot to offer," Eric observed.

It wasn't what Eric said that threatened to set Connor off, but the tone he used as he said it. Connor remained silent, visualizing the fork in Eric's carotid artery. If he were quick, the multiple prongs would be sharp enough to poke small holes, but take too long to bleed out. Maybe the fork in one hand and the knife in the other, he wondered as he simply raised his eyebrows in question.

"Connor, Clara's said it herself, she has had too many days off in her probationary time. We can't give her a positive referral so she has to stay," Eric stated with confidence. It would also give me more time to enjoy her until the money comes in. By then I will have control, he chuckled to himself as he continued to eat his dinner.

"I don't think she will be staying. A friend from the Trauma Center in the city reached out today asking about her returning to her previous position. She is that good. When I went to her place last night, she was already packing up," Connor stated miserably. He didn't have to act.

Eric was almost feeling bad for Connor. He wasn't used to seeing the vulnerable side of his older cousin. As a family, they often spent time together during various holidays, but due to the age differences growing up, they were never close. Working with them at the nursing home was the most he'd been around them his whole life. His cousins were never mean or condescending. They were, more or less, respectful, just as all the children raised in the large houses on Park Avenue.

Eric pondered as he sipped his beer. If Clara was actively preparing to leave, he had to act fast. Connor watched as Eric's mind seemed to process the current information. And he waited.

"I don't think she'll leave," Eric predicted.

"I think she will. She has been quiet lately. She doesn't like me to touch her," Connor mumbled quietly.

Ahh good, the medicine has been working. Excellent, he thought. "Give me a few days, I'll have her back to work."

"How? She has her mind made up."

"Oh Connor, how are you so naïve? You have to know by now I have a cabinet that will always help me get whatever it is I want," Eric bragged.

"What are you talking about?" Connor tilted his head in disbelief, he was shocked it was that easy. Feed the stupid prick's ego, just like his father.

"Like you don't know? You think Clara would have left with you if I didn't give her that little push?" Eric wasn't aware Connor knew about the spiked drink.

But the word push did make one wonder about the physical push down the stairs. Connor's eyes narrowed in question as he softly asked, "Did you push her down the stairs?"

Eric chuckled before he answered sarcastically, "Right. You think if I were in her house I would be hiding? And then push her? Why would I? God, did she tell you that? She is getting paranoid! Yesterday, she asked me if I killed her husband!"

"What?" Connor was thrown off by the suggestion. "Why would she ask you that?

"No idea. He was killed in the city, right? I hate going into the city. I wouldn't even have known who he was if I walked past him."

Connor agreed. Eric would have been too lazy to research the guy. And according to Matt and his father, the Howell family didn't have enough money to hire a killer.

"So, if you didn't push her literally, how did you do it? Did you drug her or something?"

"Drugging is a little strong, more medicated. I simply made her easier for you to control," Eric corrected.

Connor lost control. He immediately stood up and tossed the table aside. He lifted his younger cousin up by his collar and shoved him against the wall, keeping him pinned with his forearm, "You fucking bastard! You were drugging her? Were you also spying on her with surveillance equipment? After all these years, she is STILL not interested in you, so you drugged her?"

"Yes, I did!" Eric yelled back. "I drugged her! I listened in on her. I heard it all! But when I drug her, she always goes to you. Without me, you would never have gotten her!"

Connor was so furious! He rammed his knee into Eric's stomach. As he balled his fist to take a swing, Devan and Joe immediately pulled him back while Anthony and the sheriff grabbed Eric.

Connor was trying to break free as he yelled, "You fucking bastard. You touched her? I am going to…" he tried to advance forward.

"Yeah, I made a move on her! She was so sweet and wanting. The look of bliss in her eyes when I touched her but every single time she was drugged, she went right to you! Every fucking time!" Eric yelled back.

Unbeknown to Connor, Clara had been getting restless staying inside all day. Both Rob and Chase agreed to walk with her. They stopped in Memories to pick up dinner to bring back. They had just stepped inside as the table was ripped to the side and Eric was shoved into the wall. Clara was shocked at the sight before her. She had seen Connor's temper before, but never like this.

"Clara, my Love!" Eric exclaimed excitedly as his eyes found her standing just inside the door.

Connor turned to see Clara standing at the door, her friends standing protectively beside her. For once, he was not able to read her expression as she surveyed the scene before her. When she looked around the restaurant, everyone's eyes had shifted to her. Clara returned her gaze to Connor. Her green eyes appeared to pull him out of his insanity as he shook off his restraints and turned around, walking out the back door. Clara turned to walk out the front door, followed by her friends.

Clara sat on the low windowsill with her face in her hands. Rob and Chase stood protectively in front of her as a deputy's cruiser double parked right outside. Anthony and Joe were escorting the handcuffed Eric. At first, he walked willingly to the door, to follow his love. Once outside, Eric continued to express his love for her as a third deputy assisted with wrestling him to the car.

"Clara! We'll be together again, I promise. Clara? I love you, Clara!" Eric yelled but his voice was muffled once the door was shut, "Clllaaarraaaaaaa!"

The cruiser sped off around the corner towards the sheriff's department.

"Clara? Are you alright?"

Clara looked up to see the sheriff squatted down in front of her. His caring brown eyes were full of concern. She slowly nodded her head as she answered, "I will be."

They both stood up together. Tony needed to get back to the department. He wanted to make sure everything was handled by the book. This slime wasn't going to be getting off on a technicality because of something his people did or didn't do. Not on his watch. Tony knew this was just scratching the surface. Federal agents began executing search warrants at Eric's home and office. Devan had given the order, as Connor was shoving the table aside. Damn, the town is going to have a field day with this!

"Clara, head home with your friends. I will be stopping in to talk with you tomorrow morning, alright?"

Once home, Clara felt relaxed as she took a long refreshing shower. She felt as if a weight had been removed from her shoulders. A month ago, hell even a week ago, she never would have thought Eric Howell was capable of such acts! But she didn't believe he was the man inside her home that pushed her down the stairs.

When she returned to the family room, the food had been delivered. She sat next to Rob as she ate, grateful for her friends. At the end of the evening, she encouraged the Foxwoods to return home.

As she walked them to the door, Rob leaned down to hug her and reminded her he was only a call away then he leaned to whisper, "You sure you're alright?"

Clara nodded, "Yeah, I'm fine."

Rob paused and looked at her closely.

"What?"

"You aren't alright when you say fine. You are the opposite of fine," Rob stated as he watched her facial expression.

"Since when?"

"Since forever, I guess. I would know something was up even though you wouldn't tell me," Rob said.

Clara sighed. "Rob, I am not great but I'm not bad either. I guess I'm healing, and I will get there. Eventually."

"Alright, I'll check in with you tomorrow." He hugged her again.

"Don't worry about me, I'll be fine." Clara stopped as she realized what she said. They both laughed and she leaned up to kiss his cheek before he stepped out.

SHADOWS OF THE NIGHT

he said what?

D allas reached over to hit the snooze, then leaned back and closed his eyes. Beside him, Lila stirred with a groan, "What time is it?"

"I need to get going but no reason you can't stay and sleep. What time is your shift?" He asked as he rolled onto his side to gently move the auburn hair from her face. He leaned forward to kiss her forehead and then her lips before he slowly worked his way to her neck. Dallas smiled when she groaned softly as he slowly worked his way down...

He emerged from the bathroom an hour later, newly showered with a towel around his waist. As he went to his closet for his uniform, Lila pulled herself up to lean against the headboard and watch.

Dallas was distracted as the sheet fell, exposing her breasts. She simply smiled. He looked away as he tried to focus and remember he had a job. But tomorrow they could sleep in if he could convince her to stop in after her late shift.

Once he was dressed, he sat beside her on the edge of the bed to give her a kiss goodbye. She pulled him in for a longer kiss. "Lila, I will meet you tonight after your shift. Text me if you leave early. I'll follow you home, ok?"

She nodded before asking, "Are you meeting up with Clara today? To ask her about volleyball?"

"I can't talk about my sister while you are lying there naked," Dallas answered as he left the room with Lila's laughter following him.

In town, Clara was up early, feeling surprisingly refreshed. Her friends made her feel special and loved, she thought with a smile as she opened the door to the sheriff.

"Good morning, Clara. I hope it's not too early."

"Not at all. Despite not having a job, I am already up and about with these guys," she said as she gestured towards the kids. "Can I get you a cup of coffee?"

"Is it already made? I don't want you going out of your way," he answered.

"It's no trouble, it's a single serving maker," Clara assured as she led the way to the kitchen.

Sitting at the kitchen table, he eased her into a discussion by asking about her normal everyday routine. Then he asked her questions about work. The sheriff was trying to figure out how she was getting drugged. Connor was confident she wasn't taking any prescriptions which she confirmed. Clara also denied any mental history beside depression.

"I've never actually been diagnosed with clinical depression but I'm sure I've had it with my mother and husband's deaths," she simply stated.

"Anyone going through what you went through would have been the same," he assured her. Tony paused before he continued, "How do you think Eric has been getting the drugs into you?"

Clara shrugged. "I'm thinking the coffee. He often has one for me every morning and sometimes in the afternoon if he goes out for lunch. I normally have a cup or two here at home but this morning, I couldn't touch it. When I think back, I was more anxious on work days than on weekends. Didn't even realize it until last night."

Tony nodded as he debated internally how to broach the next topic, "Clara, how would you describe your relationship with Eric."

Clara's eyes held the Sheriff's for a moment before she answered, "We grew up in houses next door to each other. We went to school together. When I returned to start working at the nursing home, we had a simple working relationship. I was the rehab director and he was my immediate supervisor. We were never really together outside of work."

"But I have reports Eric came to your house several times," the sheriff challenged.

"True, he would stop over without an invitation. Every time someone was here with me. I just figured he was being neighborly, checking up on me." She paused as she realized he always brought her a coffee. It was prepared in a specific way specifically for her. She explained this to Sheriff Mancuso. She also told him about the morning he stopped over when no one was around, and she didn't open the door.

"And there was the one time I was with co-workers at The Lantern, he was there. That was the night I was drugged. It was different from the more recent feeling. That night I lost my filter, but in the last few weeks I have been feeling anxious and paranoid. Like someone is watching me."

"So, you never had a romantic relationship with Eric?" He inquired.

"Good God, no. He is the same as he was in high school," Clara blurted out without thinking.

The look of horror on her face made the sheriff believe her. "How so?" he asked.

Clara shrugged, "I don't know how to explain it. He's always trying too hard to be friendly and acting as if he cares, but he doesn't really respond right."

The sheriff nodded encouragingly before she continued, "In high school, we were lab partners in biology and then chemistry. He did the bare minimum, and I always had to tutor him. Always on his schedule so it wouldn't interfere with his social plans. When I wasn't available to help him study the night before a test, he blamed me when he failed and was benched for a week," Clara said. "Eric didn't talk to me that week until he realized he needed my help to pass the class and get off the bench. I wasn't very nice, but after the fathers got involved, I helped him. Not unusual behavior in a teenage boy. Before this week, I would have considered him a colleague, but never anyone to rely on for emotional support. I would never have wasted my time with him."

"Clara, have you ever had a physical relationship with him?" Tony asked softly.

"Are you asking if I had sex with him?" Horrified at the thought, Clara subconsciously shuddered as she shook her head. "Hell no."

Sheriff Mancuso wondered about Eric's mental state. He appeared to believe he had a romantic connection with her. He describes a very disturbing account of their relationship that resumed when she returned home this spring. And she's denying it.

"Can you tell me what happened in his office on Wednesday afternoon?" He quietly asked.

"In his office?" Clara was surprised by the question. She had not told anyone about it. Why would he think there was anything to tell?

"Witnesses report you were seen coming out of his office agitated," he explained. He didn't add Connor's speculations because they were just that, speculations.

Clara sighed as she stood up and walked to the sink to look out the window. Wednesday afternoon seemed ages ago. Her memories had a dream-like quality. She couldn't remember the whole conversation, but she remembered the look on his face and the smell of alcohol on his breath. Clara shook her head to focus back on the conversation.

"Nothing I couldn't handle. It was more of a HR issue than a police matter," she stated.

"If that were the case, why did you quit?"

"Because he pissed me off so much. I honestly don't recall the whole conversation just that I wanted out of there and never be near him. Something triggered a memory from the night I was drugged at the Lantern. I had a flashback of him handing me a drink and feeling different. Not anxious but more relaxed," Clara simply answered.

The sheriff watched her body language closely as he made the next comment. "Eric says you two had sex in his office that afternoon and that it wasn't the first time."

"He what?" She was totally shocked. "If there was any sex in that office, it was without me. He was certainly ready with his pants bulging. At least he had the decency to wait until after I left to pull it out. Excuse me for being so vulgar."

Tony didn't tell her the office did have a lot of DNA present that currently supported her theory. When the Emerson's get word, they'll probably have the office totally gutted. He believed Clara's version over Eric's. His son Anthony described the high school years as she did. Back then everyone believed she was holding out for Rob Foxwood.

"Clara, I will be taking off now. Here's my card. I want you to call if you have any concerns or questions. I have my sons' numbers on the back. Call whichever one of us you feel most comfortable talking to, alright? I am sorry you are going through this." He stood from the table, leaving his card next to his coffee mug. "Thanks for the coffee."

After the sheriff left, Clara decided she needed to get out of the house. She suggested a walk and the kids were interested. But just as they reached the front door, Reese requested they take the wagon instead of the baby stroller. She laughed and agreed.

Dallas Thompson barely made it to work on time. He was scouting out the various parts of the park on an ATV when he noticed vultures flying over the trees, just off a nearby trail commonly used among the weekend hikers. Probably just a dead bear. Best to take care of it now, or the vultures will have the bones wiped clean and scattered all over the park, with endless calls to follow. People always assume larger bones were human, but 95% of the time, they were from large animals, dead due to either natural causes or an injury.

As it turned out, today was part of the 5%. And it didn't look like natural causes or an accident.

should have caught on sooner

An hour after leaving for the walk, Clara was sitting in the shade watching Hailey try to eat her ice cream cone before it melted. The little girl was too disgusted with the mess, holding it away, "Mama, no!"

Reese put his hand out, "Can I have it?"

She nodded as she reached into the diaper bag for wipes. Once the girl was cleaned off, Clara entertained her with a toy as she placed her back into the wagon. She waited patiently for Reese to finish before they could head home.

"Clara?"

Clara turned to see Dallas walking up with a bag of to-go containers. She smiled as he approached. "Hello Dallas, don't you look handsome in your uniform!"

Dallas paused, not expecting a compliment and unsure how to respond. He simply nodded.

"Reese, Hailey, I want you to meet your Uncle Dallas. He's my older brother," she said as she gestured for him to join them.

Reese waved with one cone as he tried to lick the other. He was eating from both cones in a race to prevent the inevitable mess of melted ice cream.

Hailey simply stared at him.

"Why do you have two ice cream cones and your sister doesn't have any?" Dallas asked the little boy.

"Because I'm the favorite," Reese explained with confidence.

Dallas chuckled as he turned to Clara, "Really? He's the favorite?"

"Reese! You know I don't have a favorite," Clara warned.

"And because Hailey didn't want it anymore. You weren't here to claim it. Snoozers are losers," he announced happily.

Dallas laughed again, then he looked over Clara's face carefully, "What happened to your face? The last time I saw you, there were stitches and bruises. Now, there's another bruise. Are you alright?" Lila had not mentioned the bruise.

Clara simply dismissed it with a wave, "Long story. Not going to bore you."

Dallas suspected she wouldn't talk about it with the children present, he looked over at Reese still racing against the melting ice cream. Hailey was still staring at him suspiciously with her big sky-blue eyes. "Listen, I'm glad I ran into you, but there's something unexpected from work that I have to deal with. Can we meet up for dinner some time?"

"Sure, how about tonight. If you don't have high expectations, I could whip up macaroni and cheese," Clara offered.

"Mommy makes good mac n cheese," Reese confirmed between bites of his cone.

"I could always go for some mac n cheese. I'll bring dessert. Is six alright?" Dallas asked.

"That should work." She stood up to give him a hug, but held his hand before he could walk away. "Dallas, I have no issues with you. You've always been kind to me, now I understand why. But I don't want anything to do with your mother and my father or rather your parents."

"Clara, I get it. I promise you this isn't some elaborate plan to push them into your life. Hell, it's been months since I've seen my mom. Our communication is usually limited to emails and texts. Maybe an occasional phone call. I haven't talked to him since high school. He's yet to actually claim me publicly."

Clara nodded understanding as he started for his vehicle with a wave, "I'll see you later. Are you alright to get back with the wagon?"

She nodded as she waved goodbye.

Again, she was not aware of being watched or photographed.

Just before six in the evening, it happened again. Clara's doorbell rang the same time her cell phone did. As before, she opened the door the same time she answered her cell. She gestured to Dallas while Reese ran over to greet him. Hailey was still reserving her opinion, keeping a safe distance.

"Hello?"

"Clara! How is everything going?" Rob answered.

"Great, Rob. How about you?"

"Not bad. Listen, it's been awhile since you and the kids have been here at the farm. How about you all come over for lunch tomorrow, say eleven?"

"Eleven? Sounds good. What can I bring?" Clara asked.

"Just you and the kids would be great," he responded before he hung up.

Dallas followed Clara into the kitchen and placed his bag on the counter, "Still good friends with Rob, eh?"

Clara turned and sighed, remembering some stupid family dispute. Lila never could explain it. "Is that a problem?"

"Not at all. The issues were always his, not mine," Dallas dismissed. "I didn't know what to bring, but I did remember what you used to love. I brought a chocolate cake. It's not homemade because I didn't have time."

"You bake?" Clara asked suspiciously.

should have caught on sooner   341

"Sure, not difficult. Recipes give you the specific directions," Dallas said.

"How are you still single?" She wondered out loud.

"What makes you think I am?" He challenged cautiously.

Clara leaned back into the counter and eyed him. He was an attractive guy with a respectable job. And he baked. If he baked, he probably cooked. Dallas was definitely a great catch.

"Is she someone I would get along with? Is it safe to assume it's a she?"

"Yes," He simply answered as he peeked into the oven, "Is this homemade?"

"Yeah, it's one of the few dishes I can honestly claim to make. I was thinking of trying lasagna, but it looks so complicated and I don't think the kids would like it yet," Clara stated. She noted he changed the subject.

"Lasagna isn't difficult. Just don't cook the noodles, add water to the dish, and bake it covered."

"Really?"

"Sure. Next time we'll have dinner at my place, and we can make it together." Dallas suggested.

"Sounds like a plan. Will your better half be there?" Clara challenged as she pulled the dish from the oven.

"Maybe," he allowed with a chuckle.

The dinner was pleasant. Clara was relieved things weren't awkward like in high school when they occasionally found themselves face to face. She always said hi and he always seemed to want to say something more.

After dessert, Clara excused herself to get the children ready for bed. The extra running around outside left them tired and almost eager for sleep. When she returned downstairs, Dallas was closely examining her dining room wall.

"Clara, this is really impressive. If I hadn't seen the wall before, I would have sworn it was a marbled wall," his fingers were touching the wall.

"Yeah, well, I have a bit of insomnia. Painting helps me to relax," Clara shrugged as she asked if he wanted any wine.

When Shannon came home, she was surprised to find Clara alone with Dallas Thompson. She had seen the SUV out front and assumed it was Connor's. She was never really good with cars.

"Hello, what's going on?" Shannon asked with confusion. A simple question asked so much.

"We are having drinks," Clara answered. "Dallas came over for dinner."

"Clara makes excellent mac n cheese," Dallas answered, amused by Shannon's reaction. Lila described her friend Shannon as the one who always gets the hot guys. While she tries to hide it, it annoys her when guys hit on her friends and not her. Shannon obviously has no idea what is going on here.

"Yes, she certainly does," Shannon agreed slowly. Her eyes were bouncing back and forth. "Clara, how is Connor doing?"

"I don't know. I haven't seen him since, last night," Clara answered as she went into the dining room to retrieve another wine glass for Shannon. When she returned, she handed the glass to Dallas as he poured the wine and handed it to Shannon.

"How are things going with the doctor?" Dallas asked. He wasn't sure if Clara knew where Shannon's thoughts were.

"I don't know, it's complicated," Clara answered truthfully.

"I'm sure but what relationship isn't?" Dallas answered with his hands out in question, gesturing between them.

She laughed, "Good point."

Shannon sat down in the chair as she watched the two bantering back and forth, trying to figure out what universe she fell into. She sipped from her wine quietly.

should have caught on sooner   343

"Shan, I haven't had a chance to tell you, Dallas is my older half brother," Clara announced. She really should have waited until Shannon wasn't drinking.

Shannon almost choked on her wine as she started to cough. Alright, she thought, now this scene makes more sense. "How did you two figure this out?"

"The guy that raised me had his suspicions and had my DNA tested. He didn't have to search far for a comparison," Dallas provided the short version. He never told anyone about the late night visits into his room by his biological father. Carl Gibson would come over when his father wasn't home to see his mother. He would often come into his room talking to him quietly, believing he was sound asleep. As he grew older, Dallas understood the situation better.

"DNA testing? Really?" Shannon looked over towards Clara as an idea formed.

"Couldn't hurt to try," Clara agreed, reading her friend's mind.

It was Dallas' turn to look confused. But Shannon gestured for Clara to explain.

"Shannon recently found out she was adopted," she explained before turning back to Shannon. "Shan, Dallas is starting up a team to play volleyball this summer a few towns over. You want in?"

"Absolutely." Shannon with her A personality was the most competitive of the friends, "Who else do you have on the team?"

Clara gestured to the present group while he nodded.

"We should ask Lila," Shan suggested thoughtfully. "And what about Devan?"

Clara looked questionably at Dallas. He noticed something in her eyes clicked. She mouthed "Lila" and nodded her head. She smiled, very pleased with herself. The friends always knew about Lila's crush on Dallas in high school. Clara also understood why the two were likely seeing each other privately. Rob will flip, when he finds out, no doubt. And he will. Secrets this good always had ways of getting out.

"Sure, Devan would be great. Who the hell is Devan?" Dallas asked Clara while Shannon stepped away to text both Lila and Devan. His eyes were warning his sister. She nodded understandingly.

"He's the new bartender at Memories and Shan's current play toy. And he lives on the other side of that wall," she gestured towards the dining room wall.

"Play toy?" Dallas confirmed.

"I'm sorry, was that too mean? I guess lover? Hell, Dallas it's Shannon!" Clara exclaimed.

Dallas laughed. Lila actually made similar comments. Girls can be so cruel, he thought.

Shannon returned to announce Devan was interested, and on his way over. Just then there was a knock on the front door. She invited him in.

"Dallas Thompson, this is Devan Mancuso." The guys shook hands. Devan followed Shannon into the kitchen. She had grabbed another glass as she went in search of another bottle of wine.

"Shan, what am I missing?" Devan asked.

"A kiss?" Shannon asked as she leaned up to give him a kiss. He smiled and placed his arms around her as he kissed her back.

"That's not what I meant," he answered as she pulled back and topped off her glass before pouring into a second one.

"A drink?" She offered his glass, silently toasting before she sipped.

"Shannon, who is this Dallas guy?"

"He was Lila's main crush in high school," Shannon explained as she played with his collar.

"Main crush?" He asked.

"High school, Devan. If you had the hots for the captain of the cheerleading squad but she was dating someone, wouldn't you settle for the captain of the girls' soccer team?" Shannon asked.

"Possibly," Devan wasn't about to admit the analogy wasn't too far off from his senior year. But Shannon's comments also confirmed that

should have caught on sooner   345

even Lila's closest friends aren't aware they're actually dating. Why the secrecy?

"And I just learned before you arrived, Dallas is Clara's older half-brother! This is new information in the last few weeks," Shannon stated as she pulled out her cell while they returned to the family room.

"Lila is definitely in but says she can't guarantee each week because of her work schedule," Shannon announced as she sat on the arm of the chair, allowing Devan to sit on the seat. He had his arm around her low back.

"Nice," Clara stated with a grin at Dallas.

"We just need one more person," Dallas announced, ignoring his sister.

"How does this work? How many on the team?" Devan asked.

"Wednesday evenings starting at six, two games play side by side starting on the hour. I'll go ahead and register us as a team. They should have the schedule for the summer out by Tuesday. We play in teams of six. If someone can't make it, we can always get someone to rotate in," Dallas explained. "I'll leave it up to you to pick the last person."

When the evening grew late, Clara escorted Dallas to the door. Both were pleased with the turn out of the evening. After she opened the door, he leaned down to give her a hug. As he pushed open the screen to step out, he was not surprised to see Connor climbing up the steps. The men shook hands with minimal greeting.

Clara remained silent as she held open the screen door for Connor.

"Clara, we are going to take off. I have my keys," Shannon announced as she gave her a quick hug. "Hi Connor!"

Devan nodded good night to Clara and slapped Connor's shoulder.

Clara was suddenly unsure how to act with Connor. She left him standing at the door as she returned to the family room to refill her empty glass. She held up the bottle in question.

Connor was hesitant about stopping over unannounced. He hadn't planned on it, but his vehicle seemed to drive on auto. He remained at the doorway watching Clara. He missed her and was frustrated with the new awkwardness between them. Connor was surprised by Matt's level of anger Wednesday night. It matched his. Both Devan and the sheriff had to talk them both down, no easy task, to allow for proper warrants to be executed and an actual confession.

When Connor left Clara's the other night, the plan was to get Eric on drug charges. He only had his suspicions of harassment but no details from Clara to back it up. But when his brother informed him of a witness, the evening supervisor Drake Murray, the probable sexual assault was no longer just a theory. Someone else was present when Clara exited Eric's office. Drake was the one to report Clara's sudden quitting and emotional lashing out. Eric never mentioned her quitting, even when she didn't show up to work the next morning. That had his blood boiling. And the whole situation began to make sense, sadly.

Connor looked up to see Clara holding the wine and thought, why not? He nodded as he stepped into the family room.

Still not a word was exchanged as she handed him a glass. Clara sat on the sofa and he followed. They each sipped and watched the other over the rim of their glasses.

"How are things going with you and Dallas?" Connor asked awkwardly.

"Pretty good. He came over for dinner," she answered. When he didn't say anything, she asked, "How are you?"

Connor simply shrugged before he explained, "Clara, I came over to let you know your job is still yours. Matt wanted me to remind you of the capital budget and new hires for your department. We have an acting administrator starting soon. I am going to be overseeing blood testing of all the residents to assess how extensive the drugging was." Connor paused, not really sure what he wanted to say. "And the staff as well. Devan has an independent lab coming out."

What Connor didn't know how to say, was there is currently an investigation looking into other incidents of sexual harrassment and assaults besides Clara, as well as drugging, even if it was just a rumor. Matt was so furious. He called their dad to deal with Eric's parents.

Clara simply nodded non-committedly. Again, Connor was unable to read what she was thinking. He interpreted her silence as anger at him for not protecting her. Why else was she not talking?

Connor leaned forward to stand as he finished his wine, "Clara, I didn't mean to ruin what appeared to be a good evening with your friends. I just wanted to let you know the job is still yours and we hope to see you back Monday morning."

He was turning to leave when Clara finally spoke.

"That's it? I have the job? That's all you have to say?" Clara demanded.

"Yeah," Connor looked into her eyes as he finally admitted, "Actually, I also want to say I am sorry this whole stupid crap happened."

"Why are you sorry? You didn't do anything. None of this was your fault," she quietly assured him. "I don't blame you."

"I should have caught on sooner. Eric was always stopping here or at your office with the coffee. I always knew he had a crush on you. I should have seen it coming. Eric always wants everything without working for it," Connor said in frustration.

"Connor, you are not to blame for his actions," Clara stated as she stepped closer. She still sensed something off between them. When he left the other night, he asked if they were good. They hugged and made up after she yelled at him. Why is he so distant? "Connor, talk to me."

"Tell me what he did to you in his office before you came to see me," he asked in a quiet demand.

"He only pissed me off, nothing happened," Clara stated, confused.

"Eric said you two were having sex. Drake reported groaning sounds when he was in the office next door. When he came out to investigate, you were in the hallway obviously upset," Connor stated as he watched her eyes.

"Nothing happened. He tried, and I'll admit he had me cornered on the sofa, but I was able to push past him. Whatever happened afterwards Eric did on his own to himself," Clara stated. She gave him a more detailed description of the conversation. "If he did rape me, and Drake heard it, he would have heard me fighting and screaming. And if he didn't, do you really think I would have been in the right frame of mind to put myself together to go yell at you?"

She had a point, Connor thought. Her clothes weren't disheveled. The only clue he had was the look in her eyes. She was furious.

Clara put her arms around him, relieved when he did the same.

"When you refused to let me touch you in my office and when I stopped over, I immediately thought of abuse victims. And you wouldn't talk, so my mind went into overdrive. I'm sorry. After they arrested him, he talked about you as if he were familiar with your body. Anyone listening to him talk would believe there was something between you. If you heard him describe it in detail, even you would have believed him. I mean, he knew about the birthmark on your left butt cheek. How the hell would he know that?"

"Connor," Clara stepped back. "I don't have a birthmark on my left butt cheek."

"Really?" He surprised himself with his own doubt.

"I thought you said I did a strip tease that night," Clara commented.

"Yeah, you did."

"Did I take it all off?"

"I actually looked away when you stripped off the pants," Connor admitted. "And every time you flash your bottom with your thong on, it's pretty dark."

"I don't flash my bottom," Clara declared.

"Well actually, you have. When you walk around with a night shirt or nightie, it flows up when you move just right," Connor admitted with an appreciative grin. He pulled out his cell to text Joe and Matt:

"Clara doesn't have birthmark on her ass"

"He's having sex with someone and pretending she's you," Connor concluded.

should have caught on sooner   349

"Now it makes sense why the sheriff didn't believe me," Clara stated.

"Hell, I believed him. Eric was so convincing," Connor answered.

Joe read his text and reported to his father and brother, "Clara doesn't have a birthmark on her ass."

"How did he not know before?" Tony asked.

"He did mention they were taking it slow. Clara thought she was married and then her husband died. Connor must be slipping up and losing his moves," Anthony commented.

"They have always been close. He was never inappropriate, just like an older brother keeping an eye on her. He would bring her home from the park by giving her piggyback rides. Connor kept the bullies away from her and her friends. Their relationship started to evolve when she moved back this spring. Sorry, Bro," Joe teased as he slapped his brother's shoulders.

"Why would he care?" Tony asked.

"Because he had the biggest crush on Clara in high school," Joe informed their dad.

"That was over twelve years ago," the younger brother stated thoughtfully as he searched for a file on the table before him. "But you know who does have a birthmark on her ass? Specifically, her left cheek?"

"Lauren McDonald," Anthony announced when no one answered. "We now also have him lying in a murder investigation." He placed the autopsy report down on the table when both his brother and father remained staring at him. Both were concerned with how quickly the younger brother made the connection so quickly, until he pointed to the file.

Both Joe and Tony looked down at the report and back up at Anthony, "Were you guys thinking I slept with her?"

Connor and Clara sat together on the sofa, catching up on the last two days. He explained there had been an increase in turnover of staff in the last six months. Eric was given a longer leash when Matt had stepped back behind the scenes. Up until her death, Beth, Rachel's mother, oversaw everything as the director of nursing. Once she was no longer around, everyone believed Eric became more laxed in protocol. The sheriff's department is currently trying to locate the individuals who left to investigate their reasons for leaving.

"I didn't think it was unusual for frequent turnover in staff. At the trauma center, people were constantly coming and going, especially the lower paying jobs," Clara commented.

"True, but in the city, people have more options. If they don't like their current facility because the boss is constantly on their back or they broke up with the person that got them the job, it's easier to move on to something else," Connor explained. "Here, if you really did quit, where would you work? You don't have many options, you'd have to move. Moving their family makes most people think twice before quitting."

"I did actually quit," Clara confirmed.

"You know what I mean."

"I haven't decided if I want to return. I may want to renegotiate my contract first," she announced.

"What more could you possibly want? You are getting more equipment and a bigger department," Connor argued.

"I haven't decided what exactly I want. Like I said, I need to review my hiring contract." She paused when Connor continued to look at her. He was trying to decide if she was playing with him.

"Who signed the contract?"

"Just Eric and I," Clara answered. "It seemed like a standard agreement, my salary, job duties, benefits, and PTO. I'll show you later. I am heading upstairs to bed."

She brought the glasses and bottle into the kitchen. Connor followed her, assuring the doors from the kitchen were locked.

Once in her bedroom, Clara went into the bathroom to put on her pajamas. When she came out, she kissed him on the cheek and said goodnight. He pulled her back towards him, kissing her more deeply.

Clara was feeling overwhelmed as his tongue touched hers and his hands pulled her in close. She debated pulling back or letting it play out. She became breathless as his one hand was caressing her back, and the other was slowly working toward her breast.

Connor felt a slight change in Clara as he tested the waters. He pulled back and smiled down at her. Her face was flushed, and she did respond to his touch, but she was still conflicted. He kissed her forehead and walked into the bathroom.

When he returned, Clara was already asleep in the bed. He curled up beside her and smiled when she held his hand to her chest and leaned back into him. Connor surprised himself by immediately falling asleep.

it's the man!

The next morning, the sun was shining and it was warm enough to wear shorts. Summer appeared to officially arrive. The children were happy to see Connor in the kitchen as Reese pulled up a chair to assist with making breakfast. Clara with Hailey in her lap sat at the table while they watched.

Reese was telling Connor all about the Foxwood Farm and how he was going to go riding. He was very excited about the day ahead.

Connor looked over at Clara as the food was brought over, "Sounds like you all have a very busy and fun day ahead. I just have a busy day."

"Do you want to come with us? Then you can have fun too!" The young boy offered.

"I really appreciate the offer Buddy, but I have to work. It's probably going to be a busy weekend," Connor explained.

Connor left immediately after breakfast. He needed to stop at his place before he headed to work. Clara was sitting in the family room with the children when Shannon arrived. Reese again explained about the day ahead, inviting her as well.

Shannon laughed at his excitement, "Maybe I will stop in later. Are you packing extra clothes to stay the night?"

Clara laughed, "The invite was from Rob, not Lila. I am not spending the night with him."

"No, but I can text Lila. We can all hang out tonight on the porch, just like the old days," Shannon suggested as she sent out a text.

When they arrived at the Foxwood Farms, Rob was just exiting the barn. Both Reese and Hailey were excited. As soon as their feet touched the ground, both children were running towards him. Rob laughed when each child hugged his legs. He squatted down in greeting. When he stood back up, he had a child in each arm. His steel blue eyes admired Clara, dressed in a small print sundress that showed off her strong shoulders and legs.

"Hi Clara, you look good," Rob greeted as she leaned up to kiss his cheek. She smiled in answer but couldn't get a word in as Reese and Hailey were both talking excitedly.

"You want to get lunch or go see the horses?"

"Horses!" Reese yelled.

"Heehee," Hailey said.

Rob and Clara both looked at her, she neighed again, sounding just like a horse.

"Then horses it is," Rob agreed as he lowered the kids down, watching as they ran ahead of them towards the barn. Rob placed an arm around her shoulder as they followed. "I hope you brought a change of clothes. As much as I appreciate you in a dress, you can't go riding in that."

"The morning was so beautiful and warm, I wanted to wear this," Clara answered with a smile. "I do have a change of clothes but I'm going to stay on the ground with Hailey while you ride with Reese."

"You are a strong enough rider to have one of the kids with you," Rob commented.

"Not anymore. I have only been back once in twelve years. I'm more comfortable with them riding with either you, Chase, or Lila," Clara explained.

"No worries," he agreed as he hugged her with one arm. "I'm the only one here right now so they'll have to take turns. Everything going alright?"

"Yeah, why?" Clara asked.

Rob simply shrugged as he silently assessed a change in her, "I don't know, you just seem different."

Clara turned to him, "Different? Good or bad?"

"Not sure, maybe more relaxed and happier." Then a thought hit him. "Oh, yeah. I guess that will do it."

"What?"

"Connor happened," he stated expertly.

"It's not like you think but is that going to be a problem?" Clara asked. She thought the change was due to less drugs in her system, but she didn't want to get into it now.

"Not at all. If he keeps you happy, I'm happy. I will always be your friend, no matter what. It breaks my heart, but I will wait until tonight to cry myself to sleep," Rob stated as he placed his hand over his heart.

"Rob, hurry up!" Reese called out.

A couple of hours later, Clara was assisting Rob with the preparations for lunch. The children were sitting at the table coloring when Reese happened to glance at the morning paper.

"Mommy, it's the man that pushed you!" Reese yelled, pointing to the picture of a man in his young twenties. Per the newspaper article, he was found dead in the federal park the morning before.

"Someone pushed you?" Rob asked, thinking something else happened more recently.

"Just that one time when I was in the hospital and the kids stayed with you," Clara answered as she went over to read the article. Rob pulled out his cell to call the sheriff.

Within the hour, Sheriff Mancuso and his son Joe arrived. He was

it's the man!   355

carrying a collage of six photos, all men with similar hair, coloring, and age. He greeted everyone before asking if he could talk with Reese. Clara nodded.

Joe watched as Clara, pretty as a flower, sat beside her son with her daughter in her lap. The toddler was fighting sleep. Foxwood was standing behind her with a hand on her shoulder. They appeared to be comfortable together, as they did back in high school. But his brother swears they were never a couple back then. But now, Joe thought, Connor had some serious competition.

The sheriff sat in a chair next to the little boy. "Reese, how are you doing?"

"Good. I got to ride the horse today and we might go for another ride later after Hailey takes a nap. I don't think I should take one because I am older, but we will see," he answered as he continued with his coloring, using his mother's phrase even though he didn't understand what it meant.

The sheriff chuckled. "Reese, do you remember when your mother fell down the stairs at home?"

Reese held up the crayon as he corrected the sheriff, "Mommy didn't fall. A man pushed her."

It was the perfect opening, he thought as he placed the collage in front of the boy, "Do you recognize any of these people."

The boy's green eyes looked over each picture and he nodded his head. Without prompting, he answered, pointing at each picture as he talked, "Of course, that's the mailman, the man that puts the food in our bags at the store, he lives down the street in the gray house and drives a fun red car, that's the one that pushed Mommy down the stairs, I don't know this one, and that guy works at the breakfast place and I don't like him."

Rob couldn't help but let out a snort when Reese announced he didn't like the last man.

Sheriff Mancuso was impressed with the boy's answers, but he couldn't resist asking, "Why don't you like that guy?"

Reese had already returned to his coloring as he shrugged with his answer. "He has a mean smile."

Joe and Tony exchanged looks that suggested they would talk about that last part later.

"Reese has a good eye for details, Clara," Joe commented.

The sheriff nodded in agreement and thanked the boy for his time. Clara, carrying a sleeping Hailey on her shoulder, walked with Rob to escort the gentlemen to the door.

"And Clara, as far as I know, the rest of the men are law abiding citizens. We only have their pictures because they have a similar makeup to the one in question. As I'm sure you realize, he was found in the park yesterday by Dallas Thompson. Since it was on federal land, the FBI has jurisdiction. However, we now have a lead to further investigate the incident at your place. Do you recall anything more since we last talked?" Sheriff Mancuso inquired.

Clara replied, "I know who he is, he worked in the kitchen at the nursing home. Why would he be in my house? We never talked beyond a casual hello."

"We don't really know at this time," Joe answered.

Once they were in their cruiser, his father stated, "Normally I wouldn't be so happy to have a case turned over to the FBI, but now I am relieved this man was found on federal land. He had a couple of interesting cash deposits and a connection to the nursing home with Eric. Eric is currently a suspect in this murder, and we have a lead on the attack at Clara's."

Joe nodded his agreement. The new murder charges would help bring Eric's case to the federal level. Leander Howell, the current mayor and previous prosecuting attorney, was fighting to keep the case local where he thought he had pull. He believed he could get the case against his son dismissed.

"What about the last guy in the picture, Danny Thompson?" He asked his father as he steered back towards town.

"Interesting, wasn't it?" Tony chuckled. "We should take the family to the diner and see what happens. Then on Monday, we can quietly look at his background. Didn't you go to school with him?"

"I think Danny Thompson was a year ahead of Anthony," Joe stated, thinking back to the expression on Foxwood's face when he saw the picture. He remembered there was some long family history between the Foxwoods and the Thompsons.

That evening, Connor was sitting at his spot at the bar while he waited for Devan to bring his beer. It had been a busy day, taking all the patients' blood samples and answering questions. Much of the staff was hesitant about consenting. Matt was present to assure them and to answer questions, especially the ones regarding Eric's sexual misconduct.

As it turned out, there were a few younger women that did come forward with comments. Connor had not been given the details yet, as Matt was too pissed off to discuss it at the time. He was currently holed up in his office doing research. He suspected the facility's accounts were being reviewed.

Devan came over with Connor's beer. "Busy day?"

Connor simply nodded as he sipped his beer.

"Have you talked with Clara today?" Devan asked as he looked over his shoulder to assure privacy.

"Not since this morning, why?" Connor's attention was captured.

"You are aware she and the kids were at the Foxwood farm, right?" He asked, noting the irritated nod. "Well, apparently the little guy recognized a face in the newspaper. Reese identified him as the man that pushed Clara down the stairs. The guy was found dead at the park by Dallas Thompson. Did you know he's a park ranger? Anyway, he had been reported missing by his mother that same weekend."

"What was his name?"

"Billy Kingsley," Devan answered as he watched Connor's face. Devan decided to keep to himself the comments Joe made as he had described the scene in the kitchen with Clara, Rob, and the children. Joe said Rob was standing protectively close to Clara. He said they looked like a family with Rob and the kids' blonde hair all close in color. He wasn't sure why that comment was made, but knew his cousin was suspicious of something. Honestly, he was surprised Connor was so tolerant of another guy being so close to his girl. Of course, maybe she wasn't his yet if he wasn't aware of the birthmark, he thought. Connor was certainly taking his time.

"Damn, how did I not hear about this at work? He worked in the kitchen and his mother is a nurses' aide with the night shift. She called off last night," Connor commented as he pulled out his cell to send Clara a text. He was annoyed when she didn't immediately respond. "How was he killed?"

"His neck was sliced open," he answered quietly. The cause of death was being kept under wraps.

"Really? By what, a guitar string?" Connor asked, remembering Clara's unusual "you should see the other guy" joke from the night of the incident.

Devan looked surprised at his cousin's question. "Why would you say that?"

Connor shrugged as he explained the conversation with Clara in the hospital.

"Does she have psychic abilities you want to tell me about?" Devan asked.

"Hey man, I almost wonder. Clara's always made weird off the wall comments and predictions, and they are accurate."

Devan's eyes narrowed as he tried to mentally review the report on the cause of death. A guitar string could be the murder weapon, he thought as he stepped away to assist with other customers. When he had a minute, he texted his boss.

it's the man! 359

Despite working full time behind the scenes with the investigation, Devan enjoyed the simplicity of interacting with the town. And on the plus side, he was able to keep his paycheck and tips. Overall, not a bad gig. It kept him in plain sight as his investigation grew from missing people to include drugging, assualt and murder. It also served to remind him not everyone was a bad guy.

When Devan returned, he chuckled at Connor's irked expression as he read a text. Clara and the children were staying overnight at the farm with her friends. Yeah, right. Just one big slumber party with Foxwood, he thought miserably.

"Connor, it really is a girls' night. Shannon is also staying over," Devan tried to be reassuring. The look on his face suggested it did not help. "Don't you trust her?"

"Yes, I trust her, just not him," he grumbled.

Connor spent the evening wallowing in his beer. He realized it was his fault. When Clara told him of her plans to go to the farm for riding, he didn't think much of it. It was something she did as a child with her friends. Connor had been relieved she would be out of her house as he explained he would be working most of the weekend. As it turned out, he finished earlier than he thought he would. Connor had been looking forward to seeing her.

A man sat alone at a table towards the front of the restaurant. He ate his dinner in solitude, seeming to be comfortable as he lengthened his time with coffee. If one had paid him any mind, they would have thought he was lingering for a reason. As if waiting for a blind date that didn't show, but might if he just stayed a little longer. He appeared to be reading on his cell phone, often looking up and around. As the dinner hour ended and the warmer evening seemed to bring out more of the town, he remained sitting alone. It was after ten when he finally gave up and walked out the front door.

• • • •

Evil was pleased to see who was sitting alone at the bar talking with the bartender. It was obvious his Babydoll wasn't planning a trip out tonight. Well, she usually didn't have a habit of going out on Saturday nights. He left a couple of bills on the table as he casually strolled out the door. He first drove out away from town and then turned to the back roads. He returned towards town, avoiding Main Street. He went around the block a few times before he finally parked a few houses down. He slowly sauntered through the shadows. He paused when he arrived at her home, only for a moment as he listened. Hearing only silence, he faded into the home.

He covered his shoes, as always, with surgical booties before he slowly ascended the steps. He was disappointed to find the home empty as he trailed down the hall, finally arriving at her room. He slowly walked around, opening closet doors and dresser drawers, his fingers fondling her items. A look at her clock suggested she was out for the night. He went into the bathroom and studied the tub. It was covered in paint stains, something he would need to take care of when he had more time. Then his eyes moved to the shower. He opened the glass door, seeing her shampoos and body washes, he sighed with a smile.

He turned on the water, removed his clothes, and stepped inside. He washed his hair with her shampoo and cleansed his body with her wash. Enveloped in her scent, he thought of her as he brought himself blissfully over the edge.

When the water began to cool, he stepped out and dried off. He folded his towel to place on the rack and paused as he realized the others were folded improperly. He refolded the towel next to it before he went into the bedroom. He pulled back the covers and snuggled up, happy to be surrounded by her scent. He slept through the remainder of the night, thinking of his girl.

• • • •

She stood in the dark at her bedroom window just after dawn. She sighed with relief when her husband finally pulled into the driveway. It seemed to take him a few minutes to leave his vehicle and enter the home. She debated what to do. Should she go to him or wait for him to come to her?

Years ago, she worried he had found another woman, someone younger and more tolerant of his peculiar appetites. But she discovered the sex was best afterwards and gave in. As long as he remained with her, she would forgive him of any transgression. She slowly made her way into the bathroom. She pulled off her nightie to look at herself in the full length mirror. She worked hard to keep her unforgiving body the same as when she was young. Her dark hair required monthly visits to the salon, she watched the foods she ate, and she did her yoga faithfully every day. Her blue eyes were surrounded by a few wrinkles, but overall, she thought she still looked good.

As she stepped into the shower, she thought of how her family tried to talk her out of her marriage. They said he was too old and carried baggage from the previous marriage, but she laughed it off. She did have concerns a few years in, but he always came back to her. For the past few years, he had closed up, never staying out late and the sex was less frequent. But in the last year, it picked up again. He started to travel to the city more and his aggressive ways were back. When Susannah Hawks' remains were found, her suspicions of her husband's involvement were confirmed. She didn't know details but knew he was involved in her death.

And now someone new has captured his attention. Someone has him as equally mesmerized as he was years before. And she doesn't only suspect this time, she knows. Only one woman can have the same effect on her husband as Susannah Hawks. Her suspicions were confirmed when Clara Noelle returned home. He emerged from his solitude to join her in her bed again. It was their best night to date.

She closed her eyes when she heard him enter the bathroom. A moment later she felt his hands roughly grab her as he stepped behind her. He kissed her neck and whispered in her ear, telling her everything he was going to do to her...

33

her friend margarita

Clara and the children returned home in the early afternoon on Sunday, just in time for the kid's afternoon naps. After they were both in bed, she went into her room, considering a nap as well. But in the bathroom, she paused when she saw the towels folded differently as they hung on the rack. Connor is certainly a little OCD, she thought. He was the last one to shower. Clara chuckled as she grabbed all the towels and carried them downstairs to the washer. She cleaned her bathroom before moving on to her bedroom. She pulled back her comforter and removed the sheets before heading back to the washer. Once back upstairs, she made up the bed, dusted her room, and vacuumed. She wasn't sure where the sudden burst of energy came from, but felt a need to cleanse her room.

Almost two hours later, Connor was standing on her porch knocking on the door. With no answer, he realized the door was unlocked. He entered, captivated at the sight before him.

Clara was in the family room singing "Like A Virgin," and dancing seductively as she dusted. Connor leaned into the doorway and watched with a smile. Damn, she knows how to move, he smiled appreciatively. If he had not known better, he would have wondered if she danced her way through college.

Clara turned around with her eyes closed, swaying her hips to the music, as she sang, "And you're mine, I'll be yours until the end of time, cause you make me feel…"

Clara opened her eyes and immediately stopped when she realized Connor was watching her.

Connor chuckled as she blushed with embarrassment. He slowly walked towards her as he asked, "Don't stop now, how do I make you feel?"

"What makes you think I'm singing about you?" She asked boldly, reaching for her phone to stop the music.

Connor grabbed her hand and twirled her, not really to the music. When he pulled her towards his chest, he leaned down to kiss her. He let his lips linger on hers as he slowly deepened it, delighted with her response. When the next song came on, he kept one hand on her low back and grabbed her hand as he led her into a dance.

"So, if you weren't singing about me, then who? The boyfriend?" Connor wondered out loud.

"That's not even funny," she responded as she fell into rhythm.

At dinner time, Connor took over the task of preparing the meal. He grilled the chicken and vegetables out on the deck. He watched as the children ran around in the fenced in yard. Clara was inside finishing the laundry. Once the towels were replaced in the bathroom, Clara looked around her room and realized the anxiety she felt earlier was gone.

As they sat out on the deck eating, Reese informed Connor of everything that occurred over the last two days, including the visit from the sheriff, what everyone ate, and where they all slept. He described the horses and gave details of the rides. He rode with Chase on a brown and white horse while Hailey rode with Rob on an all brown one.

"What about Mommy," Connor asked. "Didn't she ride?"

"No, she was sitting on the porch with her friend margarita," Reese explained.

Connor turned to Clara and laughed. He realized as he listened, he had overreacted the evening before. And if he ever had any doubt, he just needed to listen to Reese. The kid talked constantly and told it exactly as he perceived it.

After dinner, Connor was called into the hospital. He gave her a kiss as he apologized for eating and running.

"Will you be back tonight?" Clara asked.

"Do you want me to?"

She nodded as she went to a drawer and returned with a key. He glanced at it before he kissed her, "I don't know how late I will be."

"That's alright. I don't know if I'll be awake." She responded.

too much too soon?

The following Wednesday afternoon, Clara was rereading the text from Dallas. He was confirming the first volleyball match started at seven and he was recommending they all meet up at six. He asked who would be the sixth player. Shannon had reminded her that both Chase and Rob were out of town picking up Rachel, and assisting with her move back home. She suggested Connor.

As if it were so simple, Clara thought. She really liked him, but he made her nervous and second guessed herself. She was hesitant with letting things progress between them. She wasn't comfortable with the term relationship. Clara sighed. Maybe she was in a relationship with Connor. As a young girl, she used to fantasize about being his girlfriend, something she never shared with anyone. Connor was over most nights, always seemed to understand how far he could go, and sensed when to pull back without her saying anything or making it awkward. Clara had an ongoing internal debate, was it too soon?

Though he never said it, Clara sensed Connor was annoyed she spent the night at the farm, realizing Rob was probably the issue. She had never seen the jealous side of Connor before and knew she would have to talk with him sooner rather than later. But for now, she needed to ask him about volleyball tonight.

Clara looked at the clock, she knew he was still here at the nursing home. She sighed as she went upstairs to search for him. As she was heading down the hall, a patient's yelling caught her attention. When she peeked into his room, he was staggering as he attempted to walk across the room before he collapsed onto the floor.

Clara called out for the nurse as she rushed into the room. She noted immediately he wasn't breathing nor could she find a pulse. She instructed the nurse entering the room to call 911 and get a crash cart while she repositioned him onto his back and initiated CPR.

While the one nurse was on the phone, another ran in with the crash cart. She opened the AED and pulled out the electrodes while a CNA cut open his shirt. The nurse placed the electrodes on his chest and turned on the machine.

After a moment, the machine stated, "Shock is advised."

The nurse stated, "Everyone back, clear."

Clara leaned back onto her heels as she lifted her hands up, "Clear!"

"Resume chest compressions!" The machine instructed after giving the shock.

Clara continued another round while the nurse controlled the breathing apparatus.

Connor had heard the code being called and was standing at the doorway with Josh watching the scene before him. He was impressed that everyone understood what to do and was doing it correctly.

When Clara finished the set, the machine instructed, "Stop compressions."

"Clara, hold up." Connor was suddenly on the other side of the patient, touching his neck to confirm there was a pulse. "He's back. Good job everyone."

Connor pulled out his stethoscope and listened to the man's lungs. He completed a quick assessment just as the paramedics arrived. He listened to Clara explain to the note taker what happened before providing instructions. He was immediately on his phone to the hospital, giving orders to have the patient directly admitted under his care. He followed the paramedics and the patient out the front entrance. When Connor returned to the lobby, Clara was sitting alone in a chair. He walked over and squatted in front of her with his hand on her knees. "Clara?"

Her green eyes were close to tears as they met his brown.

Connor stood up then sat down beside her with an arm around her. "Sweetheart, you did a great job. You saved him and brought him back. I am proud of you."

He noted her hands were shaking and explained to her it was the adrenaline still in her system. He sat with her for a moment before talking again, "Why were you up here? It's after four, you're usually gone by now."

"I was looking for you."

He grinned at her answer. After another moment of silence, he stated, "You found me."

She didn't respond, always like pulling teeth with her, he thought, "Clara, why are you looking for me?"

"I came to ask you if you wanted to be on our volleyball team. The first match is tonight," she answered softly into his chest.

"At the Shack?" He smiled when he felt her head nod. Connor debated before he asked, "Who is on the team?"

"Does it matter?"

"Hell yeah," he answered.

When Clara listed off the players for the evening, Connor thought the team was impressive. He realized they had planned this when everyone was at her place the other night, "What about the boyfriend?"

Clara pulled back to look at his face and sighed, reminding her she still needed to talk about Rob. Keeping it simple she explained, "Rob and Chase went to the city last night to help Rachel with the move back."

"So, I'm just a last minute thought?" He teased.

"Not really but we are meeting at six and I need to get going. Are you interested or not? We can all probably ride together."

"Sure, I'm interested, but I'll drive separately in case I get called in tonight. I'll pick you up," he explained as they both stood up.

Clara nodded her head, "Just text me when you're on your way. We'll probably eat dinner after the game."

She turned to walk away but Connor grabbed her hand to pull her back. As he leaned down to kiss her, he stated, "Seriously, good job today."

He chuckled as her green eyes flared up.

At home, Clara was ready to go. Michelle, the babysitter, was sitting with the kids eating dinner when there was a knock on the front door. She answered it just as Shannon was heading down the stairs.

"Are you ladies ready? I want to get there and do some warm-up drills," Devan announced from the doorway. His eyes were assessing Shannon appreciatively as she approached wearing shorts and a light green tank. She greeted him with a kiss.

"I am all ready, Dev. Clara is going to ride with Connor," she explained.

Clara followed them out as Connor pulled into the driveway.

He watched as she climbed into her seat and secured the seatbelt. When her eyes finally met his, she realized he was watching her. "What?" She asked.

Connor leaned toward her, gesturing she do the same. When they were close enough, he leaned over and kissed her on the lips. He grinned as he backed out and drove. "Now we are ready."

"Connor," Clara started to say but paused. What does she want to say? She found herself once again flooded with mixed emotions. Every time he touched her or kissed her, she either tensed with guilt or relaxed with happiness.

"Clara," Connor interrupted as he grabbed her hand to reassure her, "It was just a simple kiss to let you know I am happy to see you. Nothing more."

He had planned to kiss her hand, but Connor felt her tense up. Instead, he released it before she could pull her hand away. He changed to a more comfortable topic, "How are the kids doing today?"

"Good," she answered. How does he do that, Clara wondered. It was like he knew what she needed before she did. She was hesitant and awkward, but Connor always put her at ease. She sighed before she stated, "Reese wants you to remove his training wheels."

"Yeah? Do you think he's ready?" He glanced over and saw her shrug sadly, "Are you ready? You know he will likely fall a few times before he gets his balance."

Clara nodded as she remembered riding her bike with her father running along beside her in case she fell. Those seemed like easier and simpler times. It reminded her that Reese wouldn't have similar memories of his father. She wiped a tear away as she remained silent.

Connor noted the tears and pulled over to the side of the road. He reached for her, and held her as she silently cried. He debated what the issue was. He was leaning towards the fact he was pushing too much too soon, as she was still dealing with the grief of Jason's death. Connor had to remind himself that not a lot of time had passed. But she seemed to be dealing with it, he thought, or is she?

"Clara? Anything you want to say?"

She simply stated, "I'm sorry to be crying all over you."

Clara pulled back and started to wipe her tears away. Connor gently tugged her back, cradling her face in his hands as his thumbs wiped the tears, "You never need to apologize for what you're feeling. I shouldn't be pushing you. I am the one that should be apologizing to you. I'm sorry. We have something between us, no denying it. I am content with things as they are. We keep it simple and move forward as you're ready, alright?"

When Clara nodded with her head still in his hands, Connor leaned down to kiss her forehead and without thinking, he kissed her quickly on the lips. He lowered his hands as he asked if she still wanted to head to the game.

She nodded as she pulled down the visor to check her appearance in the mirror, "Don't worry, you are still Beautiful."

When the game started, Clara was up first to serve the ball. It went beautifully over the net and landed in the middle of the court. The other team, never having played together and with already one to two drinks in, simply watched the ball fly into the air, over the net and onto the ground in the center of the court.

Clara was up to serve again, this time someone did bump it, but it smashed into the net and landed on the wrong side. The third time she served, it finally returned over the net, but Dallas blocked the ball. During the fourth serve, it flew back with Lila calling it, bumping it up while Clara called it and tapped it with a set. She called it to Shannon, who spiked it over the net.

They won the first game, 15 to 2, as well as the second game, 15 to 1. Devan was so excited to be on the winning team he offered to pay for the first round and dinner. Once everyone was at the table toasting to the first won match, Dallas finally explained the girls played high school volleyball together. They brought the team to the state finals two years in a row.

"Why didn't you tell me?" He looked first at Shannon and then his cousin. They just laughed and shrugged as they sipped their drinks.

After dinner, Shannon wanted to sing karaoke. She and Lila went up to inquire and get the song list.

Sitting next to Clara, Dallas asked if she was going to sing. She shook her head, "I don't sing in public."

Connor nodded in agreement. He knew she was very self-conscious, being hearing impaired. She could sing, he heard her many times, when she thought she was alone. However, she became too self-conscious when others were around. Plus, she didn't always know the correct words, setting herself up for more embarrassment.

"Never?" Dallas challenged.

"Maybe if I have had too many shots, I might get pulled up with them but otherwise, no. They are able to sing. Rachel is really good," Clara confirmed.

"Clara saved a life today," Connor announced. He had thought to shift the attention but embarrassed her more. He laughed when she glared up at him before telling the story.

Dallas watched the interaction between the two, they were comfortable. When Connor was finished, Dallas praised her, "Clara that's great! You saved the guy!"

Connor watched as Dallas gave her a brotherly hug.

"I was just doing my job," Clara stated, hating the attention.

"I'm proud of you. Not a lot of people respond and do what needs to be done. You did everything correctly and brought him back. Awesome," Dallas stated.

Connor found he liked the guy. Dallas acted as an older brother would and noted they were both comfortable with each other. It surprised him to see Carl Gibson's children so hard working and successful in life. He struggled to find positive traits the man possessed, reminding himself certain traits often skipped generations. That made him think of his relatives.

Shannon and Lila returned all excited, talking about what songs were on the list.

Clara sat back and enjoyed herself as her friends went up to sing.

She wasn't aware of being watched with disdain as someone from Connor's past became envious and anger grew silently each time Connor touched her…

Why is he still so smitten with the woman? How has she kept his attention for so long while he continued to ignore her?

35 time to head home

Six hours away in the city, Daniel Emerson rolled his eyes at his wife as he listened to his sister on speaker phone. His wife was smart enough to remain quiet as she patted his hand encouragingly. He had been expecting the call, and was surprised she waited this long. She still didn't grasp the bigger picture.

"Daniel, you have to do something to help, he's your nephew," Kathleen Emerson Howell desperately pleaded.

Dan was relieved it was over the phone and not in person. He was grateful she was too lazy to drive herself down to the city. "Kath, what do you expect me to do?"

"Get the charges dropped! Haven't you been listening? Last week they accused him of drugging the girl and sexual harassment! This week they are talking about murder charges. Eric needs someone to step in and take his case. Matthew won't even take my calls," she complained.

His son was obviously smarter than him, Dan thought, relieved he was mostly retired. He had recently stepped back in the law firm. He continued to monitor operations of the city branch while Matt ran the smaller branch in town. He also looked over everyone's shoulder at the nursing home. He sighed as he prayed for patience and repeated the question, "What do you expect me to do? From what I heard, he openly admitted to drugging and sexual misconduct."

"He was coerced into saying it!" The voice screeched from the speaker.

"He yelled it inside Memories. Half the town heard it," Dan replied in a patient tone.

"Eric would never have willingly said anything if Connor didn't put him up to it. Bad enough he is also sleeping with that slut. Connor is ridiculously jealous of his little cousin. I mean really Daniel, if Shelby Hawks were alive right now to see how far her family has fallen! Daniel, please help us here," Kathleen pleaded again. It never dawned on her that she was insulting her brother's son.

"Kath, we keep going around in circles here. I have no control in the matter. I am not in a position to take his case. Last I heard, it is in the hands of the federal courts," Dan slowly explained, using the tone he used in the courtroom when he addressed the jury.

"Well, could you at least talk to those sons of yours? Make them understand the situation?"

"Kath, I promise you, if I don't talk to them tonight, I will call them first thing tomorrow morning. I need to go now. I have another call coming in. It could be Matt." Dan's hand tapped the end button to disconnect the call. He groaned out loud as he looked over at his wife. "I need to start screening my calls better."

"Are you really going to call the boys?" Heather asked.

"Yes, I said I would, didn't I? She wants me to make sure they understand the situation and I will. I want them to understand our facility does not tolerate sexual harassment. Administering drugs to another person without their knowledge is unspeakable. Do not even get me started on the dispensing of drugs without a proper prescription. What the hell was he thinking? Those drugs have serious side effects that require ongoing monitoring with blood tests and therapy. Eric doesn't have the proper background to understand the medications he was playing with. He couldn't follow in his grandfather's footsteps to be a pharmacist because he couldn't pass the basic chemistry classes. Connor was right to have doubts about the kid being in the administrator's office. We should have found a different position for him. This is partly my fault for allowing him to be in the position.

"As for the murder charge, I honestly don't believe Eric did it. He's too lazy and has never processed through a situation. He used to whine about carrying wood inside for the fireplace, for heaven's sakes! How would he have carried a body that far into the forest? He doesn't even go into the woods as it is. I don't believe it for an instant. And if I am correct, then the evidence will show it. Anyone would be able to clear him of the murder charge. I am glad this is out of our hands and in the federal courts. If all this is true, holy shit!"

His wife nodded in agreement, even after almost forty years of being in the family, the differences in her husband and his younger sister still amazed her. They were raised in the same household by the same set of parents, but both had different sets of values and priorities. Her mother-in-law blamed it on gender roles as they were growing up and her wild, rebellious teenage years. Her mind drifted to her own offspring. She had been convinced Connor would never settle down and now he is with Clara Noelle, the little girl from next door?

"When did Connor and Clara start seeing each other? Did you know about this?" Heather asked.

Dan simply shook his head, "Matt assured me they just started seeing each other, maybe in the last couple of weeks. Said they were just getting close. He doesn't believe they've been intimate yet."

"How would he know?" Heather wondered out loud. She knew the age difference between her son and stepson brought tension between the brothers. Matt was the last person Connor would confide in, especially regarding details of his relationships.

"He said Connor wasn't even aware that she didn't have a birthmark on her bottom," Dan stated as he explained the comment. When he finished he said, "I know you want to head back into town, but I think we should stay here in the city, keep our distance unless the boys need us closer."

Heather squeezed her husband's hand as she agreed, "Have you talked to either one of the boys today?"

"Yeah, I spoke to Connor briefly. He was heading to a volleyball game. Apparently, he and Devan are playing with Clara and her friends. He's keeping a close eye on her." Dan didn't mention Devan was seeing Clara's friend Shannon.

"Volleyball?" Heather's brown eyes widened in surprise. Maybe Clara is what her son needed. Hopefully, she could also get him to enjoy his beautiful lake house. "Well, if Connor and Devan are both playing volleyball, they must not be too concerned."

Ten blocks north, Rachel MacKenzie was slowly walking around her apartment to make sure she had everything. She was staring out the window one last time when Chase returned.

He gave her a minute before he said, "We have everything all packed and secured in the truck. We are ready when you are."

Rachel turned around and nodded as she sighed, "Yeah. Time to head home."

Chase stepped out into the hall as she locked up the apartment. He grabbed her hand as they headed down the stairs. She dropped her key into a box before they walked outside.

"It's close to rush hour. If we try to leave now, we will just be sitting in traffic. Why not get dinner first?" Rob suggested. They both agreed.

"What are you guys in the mood for?" Rachel asked.

"Your last night, you choose," Chase answered.

"Well, we can get American at home, as well as Chinese, and Italian. How about Korean? There's a place right around the corner. We can leave the truck here and walk," she said as she looked between the cousins. When they both nodded, she linked her arms with theirs as they strolled down the street.

After they ordered, Rachel asked about the latest happenings at home. Rob and Chase took turns telling her about the latest incident involving Clara and Eric. Chase noticed that Rob skipped over the details a bit regarding the doctor. The topic shifted to Reese identifying the man found dead in the park as the one in Clara's home. Rachel was absolutely shocked at learning Eric was a suspect.

"Wow! I don't believe it! I grew up next to him! You guys really think he's a killer?" Rachel asked.

"Who knows? I'm still struggling with the drugging thing," Chase stated.

"He's always had a thing for Clara, even in high school. I warned her about him," Rob stated.

"Yeah, you warned her about him and every other guy in the school," Chase commented.

"But seriously, you guys really think Eric is a killer? Neighbors always say the killers were quiet and kept to themselves. He is anything but. I don't think he did it. He's not smart enough," Rachel decided. "Plus, he's lazy. I don't see him carrying a body and digging a hole, he would get sweaty."

"Yeah, whoever the killer is was not even smart enough to hide the body better," Rob stated as he sipped his coffee.

Chase laughed as he nodded in agreement. As they were finishing up, he leaned back next to Rachel with his arm stretched out on the back of the booth. When a man came up to the table, Chase's arm fell possessively down around her shoulders.

"Rachel! I am so glad to run into you! I thought the movers were coming today," the man asked.

"Max, hi!" Rachel acknowledged cheerfully. "These are my friends from home, Chase and Rob Foxwood. Guys, this is Max Kaufmann."

Rob stood up to pay the bill, he shook hands with Max before heading to the cashier. Chase reluctantly stood up to shake hands and join his cousin, to give Rachel a few minutes with her friend.

When Rob glanced back while returning his wallet to his back pocket, he saw Max reach out to touch her face before he leaned down to kiss her. Oh shit, he thought as he stepped in front of his cousin, body blocking him. Not one to make a scene in public, Chase was forced to step outside.

"Who the hell does this guy think he is?" Chase demanded.

"Chase, Rachel's a beautiful girl. She's bound to have many admirers but she's LEAVING this city and heading home with us tonight. We aren't likely to see the guy again."

Chase seemed appeased but when he peeked into the window, they were still kissing, "I can't believe she's letting the guy kiss her like that in public. What the hell do you think they've been doing in private?"

Rob glanced over his shoulder, careful to keep between his cousin and the door, "Don't let him rattle you. He's only attempting one last time to win her over. If she really felt anything for him, wouldn't he be the one assisting her with the move home, not you?"

Max Kauffman was two years younger than Rachel. They met over a year ago when she decided to join a gym. The membership provided six free sessions with a personal trainer. Max was her trainer. He fell fast for the beautiful girl with long blonde hair and baby blue eyes. She was soft spoken and always in an easy go lucky mood. Once she completed her free sessions, he scheduled his personal work out times to coordinate with when she would be at the gym. Their relationship progressed to a drink post-workout at the juice bar, to casual coffee dates down the street, and finally she agreed to be his date for his cousin's wedding. Max had a great time but afterwards, Rachel declined the invitation to his apartment. Rachel never invited him to hers. She explained, many times, she wasn't interested in anything serious and preferred they remain as friends.

Max accepted the challenge, even thrived on it.

Until her mother died unexpectedly.

He was heartbroken when he couldn't be at her side during the week when she likely needed him the most. He thought for sure Rachel would return in need of his comfort. Max was more than happy to provide it. He was counting down the hours until she returned to the city. Instead, she delayed seeing him for another week. She shocked him by not needing his manly comfort and again declined the invitation to his apartment. And then she announced she was returning to her hometown.

Rachel was the only woman to change the rules of the game. He felt a panic unlike anything he ever felt before. He could not lose this challenge. The clock was ticking down until she left permanently. Max was so close a few weeks back. He had a whole casual day planned with her. Then he would pretend to get a call from a friend for a free dinner. She would need to stop by her place to change before they went. He had it all planned out, reservations and everything. But then she canceled. Claimed her friends were coming to stay while they all went to a memorial service. Or so she said. He knew differently.

Max was always suspicious she had an on-again off-again relationship with someone from home. Rachel always denied it. Said she was returning home to be closer to her grandmother. While that was probably true, he saw her walking out that weekend with a guy, holding hands and acting all comfortable with him. Max knew she was holding out on him.

But when he saw her sitting there comfortably with two guys, one sitting close to her as she laughed with them, the guy's gray eyes gave it away. They had something going on. When he kissed Rachel, his reaction proved his theory. But don't worry Rachel, I never walk away from an accepted challenge until it has been met. And you are still unconquered.

Rachel allowed him to hold her hand as he led her towards the front of the restaurant. Before they exited, he paused and turned towards her. "Rachel, stay the night. One last night," Max pleaded as he looked into her blue eyes, gently moving a strand of hair from her face. "We can spend one last night on the town together. I will drive you home in the morning."

"Max, we've been through this before. I need to get back home with grandmother and these guys are my ride. They have my stuff. I need to be with them so they can unload the truck. You take care," she squeezed his hand as she continued out the door.

Max had no choice but to shake their hands and wish them a good trip before he walked away. It was everything he could do to not look back to see if she was watching him. He could feel her eyes on his back, he smiled. This challenge was definitely the hardest, but he was up to it. It would require more than he's ever given with his previous challenges, but Rachel would be worth it. The reward would be like nothing he's ever experienced before.

As it turned out, Rachel didn't turn to watch Max walk away. She literally did not give him another thought as she latched onto Chase's arm and asked if the guys were ready for the drive home.

During the long ride, Rachel sat between Rob and Chase. They continued their easy talk and bantering. Everyone was comfortable when the cab grew quiet.

"Rachel, we're approaching a rest area, do you need to stop?" Chase asked.

"Yeah, I better," she agreed. "I might even get a coffee."

When she came out of the ladies' room, Chase was standing nearby with a tray of coffee, "You still drink with two creams and two sugars, right?"

Rachel smiled as she accepted the coffee. When they returned to the truck, Chase opened the door and assisted her up. Once he was settled in, Rob started on his leg of the drive.

Rachel enjoyed her coffee as she listened to the cousins discuss employee issues on the farm. She leaned into Chase's side as she thought of the farm. She was reminded of a time when she was a teenager, staying the night with Lila. All four girls were camping out in the sunroom playing truth or dare. They were supposed to be working on their summer reading. Rachel was the only one who had a book within reach. When it was her turn, she tried to skip and opened her book. She hated the game. She was always too embarrassed to give the truth, stupid questions every time, but the dares always made her nervous. Rachel never liked getting caught.

This time, she somehow got roped into a dare. To this day, she still can't believe she even agreed to it. They dared Rachel to walk alone, to the old cabin in the woods and return. They would know if she made it all the way as Shannon had conveniently left her friendship bracelet on the table inside.

When Rachel left the sunroom, it was still daylight, but dusk was approaching. She felt a bit of panic when she reached the ravine. That was when she knew without a doubt. She was lost. The ravine was nowhere near the old cabin. Just as she decided to cross it, the storm arrived. It was fast and sudden, darkening the sky so much it appeared to be midnight. When Rachel got to the bottom, the water was quickly rising, turning the ravine into a river with fast rapids. She was trying to climb up the other side of the ravine when she was pulled into the rapids. She finally understood the term flash flood.

Never really a strong swimmer, Rachel began to panic as she tried to swim towards the riverbank and grab onto the roots. She was confident she was going to die with her body never to be found, all because she had no sense of direction. If she did, she would never have been anywhere near the ravine.

Then she thought she heard her name. When Rachel looked back, Chase was swimming up behind her. He had one arm around her waist as he continued to swim towards the nearest bank. When he was able to grab onto a root, he pulled her over, instructing her to grab onto the roots and pull herself up. Chase remained behind her, catching her the few times she lost her footing. When they reached the top, he climbed further up the hill, pulling her with him. He found a spot under a large boulder, almost like a shallow cave, to protect them from the storm.

Once they were settled out of the pouring rain, Chase shouted, "What the hell are you doing out here by yourself in the storm?"

"Don't cuss at me. You know I don't like it," Rachel snapped back.

Chase just rolled his eyes. Always prim and proper, their Rachel was. He had been surprised when the foreman told him Rachel left the house alone. Because it made no sense for her to be walking up the trail towards the mountain top, Chase decided to follow her. When he finally caught up, he was horrified to see she was being pulled into the flooding ravine.

"Well?" When Rachel started to cry, Chase almost felt bad. Almost. He placed an arm around her as he realized she was probably more terrified than he was. He was a strong swimmer and knew his way around the woods. Rachel was the weakest swimmer in the group, not an insult, just a simple fact. She also had the worst sense of direction. She could not point out west if the sun were setting.

"I'm sorry! I didn't want to play but they made me! I didn't want to answer a stupid question, so I picked a dare! They made me go to the old cabin and return again," Rachel sobbed.

"Why didn't you just cheat?"

When she simply looked at him, Chase explained, "Go into the woods and hide for an hour and then come back."

"Because I had to get a bracelet left on the table to prove I actually went to the old cabin," she cried again.

Chase shook his head in disbelief. The girls were tight, but they were cruel when they played this game. He and Rob always left the group when the game was even suggested. He tightened his hold on her as she cried.

"Are we going to be out here long?" Rachel wondered out loud.

"The storm is supposed to be strong, but it will not last all night. We should be alright here until the rain lets up some, then we can head back," he answered. Chase closed his eyes to rest. He was comfortable and enjoyed having Rachel cuddled up to him. "Rach?"

"Yeah?"

"Just so you know, you are nowhere near the old cabin," he couldn't resist teasing.

Rachel sighed as she answered, "I know. I have no idea how to get back either."

Chase laughed.

Once the rain had stopped, they detoured to the old cabin before he led her safely back to the farm. Rachel smiled as she remembered the harsh words he had with Shannon and Lila. Chase somehow knew whose idea it was and knew who should have known better and overruled based on common sense alone. Sending the one person without any sense of direction out alone close to dusk was the stupidest thing. The adults never learned of the incident and Chase wore the bracelet for the rest of the summer.

Rachel snuggled comfortably and sighed when he tightened his arm around her. She slept the rest of the ride home.

start the ball rolling

Rachel stayed overnight on the farm after the truck was unloaded. Lila returned with her to her Taylor House the next morning to help her unpack. Clara and Shannon were so excited to have the fourth friend home for good, they both arrived to work early, worked through lunch, and arrived at Rachel's in the late afternoon.

Inspired by Dallas Thompson's story of DNA to confirm his parentage, Shannon had purchased DNA tests and was excited to have them arrive that afternoon. With enough for all the friends, including Rob and Chase, she easily convinced them to each have their DNA tested for fun while she hoped to have a connection to her biological family. They discussed possibilities as they assisted Rachel with unpacking and organizing her clothes.

"We could all be like distant cousins," Lila said.

"Maybe you'll be related to someone famous!" Rachel said.

"Would you set up a meeting with your biological parents?" Clara asked.

"I don't know what I'll do," Shannon admitted. While she wanted to know her own story, she worried about secrets that should be left unknown.

As the afternoon grew into evening, Shannon drove the friends to Clara's where they would all probably spend the night. They could safely walk back, regardless of how much they had to drink.

The dinner crowd was thinning at Memories when the friends entered laughing. Rachel and Clara found a table in the back while Lila and Shannon went to the bar to get the first round.

"How are you doing, Clara?" Rachel asked. She felt bad she wasn't home during what had to be the worst of weeks.

"I don't know. I guess I just am. I'm taking it one day at a time," Clara sighed as she answered. Rachel nodded as Clara continued, "It's just so weird, being back here. Everything is so different and yet so much has remained unchanged. I never would have predicted I would willingly move back alone with two children before I was even thirty."

"I am sorry you had to go through this," Rachel said as she took her friend's hand and squeezed.

"Yeah, me two. I want to be happy and live my life. I want my kids to grow up happy and experience life. Not to watch me dwelling on my grief. It's weird, when I first moved back, people thought I was a single mother and available. Always trying to pull me out and set me up. But I was dwelling on the fact that for the second time in my life, one of the most important people chose to leave me. It really killed a piece of my heart. Then suddenly, in a short time I find out they were each not only dead all this time but maliciously taken away from me. Is it so horrible to admit I was slightly relieved to know they didn't leave me?" Clara sighed sadly. "And yet, people continue to encourage me to move on and date. But I'm afraid to be happy with someone. That means I'm glad Jason is gone."

"Oh Clara, I don't think Jason would think that. He absolutely adored you! Everyone could see it in his eyes how much he loved you and those kids. I really believe he would be alright with you moving on with your life and even meeting someone special," Rachel declared.

"I don't know, it doesn't seem appropriate," Clara commented after a moment

"What's not appropriate?" A male voice asked from behind.

Rachel looked back and smiled, noting Clara's slight shake of the head.

Connor sat on the other side of Clara, casually placing his arm around the back of her chair as he talked comfortably. He looked amused at Clara's discomfort, "Rachel, welcome home. I hear you are back for good this time. Your grandmother will love seeing you more. You ladies are without drinks. What would you like?"

"Shannon and Lila are already on it," Clara answered. She looked over her shoulder and realized the drinks were made and waiting for delivery on the bar in front of Lila and Shannon. Her friends were too busy chattering away. She was about to go get them, but Rachel was up quicker.

Connor looked over at Clara as she appeared to be trying to avoid him. He reached over for her hand as he quietly said her name. When she finally looked up into his eyes, he could see she was having another bad moment. She was working hard to not cry, he could tell. He squeezed her hand and gave her a little hug, "Do you want to talk about it?"

Clara shook her head.

"Do you want me to leave you alone?"

Clara shook her head again.

"Do you want me to stop touching you?"

Clara shrugged. Connor watched her face as he brought her hand up to kiss. She didn't pull back and allowed her hand to remain in his, resting on his lap, "Hey Beautiful, I love you, as I always have. I told you before, I will be whatever you want me to be. I will stay within the boundaries that you set. We go forward at your pace. You and I together, alright? Whatever we have here is for us to decide. We don't need to put a label on it. We have no timeline and no agenda. There's just you and me with those adorable kids of yours."

"What's going on between those two?" Rachel asked when she arrived at the bar. She reached for her drink as Lila and Shannon both turned to look over her shoulder.

"I don't know," Shannon answered. "When I first returned home, Clara was back and forth between him and Rob but I think there's more sparks between her and Connor."

Rachel glanced over to Lila to get her take. She was nodding agreement.

"Yeah, it's like he helps her escape from it all, but then she falls face first into reality. She has had a rough time these last few months. Connor always seems to be around when she needs him," Shannon concluded.

"You know, they were always close," Rachel responded. "She used to sit at her bedroom window and watch him play basketball with his friends or wave goodnight to him. She often went into his treehouse after he left for school. They never lost touch, not even when she got married. Connor always checked in with her, made sure she had what she needed, and was safe. They even double dated a few times."

"Really? I knew she always had a thing for him, but I never knew they kept in touch," Shannon stated as she sipped her drink.

Lila nodded. "Connor, Clara and I worked at the same trauma center. I would occasionally see them eating lunch together. I'm not really surprised they grew closer. He's always been somewhere in the background."

"I can't believe I never knew all this!" Shannon exclaimed. "I do remember she would make us go to the park so she could drool over him. I wonder what happened to that cute one that was only around during the school breaks."

"Isn't he that bartender over there?" Rachel asked, "Anthony Mancuso's cousin?"

Shannon and Lila both followed Rachel's finger then they both looked back at each other and laughed.

"Rachel, you are so right! Oh my God! I can't believe you didn't know that!" Lila laughed so hard she was almost crying.

"What is so funny?" Devan asked from the other side of the bar with a smile. The laughter was contagious, but he felt left out. Especially when Shannon and Rachel laughed even harder.

But Lila felt bad, "Shannon just learned what happened to the cute kid from the park when we were kids."

"Oh? What happened to him?" Devan asked, causing the girls to all laugh even more.

"It's you!" Shannon stated between giggles.

"Huh?" He looked between friends and it all clicked. When Devan came to visit, he was always aware of Clara because she was like Connor's little charge that was always into trouble. She often had three friends nearby, the polite blonde, the bossy brunette, and the peacekeeper redhead: Rachel, Shannon, and Lila. Damn, small world in a small town. And the bossy brunette thought he was cute!

"Hey, did you all ban Clara from drinking? Why is her drink sitting here melting while she's back there dying of thirst?" Devan demanded. He grabbed Shannon's hand before she could walk away, he leaned over the bar and kissed her. He was rewarded with a suggestive smile.

Across the room, the man who sat alone was back. He was in his early thirties. He was finishing his dinner when the group of friends entered laughing. He was pleasantly surprised how well his evening was going. The food was beyond his imagination for a fracture of the price at home. The women were plenty and hot. And most importantly, it looked like he found the one. He held his cell phone up as if he were reading while he ate. He was comparing the picture to the women in the place. Initially he thought it was the one in the back in a purple top. She had a similar facial structure, but she was too short and had curly hair. But the one at the bar seemed to hit all the boxes. Her hair was longer than in the picture but when she smiled in his direction, he was convinced. Maybe he could kill two birds with one stone. He could pick her up and take her back to her place. They could have themselves a fun weekend while he assessed her life. His current instructions were to simply locate her. Likely the boss would want him to find where she lived and worked. Then, he would receive instructions to complete the job.

It couldn't hurt to start the ball rolling he thought as he admired everything about her. It was obvious she worked out. She would bring a lot of pleasure. Why not let her have a few rolls in the sack before she said good night?

Then she crushed his plans by kissing the bartender, damn it. That certainly complicates things.

"Would you like anything more, sir?" Jill, the young server, asked.

"I'm finished with my dinner, but I think I'll hang out for a bit. This place seems to be coming alive. I will pay the check, and then can you help with one last thing?"

· · · ·

Evil watched from the end of the bar as his Babydoll cuddled up with another guy. A week ago, he was pissed when the kid openly admitted he was sexually involved with his girl. He even considered killing him when he gets released on bail. But when he learned she denied it and his description was made up, he relaxed and forgave. And when the kid was accused of murder, Evil laughed so hard he almost cried. A new plan literally fell into his lap. The boy's mother had officially lost her marbles, he thought with a chuckle.

Naturally, he believed the kid when he said he did not do it. The kid was finally good for something, Evil thought as he requested another drink. He just needed to lie low until the kid was out. Shouldn't be much longer, he thought as he glanced at his watch. The excitement of the week brought out so many possibilities as he planned the future.

Evil glanced around the bar as he debated the woman beside him with the big tits and tight clothes. He knew from experience she would let him have his way with his excessive tastes, things his own wife hesitated to do. She allowed her leg to lean up against his as she leaned closer to whisper in his ear, he had no idea what she said. His eyes were distracted by the full view of her tits. His pants were getting tight as her hand trailed up his thigh, lingering close to his crotch.

What the hell, the night was young. He could spare a couple of hours up in his office before he returned home to his wife.

just a little hot

As the evening progressed, Connor left the girls to sit at the bar and occasionally talk with his cousin. Joe had stopped in with his brother for a round before heading home to his family. His nephew even stopped in for a bit. To his amusement, Joshua almost drooled as his eyes seemed to immediately lock on to Clara with her friends in the back. When he realized his uncle was watching him, he mumbled something about heading across the street.

"How's it going?" Dallas asked as he ordered a drink. Since meeting Devan at Clara's, Dallas was now comfortable around both of the guys. He had a great time the other night getting to know everyone during the volleyball game.

"Dallas, have you talked with Clara lately?" Connor asked.

"Not since the other night, why?"

"I don't know she seems off tonight," Connor shrugged.

"Well, I'm heading over now to say hello," Dallas stated as he grabbed his drink.

When he joined the women, they all cheered and laughed. He almost blushed. Each stood up and gave him a hug as they moved around the table like they were playing musical chairs. When he sat, he was sandwiched between Clara and Lila.

When Chase later joined them, the friends again stood up and hugged him as they rearranged the group. When Dallas sat, he was still sandwiched between Clara and Lila, but they were on opposite sides. He glanced over at Clara. Connor was right, she was quieter and looked a little pale.

Clara was initially excited to hang out with her friends, but as the evening progressed, she was overwhelmed by a sense of being watched. She felt as if the shadow was in her peripheral but when she looked over her shoulder, he faded into the crowd.

"Hey, are you alright?" Dallas asked.

Clara simply shrugged.

"Ladies, are you ready for the next round?" Jill lowered her tray onto the table, handing each one a shot before she collected all the empties. She didn't say anything about why the guys didn't get a drink, nor did they ask.

Clara excused herself to go to the restroom. She was relieved there wasn't a line. She splashed cold water over her face as she wondered why she was feeling so anxious. She had a moment of panic, thinking maybe she was drugged again, but she reminded herself he was in jail and it happened at the other bar, not here. When she looked in the mirror, she gave herself a quick pep talk, "You are just a little drunk. You have not done this much drinking since what, college? Now stop and get out there. You are good!"

The pep talk didn't really help. Clara decided to use the bathroom since she was already there. When she stepped out, she was embarrassed to realize she had been in the Men's room. There was a man there waiting. He was about her age dressed as if he just arrived from the city. She didn't recognize him.

"Sorry, I really had to go," she apologized.

"No worries," he said with a smile. He admired her openly, "Meet me at the bar and I'll buy you a drink. You can tell me all the good hang out spots in town."

"Oh, I don't think I'll be any good. I don't get out much," Clara declined as she stepped away.

Connor had watched her disappear into the Men's room. When she came out, her face turned red as she talked to the guy waiting in line. He figured the guy was hitting on her. Connor was silently pleased when she shook her head and walked away.

When her green eyes met his, she walked over. Connor vacated his seat and gently prodded her onto the stool, "Are you alright?"

Initially she was feeling the beginnings of a panic attack, but she relaxed once she saw Connor. Clara shrugged. "I don't know. Maybe I'm just a little hot."

"Well, Sweetheart, that goes without saying," he answered with a chuckle. "Do you want to head out?"

When she nodded, Connor nodded good night to Devan as he grabbed her hand to lead her out the back entrance. As they approached the restrooms, the guy was coming out. He smiled when he saw her walking in his direction. Clara smiled and wished him a good night.

His smile vanished as he realized she was holding onto Connor's hand. Damn, he thought. Another hot one already taken for the night.

Connor led Clara upstairs to his loft, asking her if she wanted anything to drink. She just wanted water. When he handed it to her, she held the cold bottle up to her forehead and then her neck, he simply chuckled.

Clara looked over at him as she drank her water. His warm brown eyes smiled as he looked at her. She felt her heart melt. I really do love him, she thought, as she wondered what it would be like to peel his clothes off, touch his chest, squeeze his tight butt, and feel him inside. Well, girl, you can keep fantasizing or go find out.

Feeling unexpectedly daring, Clara slowly stood up and walked around the counter towards him, unbuttoning her blouse. When she was almost touching him, pulled him down and kissed him with everything she had.

Connor allowed the kiss to play out, but reminded himself she had been drinking. He looked questioningly into her eyes.

"I'm alright, I promise you," she assured him as she slowly unbuttoned his shirt, rubbing her hands on his chest as she continued to whisper, "I want to touch you, taste you, feel you."

Connor needed no further encouragement. His lips were instantly on hers. As their tongues met, she softly moaned with delight as her hands slowly moved, exploring his body. He felt her hand slowly caress him through his pants. Within seconds, he had her completely naked, only her sandals remained. His shirt was open, as were his pants, as he braced Clara up against the wall. He kissed her neck as his hands touched her shoulders and breasts. He lowered his lips to a nipple and sucked. Encouraged by her groans, his tongue played with the other nipple as his hand went lower, exploring her body. His fingers played as she groaned with pleasure.

He brought her arms up around his neck. As he lifted her from the floor, he looked into her eyes…

Clara was suddenly overwhelmed with pleasure as she looked into his warm brown eyes, she couldn't process anything. She could only feel incredible intense pleasure as she climaxed. She had no time to recover as she was lifted up and hit by another wave. It pulsed through her, washing over her again and again. She closed her eyes and lowered her head onto his shoulder as she tried to catch her breath. She was vaguely aware of his heart pounding and could feel his breathing in her ear. When she lifted her face towards his, he smiled and kissed her on the lips, letting the kiss linger…

And then they both heard a cough.

Connor was able to register first; they were not alone. He looked over his shoulder in anger at who would dare enter his place without an invitation.

"What the hell do you want?" He growled at his brother, who was standing in the doorway, trying to be discreet by looking away.

"I need to talk to you. You didn't answer your cell," Matt explained.

"I am busy, can't this wait?" Connor demanded as he slowly lowered Clara onto her feet. He zipped up his pants as he stood in front of her, removing his shirt.

"Clearly. I'll be in the front room," Matt replied with a chuckle, already halfway down the hall.

Connor turned to Clara. She was still leaning up against the wall as she looked up at him. Still dazed, her face was flushed from embarrassment. He handed her his shirt. He tilted her chin up and asked, "Sweetheart, are you alright?"

She could only nod. He kissed her forehead and then her lips. "Put this on and have a seat. I'm going to go see what the hell is so important and get rid of him."

Clara was slow to move, causing him to smile as he walked away.

When Connor entered his front room, Matt was standing at the large window which covered the top half of the length of the wall, and overlooked Main Street. Matt had a similar view in his waiting room across the hall. He turned when he heard his little brother.

Connor was standing before him shirtless, "What the hell is it that can't wait?"

"I guess you can now confirm if she has a birthmark or not, eh?" Matt couldn't resist teasing. But then he was suddenly serious. "I came to warn you. The judge has signed off on Eric being released on bail. He's likely to be out sometime tomorrow morning. I took the liberty to act on Clara's behalf as her attorney. I've petitioned for him to be under house arrest with an ankle bracelet. I've also asked for a restraining order forbidding the bastard from being within fifty yards of Clara, her children, either of her homes, the daycare, and the nursing home. Dad and I are both confident he will break the terms of his bail and be sent back. We just need to be prepared."

"How the hell did Lee come up with a million dollars for bail?" Connor demanded. "How did Devan not hear about this?"

"Dad was alerted when Kathleen requested special access to her trust fund yesterday. As for Devan, I can only say he's too busy burning the candle at both ends of the stick. Listen, Dad and I have been reviewing the terms of his release on bail. He's very likely to get past everything. We suggest you get her and the children out of town for a few days while we get better security in place. Don't let her out of your sight. I'll keep you posted as I learn more."

"Who is representing him?"

Matt chuckled, "Would you believe his father is?"

"Interesting. What about the mayor position?"

"The rumor is he's resigning, but I don't see him doing so voluntarily," Matt answered as they walked together towards the kitchen.

Clara was sitting on a stool, leaning onto the island wearing Connor's shirt.

"Clara, it's always a pleasure to see you, my apologies for the intrusion," Matt called out. When he closed the door behind him, he had to pause to center himself. Seeing her sitting shyly in the kitchen with her messy hair made him think of Susi. He needed to get her out of his mind before he returned home to his wife.

a little too drunk

Downstairs, the three remaining friends continued to laugh and talk together as they drank. Both Chase and Dallas were surprised by the excessive drinking.

Shortly after Connor left with Clara, Devan became aware of counterfeit twenties in the register. Shit, he thought. Just what this town needs, a bunch of fake money to be thrown all over the place. He removed the pile, placing it into a secured drawer. He sent a text out to his boss as he looked around for a potential suspect.

Across the room, Chase was very aware of Lila's interest in Dallas. How could he not be? She was touching his knee, holding his hand, leaning into him, and even rubbing his back. He was less obvious, but he seemed comfortable, reminding him of his theory she was seeing someone. It also explained why she kept it secret.

Shit, he thought. Uncle Mitch and Rob are going to have a heart attack when this gets out. How long has this been going on? He leaned over towards Dallas as he asked, "What the hell is going on between you and my cousin?"

Dallas felt a moment of panic but reminded himself this was the nicer one. He is less likely to punch. He took a deep breath before he answered, "You need to ask Lila that yourself. Preferably when she's sober enough to remember the conversation."

When Chase's only response was a slightly puzzled look, Dallas changed the subject, "Do these girls drink like this often?"

"Not really. At least not since college anyway. I haven't seen any of them opening their purses either. They must have a hell of a tab running. I'll go check on it." As Chase approached the bar, he thought why not ask the new guy. Devan's with Shannon and might have a better idea of what was going on.

"Chase, you and Dallas want another round? It's last call," Devan asked.

"No, it's safe to say we are the designated drivers tonight unless you think we can all crash upstairs at Connor's?" Chase suggested. When Devan chuckled, he continued, "I'm checking on the girls' tab. I'll close it out."

Devan nodded as he went over to ask Jill. Interesting, he thought. He came back looking slightly confused as his eyes scanned the room, "Jill says a guy was here earlier and paid it up front. It's already closed."

Chase's eyebrows went up in surprise. "It wasn't Connor?"

Devan shook his head as he repeated, "Some guy she's only seen recently. She didn't catch his name."

Both thought it odd to have a total stranger pay for the evening. Chase wondered if he would have been able to place him. "Alright, I guess that saves me a few hundred dollars."

Chase hesitated a moment but decided, what the hell, "Hey Devan, what do you know about this Dallas guy?"

Devan wondered when someone else would start noticing. He suspected Clara already knew, but didn't discuss it. "He's local, like you. I know he was in the army. He's a ranger at the national park. Shan says Lila's had a crush on him her whole life, and just last week, I learned he's Clara's older half-brother. That last part seemed to be new information this summer. Listen, you all get home safely. I'll make sure

Shannon gets home."

Chase turned around as he repeated the last part in his head, Lila's had a crush on him her whole life? He's Clara's older brother? What the hell?

Just then, Lila was standing in front of him with a big smile as she slurred out, "Hey big cousin, I am going home with Dallas. Tell my brother I won't be home for the weekend."

Dallas was suddenly standing beside her, shaking his hand, "I guess she's going home with me."

"Yeah, that's what I told him," Lila said as she hung onto his arm.

Chase pulled her aside, "Lila, aren't you a little too drunk to be leaving with him? Let me take you home."

Lila laughed as she reached up to hug him. "I'm alright. We have been together longer than this week. We are good. I promise you. He won't hurt me, he loves me."

Chase was frozen in place with shock. Thank God Rob had to stay home to monitor the mare, he thought. He felt a tug on his arm as Rachel came up behind him.

"Chase, are you alright to drive me home?" She asked as she gently rubbed his chest. Oh, it's going to be a long night.

Clara was surprised to find herself sitting on the bench looking over the river. She closed her eyes as she felt the cool breeze. She could smell fresh bread and warm meats from nearby food carts. She couldn't remember the last time she sat here.

"Hey Babe."

She turned to see the sky-blue eyes that she loved so much. He looked as he did when they first met. His blonde hair was longer and blew in the gentle wind. His face was slightly tanned. He was wearing a t-shirt with their college on it and an old pair of jeans. He smiled as he leaned forward to take her hand and guide her along the river.

"Are you coming back?" She asked hopefully.

He shook his head as they continued walking.

"I miss you. I am sorry I was so angry when you wouldn't answer my calls. Will you forgive me?"

"There isn't anything to forgive, Clara. I wish we had more time together and I could have protected you longer." He turned to look into her eyes. He smiled as he brushed a curl from her face. "You never did anything wrong. I love you, always, no matter what. Tell Reese and Hailey I love them."

He leaned in to kiss her as he slowly faded…

"No! Nooo! Don't leave me please, Jason, no!" Clara sobbed.

Connor sat straight up as he heard Clara yell. A quick glance around the room assured him there was no danger. He looked down at Clara on her side as she sobbed in her sleep. He heard her mumble, no, don't leave me, and he was sure he heard her say, Jason.

He laid back down, cuddling up behind her as he pulled her in close. He held her as she cried for her late husband. He knew she wouldn't hear him, but he still spoke softly as he attempted to reassure her she wasn't alone.

Is this what was wrong? She was having trouble letting go? Connor remained awake as he laid beside her the rest of the night. Just before dawn, Clara stretched out and rolled over onto her back. He remained on his side as he watched her face, gently touching her cheek. He softly kissed her forehead then her lips. He whispered he loved her. She smiled and sighed as she continued to sleep.

39 like a couple of teenagers

When Clara woke up a bit after dawn, she felt refreshed as she stretched out on the bed. On her way to the bathroom, she picked up Connor's shirt that was casually thrown over a chair. She smiled as she thought about the night before. And then she groaned when she remembered his brother stopping in. Not embarrassing at all, she thought sarcastically.

Wearing only the shirt, Clara went out of the room in search of Connor. She found him sitting at the counter wearing only a pair of gym shorts. He was going back and forth between his tablet and cell phone. She remained at the doorway watching him with a smile as she remembered his hands and his lips…

Connor had been awake awhile. He waited until dawn to leave the bed as his brother was providing updates as promised. Both brothers required only a few hours a night to function which allowed them to have so many work projects going. Sensing her presence, Connor looked up to see her watching him. Man, she was so beautiful first thing in the morning. Wearing only his shirt with her curly hair hanging over her sleepy eyes. He smiled as she slowly approached him, turning on the stool as she neared.

Clara kept her eyes on his as she stepped between his legs. Her hands moved up his thighs as they caressed their way up to his shoulders. He would always refer to that as "her move," Connor thought as she gave him a good morning kiss.

When she stepped back, Clara smiled. Her hands trailed along his back as she walked around to get a bottle of water. She returned to sit beside him, sipping her drink. Her bare feet were propped up on his stool with their legs leaning together.

He noted she didn't touch the coffee. Before Conner could ask, he was distracted by a text and responded quickly as he turned off his tablet. He propped an elbow on the counter and leaned his head onto his hand as he watched her.

She looked up at him and asked, "Problem?"

Connor laughed as he shook his head, "Not at all. When you take a step forward, you leap."

"A problem?" Clara repeated. "Was I too forward last night?"

"Nothing I can't handle," Connor answered as he pulled her legs up into his lap, gently massaging her feet and calves. He noted the thin scar on her left ankle from an IV during her hospital stay as an infant. The scar on her right knee from when she was dragged around the merry-go-round when she was five. He had to give her a piggyback ride home that afternoon. Now he knew, she had a birthmark on her right side, the size of a dime and a mole on her lower abdomen to the left. He sighed as he thought back to the night before. Nothing prepared him for the intensity of their first time together. Something Connor had never experienced.

His cell chimed again and he was anchored back to reality. After a quick glance, Connor asked Clara if she was hungry.

"Not just yet. I need to head home and relieve the babysitter," Clara answered. Neither one moved as they both watched each other.

"What are your plans for today?" Connor asked.

Clara sighed as she thought about it, "Oh you know, the usual, grocery shopping, laundry, cleaning, the park, lengthy discussion why we can't have ice cream for dinner."

"How about you, Reese, and Hailey all join me at my lake house today?" Connor suggested. Matt advised him to get her out of town and that was his current mission.

To his surprise, Clara looked thoughtful as she considered before she nodded. Why not? The kids would enjoy it, and it would be a treat to spend a whole day with him.

"The weather is promising to be great for riding in my new boat and we can stay the night," he continued as he lowered her feet and pulled her up and over towards him. He kissed her between words.

"Connor, it will take me a while to get home and pack for a weekend," Clara started. It was one thing to be gone for a day, but for the whole weekend? She already spent last weekend at the Farm and got nothing done at home. But Reese and Hailey really enjoyed themselves, she reminded herself.

"What do you have to do?"

"Pack their clothes, toys, and food," she said. While Connor spent a lot of time with her, she wasn't sure he was aware how the children's needs dictated her day. There were naps and mealtimes. Before she had the children, she and Jay used to be able to have brunch and a later dinner. When the kids came along, they required three meals a day with snacks.

Connor watched, amused and aware of her thought process. "Clara, how about I drop you off, so you can pack a bag for the night. You only need an outfit, maybe two for the kids, pajamas, which is really pointless for you, and swimsuits. I will see to the rest and pick you up thirty minutes later."

"Connor, I don't have life jackets for them," Clara started.

He simply kissed her and walked out. Connor returned a few minutes later dressed in loafers without socks, cargo shorts, and a short-sleeve, button-down shirt. He had a small overnight bag on his shoulder. He placed his tablet into his bag, and set it at the door. He left her clothes on the stool beside her. He reached for his mug to rinse before placing it into the dishwasher. He emptied the coffee maker and washed it out.

Clara eyed him as she dressed, suddenly shy.

When Connor dropped her off, he looked at his watch and told her the time, "I'll be back in thirty minutes, Beautiful."

Twenty-eight minutes later, Clara had showered and donned a short summer dress. She was heading down the steps with the children, carrying an overnight bag for clothes and a bag of swimming gear with sunblock, hats, and sunglasses. A third bag was full of toys, books, and crayons. She supervised Reese while assisting Hailey with their sneakers as she mentally checked anything possibly needed for the weekend. When the doorbell rang, Clara opened it without looking, confident it was Connor.

Instead, it was Felicia Thompson, Dallas' mother and her father's girlfriend. Oh shit, she thought. This visit does not fit in the allotted thirty minutes. Clara contained her annoyance at the unexpected early morning visit. What could go wrong, she thought sarcastically.

"Ms. Thompson, hello," Clara answered. Keeping the view behind her blocked with the door as she held onto the screen door.

"Clara, darling, I've told you before, you may call me Felicia. Please, aren't you going to invite me in?" She asked with a condescending tone.

"I'm not available for a visit right now, Felicia. We are about to head out," Clara answered firmly.

"Clara dear, really? You are being very inhospitable. I would have hoped your mother raised you better than that," Felicia commented as she attempted to open the screen door.

Despite the rude reference to her mother, Clara reminded herself the woman was Dallas' mother and her father's girlfriend. Even if she never saw it, the woman had to have some redeeming qualities. She tried to keep her tone low but firm, but Clara couldn't keep out the sarcasm. "Well since my mother died when I was nine, my social skills are obviously lacking since I then grew up without a proper role model. As I just informed you, I already made plans for this morning. I was not aware of your intent to stop over. If I had been, I would have informed you that the visit would have to be scheduled for another time. I suggest you call ahead to assure I will be available before you go through the trouble of driving over next time. Can I call Dallas for you?"

Felicia was shocked Clara had no intention of letting her inside. She was so sure her ability to control the father would work on the daughter. She realized too late, Clara really was her mother's child, stubborn as hell and very selfish. Felicia was absolutely appalled. "No, I don't need you to call him. That no good son of mine has not been answering my calls as it is. I will leave. If I ever have the foresight to stop over again, I will be sure to call first."

Felicia turned around and stomped back to her old model SUV. Clara remained at the door watching her drive off as Connor pulled into the driveway. She pulled out her cell and left a voicemail. "Hey Dallas, this is Clara. Sorry to call so early but your mother just stopped over unexpectedly and left upset because I was heading out the door. Sorry about breaking the rules. Call me."

Connor was heading up the steps, pleasantly surprised to find everyone was at the door and ready, "Hey Beautiful. You did it! You showered, packed, and had time to spare to make a call."

He grabbed her keys and her bags. Clara followed Connor out as he placed the bags in his vehicle. He unlocked her car, then returned the keys to her as he removed the car seats.

"Connor, do we need the stroller?" Clara wondered.

"I have no idea," he shrugged.

Connor followed her back to her car and pulled out the stroller as she went back inside. She returned a moment later with another small bag followed by the children skipping behind her. Two minutes later, they were buckled in and backing out.

like a couple of teenagers   411

"I love this! We made plans an hour ago and we are already on our way. I can get used to this. The day is too gorgeous to waste half of it planning," he said as he grabbed her hand and kissed it. He continued to hold it as he and Reese engaged in conversation.

Clara reached for her cell. "Hello?"

She paused for a moment and nodded. "Yeah, it was totally unexpected. She wasn't happy when I told her twice, we were all heading out. When have you seen them last?" She paused again and then asked, "So you have no idea where they are?" She paused, then answered with a snort, "Yeah right. That will be the day. I am heading out with Connor and the kids to his lake house." Pause. "The rest of the weekend." Pause. "Thanks. You, too."

Clara dropped her phone back into her bag, looked back at the children before she leaned back to watch the scenery. Feeling his eyes on her she looked over. "What?"

"You really enjoy doing this, don't you?" He accused.

"Doing what?" she replied, totally clueless.

Connor sighed, "Who doesn't know who or where they are staying?"

Clara laughed, "Oh, sorry. Dallas' mother literally just dropped in unannounced before you arrived. She wasn't happy about me not letting her inside. I have no idea what she wanted and didn't feel like ruining the day. I was adamant she call first instead of just dropping in. I tried to be polite, but that b…" she caught herself in time and changed the word, "*woman* gets on my nerves when she makes comments about my mother."

Connor could understand that. He had few interactions with Clara's father while she was growing up and only knew about the girlfriend by reputation. He was pleasantly surprised Dallas was different. "So I take it Dallas was the one you were leaving a message for when I arrived. What rule did you break?"

"He hasn't heard from her in months, but Felicia called him this morning and he let it go to voicemail. He didn't want to ruin a potentially good day either. When Dallas first told me he was my brother, I was hesitant to let him get to know me and the kids. I mean, hello, look who his parents are. But since we share the same father, I can't really talk. I've known him most of my life and he's never been anything but kind to me. He stopped in to see me at the hospital. Another time, I ran into him while I was running. He offered me a drink and a hug, as I pictured an older brother would. We agreed, we would hang out, play volleyball, whatever, but we would not talk about his parents. And we would especially not report to them what the other one is doing," Clara concluded.

"Sounds fair," Connor commented.

Lila woke up with a pounding headache worsened by the bright morning sunlight when she opened her eyes. She leaned back onto her pillow and groaned. A moment later, she felt the bed give a little as Dallas sat beside her. He leaned down to kiss her forehead. When Lila opened her eyes, he smiled and kissed her lips.

She sat up against the head of the bed and smiled. He handed her a couple of Tylenol with a glass of water. She took a small sip and handed back the glass.

Dallas held her hands and guided the glass back up to her lips, "It works better if you drink it all."

After a moment, Lila leaned back and sighed. "Boy we drank last night! We must have sipped the place dry! We had a drink like every half hour, followed by a shot. I haven't partied like that since college."

Dallas agreed, "Yeah you ladies were drinking it up. What do you remember about last night?"

"Clara left early with Connor. Rachel left with Chase. I think things are finely heating up between those two." She smiled mischievously. "And Chase has figured us out."

Dallas wasn't sure which couple she meant, but let it go. His focus was on her family. "And how do you feel about that?"

"What do you mean?"

"Chase knows about us. Hell, he even suggested you were too drunk to leave with me as if it was just a casual hook-up. But you set him straight. I am proud of you," Dallas said as he leaned down to give her a kiss. "You also said you were staying the weekend, does that still hold?"

Lila smiled and nodded as she scooted to the edge of the bed.

When Lila stepped out of the shower, she smiled at her mug of coffee on the counter. During her shower, Dallas had appeared to hand her the needed coffee. After drinking half the mug, she handed it back to him, and he kissed her before leaving. Lila felt much better. Once dressed, she followed the smell of food and the sounds of music.

At the doorway, Lila paused as Dallas expertly danced around the kitchen, moving to the beat and singing along. He executed a fancy turn and smiled as his eyes met hers. Keeping his rhythm, he grabbed her and twirled her around the kitchen.

At the end of the song, Lila laughed as she dipped back. Dallas lifted her up and kissed her before leading her out to the back deck. He pulled out her chair, scooted her closer to the table before returning to dish up the food. When he sat beside her, he looked over and smiled before starting into his omelet.

"What has you in a good mood?"

"You," Dallas answered with a smile as he brought a forkful of food up to his mouth.

"Me? This has to be the first time I've stayed the whole night without us having sex. How can that possibly make you this happy?"

Dallas laughed. Lila had fallen asleep during the ride home. He had carried her into the house and undressed her before tucking her in bed. He was content to have her sleep beside him. "True," he said, "Signs we've been together a while. Usually one of us, if not both, are rushing off in the morning. But you, the love of my life, are staying the whole weekend. We need to pace ourselves. Plus, we are celebrating."

Lila smiled. Dallas always found ways to keep everything positive. If they had only a few hours, he assured her it was quality time. If it were too cold, they could use their bodies to make heat. The walls are literally falling down around them, but that gave them privacy with time to get to know each other. And today, they were celebrating.

"What are we celebrating?" Lila asked as she cut into her omelet.

"We are officially out," Dallas answered excitedly. "I may be dead before the weekend is over, but we are out as a couple."

"Not everyone knows about us yet. And why will you be dead?" Lila looked over with confusion.

"Everyone at Memories saw you all over me last night, including Chase. If he knows, your brother will soon. Those two are tight," he answered cheerfully, not really too concerned about his pending doom.

"Clara left early. She doesn't know," Lila stated as she mentally replayed the previous night.

"Oh, she knows. Clara figured it out last week when I had dinner at her place," Dallas dismissed. When he looked up, he chuckled at her expression before he told her about the conversation.

"You already knew I had a crush on you in high school. That wasn't top secret," she commented.

"But you talked about me with your friends!" Dallas tapped his heart mockingly before he continued, "It touches me that you were risking your own life by sharing your love for me with your friends who are also tight with your brother."

"I don't think Chase will tell Rob. He's too smitten with Rachel right now. He's going to make his move. As long as I remain among the living, Chase won't give it much thought."

"I hope so," Dallas stated. He leaned back and watched the beautiful woman sitting with him. "In honor of our celebration, you get to pick what we do today."

"Oh yeah? Any suggestions?"

"We can barricade ourselves in the bedroom with a case of water,

like a couple of teenagers   415

we can go hiking up to the peak, we can ride through town and have dinner at the new fancy restaurant, we can go skinny dipping in the lake, whatever you want. As long as we are together," Dallas clarified.

"What were you already planning to do?" Lila asked as she stood up to sit on his lap. She kissed his neck as he talked.

"Mow the lawn, weed the garden, chop wood," he stated until he was distracted.

Rachel was awakened by the smell of coffee and bacon. She rolled over and sighed at the thought of breakfast with bacon. Her mother never cooks bacon anymore.

Then she remembered her mother was no longer with her and her eyes shot open as she scrambled to the edge of the bed. Who is downstairs cooking the bacon? Rachel wondered, looking down at her clothes.

She was wearing the pale blue nightie that matched her eyes. She reached for the matching robe as she debated what to do. Who could possibly be in her kitchen? Really Rach, a burglar isn't going to take the time to make bacon. Hell, she didn't even have bacon in the house yesterday.

It must be Chase. She remembered inviting him in when he brought her home. Rachel also remembered kissing him before he brought her upstairs. What the hell did she do? She tried to remember as she headed down the back stairs.

In the kitchen, a fully dressed Chase was slicing up a frittata, and placing strips of bacon onto a plate. When he turned around, he paused at the sight of Rachel in a short blue robe standing on the bottom step. She looked a bit confused with his presence in the kitchen on a Saturday morning.

Chase placed the plates on the table before he went to the stairs. He reached for her hand as he pulled her over to the table. He kissed her on the lips, pleased that she continued to respond instead of pulling away during the light of day. Once she was sitting, he poured the coffee and orange juice before joining her.

She probably doesn't remember what happened last night, Chase thought. I could have fun with her. "Rach, what is wrong?"

"What happened last night?" She asked suspiciously.

"A gentleman will never kiss and tell," he answered with a wink, chuckling when she blushed.

"Rachel, we didn't do anything wrong," Chase started, but decided he needed to be more specific when she looked panicked. "We didn't do anything you wouldn't have agreed to doing totally sober. Trust me, if we did, you would remember it."

"But we kissed," she almost shouted.

"Yes, we did," he agreed happily. "See, I told you, you would remember. There was also some touching, but I fought hard to stop you, and unfortunately, I won the battle. Next time you undo my pants and stick your hands in, I'm not stopping you. That's the only warning I'm giving."

Rachel's face reddened as she remembered, "Why did you stop me?"

"I wanted you to want me for the right reasons, and if you had continued what you were trying to do, I would have lost my will power and let you have your way with me. The hell with the consequences," Chase explained. "Rach, eat your breakfast, it's getting cold."

Rachel did, surprised at her hunger. When she was up retrieving the coffee pot, Chase casually asked what she had planned for the day.

Rachel remained standing at the sink, looking out the window at Gigi's gardens. Her mother had been keeping up with them over the years. She sighed as she remembered helping her mother and grandmother, asking questions. They taught her the names of the plants, the amount of sunlight needed, and when they bloomed. Rachel was surprised when the tears came. She wanted to pull herself together before she turned back around. Instead, she felt his strong arms around her as he pulled her into him for a comforting hug. Rachel lost her control and cried.

Chase had an arm around her waist and the other around her shoulders. His head rested on her shoulder as she leaned her head on his. He was very aware of her strong bond with her mother and understood the return home would be painful. Rachel was raised by her mother and grandmother. Her father was gone at an early age, she had little memories of him.

He was the opposite, his mother passed when he was too young to remember. Chase was raised by his father with the help of his aunt and uncle. While he and his father didn't currently live in the same town, they talked or texted almost daily. He could only imagine how devastated he would be if something happened to him.

When Rachel's tears seemed to slow, he led her over to the sitting area and sat on the large overstuffed chair, pulling her down into his lap.

After a few minutes, he felt her tense up as she tried to pull back. "I'm sorry."

"For what?"

"Being a cry baby. I need to get up." She tried to move but he held her. "Chase, we can't be sitting like this."

"Rachel, you don't need to apologize for having emotions. It's me, no one else is here. And as for sitting with me, I like having you close," Chase admitted.

"But it's not proper," Rachel began.

"Says who? Who will know what we do or don't do? You sat on my lap last night at Memories, so half the town already has their own ideas of what we've been doing together," Chase quickly answered as he watched her face closely. "Does it really bother you what others think? Am I making you uncomfortable?"

"I guess not," Rachel admitted after thinking about it. She placed her hand palm to palm into his, interlocking their fingers.

He watched as her hand played with his and she leaned comfortably into him. "Rach, I don't ever want to do something you don't like or aren't ready to do. Please tell me, alright?"

Rob walked out of the barn when he heard his cousin's truck approaching. Chase barely had his feet on the ground when Rob called out, "Have you heard from Lila?"

Chase paused for a moment, assessing Rob's level of anxiety, "No, did you have plans with her today?"

"No, but she's not answering my calls," Rob answered as he followed Chase up the stairs to his apartment.

"Rob, what is the urgency? It's not even eleven in the morning. She may have forgotten to charge her phone. She's a grown woman," Chase stated, thinking of the ways Lila would make it up to him.

"Shannon and Clara aren't answering their phones either," Rob replied, thinking it would help him understand the severity of the situation.

Chase was sitting on a bench by his door changing his shoes to his work boots. "What's with all the urgency? Do the girls all usually text you every morning?"

"No, of course not," Rob answered.

"So, what's the problem?"

"Eric is being released," Rob reported.

"Yeah, I heard about that in town," Chase said. He finally understood the anxiety. That was the same reason he made sure he knew Rachel's schedule and would be back by early evening. Chase stood up and returned down the steps as he mentally listed the chores he needed to complete before heading back. He planned to bring the paperwork with him. "Rob, I promise you, each of the girls were safely tucked in at one place or another last night. They are all good, most likely very hung over from the excessive drinking."

"Are you trying to not tell me Clara left the bar with Connor again?" Rob demanded.

like a couple of teenagers   419

Chase simply closed his eyes as he prayed for restraint. Otherwise he would risk hurting his fists and spending too much time in the emergency room if he punched him.

Rachel enjoyed the morning with a walk to see her grandmother. After a couple of hours, she decided to get ice cream. While Rachel enjoyed her cone, she sat on the bench outside and watched the traffic and people. When her cell rang, she answered without looking at the caller ID, "Hello?"

"Rachel, Baby! How are you? Miss me?"

It was the last voice she expected to hear. She glanced quickly at her phone to confirm she guessed correctly and groaned.

"Max, hi." Rachel answered cautiously.

"Are you missing city life yet? I looked up your town, it only has about a dozen restaurants, a couple of motels, and only three bars. No night clubs. What the hell do you all do at night?" Max asked.

Go to bed at a decent hour, Rachel thought. But fortunately, he began talking so she didn't have to answer.

"There are many farms of every kind. You don't live on a farm, do you?" He asked with concern.

"No, I live in town," she answered.

"I'd like to come visit you," Max blurted out, hoping she would take the hint and give him a formal invite. "School doesn't start until after Labor Day, that's over two months away. You will be bored with nothing to do. You can show me around and help me understand why living in a small town is the new best thing."

"Max, why would you want to? You just said there's nothing to do. I moved back because this is my home. I want to be near my grandmother and I also need to settle my mother's affairs," Rachel patiently explained. "I am never bored here. I am also working. Just because the kids don't start classes until September, doesn't mean I don't have anything to do. I have to plan my lessons, and meet the teachers and parents. I won't have much time for you. You will be bored."

She allowed a slight fib as she wasn't actually meeting anyone until August first, but she didn't want to encourage him.

"Baby, I get why you did it, I really do. I understand the importance of family. I just wished it weren't so Mayberry, then we'd have a better chance," Max calmly explained.

"Better chance at what?" Rachel asked, totally confused.

"Being together, I miss you. I miss seeing your beautiful blue eyes and your bright smile. I want to visit, stay with you, and give you a chance," he stated in what he thought of as his bedroom voice.

Rachel was too stunned to process what he was saying, he wants to give her a chance at what? Suddenly she heard her name being called. She looked over her shoulder to see a friend from high school calling out as she approached.

"Max, I need to go," she said as she hung up the phone.

Max smiled and put his cell into his pocket, she did not say no.

Rachel talked with her friend for a few minutes and was about to head back home when her phone rang again. Lesson learned, she checked the caller ID before answering.

"Hey Clara, I am so glad you called," Rachel answered, very relieved. "Are we still on for brunch tomorrow?"

"That's why I'm calling. I can't make it. Connor invited me and the kids to his lake house for the weekend. I also want to apologize for bailing last night. It was your first night back, and I left early. I am so sorry," Clara stated.

"Clara, it wasn't a problem. We all had fun and mingled. So, you and Connor, eh? You have been holding out on me. But Chase brought me home and stayed with me. He made breakfast. It was nice," Rachel said thoughtfully.

"Really? You and Chase spent the night together?" Clara asked, slightly surprised as Rachel was the most prim and proper in the group.

Her current plan was to wait until she was married.

"Well, he spent the night, but we didn't sleep together in the same room," she stated sheepishly. "We've made plans to have dinner tonight. He's going to take me out."

"Wow, dinner and breakfast, all in one day. Aren't you lucky?"

"I don't know, maybe he just feels sorry for me," Rachel answered, showing her insecurities.

"Rach, Chase is a great guy. He's definitely in my top 5 favorite guys, but he's not going to spend the better part of a weekend with a girl because he feels sorry for her," Clara confirmed.

"So, you think it's a date?" Skepticism was evident.

"I think so. What are you going to wear?"

When Clara was finished with her call, she placed her cell on the table as she leaned onto the rail of the deck. She looked out over the lake and smiled as she felt the breeze on her face. What a beautiful day! When she closed her eyes, Clara could actually hear the water lapping on the bank and the motors from the boats. How did I not know what I was missing before, she wondered as she silently played her game, with her eyes closed, identifying the sounds.

Connor stepped out onto the deck, watching her as she remained at the rail with her eyes closed. As he approached, she turned towards him. He handed her a drink and eyed her carefully. He really needed to tell her about Eric. Clara was bound to find out from one of her friends, and he knew she'd already talked to Rachel. He slowly went to sit.

Clara sat beside Connor with her drink as she wondered what was wrong. He was usually the easy going one in this relationship. She sipped her drink and then just asked.

Connor struggled to find the right words, reminding himself they have always been honest. Just be honest with her. "Clara, Matt stopped in last night to warn us Eric is being released today on bail. With the weekend approaching, he assumed the role of your attorney. You can always have it changed. But he petitioned to have him under house arrest and a restraining order. He plans to stop in later to explain and answer questions you may have."

"So that's the real reason you invited me here? Because Eric is getting out?" Clara asked.

"No, I had already thought to ask you. As much as I loved the idea of you staying the weekend, I was hesitant. Until last night. I wanted to spend the weekend with you. We never just hang out all weekend. It's usually me in and out. The other crap was just the icing on the cake."

Connor was quiet as she returned to the rail. Leaning down on her elbows, she looked out over the lake. It was so peaceful and relaxing here. She really needed this and if she were honest with herself, she really did want to build something with him. She wanted to see where they would go together. She knew he loved her and she could trust him.

When she turned around, he was standing a few feet from her. He looked worried.

"Connor, please just tell me next time. I'm not a delicate flower that withers with bad news. Something this important doesn't just involve me or you. I also need to think of my children. I can't have you and your brother making decisions on my behalf without my knowledge. I'll give you a pass this time because you worried I'd pull away when you were finally getting lucky," Clara answered with a grin.

"So, you aren't angry with me?" He asked as he started towards her.

"No, you are being protective. You did tell me. But I think you should make it up to me for being sneaky," she stated as she allowed him to hug her.

"How long will they be sleeping?" Connor wondered as he thought of a few ways.

"Usually an hour and a half or two," she answered as she caressed his butt.

Connor's eyes sparkled as he kissed her. Clara let the kiss play out before she pulled back with her eyes on him, she pulled her dress up over her head to reveal her bikini. When he stepped closer, she stepped back again as she tossed her dress onto a chair, "Let's check out the hot tub."

Without waiting for an answer, Clara turned around and headed down a flight of stairs towards the lower deck. The house was locked up from the front with a fence around his property. Someone either needed a key to enter or would enter by the lake. The top deck had a gate. Connor would hear the kids when they woke up.

He smiled as he followed her down.

It didn't seem like much time had passed, but it was actually close to an hour. Clara's bikini top was floating in the water while she sat straddling him. They were kissing as his hands were all over her when they heard, "Good God! You two are like a couple of teenagers! Going at it at every opportunity! And outside in broad daylight! Where are the kids?" Matt looked up towards the deck.

"They are napping. We were getting ready to check on them. What the hell are you doing here?" Connor snapped back.

"You invited me over. I came over, even sent a text. I'll wait upstairs." He shook his head in amazement, relieved none of his sons were with him. He never saw his brother this loose before.

Matt arrived up on the deck, figuring he would give them some time to regroup or whatever. He looked out over the lake, noticing the boat at the dock. He smiled as he thought about coordinating when they could go water skiing with the boys. He turned when he heard a knock.

The little girl was standing inside the glass door holding her baby doll. He had seen the children around town with their mother, but never up close. He opened the door and squatted down.

"Hi Hailey. I am Matthew, Connor's older brother. How are you?" Matt asked in a soft voice.

She smiled and held up her baby doll.

"Would you like me to bring you to your mother?" When the little girl nodded, he held out his hands and was pleasantly surprised she stepped into his arms. He picked her up as he stood. He talked with her for a few minutes, asking her about her dolly.

"Mama! NaNa!" The little girl yelled with delight as she saw her mother with Connor at the top of the steps. They were each wrapped in a towel.

"Mama, Mamu, Mama. NaNa, Mamu, Mama." Hailey beamed at her mother.

Clara laughed softly, "Yes Hailey, that's Connor's brother Matthew. Let's get you changed and check on your brother."

She opened her hands and the little girl reached out. Once in her mother's arms, she looked over her shoulders and waved.

"I didn't understand a word she said," Matt stated as he handed a couple of files from his briefcase over to his brother.

"Reese is the only one that seems to always understand her, but I suspect he's making it up to fit his agenda," Connor stated as he glanced at the papers. They talked for a few minutes.

"Connor?" Reese was yelling as he came running out onto the deck. He paused when he realized there was another person with him.

Connor squatted down, and the boy didn't need any further encouragement. He jumped into his arms. Reese was still eyeing the stranger. Connor introduced them.

"Are we going back on the boat? Can I drive again? Are you going out with us on the boat, Matt and see me drive the boat?"

"Not today, Big Guy. Another day, I promise. And I will bring my boys to play with you," Matt promised.

"You don't want to ride with me in the boat?" He asked sadly.

"Oh Connor, you two will have your hands full. I suspect I've embarrassed Clara enough this weekend and she's hiding until I leave," Matt chuckled as he said his good-bye.

Lila stepped out onto the back deck after refreshing their drinks. "I

like a couple of teenagers   425

just checked in with Chase."

"Yeah? Is he relieved you are alive and well?" Dallas asked as he accepted his glass.

"Honestly, he didn't seem bothered either way. He was preoccupied completing his chores and getting back to Rachel's," she stated. She sipped from her glass. "He wanted me to call Rob. He's got himself all worked up in a frenzy. Apparently, Eric is getting out on bail today under house arrest. Chase isn't too happy either with Rachel's house next to his."

Dallas' blue green eyes looked at her in surprise. "What? How is that bastard getting out on bail? After all the things he did?"

Dallas reached for his cell to call Clara.

"Hello?"

"Clara, how is the lake house?" Dallas asked as he looked at Lila with a shrug.

Lila leaned back in her seat and smiled. Yeah, he's a big brother alright. She had seen the signs during high school. He always wanted to make sure Clara was alright. Dallas was constantly redirecting his cousin Danny away from her. Lila had been aware of Dallas' interest in knowing Clara back in high school. She wanted to help the siblings' relationship but was sworn to secrecy. She liked how everything was finally coming out in the open. Well, almost. Her brother and parents were still unaware of Dallas.

Clara laughed at the hidden agenda, "It's such a beautiful day. Connor's lake house is beautiful. He brought the kids and I out for a boat ride."

"Oh yeah? Is it nice? I heard about the boat and jet skis. His place is not too far from mine. Why don't you all come over for dinner?" He looked questionably at Lila. She just smiled.

"Hold on a minute," Clara answered. He could hear her talking to Connor. "It's Dallas. He is checking up on me without it looking like he's checking up on me. Likely, he has heard about Eric. He's inviting us to his place for dinner." Then he heard Connor's voice. "We have plenty of food. Have them come here."

"You talk to him," she said as she handed him the phone and went to grab Hailey and the stick she found. They were out in the backyard enjoying the warmth of the sun and husking corn on the cob. The little girl was distracted by the new environment. Reese was still helping, pulling one piece of silk string at a time.

A moment later, Connor placed her cell on the table and announced two more were coming for dinner in the next hour. He watched as Clara, walking around in her bikini, grabbed Hailey before heading up the steps.

"Where are you going?" He called after her.

"Changing!" Clara called back, already half-way up the steps.

"Why? I like what you are already wearing."

Clara turned back and smiled. "Don't worry Connor, I'll make sure you like what I have on."

It wasn't what she said, but how she said it that made him quietly groan.

Dallas hung up his cell and looked apologetically at Lila as he leaned in for a kiss. "I am so sorry. I promised we would let you decide what we do today and I overruled without asking you first. We'll reschedule skinny dipping first thing tomorrow, I promise."

Lila laughed as she went inside to prepare for the outing. The skinny dipping was his idea.

a lot to process

Dallas and Lila arrived shortly after the conversation. Lila hung out with Clara on the deck with the children while Connor brought Dallas down to check out the boat and jet skis.

"Sorry we came crashing over," Lila stated as Clara brought her a glass of lemonade.

"Oh, don't worry. Connor has warned me this is what big brothers do, constantly harass and put their noses in our business," Clara said.

"Yeah, don't I know it. You have to admit, Dallas is more subtle than Rob ever was," Lila responded.

"He certainly is. It doesn't bother me that he called to check up on me. It's nice having a sibling," she answered. "How is Rob handling you and Dallas together?"

Lila shrugged. "I don't think he really knows yet. He's probably hearing through the grapevine the bunch of us were playing volleyball together, hung out afterwards, and were at Memories last night. But I have no idea what he's hearing about us specifically."

"Hmm, I'd love to be a fly on the wall when he finds out," Clara chuckled.

"Have you heard from him today?" Lila wondered.

"Yeah. When I checked my messages around noon, he had left eight texts and four voicemails. It's too nice of a day to listen to his third degree on everything. He would demand to know where I am and come right out. He and Connor would probably get into it and honestly, for what? Eric can't get to me here without getting noticed. Back in town will be another story, and we'll deal with it. One day at a time like we do with everything else in life," Clara said as she shrugged.

"How are you holding up?" Lila asked.

"Alright, I guess. Nothing has really hit yet. He's out on bail, Connor's brother confirmed it and notified us earlier. I just can't believe he's actually the one doing what everyone is reporting. I grew up in the house next door to him, it shocks me," she answered.

"I know, me too," Lila agreed. "Rob and Chase say he always had a thing for you in high school."

"I don't know. He never made a move or anything," Clara answered thoughtfully, but found herself remembering what he said the day he got arrested.What the hell did he mean by every time she always went to Connor? Did he drug her other times? If that were the case, how long has it been going on?

Dallas walked around the dock, checking various parts of the boat, and asked why the jet skis weren't in the water yet.

"This is the first weekend I've been here since I won them. One of us has to stay back with the kids, and it's not as fun to ride by yourself. However, you both come back another weekend with your suits and we can go at it. We can even water ski," Connor suggested.

"That would be great. It may take a bit between mine and Lila's schedule," Dallas answered as he surveyed the surrounding area, seemingly keeping an eye out for trouble.

"You don't have to hide your intentions, Dallas. You can come right out and ask questions. You're Clara's older brother. You are one of the few that have the right to ask about her. I warned her it's what older brothers do," Connor said. "But I can appreciate your not rushing over here and shoving your way in trying to get answers. There are terms to Eric's release. He is under house arrest with an ankle monitor. However, Matt and I are confident he can find his way around that. He cannot go within fifty yards of Clara, the kids, either of her homes, work, or the daycare."

"So, does Clara have to notify Eric to move to the other side of his home if she goes to the Hawks House?" Dallas asked.

"I don't see her going there anytime soon, so Matt didn't force the issue. Clara's getting a security system in place this week. I have talked to the hospital about the daycare security, and we are having a better system installed at the nursing home with added security. I already have security systems at both my places," Connor stated as he sipped from his beer.

"Sounds like you have all your bases covered when she's home and at work, but if I know anything about Clara, she's Miss Independence. She will be going to the store, volleyball, Memories, even Rachel's. Do you have an armed escort assigned to her?" Dallas inquired.

"Yeah, I wish. She won't allow that. I didn't even suggest it. We have to trust she will use her common sense and not do anything stupid. She's had self-defense training," Connor informed him.

"Really?"

"Yeah, I showed her the basics when she was in middle school, and had a friend give her a few personal classes when she was in high school," he explained.

"That's good, I guess, if she remembers what she was taught. She may need a refresher course," Dallas suggested.

"You get her to agree and I'll set it up," Connor answered.

After Dallas and Lila left, Connor was sitting out on the deck with a glass of wine while Clara was checking on the children. When she joined him, she was dressed in a simple berry colored nightie. Without a word, they both watched the moonlight reflecting on the water.

"Kids settled in alright?" Connor asked a few minutes later as he pulled her legs up over his lap.

"Oh yeah. They were exhausted. Even with the nap, they should sleep well tonight," she relaxed as she watched his hands on her legs, and sipped her wine.

"What are you thinking?" Connor asked after a moment. His hand was slowly caressing her legs as they talked.

"I don't know. A little bit of everything, I guess. It's beautiful here. I can't believe I'm sitting here with you, and we spent a Saturday evening with another couple as a couple; Dallas is my older brother, and Eric is a possible murder suspect!" Clara shook her head and sipped again. "I don't know which one is the most difficult to believe."

"Yeah, I guess you have had a bit to process," Connor agreed.

"I wonder if everyone is overreacting. Eric has never harmed me. He didn't force himself on me in his office. It was more his body language suggesting we could be more, I guess. I just don't think he would hurt me," she reported.

Connor's hand paused as he looked at her in the moonlight. "Clara, putting a date rape drug in your drink and leaving you vulnerable may not have caused you physical harm that night, but he did open you up to potentially getting hurt. It pisses me off every time I think about it. What if I wasn't sitting there that night and another guy got his hands on you. Worse, what if Eric had guided you out."

He simply kept the rest of his thoughts to himself. He was thankful those scenarios didn't happen. And he had to remind himself each time his mind went down that road.

"You know, I can remember everything about that night. I thought people black out with that stuff," Clara commented.

"You've always been intuitive and smart. Maybe that's how your body has coped," Connor suggested.

Clara thought about the times she left her bed as a child and hid in his treehouse. She could never explain why she did it and he never questioned her. Of course, he didn't know how often she climbed up for the night.

They sat together in silence, each in their own thoughts, sipping wine as his hand resumed gently stroking her legs.

"You aren't having trouble with us as a couple, are you?" Connor asked as his hand started to slide further up her legs.

Clara giggled as he reached for her glass to place it on the table...

Eric was glad to finally be out. He had to sit through the humiliation of lectures first from his father, then his grandfather. If that wasn't bad enough, his mother was beside him arguing with his father. Eric was relieved when he was allowed to return to his suite up on the third floor. He had to disguise himself with different color contact lenses, a wig, and bigger clothes before he could head out for the night. Disabling the ankle guard wasn't even worth mentioning. He simply hacked the computer into a loop, showing he was wandering around his suite. The codes to hack into the sheriff's department were easily retrieved from his father's office.

He felt good just walking around outside, but he kept to the shadows and avoided the main streets. His normal hang out was packed when he arrived after ten. Initially, Eric sat at the bar, pleased to hear he was the main topic of conversation. But it quickly pissed him off when he realized the comments were unfavorable.

Annoyed that his town had turned against him, Eric grabbed his beer and retreated to the corner. His arrogance and self-pity kept him from focusing on his surroundings. He was never aware he was being followed. Of course, it is debatable if it would have made a difference.

Without intending, the brooding, loner aura worked in his favor. A younger girl sat beside him. He wasn't sure of her name, but he thought he may have gone to school with her cousins. She was pretty, shoulder length brown hair with waves. Her eyes were green. When she smiled, a crooked incisor showed, but added to her charm.

Within a half hour, Eric was following her out the front door. She had an apartment a block over, on the third floor, in the back towards the alley.

Neither was aware of being followed. But, if they had looked back, they still probably wouldn't have seen anything as he kept to the shadows.

• • • •

Evil could not decide if this was a good or bad thing as he followed the kid with the young girl. He wasn't surprised he would attempt to get out, curious to know how he overcame the ankle guard. The girl, while young, could be useful, he thought as he followed just long enough to determine where she lived before continuing on to see his Babydoll…

the prom

The longer days of June made for longer daylight, allowing the Foxwood cousins more time to work on the Hawks House. The following Monday, Rob was in one of the bedrooms upstairs fiddling with a loose board in the wall. He was surprised the piece gave way, revealing a hidden pocket. He reached inside and pulled out a loose cloth, "What do we have here?"

Clara already had the children in bed and was preparing for the next morning when she heard the knock on the front door. Glancing at the clock, she was surprised by the late visit. Hesitantly, she peeked out the window, relieved it was only Rob standing on the porch holding a box.

"Rob, come in. Is everything alright?"

"Clara, I should have called first. I forget how late it actually is with these longer days. I found something I'm sure you want back," Rob explained. He was about to remove his work boots, but Clara told him not to bother.

He followed her into the kitchen, placing the box on the table as she asked if he wanted a drink.

"No, hell I shouldn't even be in here. I'm covered in sawdust and drywall crap. I just wanted to drop these off. I don't think you want these falling into the wrong hands," Rob explained as he gestured towards the box.

"What's in here?" Clara asked as she looked inside the box. It was full of old composition books.

"I'm guessing your journals. You had a pretty sweet hiding spot in your room," Rob answered. He watched as she looked confused, grabbing a book.

"I never had a journal," she whispered as she opened it. Her heart skipped a beat as she recognized her mother's handwriting. Clara quickly skimmed a few lines of her mother's description of the rose garden behind Hawks House. She hugged it to her chest as she looked up into his steel blue eyes. "These were my mother's. Thanks Rob."

Rob's heartbeat quickened when she came over to kiss his cheek. He turned to leave but stopped at the doorway of the kitchen, "Listen Clara, you are being safe, right? Taking all appropriate precautions especially since that bastard is out of jail."

Clara held onto her patience at the simple question, telling herself he was only being protective. She gently placed the notebook back in the box as she sighed before turning back with a questioning look, "What are you talking about?"

"You opened the door pretty quick," Rob answered.

Clara heard the familiar condescending tone he used in high school and immediately expressed her irritation, "Rob, I get enough lectures from Connor, Matt, and Dallas. I don't need it from you."

"I get Connor is your boyfriend, it's expected he'd be looking out for you, or I'd say get rid of him. It's a stretch for his brother but what right does Dallas have to be lecturing you? Who the hell does he think he is?" He demanded as he stepped towards her.

"Rob, boyfriend or not, Connor has always been supportive and protective without being condescending. Matt has been retained as my lawyer. He's the one that petitioned the judge to have Eric put under house arrest," she said as she tried to contain her patience. Then it dawned on her. "You don't know, do you?"

"Know what?" Rob asked with a slight panic. Did she elope again?

"Dallas is my brother," Clara proudly stated. Feeling slightly juvenile as she was able to jab back at him after the times he tried to keep them apart. She was confident Dallas would have approached her sooner if not for Rob's constant interference.

"What! How the hell did that happen?" He was so shocked by the news, he stepped back, leaning onto the dining room table.

"Probably the normal way. Good old Daddy couldn't keep it in his pants, but to be fair, the affair was before he married my mother," Clara rudely answered. But probably while they were engaged, she had already speculated.

"He's your fucking brother? You have got to be kidding me! This has got to be the worst summer yet. First, you hook up with the good doctor, and now you are fucking related to the town asshole? What the hell!" Rob almost shouted.

"What the hell is your problem? Can't you be happy for me? Why are you making this into a big deal?" Clara's voice was rising with each question.

"Because I'd hoped you would give me a chance when you returned. That's all I have ever wanted. A fair chance at starting something with you," he finally admitted for the first time. "You were supposed to stay the summer after graduation, instead you left. I thought we would finally get together. But you were gone without saying goodbye. When I returned to the city that fall, you kept your distance. And now years later, you come back and I lose my chance again."

Clara was stunned quiet as she stared into the familiar blue eyes, but felt her tempter rise as her mind replayed the scene from the prom. "You had a chance. You were the one that hooked up with Isabella Daynee."

"Clara, she was stumbling around. I was just helping her, keeping her from falling," Rob attempted to assure her.

"Rob, I was sick that night. I literally stumbled out into the hall, fell over, and picked myself up from the floor before I threw up my dinner. I may have even passed out. When I came out, you were making out with her." Clara's voice was dangerously low.

"Clara, she kissed me," Rob answered defensively.

Clara laughed harshly, "Yeah, I believe that's how it started, but that isn't how it finished, is it?"

"What the hell are you talking about?" He asked, fearful of what she would say. How did she know? To this day, he still couldn't figure out how it happened.

"All these years later and you are going to lie about it? What's the point? I know you were having sex with her," she whispered.

"What? Who told you?" Rob's face paled.

"I saw you two in the back of your car. Plus, she was bragging about it at school the following Monday. Every time I turned around, there she was talking about you and what you two did. Why do you think I left town? You were my date. You embarrassed me by having sex with the class slut at my prom, you idiot! If you were going to be having sex that night, it should have been with me!" She yelled back. She had stepped back into the wall. She forced herself to breathe as she willed to herself to calm down. That was years ago, she could not possibly still be upset about this, could she?

"You were always picking any girl that would give it to you over me. You never even tried anything with me. You never attempted. I finally realized you weren't interested in being with me," she whispered.

Rob was utterly shocked! If he had not already been leaning, partially sitting, on the table, he would have fallen to the floor. Clara was expecting him to make a move on her at the prom. Instead, she saw him with Isabella. All these years, and she never said a word. He embarrassed her and still she never confronted him. But why would she?

She wasn't like that. Instead, he let his hormones dictate his actions. Rob had not even considered the possibility that his actions would get back to her. And it ruined his chance to be with the one person he wanted. He was a real jerk back then, just like Lila said. And now, the truth was finally out.

"Clara?" Rob stepped closer to her, daring to place a hand on her shoulder. When she didn't answer or look up, he continued anyway, "I am so sorry for hurting you. I get why you weren't interested in giving me a chance. I blew my chances back then. I've been dishonest about it. I even tried to keep it from you. That was foolish, especially in this town. I am sorry."

She finally looked up. The sadness in her eyes made him feel even worse.

"Rob, it was high school. I'm over it and have moved on," she answered. "The weekend after the prom, I finally realized I had no reason to remain in town, no real ties. I was free to do as I wanted with my life."

"Yeah, you certainly have. Now I have to let your boyfriend beat me up," he sighed as he wiped a tear from her cheek.

"Why would he?"

"Because I hurt you and made you cry," Rob answered honestly. "It's what I would do if anyone hurt you."

"He's not like that," Clara assured him.

"I saw him rightfully go after Eric. He is like that, a guy protecting his girl," he stated. He heard a vehicle pulling in. "I'm going to take off, Clara. Are we good?"

She nodded as he kissed her forehead. "Rob, thanks for bringing over my mother's journals."

Rob was walking towards the front door as Connor entered. He already knew Foxwood was inside, he saw his truck out front. He was certainly curious to know why he looked so sad, but the guy remained silent as he nodded before walking out the door.

Clara wasn't aware Connor came home. After Rob had stepped away, she slid down the wall onto the floor with her face buried in her knees. She wasn't sure how long she was sitting on the floor before she became aware of him sitting next to her.

"Hey Beautiful," Connor greeted her. He placed an arm around her and hugged her when she leaned into him.

"Did you two have the long overdue talk again?" He felt her nod.

"Want to talk about it?" He felt her shrug.

"You might feel better," he advised. He heard her sigh.

"He doesn't like Dallas and just found out he's my brother. He still doesn't know about him and Lila either," she answered.

"Why doesn't he like him?" Connor was curious.

"I don't know. Old family feud goes back generations," Clara answered. "Possibly before we gained our independence."

"Is that it?" There had to be more. This was old news, he thought as he felt her tensing up. She was always protective of Foxwood. "Why did he leave?"

"He doesn't want you to kick his ass," she answered honestly.

"Why would I kick his ass?" Connor wondered. Not the answer he was expecting. He smiled at the thought. He had considered it a few times in the past but knew it would upset her.

"Because he hurt my feelings," Clara admitted.

"Why did he make my girl cry?"

"I'm not crying," she denied as she wiped a tear before it fell. "He just found out I already knew. He didn't know that I knew."

Connor rolled his eyes. He felt like she was back in high school.

"Would you like me to kick his ass? I will if you want me to," Connor assured her.

"No, that's alright. I told him I was over it and have moved on," Clara declared sadly. It made him wonder how over it she really was.

They sat for a bit longer.

"Clara?"

"Yeah?"

"How much longer are we going to sit here on the floor?"

"Do you have something better to do?"

"Honestly, about ten things come to mind," Connor admitted.

"I don't feel like stripping right now," she informed him.

Connor chuckled as he stood up. He reached down for her hand, pleased she put her hand into his, and pulled her up. He cradled her face, using his thumb to dry her cheek. He leaned down to kiss her. "Alright, I'll wait until later to watch you strip. Even though it was the one thing keeping me going today," he teased.

"Sorry," she answered miserably.

"That's alright, I still love you. Have you eaten yet? I'll go pick something up. Do you want your burger or club sandwich?" Connor asked, already texting.

"The burger," Clara sighed.

Connor reached for her hand as she started to turn away. He pulled her towards him and backed her into the wall as he leaned down to give her the hello kiss he imagined during the drive over.

"Connor, should we be doing this now? Your brother could walk through the door any minute," Clara stated sarcastically.

Connor's head fell to her shoulder as he laughed. When he stopped laughing, he asked, "Did you give him a key?"

"Good God, no! He would probably use it," she concluded.

"No doubt. Learn from my mistakes, don't give it to him, no matter how many times he asks for it," he cautioned her. "Are you alright? I'm going to head out now and grab a beer with Devan and Matt while I wait for the food."

He kissed her again, "Maybe you'll feel like stripping for me later."

"I'd rather watch you strip," she answered thoughtfully.

"I don't have anything underneath as exciting as you do right now," Connor predicted.

"I might not have anything on for you to get excited about," Clara stated as she walked out of the room.

Connor groaned quietly as he debated following her. A part of him was surprised by her carnal side slowly emerging in the last few days.

Connor pulled up behind Foxwood's truck in front of Memories. He even sat next to him at the bar.

"Foxwood," Connor greeted him cheerfully, nodding his thanks when Devan placed a beer in front of him.

"I suppose you're here to kick my ass," Rob speculated.

"Do you want me to kick your ass?" Connor asked as he brought his beer up for a sip.

Devan's eyebrows went up in question as he listened to the conversation.

Rob shrugged. "I would if it were reversed."

Connor laughed as he looked over at Foxwood. He looked miserable.

"I should have known she would find out. I can't believe she was there then when it happened," Rob would later wonder why he was so open, to the good doctor, of all people.

Connor simply nodded. What did she witness? The suspense was almost killing him, but he was determined to not ask.

"I can't wrap my mind around the fact that she saw me having sex with the class slut at her prom. That's why she left for college early that summer," Rob concluded.

Relieved he wasn't drinking at that moment or he would have choked, Connor had no doubt. He tilted his head as everything finally fell into place. Twelve years later and he now understood Clara's anger that weekend. And fortunately, she did not tell him back then what happened. Connor would have gone out to the farm to beat Foxwood's ass.

"I have no idea how it started. I could barely remember the evening, only bits and pieces. One minute Clara and I are dancing together, sharing a glass of punch, then the next thing I know, I'm in the backseat with Isabella. Clara wouldn't talk to me that weekend and I never learned how she got home," he shared. "All the other girls got rides home with their dates and had no idea either."

Connor waited a beat before smiling with a wave of his hand.

Rob paused to look at Connor. "You? You gave her a ride?"

Connor nodded, "It was purely coincidental. I was coming home for Mother's Day weekend when I saw Clara Noelle alone, on the side of the road, in the dark. Not sure who was angrier, me or her. She sat silently in her seat, fuming, as I lectured her on common sense and safety. Honestly, I suspected she turned her hearing aids off."

Rob stared at him for a long moment. The good doctor just happened to be driving home along that route while she was walking home. Damn, if that isn't fate, what is? He not only screwed up royally twelve years ago, but his actions pushed her into his arms.

"How does it not bother you to come home and find your girl in tears after having an argument with another man? Don't you ever get jealous?" Rob asked.

"Not really. I've been through drama before with other women I've dated, but Clara is not like that. She's not going to do or say something to purposefully make me, or even you, jealous. It's not her style. At the end of the day, it's about trust and honesty. We've always trusted each other and have been honest, even when she was young," Connor shared.

"Honesty and trust," he repeated, as if they were the words to an evil spell.

"Hey Loverboy, sorry I'm late," Matt said as he slapped Connor's shoulder and sat on his other side. He looked around the bar.

Connor and Rob both turned to look around as well.

"Who are you looking for?" Connor asked. He already knew their cousin wasn't here.

"Looking for your girlfriend," Matt answered.

"Matt, you want a beer?" Devan called out. He wasn't sure if Connor picked up on what Foxwood just said, or rather hinted at. Rob admitted to limited memory of the prom after sharing a drink with Clara. Devan suspected the drink was spiked, causing Clara to be sick and Foxwood easily distracted by another girl. He wondered if Eric was at the prom.

"No, I better not. My wife will be upset with me if our dinner is cold and she smells beer on me," Matt answered.

"Clara is home with the kids," Connor answered cheerfully, unintentionally irking Rob.

"Oh? Is that what you tell yourself? How do you know she doesn't tell you that so she can have her boyfriend over?" Matt couldn't resist teasing his little brother.

"I have nothing to worry about, he's right here," Connor said as he pointed to Foxwood.

Matt leaned back to look around his brother at the accused.

"Robert Foxwood, huh? Still carrying the torch after all these years," Matt teased as his brother chuckled.

"Don't you have a motion to file or something?" Rob asked with irritation.

"Indeed," Matt grew serious as he informed his brother of the latest, "Lee has filed a petition for a restraining order against you. You are not to go near our wonderfully stupid fuck of a cousin, or you risk getting arrested."

"What? How can I even touch him, let alone kick his ass, if he stays where he's supposed to be, under house arrest? If I ever catch him where he has no business being, you can bet I will," Connor started before his brother cut him off.

"Please do not finish that statement. It is so much easier to fight the charges when there isn't a room full of witnesses, trust me," Matt said as he held up his hands defensively.

"What if I kick his ass?" Rob wondered out loud. It was something he thought about all through high school.

"I don't advise it. But, being the boyfriend and all, you do have a good reason. But just in case, here is my card. Don't say a word until I am present and we've had a chance to talk, no matter what the police try to tell you," Matt advised as he passed a card along the bar, then grabbed his brother's beer.

Connor chuckled.

Rob reached for the card, placing it in his wallet. Wouldn't hurt to have a lawyer handy, he decided.

"If you lose it, Clara can hook you up," Matt stated after he finished the beer. "Hey Devan, when will my order be ready?"

Devan placed a bag in front of Connor with the check as he spoke, "Matt, yours will be ready in a few minutes. I ask that you guys stop talking about premeditated murder, it makes me itchy. I don't want to be subpoenaed as a witness."

"All you need to remember is Foxwood is the boyfriend," Matt answered.

Connor pulled out a few twenties, gestured to his cousin he was picking up the others' tabs. He grabbed his bag and wished everyone good night.

• • • •

Evil had been watching the house, pleased to see his Babydoll was left alone after a late visit from the farmer, and a surprisingly short visit from the doctor. He was going to sneak inside once the lights went off, then wait an hour before sneaking into her room. But to his annoyance, the doctor returned. Oh, Babydoll, it'll have to wait another day...

The lone man tried a different tactic this evening. He sat across the street at The Lantern, alone, nursing his club soda. He was fortunate enough to have a seat near the window. He watched the streets, pleased the woman did indeed return. He was amazed at the activity for a Monday evening. He remained alone as a small local band started up, and the crowd grew on the pathetically small dance floor. As he observed the many beautiful women dancing, he remained alone as he planned his next move. His intent was to follow the woman home to determine where she lived. Then he could plan the next phase of the job. That was his intent but he became distracted when a woman sat beside him. Things were looking up after all...

SHADOWS OF THE NIGHT

42 spoken like a true foxwood

During her lunch hour on Tuesday, Clara received a text from Dallas inviting her and Connor to join them that night for country dancing a few towns over. Clara sent a text to Connor asking where he was and another to Michelle about babysitting. She looked up when there was a knock on the door, and smiled when Connor stepped inside.

Connor looked around, realizing she was alone, he closed the door behind him before going over to kiss her. He initially intended it to be a quick kiss, but Clara somehow pulled him deeper into it. And then there was another knock on the door.

Matt walked into the therapy room, expecting a private moment with Clara while her department was at lunch. He wasn't expecting to see Connor leaning against her desk with Clara standing between his legs, the two heavily kissing. Matt shouldn't have been surprised after what he saw over the weekend. "Seriously? At work? Don't you two ever stop? I need to review the kissing policy."

"We have a kissing policy?" Clara repeated with confusion as she tried to step away, but Connor tightened his hold.

"I'm seriously considering it. It's never been a problem until now with you two." Matt's face remained serious as he teased.

"What do you want?" Connor asked, ignoring his brother's comments.

"Clara, I have these files for you. There are a couple of patients we are considering for admission, but their cases look more complicated than what we are used to treating. If you could make a recommendation either way, that would be great. I also have the forms regarding the budget and a list of resumes already in HR if you want to look them over and set up interviews. And last is your copy of the paperwork." Matt handed her the files, then smiled when Connor had no choice but to release her.

"Alright, Sir, I will look over this now. When do you want the answers?" Clara immediately opened the first file to avoid eye contact.

Matt smiled with amusement when she called him sir. *She is definitely embarrassed.* "I'll be in Connor's office until four. It'll be good to have an answer by then. Also, the security system will be put in tomorrow around noon. Who will be there?"

"I will, I have the easiest schedule to work around," Connor answered as Clara continued to look over the paperwork at her desk.

Matt nodded before he turned to leave, but stopped at the door, "Can I trust you two to behave until at least after four?"

"Get out of here," Connor waved him away. Matt's laughter trailed in his wake.

Clara had the files on her desk. She found the personal one and placed it into her briefcase. She skimmed the list of applications. A few names were familiar, but none she could place. She wanted to go ahead and set up a few interviews, at least for prn coverage. Next, she turned to the potential new admissions.

"What did he give you?" Connor asked as he watched various emotions play on her face.

"Paperwork regarding the wills," Clara answered softly, reaching for her cell to check a text.

"And why are you looking for me?" Connor asked.

"What?" Clara looked up confused.

Connor pulled her back into an embrace as he spoke, "You texted me asking where I am. Here I am and why do you ask."

"Oh, yeah. Dallas invited us to go dancing tonight at some country dancing place, but it's moot. I can't get a sitter. Michelle already commits to Wednesday and Friday nights and doesn't want to give another," Clara answered sadly. Her focus had shifted to the unpleasant task of dealing with the wills and estates.

Connor heard the others from her department returning and released her after a quick kiss, "If you find a sitter, let me know. I would never turn down an evening dancing with you."

"You two-step?"

"Not really."

"Why would you want to go?"

"Good company, music and you. I'm always game for that, Beautiful," he winked as he turned to leave.

Kim and Marie entered the room. "Clara, what's wrong?"

"Oh, we were invited to join another couple tonight, but my usual sitter is busy," Clara explained as she continued to look over the paperwork on her desk.

"What about my niece? She watches my kids all the time. I'll give her a call." Kim pulled out her cell to call.

Jordan was available and excited to be earning extra cash. Her older brother was able to drop her off and pick her up. Jordan's mother worked at the facility in housekeeping. Clara already knew the niece.

That evening, Clara and Connor entered the dance club close to sunset. She looked around at multiple small bars set up around the perimeter of the large room with small tables scattered all around. In the center of the room was a large dance floor already covered with couples two-stepping to George Strait singing about a fool-hearted memory. When Connor finished paying the cover charge, he grabbed

Clara's hand as he looked around. He spotted Dallas waving them over.

"Clara, I'm so glad you guys made it!" Lila hugged both Clara and Connor. She was happy she and Dallas could finally hang out with her friends as a couple, without fear of it getting back to her brother.

"I'm going to go get drinks. What would you like?" Connor asked.

"Jameson and ginger ale," Clara answered without thinking, not seeing Connor and Dallas share a look, each chuckling.

"I can't believe you've never two-stepped before, Clara. I learned when I lived in the city," Lila was saying. "But don't worry, it's not difficult. If I can do it, you definitely can."

Dallas nodded agreement. As he sipped from his beer, one of his favorite songs came on. He grabbed Lila's hand as he placed his drink down and led her to the large dance floor.

Clara watched them dance, surprised at how good they were together. Lila looks so happy and in love. How long have these two been together? She found herself wondering again.

"Considering I've known you all your life, I am amazed you can still surprise me," Connor stated as he placed the drinks on the table. She looked at him in question. "I never thought of you as an Irish whiskey girl. I only knew about your love for tequila."

"Well, this seems like a good Irish whiskey evening," Clara said as she watched couples dancing. "Have you been here before? You know how to do this?"

"Yeah, I've been here a few times," he answered vaguely. They both watched as Dallas and Lila reversed and he twirled Lila without breaking rhythm. "But I am not that good."

"They really are good, aren't they?"

Connor and Clara watched their friends dancing, not aware they were also being watched by many others.

When the song was over, Dallas and Lila returned to the table as Clara complimented, "You two are really good. Dallas, I didn't know you were such a good dancer. Color me impressed."

Dallas laughed as he reached for her hand, "Come on, I'll show you."

Clara hesitated, but Connor smiled and nodded in encouragement.

Lila and Connor talked as they watched Dallas give Clara instructions. Within minutes they were dancing around the floor. They were two-stepping forward and back. Dallas said something, causing Clara to shake her head, but he nodded encouragingly and then twirled her, leading her back into the two-step without losing the rhythm. Clara laughed with excitement.

"I thought Clara said she's never two-stepped before," Lila commented. "She just twirled without a misstep."

"That's what she says. Either she's a natural, or Dallas is a really good teacher," Connor responded.

"Yeah, with them being related it's probably both. He dances around all the time at home. The more I see them together, the more I see the similarities," Lila answered.

"Yeah? How long have you known?" Connor asked. He agreed with Clara, and suspected Lila and Dallas were too comfortable with each other to have just recently started dating.

Lila sighed at her slip but answered honestly, "Since high school."

"You two have been together since high school?" Connor was shocked they had been able to keep it a secret for that long. . Especially with the town's ability to speculate and gossip. "Why didn't he tell her he was her brother sooner?"

"We were on and off when he joined the army but always kept in touch. I think he was worried about Clara rejecting him," Lila guessed. "I'm sure you're aware of his mother, not really around as she was too busy. And the man that raised him disowned him when he was twelve."

"What about their father?"

"You know how uninvolved he was with Clara, his legitimate child. Do you think Carl Gibson would be more involved with his illegitimate child?"

"Good point. Clara says she was hesitant at first, but looking back, she remembers him to be kind and polite towards her. And he proved that again this summer."

Lila nodded as Dallas and Clara returned to the table. Dallas went to the bar for drinks as Clara talked about how easy it was.

"They have lessons here at six on Thursdays and Saturdays before it opens to full dancing at eight. On Sundays, it's open in the early evenings with lessons and family night. People bring their kids. It's closed on Mondays and Wednesdays," Lila explained.

Connor watched as Clara's face lit up with excitement, "I am not as good as Dallas, but do you want to give it a try?"

Clara nodded as she took Connor's hand. Once out on the floor, she remained still as she tried to place the song. Being hearing impaired, she often could only hear the music but not understand the lyrics. But since she had her cochlear implant, she was better able to understand the songs playing, although it still took her a moment to place the song.

Connor remained standing in front of Clara, who was standing still with her eyes closed. "What are you doing?"

"This is our first dance together, I'm trying to place the song so I can remember it as our song," Clara explained patiently. Her eyes opened and she smiled. "It's Martina McBride's Independence Day."

"We've danced before, and I don't want this to be our song. Do you even understand the lyrics?" He asked as they started dancing.

"Not at all. I just like the music and her voice," Clara answered honestly.

Connor nodded, very aware of her love/hate relationship with music. When she was in middle school, Rachel had written out the lyrics to many songs to help her understand what was being said. He remembered a time when she was helping him wash his car and she tried to sing along with the song playing. She had the words totally wrong, not even the right topic. He burst out laughing. She got embarrassed when he explained the words, and he felt terrible. That was why she rarely sang in front of others.

They continued dancing through three more songs and even tried the twirl a few times. It wasn't bad, but it wasn't as smooth as Dallas and Lila's. "They really look happy together. I'm glad you agreed to come out tonight."

As they danced, many pairs of eyes followed them as they laughed, obviously enjoying themselves.

"Me too," Connor leaned in to kiss her as the song ended.

Everyone met back at the table, the conversation was kept easy and fun.

"Hello Connor, I thought that was you out there dancing. You are still looking good," said a voice from behind him.

Everyone turned to see a woman, almost his height, dressed in full country-western attire, including a hat and boots. Her long blonde hair had highlights and lowlights, and her face was fully made up, just the kind of woman Clara was used to seeing on Connor's arm when they lived in the city.

"Hello Amanda," Connor answered non-committedly.

Clara saw a brief instance of annoyance when he first saw her, but then he covered it. Yeah, she was one of his previous girls, she thought with amusement. Amanda had initially been standing behind him but stepped closer, between him and Clara, when he acknowledged her. That only served to validate her theory.

"How about a dance," Amanda asked in a low sexy voice that seemed to caress him as she placed her hand on his arm.

"No, I am hanging out with my friends," Connor answered. Since his mother raised him to be polite, he found himself introducing everyone, "Clara, her brother Dallas, and his girlfriend Lila."

Amanda noted his dance partner wasn't labeled as his girlfriend, believing that meant he was still up for grabs. She was determined to join the group and pushed herself into the conversation. She turned to Clara, "You look pretty good out there, but I've never seen you here before."

"This is my first time," Clara pleasantly answered.

To Connor's annoyance, Clara appeared to be enjoying the interaction. He was concerned it would only fuel Amanda's inquiry and keep her at the table longer. He really didn't want them talking together.

"Oh? Did you learn to dance back home?"

"No, I just learned the two-step tonight. It really isn't difficult."

"Where are you from?" Amanda asked, trying to figure out the connection.

"I'm from here. I went away after graduation. Just returned home this spring," Clara answered with a smile.

"You grew up here? Where?"

"In the house next door to him," she said, gesturing towards Connor. Then, Clara politely excused herself to go to the ladies' room, joined by Lila.

"I can't believe the nerve of that woman!" Lila stated as she linked arms with her friend. "Doesn't it bother you that another woman is poaching on your man? That would so piss me off."

"Why? It's not like Connor is taking her up on her offer. He can't control the actions of others." Clara shrugged dismissively.

"Oh my God, I can so see the similarities between you and Dallas!" Lila exclaimed.

Clara paused before entering the stall, "Is that an insult? The words themselves sound complimentary but the tone suggests otherwise."

Lila laughed. When they met up again at the sink, she continued, "It may have been meant as a slight insult. Dallas has the same laidback attitude. It does not bother him when guys flirt or ask me out, but it really pisses me off when a woman tries to pick him up. He just politely declines."

"Why does he need to react? You aren't accepting the invitations, are you? Dallas probably likes knowing he has the girl every other guy wants. A boost to his ego. I believe he would react if there was a reason, like if the guy was being too pushy or hurting you," Clara stated confidently.

"I guess that's one way to look at it. I can't simply sit back and watch a woman get all touchy feely with my man. I'm too jealous," Lila admitted.

"Spoken like a true Foxwood," Clara stated understandably.

"Oh my God! You just put me in the same category as Rob, didn't you?" Lila laughed.

"Lila, I just believe at this age, we should be with who we want to be with and not play games, that's so high school. How is it a problem if he's not responding to it? If he is, then what is the point? Drop him and move on. Life is too short to be with someone you don't trust. Connor and I have barely started, and the women have been coming out of the woodwork. I don't want to ruin every time we go out in public. Our time together should be positive, not spent constantly second guessing if he'd rather be with her than me. Those other women have already had their chances and for whatever reasons, things didn't work out. Now it's my turn," Clara explained just as they joined the guys. As anticipated, Amanda received the message that Connor wasn't interested, as she was no longer hanging out..

Connor and Dallas both escorted their women back to the dance floor.

Connor watched Clara's face for any signs of annoyance caused by yet another one of his ex-girlfriends. He was slightly embarrassed she kept getting approached by his past, but she obviously wasn't bothered. It was such a breath of fresh air after dating women with an excessive need for drama. He leaned down to kiss her.

"I can't believe she's not upset about this," Lila said as she watched her friends dancing.

Dallas smiled in amusement. He didn't understand the jealousy issues, he wasn't the type. "I can't believe you are more upset about this than Clara is. Let it go."

"What happened when we left?"

"She finally got the hint," Dallas said with a shrug. He would have left it at that, but Lila wanted the specifics. "Amanda asked him again to dance and Connor declined. The tone and the look he used gave me the impression their past relationship didn't end on a good note." He didn't feel it was necessary to share how Amanda changed tactics by sliding over towards him. Dallas wasn't sure if she was trying to make Connor jealous or simply move on to the next guy. He laughed when she placed her hand on his arm and smiled at him. Dallas was saved from having to say something when Connor stated softly that she needed to leave before she further embarrassed herself. Amanda hesitated and looked up at him as if he would defend her. Instead he said, "I'm enjoying myself too much tonight. It won't be pretty if you're standing here when Lila returns. She's not as understanding as Clara."

When she did finally walk away, he looked at Connor and said, "She is persistent."

"Annoyingly so, sorry about that," Connor stated apologetically. "I hope she doesn't cause any issues between you and Lila."

"As long as Lila doesn't learn she made a move on me, we won't have a problem. Lila does have the Foxwood jealousy trait," Dallas admitted.

Connor laughed, he was very aware of Rob's antics.

"She's a horrible bitch!" Lila couldn't help herself, bringing Dallas back to the present conversation.

Dallas laughed as he kissed her. "Clara's obviously not bothered by this. Let it go."

Lila turned to see Connor kissing Clara while they danced. Why was she the only one upset about it? Clara was right, she is a true Foxwood after all. She groaned inwardly, not one of the better family traits.

Dallas smiled down as Lila continued to watch the other couple, "Does it bother you Clara's with Connor and not your brother?"

"Not at all," Lila answered without hesitation, comprehending Clara's earlier comments. She had been referring to her experience with Rob during high school. "Clara's much happier with Connor. Rob would be driving her crazy and she would be dumping him pretty quick. She has grown and matured since high school, but Rob, not so much. They would be broken up by the end of the summer. Besides, you wouldn't want to double date with him, would you?"

"Good point," Dallas answered as he twirled her around the dance floor. He didn't give the other woman another thought.

But the other woman continued to watch both men as they danced. Each appeared to adore his dance partner, both who were ridiculously less sophisticated than she. Knowing what she could bring into a relationship, Amanda could not fathom what they had that she did not. How could Connor be so smitten?

• • • •

Further back in the shadows, a pair of blue eyes watched as his Babydoll twirled on the dance floor. She is so graceful, Evil admired. He remembered when they last danced, her green eyes sparkled as her silky hair trailed behind her as he twirled her around.

Later, Clara was standing in front of the mirror, reapplying her lip gloss when Amanda came alongside her. She started to brush her already perfectly straight hair before she stated, "You know, Connor's not going to give you what you want."

"I don't know, he's doing a good job of it now," Clara's eyes sparkled as she talked.

"He's not going to stay long with a girl like you," the woman stated harshly. "You won't be able to keep him happy in the long run."

"Connor has never been with someone like me. Besides, it's not what I do that's important, but what he does to keep me happy. That will dictate how long we stay together. I've not had a full night's sleep since we've started. And honestly, I haven't heard any complaints from him," Clara explained with a smile as she turned away.

Amanda could only stare as Clara walked away, embarrassed by the smirks from the other women.

As Clara stepped into the short hall leading from the bathroom, she was texting the babysitter. She didn't see the man until she literally bumped into him. She dropped her cell.

"I am so sorry! I wasn't even paying attention," Clara stated as she and the man both squatted down to retrieve her phone.

"No worries, Babydoll. Let me get this for you." Evil was wearing a brown Stetson pulled down low, preventing her from seeing his familiar blue eyes. He picked up the phone, quickly glancing at it before he handed it back, "Looks as good as new. We'll meet up again tomorrow?"

Clara was so embarrassed, she avoided looking up at his face. The loud background noises kept her from processing what he said. But when he leaned towards her ear to talk, his cologne triggered an unsettling emotion, distracting her from understanding his words. Clara remained in place, only able to nod her head in thanks when he handed her back her cell. As she tried to recall the memory, it faded with his cologne when he stepped away. Clara felt a slight chill as she returned to the table.

Amanda had followed Clara from the bathroom. It further annoyed her to see another man hitting on the girl. While he was older, he obviously had money. What am I not getting, she thought again? How can Connor fall for such a plain ordinary woman? She pondered on what to do as she watched Connor's face light up when Clara joined him.

43 the journals

The following night, the second volleyball game had the same players. Chase and Rachel came out to support their friends. When they first arrived, Rachel was approached by an old teammate from high school, asking if she would consider playing with their team that night. Rachel simply laughed and declined the offer.

Dallas was pleased his team won the match. His initial intent was to have fun and to get to know his sister better, but he found himself watching the team they were scheduled to play the following week, also undefeated.

"We'll beat them. They're too arrogant and don't play together as a team," Devan observed from beside him.

"Maybe but they all have the skills," Dallas acknowledged.

"Why are you two out here? The drinks are inside," Lila stated from behind.

As the evening progressed, the girls, sans Clara, were ready to do karaoke again. They all went to sign up and review the list of options to sing together. When they returned, they announced the song and requested Clara join.

"Absolutely not," she responded.

"Clara, we haven't all been up there since," Rachel paused as she turned to Shannon, "When was the last time, when Clara turned twenty-one?"

Shannon was sipping her drink as she thought back, "I want to say when we all went out one last time before Lila moved back home. We sang 'Get Into the Groove' by Madonna."

"Yeah, that's right. We got a standing ovation that night," Lila remembered.

"That's because Clara did her little strip tease routine," Shannon laughed.

Connor had been sipping his beer when the last comment was made, he ended up spitting out his beer, causing everyone else to laugh harder.

"Excuse me, what strip tease routine?" He asked after wiping his face with a napkin.

"Oh, she hasn't told you? Tequila makes her clothes fall off," Shannon exaggerated with a laugh.

Chase, having heard the stories already, laughed at Connor's reaction.

"Strip teasing is your thing? You strip in public? Clara Noelle!" Connor exclaimed, seriously shocked.

"I believe it," Devan couldn't resist. He was a witness to her dance routine the one night at Connor's.

"Yeah but it wasn't like she was totally undressing. She was the only one wearing a button down shirt with a tank underneath. We were in a competition," Rachel explained.

"We won," Clara answered. "It was more of a dance than any real clothes coming off."

The girls all laughed and nodded.

"Is it just Clara that does the routine or all of you?" Devan wanted to know. He lifted his hand to get the server's attention. When she came over, he ordered another round for the women and tequila shots. The guys all laughed.

The next night, Connor was working late. Clara used the solitude to start reading her mother's journals. With a cup of tea, she settled into the chair in her room. The first journal was easy reading. Her mother talked about her friends and school. It gave her a better understanding of her family, people all gone before her time. Well, her grandparents died after she was born but she did not have any memories of them. Her mother never talked about her older brother that was killed in a freak accident just after he graduated from high school. It made her stop to think about family in general, Clara didn't know anyone but her father. Did he have any family? Maybe her mother's journals would give her some answers:

September 4
Tomorrow is the first day of my freshman year of high school. I am very excited!! M said he'll pick me up and we can walk together. I can't wait. I wonder if he'll hold my hand.

September 9
High school is fabulous!!!! E wanted to try out for cheerleading but I passed. I can't imagine standing in the cold wet rain trying to follow the ridiculous game! There's a hot guy in my PE class. He has the most handsome colored eyes! And a smile that melts my heart. But A saw him looking at me and told me to stay away from him. E agreed, said he was trouble.

October 30
Went to the harvest festival. E and I were lost in the scary maze! Took forever to find our way out. Thankful HG was there and helped us find our way out. I didn't tell M nor A.

Clara found herself speculating who people were: E was mostly likely Elizabeth, Rachel's mother. A was her brother, Aaron but it took her a few minutes to catch on that HG was "Hot Guy", not really much help. She decided to let her mother's words tell the story, Clara was confident the names would all fall into place.

not going to be reasonable

The owner of The Shack was pleased this summer season brought an increase in spectators to watch the volleyball games. He had not initially been aware, but four of the teams had multiple players that competed at the state championship level during high school. It was as if the old rivalries were either attempting to steal the title or fighting to keep it. Regardless, it over doubled his business just on Wednesday nights alone. For this reason, the players on the winning teams were given a special stamp for free drinks after the games. Not the "managers" or "substitutes," just the actual players, up to six per winning team.

Everyone was enjoying themselves except Rob. He was more irritated than usual. The team was mixed up during the third game as both Connor and Lila had to work. Rachel and Chase both stepped in to assist with another winning match. Rob tagged along to support his friends. As expected, he did hear about his sister dating Dallas. It still annoyed him that Clara was related to the guy. Fortunately, he didn't have to watch the guy drool all over his sister. But to watch the guy interacting with Clara all evening did not sit well. Rob didn't think the words to describe his thoughts even existed.

Chase had made a point of keeping close to his cousin and not drinking. He thought his job would be easier since Lila was working. When Lila had informed him earlier that she wouldn't be present, she called it "easing Rob into it." It was probably better than him watching the two sparkle as the couple looked at each other with such adoration. The good news was that the relationship was out in the open, and Chase may not need to bail his cousin out before the night is over. Always a plus.

Rob, thinking he needed a break, left the table. He sat on a stool next to Theodore "Bear" Johnson. In school, only the teachers called him Theodore. He was called Teddy by his grandmother. His younger cousin Livy had taken to calling him Teddy Bear when she first learned to talk. It stuck during elementary school as she was only a year behind him. As Teddy Bear grew, he was always one of the tallest in his class. He was in the starting position in football, all the years he played. By the time he hit high school, he was six foot five and as wide as the doorway. The Teddy was dropped, and he was affectionately referred to as Bear.

"Hey Rob, how is it going?" Bear asked. He was surprised and impressed to see Foxwood sitting civilly at the same table as Dallas Thompson. Throughout their school years, he had to pull Rob back from fighting with one Thompson or another.

"I've had better nights. You?" Rob asked

"Been busy. You know how it is. I've been helping my uncle with my grandparent's farm when I'm not working. My grandmother had that bad fall," he said, then sighed.

"I heard about that. My sister was in the emergency room when she arrived. They were concerned she might not be able to walk again," Rob commented.

"Yeah, but when she went across the street to rehab, Clara had her back on her feet in no time. She's expected to be coming home next week," Bear stated. "She's the best."

"She is," Rob agreed. Even though he didn't have firsthand knowledge, her personality alone would make her shine at her position.

"Your Clara is working at the nursing home? Wasn't she sleeping with the boss? Isn't that how she got the job? By sleeping with him? And now she's moved on to the next big man. Did she finally drop you or is she still letting you bang her as well?" Rob heard from his other side. When he turned in his seat, Danny Thompson was sitting beside him with a drunken smile.

Oh shit, Bear thought as he tried to mentally tell Foxwood to let it go. He went to school with both of them, he knew from experience time hadn't matured either of them enough to just walk away. Bear started to stand up in preparation.

"I don't think it's Clara you are thinking of. I'm pretty sure it was your sister that got the job by sleeping with the boss. We all know that's the one thing she is good at," Rob commented as he stepped away from the bar. He knew it was coming. He stepped back as the blow came to his face. Then he ducked the second swing and blocked the third before going in with an unexpected swing from his left.

Back at the table, Dallas noticed his cousin, well not really anymore, purposefully sat down beside Rob. He knew it was just a matter of time before the fists would be swinging. He jumped up, "Shit, this is not good."

Everyone turned as a group, but Chase understood first and followed. Clara was right behind him.

Devan was the only one not understanding, eyes were following everyone towards the bar, "What the hell is going on?"

"Oh man, blast from high school past. Rob and Danny Thompson can't be together five minutes before the insults and fists start flying," Shannon explained.

"What's their issue?"

"Unfortunate family legacy," Rachel stated.

"With a little Clara sprinkled in," Shan added.

"What?" Devan turned back to Shannon. He had debated assisting in keeping the fight from turning into an all out brawl.

"Never sure of the details. Rob has assured us over the years Danny's comments are too vile to repeat." Shannon shrugged.

"Danny didn't take it too well when Clara turned him down in ninth and tenth grade," Rachel commented. "He was stupid enough to try again in eleventh and twelfth as well."

"Neither did Rob." Shannon explained. "He was pissed Danny would even consider looking at her, let alone trying to ask her out."

Dallas arrived just as Rob swung the unexpected left hook. The blow caused Danny to fall onto the bar. As he pushed himself back up, he grabbed his beer bottle to smash it open on the bar. He was just lifting his arm up in preparation to swing at Rob when Dallas grabbed his wrist, slamming it into the bar to release the bottle. He twisted his arm behind his back as he shoved him towards the door. The bartender and bouncer were immediately beside him, dragging and shoving Danny out. The owner was already on the phone calling the sheriff's department.

"You are an embarrassment to the family, banging the Foxwood girl!" Danny yelled at his cousin, not aware of Dallas' true parentage. Dallas kept his fists tightened at his side as he contemplated taking a swing. Fortunately, the bouncer took over the task, and remained at the door to prevent him from attempting to reenter.

When Dallas turned back around, Bear was still restraining Rob while both Chase and Clara were calming him down.

It was close to midnight when the group started out into the lot. Clara was walking ahead with Rob and Chase as they all headed back to their vehicles. Rob was the first to see it, all four of the tires on his truck were slashed.

"That stupid fuck! Where the hell is he?" Rob yelled as he turned to search the parking lot.

"Shit," Chase muttered. I should have known this wasn't over, he thought as he also scanned the shadows of the lot.

"Right here, Asshole! Clara, it's good seeing you again. You are looking as sexy as ever! Hop in and I'll give you the ride of your life. You can't possibly be satisfied by this poor excuse of existence," Danny called out as he casually strolled away from the shadows, towards Rob.

Clara did not hear it, but the guys did. It was the click of a switchblade opening. The cousins immediately stepped in front of her while Rob continued forward, keeping his eyes focused on the knife. He knew Danny was under the influence of something more than beer and would get sloppy. He always did. Rob waited for his opponent to strike first.

Chase, not wanting to distract, kept an eye out for anyone else coming to help Danny. He was not known for hanging out alone.

Dallas and Devan were already on the lookout when they exited the bar. Dallas knew his cousin often carried and hoped he didn't have his gun. He instructed the girls to stay near the entrance and keep everyone clear until the deputies arrived. Then he realized Clara was already in the parking lot with Rob and Chase. Damn it!

"He's got a knife out," Dallas informed Devan, relieved to recently learn he was an FBI agent.

"Great! This guy is your cousin?" He tried to clarify. "Any way you can talk him down?"

"We were raised as cousins, but we aren't really. I don't think he knows. But if Danny was stupid enough to break open a bottle inside a bar where there's security video, he is likely high or drunk and not going to be reasonable. Don't you have a gun? Can't you just shoot him?" Dallas suggested.

Devan laughed as he looked back to assure Shannon and Rachel were out of danger, "I don't have it on me."

Rob stepped forward and kicked the knife out of Danny's hand, then he quickly advanced and punched him in the face.

When the deputy cars arrived, Danny was on the ground and Rob was being pulled off him by Chase and Dallas. Clara moved to stand in front of him, trying to calm him down.

Devan was keeping close to Danny. He was already in the process of standing up, still yelling insults at Rob. Rob was too hyped up to easily be talked down. The deputies, Joe Mancuso and his partner Walker Keluski, had no choice but to arrest them both. Once a second vehicle arrived, they each sat alone in the back seat of a cruiser while the deputies took statements and gathered evidence.

"This is like high school all over again. We need to call Rob a good lawyer," Shannon stated.

Clara nodded in agreement as she pulled out her phone.

It was close to three in the morning when the sheriff and deputies agreed with Matt. Danny approached Rob, threw the first three punches, and even attempted to use a deadly weapon, the broken bottle, before Dallas stopped him. After he was thrown out of the bar, the parking lot surveillance showed Danny getting into his truck. He drove around the lot then backed up next to Rob's blue truck. After he sliced all the tires, he hid in the shadows until Rob exited the building. That's when he pulled out his knife.

The paramedics had been on the scene to determine if either needed to be taken to the ER, but both refused. Rob's alcohol level was well below intoxication, but Danny's was another story. There was a good chance he would have DUI charges added since the video also proved he was behind the wheel.

Clara, Dallas, and Chase were waiting in the lobby of the sheriff's department. Devan had returned home with Shannon after dropping Rachel off at home. Clara sighed with relief when Matt came out with Rob. Initially, the deputies were going to keep Rob until the judge dropped the charges. However, the surveillance videos were enough to prove Rob was targeted and provoked, and was simply defending himself and Clara.

Matt had been home in bed with his wife when he realized the late call was from Clara, suffering a moment of panic as he answered. He was surprised the call had nothing to do with his cousin breaking the terms of his bail. He was annoyed when he learned it was regarding a senseless bar fight, over a girl belonging to neither of the men. He cringed when he saw the video and realized how close Clara was to the altercation.

"Rob, please learn to walk away from the guy and not bait him. I'll keep you informed. If he gets out on bail, I suggest you keep your distance and watch your back," Matt advised.

They were interrupted when Clara first hugged Rob, asking if he was alright. His face was starting to bruise and swell. Then she hugged Matt, thanking him for coming out late at night. Rob went over to Dallas to shake his hand, "Thanks for having my back. I never expected you to be on my side against your cousin."

"We aren't related despite being raised as cousins. He's never been logical, nor does he fight fair. I've never understood his fascination with Clara or if it's simply his way of pushing your buttons. Regardless of his reasons, seems to still be working," Dallas responded as he shook his hand. "Just keep an eye when he gets out."

"Here's my card. You can send the bill to this address," Chase said to Matt as he came up beside Clara. The interaction between her and Matt was curious. He couldn't put his finger on it, but Matt's eyes seemed to follow her even after she stepped away.

Matt accepted the card as he watched Clara with Rob and Dallas. How does she hold this influence over everyone, he wondered, as he found himself saying what he never says. "Don't worry about it, they don't have a case. If anything, they'll probably call Rob as a witness."

"You were called late at night, pulled out of bed, and away from your wife. No, send the bill and please charge him double for bringing you out so late. Then, maybe my idiotic cousin will understand we aren't in high school anymore when he's writing that check," Chase stated loud enough for Rob to hear.

"I would have left it alone, but he went after my truck and Clara. No way was I standing down," Rob answered. "Not with a knife out."

"Rob, save the receipts for the towing and the tires. We'll go after him for personal damage," Matt suggested.

Clara turned to walk with Dallas for a ride home but stopped when she saw Connor in the parking lot, leaning against his SUV.

Connor had received word there was an altercation after the volleyball game. It annoyed him that Clara was in the midst of it. His cousin had given the details, concluding Clara was still at the sheriff's department. He remained in the shadows, watching as his brother came out with Foxwood, followed by the others. He also remained silent as he watched his brother's interaction with Clara. His irritation grew as he watched, because Clara had yet to answer his texts.

But Connor forgot all this the moment she turned her attention on him. Her smile of surprise and joy when she saw him made his heart melt. Clara turned to Dallas, giving him a hug before she walked toward Connor.

"Hear the aftergame celebration got out of hand," Connor stated as Clara hugged him. He opened the door for her as she shrugged.

"Are you going to tell me about it?"

"Not really anything to talk about. Danny and Rob always seem to have it out for each other. Today was the worst I've ever seen," Clara said. "It was almost the perfect evening until the altercation happened."

"Almost perfect?" Connor asked as he studied her face.

Clara turned towards him with a tired smile, "You weren't there. I missed you tonight. I was going to text you but my cell died."

"Your cell died? That explains why you didn't answer my texts," Connor acknowledged. "Didn't you charge it before you left?"

"Yeah, I thought I did. It may be time to get a new phone. The battery seems to drain as soon as I step out of the house," the annoyance could be heard in her voice. "I don't like the sitter not being able to reach me if there's a problem. And that's why I asked Devan to call you and let you know I was going to be later than usual."

When Connor and Clara arrived home, the babysitter was still awake, but she needed a ride home since her boyfriend had borrowed her car.

"I'll take her, it's only two minutes away. Head up to bed," Connor stated as he kissed her forehead.

"I'm all yuck, I need to shower first," she mumbled as she dragged herself towards the stairs.

"I'll hurry back," he answered with a sparkle in his eyes.

Clara peeked into Hailey's room first and then Reese's. She pulled up their covers before giving each a kiss. When she stepped back into the hall, she noted the linen closet door was slightly ajar. She paused for a moment to close it before going into her room. Exhausted, Clara was tempted to simply crash onto her bed, but instead she kicked off her shoes and stepped into the bathroom to start the water. She quickly removed her clothes and returned to her room to drop them into the dirty clothes basket, not noticing the closet door was slightly open. She walked naked back into the bathroom and into the shower.

• • • •

The second the shower door was closed, the closet door slowly opened more. Evil cautiously stepped out of the narrow space. Maybe not a wasted night after all, he thought as he touched himself. The image of her as she undressed in front of him more than made up for the wait. Remaining in the shadows, Evil walked across the room. He paused for a moment to grab the shirt his Babydoll just dropped in the hamper. Holding it close to his face, he sniffed her scent as he watched her through the clear shower door. She turned towards him and smiled as she closed her eyes, tilting her head back as the water flowed over her soft skin. He watched as he visualized his hands as hers touching her magnificent curves. He was about to climax when the flash of the headlights bounced across the room, announcing the fool's return.

Damn it, he thought miserably. The worst timing. Evil slowly faded deeper into the shadows with her shirt still in his hands.

Clara felt the sudden cold draft of the shower door opening, she opened her eyes to see Connor stepping in to join her. She smiled as he came closer...the steam providing camouflage.

· · · ·

In the shadows, Evil slowly emerged, watching. He visualized it was him, taking her from behind under the steaming water. He closed his eyes as the sounds of her groans brought him closer with each thrust. This time he climaxed. He watched for a moment longer before he faded back into the shadows.

Clara was drying off in the bathroom, watching as Connor paused with his head tilted slightly to the side, as if listening. She couldn't hear a thing, her hearing aides were off for the night. He gestured he'd be back as he wrapped the towel around his waist and walked out.

Connor thought he heard footsteps. He glanced across the hall. The young boy was sprawled across his bed, uncovered after Connor had covered him not too long ago. He slowly headed down the hall, he could hear whimpering and light footsteps. As Connor was about to turn into her room, Hailey appeared at the doorway with tears in her eyes. She screamed when she saw him.

He picked her up and noted she was flushed and warm to the touch. "Hailey, what's wrong? Are you sick?" He asked softly.

Clara met Connor in the doorway of their room, already dressed in a nightie. She looked up to read his lips, "She feels warm."

Once Hailey was in her mother's arms, she threw up.

Clara returned to the shower with Hailey as Connor cleaned the rug. When both mother and daughter were freshly clean and dressed in new pajamas, the little girl insisted on staying with her mother. Exhausted, Clara dimmed the bedside light and closed her eyes with her daughter settled beside her in her arms. A moment later, she felt a sudden flow of smelly dampness.

Hailey started to cry as she once again vomited all over her mother.

Connor was sitting in the chair across the room. He looked up when he heard Clara groan and the little girl crying. Clara was again covered in emesis. He was shocked by the amount of projectile vomiting from such a small person. Connor brightened the light and reached for Hailey before she could curl up to her mother.

"She did it again! I didn't think she had this much to eat last night," Clara stated as she slowly tried to slide out of the bed without causing the mess to spill over.

Connor handed her a towel before bringing Hailey into the bathroom to wipe her mouth. When he turned around, Clara was standing with a towel wrapped around her, "She still looks warm. Do you think it's a good idea to try to give her a drink?"

"It wouldn't hurt, if she can keep it down. Where's the thermometer?" Connor asked, looking directly at her so she could read his lips.

"It's in the medicine cabinet in the other bathroom. The baby Tylenol is in there as well," Clara answered as she stepped back into the shower.

Spared another shower, Hailey remained with Connor while Clara showered again. When she came out, Connor was slowly pacing the room with the little girl leaning up on his shoulder, almost asleep.

"Her temp is 101.1. I gave her Tylenol. She would only take a few sips," he gestured towards a cup on the table. "Do you want to take her while I change the sheets?"

"She's almost asleep. Keep her until we're sure she won't throw up the Tylenol and water," Clara stated. "I won't need another shower."

Connor chuckled while he continued to pace the room.

Clara dragged the soiled bedding downstairs to the washer. When she returned, Hailey was finally asleep on Connor's shoulder while he also slept in the chair. Clara watched the two sleeping a moment before she went out to the linen closet to retrieve another set of sheets and

not going to be reasonable   473

blankets. She was too tired to realize the door was once again ajar. After getting the bed prepared, she didn't have the heart to wake him up, and was also concerned that Hailey would wake up and not easily fall back to sleep.

"It's a rarity for you to be sleeping and me awake," Clara whispered as she took a picture before getting into bed.

It seemed her head had just hit the pillow when Connor was leaning down kissing her forehead. He was holding a newly changed Hailey with a dressed Reese standing beside him. The little girl immediately held out her arms for her mother.

"Good morning, Beautiful," Connor greeted as he sat on the edge of the bed, allowing the little girl to crawl down and cuddle with her mother.

Clara groaned as she sat up and felt Hailey's forehead, "What time is it?"

Connor handed her the hearing aids before he answered, "It's almost seven. Her fever's gone and she hasn't thrown up again."

"I need to call work and have Jerry come in to cover for me. Hailey can't go to daycare until she's gone twenty-four hours without vomiting," she slowly sat up on the edge of the bed.

He eyed Clara carefully, touching her forehead. "How are you feeling?"

"Like I didn't get any sleep." She stood up to go use the bathroom. When she returned, everyone was sitting on the bed. "Reese, you can stay home with me and Hailey."

"But Mommy, I need to go to school. Cheyenne's mommy is bringing cupcakes today!" The young boy explained.

"I can drop him off. You two both look like you need the rest," Connor stated. After a quick discussion and a phone call later, Connor and Reese both kissed her goodbye and left.

Clara and Hailey went into the kitchen for drinks. Within the hour, both were too tired and irritable to do much of anything. Clara went upstairs to get pillows and blankets to set up camp in the family room on the sofa. After she laid down, she realized she forgot her journal. Because the little girl was already curled up beside her, she decided to close her eyes for a moment...

Clara dreamed she was once again a little girl, awakened by the cold draft in the room. She pulled the covers up to keep from shivering. When she opened her eyes, the familiar blue eyes met hers as she mumbled about being cold and rolled over. She felt the hand pull her covers up to her shoulders and gently touch her hair. She smelled the stale breath mixed with beer when his lips touched her forehead. She could feel the breath flowing as he whispered in her ear, but she had no idea what was said. Clara drifted back to sleep...

• • • •

Evil sat on the edge of the couch as he touched her hair. He smiled when she briefly opened her eyes and mumbled something about being cold. He reached for another blanket, covering up both mother and child. He leaned down to caress her cheek before kissing both on their foreheads, "Sweet dreams, Babydoll. Feel better soon. I love you."

Then Evil exited the home. As he stepped into the late afternoon shadows, he checked to assure his tokens were secured in his pocket. He smiled as he thought of the gifts he left: sleepy time tea to ensure she'd have sweet dreams to enhance his visits and a matching bra/panty set in a green that matched her eyes. Sighing as he mentally imagined her wearing only them during his next visit...

not going to be reasonable   475

what man was here?

Connor was consulting in the emergency room, but hoping to head out. He was relieved the patient didn't need surgery. He signed off on the case before heading to his office. Clara had yet to respond to his texts or calls. He tried one more time before he decided to call it a day. Once he had his bag, Connor headed down to the daycare to pick up Reese.

When he entered the house, Connor immediately noted the alarm was off. He didn't think too much of it as she doesn't usually set it if she's hanging out inside the house, or going in and out to the back deck. It's a nice enough day. But when he looked into the family room, Hailey was playing on the floor while Clara was sound asleep on the sofa.

The little girl jumped up when she saw her brother and Connor. She clapped her hands and hugged them both. She talked, and appeared to have a lot to say, but he had no idea what she said. He picked up the toddler, feeling her forehead. The fever was gone.

"Feeling better, Hailey?" Connor asked as she nodded and continued to talk, pointing at her mother.

"Mommy's sleeping. She's sick," Reese translated. "And the man was here earlier to get them drinks."

Connor paused as he went over to the sofa and sat beside Clara on the edge. She was shivering, her face was flushed and very warm to the touch. "What man was here earlier?"

"No idea," Reese stated as he went to open his bag.

Clara opened her eyes, vaguely aware of her surroundings and mumbled she was cold before she closed her eyes.

Crap, Clara caught Hailey's stomach bug. Too distracted to ask further questions, Connor was busy for the remainder of the evening. Relieved that the little girl was obviously feeling better, he hoped Clara would be better by morning. He went into the kitchen, followed by both the children, to get drinks for everyone. He promised to get them dinner as he instructed both to remain downstairs while he carried Clara up to her bed.

When they entered the room, Connor noted the bed was perfectly made, including the shams and decorative pillows. Not something she worried about each morning. He was the more anal one that liked everything in its place. It didn't register that the room had also been dusted and vacuumed. Nor that the bathroom was cleaned since he last stepped into it. The faint odor of bleach still lingered, and fresh clean towels hung on the wall. The different folding pattern should have triggered a warning that something was off.

But it didn't. Connor was too focused on getting Clara settled into bed as he quickly completed an assessment.

A few minutes later, Connor confirmed Clara had a fever of 103.2. Sitting beside her, he gently woke her up and encouraged her to take the Tylenol and water he brought her. He thought she mumbled something about the shadow and blue eyes. He left her to rest as he returned to the kitchen with the children.

After dinner while he was cleaning up, Connor noted the extra dishes in the dishwasher. There were three mugs, a glass, two plates, and a small frying pan. So Clara had been up and about, eating and drinking since he left that morning.

An hour later, the children were bathed and Connor was getting ready to read a story to them. Reese said they each always pick two, but Connor was sure the little guy was playing him. He went downstairs to make a few calls and completed some work on his laptop. After he gave Clara a second dose of the Tylenol, he checked in on the children, taking their temperatures before he settled into his chair.

When Connor opened his eyes in the early hours of dawn, he was greeted with cheerful sky blue eyes. Hailey climbed up into his lap, talking to him in her incomprehensible gibberish.

When Clara opened her eyes, the room was dark. She was disoriented and thirsty. She had no idea what day it was. She drank the glass of water at her bedside then got up to go to the bathroom. Exhausted and sticky, she immediately stepped into the shower.

Connor was sitting at the kitchen table going over files with Matt and Devan. They were reviewing employee files from those that left the facility for one reason or another in the last year. They were trying to assess if the departures were due to Eric's influence. He had heard the shower running upstairs and quietly sighed with relief. He had meant to head upstairs when the water turned off but was distracted with specific names on the list.

Devan was first to notice Clara standing in the doorway and greeted her with a smile, "Well hello sleepy head."

Connor turned to see Clara standing in a bathrobe with her hair wrapped in a towel. He realized she probably wasn't expecting Matt and Devan to be present this late in the evening. She also looked confused, "She's not wearing her hearing aids, she can't hear you."

"How can you tell?" Devan asked as Matt turned around.

"She doesn't usually initiate conversation when she can't hear. Plus, I don't think she was expecting you two," Connor waved her over and pulled her down on his lap as Devan hid the list of names.

But not quick enough, Clara was able to read Beth Taylor's name before it was covered.

"Feeling better?" Connor asked as he assessed her appearance. Clara simply shrugged. "Hungry?"

Matt was up a second later getting her a cold drink as Clara reached for a banana from the fruit basket.

"Thanks," she stated when he brought her the glass. After she drank half the glass, she placed it down on the table. "What are you all doing?"

"Just going over the investigation at the nursing home," Devan explained, careful to look at her when he talked.

"I won't keep you. I'll head back upstairs," Clara stated as she stood up, surprised everyone did as well. "Good night."

A few minutes later, Connor joined her in the room. Clara was in the big chair, just sitting. He sat down on the ottoman opposite her, "How are you feeling? Are you hungry?"

"I don't know," she shrugged. "Connor, you can go back to your work downstairs. I don't need you to be nursing me."

"Clara, they left. It's getting late. I can bring you some food. You haven't eaten anything in a while," he stated.

"I just had a banana. I'll be alright until the morning. I should get the kids' bags together for tomorrow," she stated as she started to stand.

Connor gently touched her, encouraging her to sit back down, "Clara, tomorrow is Sunday."

"What? What happened to Friday and Saturday?" She asked with a slight panic.

"You slept through them. You had a fever Thursday afternoon. It seemed to break on Friday mid-morning, but you kept sleeping," he answered. Connor was surprised she didn't remember anything from the last few days. When she still had the fever Friday morning, he remained home with the children as he kept the fluids in her. She would sit up to drink, and even had a few conversations with him. Friday afternoon, Connor had taken the children to the playground and then out for ice cream. When they returned, there were signs she had been up and about. She had moved from her bed to the sofa, her cold drink was gone, and an empty mug of tea was on the table beside her.

Connor had been pleased to see her moving around, and figured her body just needed time to recharge. Clara had been under tremendous stress the last few months. But when she continued to sleep into Saturday, he was a bit concerned. If she hadn't improved by Sunday morning, he would have taken her to the hospital for a full work up.

"Why don't I remember anything? What about Hailey and Reese?"

"Hailey was better by the time we came home Thursday afternoon, but you were sick. Reese never had a fever, but I figured we'd all stay in, just in case," he answered, handing her another drink.

"Connor, I'm sorry you missed work, but thank you for taking care of the kids. And me. I didn't get you sick?"

"No, neither Reese nor I had a fever. I kept checking his temperature to be sure." Connor shook his head. He narrowed his eyes as he eyed her closely, Clara seemed dazed and disoriented.

· · · ·

Across town, Evil turned in early. He couldn't seem to tolerate his wife's company and hoped she would take the hint when he locked himself in the other bedroom. This guest room had a queen-sized bed that perfectly fit the unwashed sheets. Once in bed, he was surrounded by her scent as he pulled her shirt close to his face. Closing his eyes, Evil was able to visualize his Babydoll lying beside him as he inhaled her sweet scent. His mind believed it was her hand touching him as it slowly lowered down...

When Clara resumed her usual activities Sunday morning, Connor knew she was feeling better. But he still stayed home with her. He assisted her with the household chores throughout the day. They went for a walk with the children riding in the wagon, stopping first at the playground before, to Reese's delight, they got ice cream.

The evening of the next volleyball game, Connor was delayed at the hospital. Clara was reading his text as she arrived home after work with the children. As they were eating, Michelle arrived to sit with them in the kitchen while Clara went upstairs to change.

Opening her drawer, she was slightly surprised to see her t-shirts and tanks folded professionally. Initially she chuckled at the consequences of having Connor the neat freak assist her with laundry. But when she couldn't find her volleyball t-shirt, Clara became agitated and irrational, convinced he threw it out. With limited time, she grabbed the one on top before hurrying to get ready.

the e in his middle name stands for evil

The next night, a freshly showered Clara sat in the chair with her feet elevated on the ottoman. A warm cup of sleepy time tea sat beside her as she read from her mother's journal. Connor was working late at the hospital. Clara turned the page as she read. Her hearing aids were removed and she was enjoying the silence as only the hearing impaired can. She hated wearing them when she was alone at night. She always thought she heard footsteps, or doors opening and closing, just as she did as a young child in her old house. Her mother always said that older homes have more creaks. Clara closed her eyes as she felt the evening breeze blow in from the open windows. She was sure she smelled flowers. She returned to the journal, saddened when she realized the dates. This had to be one of her mother's worst years, Clara thought.

April 30

The April showers certainly do bring a lot of rain, but today it was actually dry enough for a hike in the woods. The weather was warm enough, so I suggested a quick dip in the lake. M laughed, said it was too cold yet to swim. His tone suggested a challenge, and I don't think he believed I would do it. I stripped down to my underwear and jumped in. He was right, it was FREEZING! He was smart enough not to jump in after me. He loaned me his flannel shirt to dry off before I put my clothes back on. And just in time! A and his friends came out on horses! I forgot they were riding today. M almost shit his pants!! When I told E all about it later, we laughed so hard until we cried!

May 5

Today the town is celebrating spring. There was a carnival in town at the park. I went on the ferris wheel twice, once with E and again later with M. L had offered to go up with me, but I declined. A said the E in his middle name stands for Evil. He's not wrong. The guy gives off weird vibes. M doesn't like how K has been hanging out with him. But she is a bit off too. They would make an interesting couple. His wife recently passed.

May 29

The day was beautiful! M and I went for a walk in the woods. We hiked up the hill to my favorite meadow, it was covered in a blanket of wild flowers of every color. We laid back to watch the clouds gently moving in the warm spring breeze. He leaned up on his elbow and moved a hair from my face before he leaned in to kiss me. He's such a great kisser. But then we heard a twig snap. He immediately stood up and reached down for my hand, he said something about us needing to hurry back. He's still nervous about A after the swimming incident.

June 2

We begin finals this week. I hate taking tests!!

June 7

Tonight is the senior prom. A looks so handsome in his tux! He went to pick up B and returned home for pictures in the garden. They are a beautiful couple! Too bad she's not a nice person. I can't wait for my prom! I think I'd get a purple dress with matching shoes!

June 21

I can't believe A graduates tonight! In the fall, he'll be going off to college! Things won't be the same without him here. At graduation, HG waved to me. I gave him a hug and congratulated him. I asked him what his plans were for the fall, he's not sure. I don't think I'll tell anyone about the hug. Don't want M to get upset.

June 22

When I went to sit in my favorite spot in the garden, A was already there arguing with B. I didn't intend to eavesdrop, but she was crying and he was furious! He told her it was over! My heart jumped with joy! I never liked her. He said something about her kissing another guy at the prom! Such a Bitch!

Damn, Clara thought as she read. Apparently going off with someone else is common at these proms! She shook her head in sympathy, I know exactly what that's like. But who is B and who was she cuddling up with, she wondered before she continued reading:

June 23

Today I felt like I was being watched. I was sitting out in the gardens by the roses reading. I couldn't shake the feeling of creepiness and came back inside after an hour. A told me not to sit out there alone any more. What did I do wrong?? I wonder if his new grumpiness is the result of his recent breakup.

June 27

I was awakened during the night. The sheriff was at the door when Father opened it. It was not good. There was a horrible accident. I can't even bring myself to write it, my heart is so heavy and sad. E came over to sit with me while her parents sat with mine. When they left, I went out back to sit in the garden. M came to sit with me. He has a way of being there without saying anything. I can't seem to cry.

July 4

It's been a rough week. My parents are different. My father locks himself in his office while my mother sits alone in her sitting room rocking. The cook has been dismissed. I had been looking forward to the parade today. I planned to go with M, as E was in it. Then we would go to the fireworks tonight. But when he arrived, he told me he's not allowed to see me anymore. Said our fathers forbid it. Our fathers forbid it? How? Why? He wouldn't even explain, just walked away after his big announcement. I went up to my room and cried.

August 4

It's been a month since my heart was shattered and almost 6 weeks since the dark cloud came over my household. I have nothing to write. No thoughts. Nothing. My parents don't talk, we sit at the dinner table in silence pretending to eat.

How horrible, Clara thought. She always knew about her mother's older brother, but no one ever talked about him. Clara wiped the tears and put the journal away. That sleepy time tea really works, she thought as she stumbled towards the bed. So exhausted, she simply plopped down on the bed. Her eyes were closed before she hit the pillow.

. . . .

Moments later, Evil slowly slid out of the closet. It was so much easier when he knew the schedule. She always prepares for bed earlier, he sighed with a smile. Always a treat seeing his Babydoll. He smiled at her habit of bringing tea upstairs before bed. Always helpful, he chuckled softly.

He slowly walked to her side of the bed and watched her beautiful face as she slept. He sat down beside her, gently caressing her cheek and her lips. He smiled when her green eyes opened in her sleepy, drugged haze, and she mumbled something. Evil let his hand linger over her shoulder and down her side as he leaned down to kiss her lips. He stood up and slowly lifted each toned leg over toward the center of the bed, then covered her up. He kissed her once again as he tucked the sheet under her chin. Her green eyes followed him as he walked around the dark room...

Clara knew the shadow was back when the breeze from the cool summer evening turned ice cold. She wanted to keep her eyes closed but she couldn't. She opened them as if by reflex, and saw the familiar blue eyes that haunt her as they faded in and out of the shadow. She wasn't aware when she fell back asleep. She slowly lifted her covers and decided she would follow it this time. She wanted to see where it goes when it's here. Mommy's friend called it Evil and Mommy laughed. She said it was fitting. When Clara arrived at the top of the back staircase, she squatted down, overlooking the old wooden banister. She could see her mother standing in the dim light wearing her robe, and the shadow standing in front of her. And without warning the shadow struck her. Within seconds, her mother was lying over the cornflower blue tablecloth on the floor. Blood appeared to be trickling from the corner of her mouth. Fear had her frozen in place as she silently watched. "Open your eyes, Mommy," her mind screamed, "open your eyes!" Then, as if she heard, her mother opened her eyes. For a moment, their green eyes met. In her head, she heard her mother's voice as her lips moved, "run"...

heavy weight of anxiety and despair

It was early morning, when Connor finally arrived at Clara's. He simply removed his clothes and slid into the bed beside her. He had just fallen asleep when Clara sat up suddenly with a loud gasp, struggling to catch her breath. Connor, used to her restless dreams, sleepily placed his hand on her back, to reassure her she was safe.

The physical contact pushed her fear into panic as she screamed and jumped from the bed.

Connor started to follow her, but in the darkened room, she could only see his shadow. Aware of her fear of shadows, he quickly turned on the light. The sudden bright light seemed to shake her out of her sleepy nightmare. When her fearful green eyes looked up into his brown, she burst into tears of hysteria as she stepped back into the wall and slowly slid down to the floor.

Connor sat beside her without touching, afraid his touch would cause more distress than comfort. It was a bit of time before she leaned into him, encouraging him to put his arm around her as she shivered.

They remained on the floor for the rest of the night.

As the early light of dawn appeared, the terror of the night seemed to fade away with the shadows. Clara sighed with embarrassment at her irrational fear of shadows. She pulled her knees in close as she closed her eyes in an attempt to recall the horrible dream. But she could not. She only knew Evil was there but the details of the dream faded with the darkness, leaving her with the heavy weight of anxiety and despair.

Clara felt Connor shift beside her, no doubt he was getting restless sitting on the floor. Not ready to look at him, she slowly stood up and went to the bathroom. When she came out a few minutes later, she was relieved to find the room empty. Clara sat on the bed and debated what to do. What is there to do? You need to pull yourself together, Clara Noelle! A guy like Connor isn't going to stick around with a hysterical girl who can't seem to keep herself under control. She closed her eyes to take a deep breath, and a distant memory flashed through her mind of her mother's face, eyes wide with fear as she looked directly at her, and that was all Clara could recall.

Connor heard her coming down the steps and went to prepare her tea, her early morning drink of choice since Eric's arrest. When Clara entered the kitchen, he watched as she approached him. Clara appeared to be trying to act as if it were just another typical morning. He placed her mug on the table as he pulled out her chair. She accepted his kiss before sitting down.

"You want to talk about it?"

"About what?" Clara asked, how can she talk about something she didn't even know? When her green eyes met his brown, she felt her anxiety increase.

"Your nightmares seem to be getting worse. Have you been having them all these years?"

"No, just since I returned," she clarified. Neither one wanted to point out that they started getting worse when Clara found her mother's remains.

Shit, Connor thought, that would give anyone nightmares. He thought back to the morning when he found her sitting alone on the step. Knowing what he knows now, is it possible she saw something that night? Does she know what happened to her mother? Has her young mind protected her all these years, but now something is causing the memories to surface while she sleeps?

"Tell me about it," he suggested as he squeezed her hand.

"Connor, I don't remember. I never do," Clara started, struggling for words. It just leaves me feeling fearful, she thought. It seems so real. In the last few weeks, her dreams had become more vivid. She could smell odd odors, feel the touching and even the coldness of the room. More than once she believed someone was in her room. The weird sensation when you think you're sleeping, but when you wake up, you're actually still in the dream.

He watched her as she appeared to be processing something. Was she remembering more than she shared? "I have to work this weekend at the hospital, but you and the kids can go to the lake house. It'll give you an opportunity to relax."

"I wouldn't be comfortable out there by myself with them. Too much water and steps," Clara said, immediately dismissing the suggestion. She didn't say out loud that she would worry too much about him remaining behind. She feared Evil would also take Connor from her. "I am really sorry you didn't get any sleep last night. You should stay at your place."

Connor sat back in his chair, his eyes narrowed in question. "Why are you trying to push me away?"

"I'm not. You suggested I leave you first. It just makes more sense for you to stay at your place. You need your sleep as much as anyone," Clara said.

"Limited sleep is a prerequisite for surgeons. Doctors in general are used to getting calls all hours of the day," he picked up her hand to kiss it. He watched her eyes as she watched their hands together. She didn't pull back. "I like coming home to you each night. I like you being the last person I see when I close my eyes and the first one when I open them. I am crazy about you, Clara Noelle. Keeping me awake will never

heavy weight of anxiety and despair   491

be a reason to get rid of me. I will only leave when you say you don't want me beside you any longer."

Clara felt a tear slide down her cheek as he showered her with words of love. She was tempted to lie as she weighed his safety versus his trust. 'Tell him you don't want him anymore,' she heard in her head. 'But you've never lied to him before,' another voice argued, 'And you aren't going to start now.' Connor kept it simple, no demands of commitment or plans for a future. He knew her too well.

"You won't tell me what's going through your pretty head?" Connor wiped a tear before he continued, "Tell me why you are crying."

"I can't, I can't even explain it," she honestly admitted as she pulled back, wiping the tears.

They sat in silence as tears continued to flow down her cheeks.

Connor heard a giggle from above, "The kids are up."

Clara nodded, "I need to get them ready for the day."

He grabbed her around the waist as she walked by, pulling her down onto his lap. He gave her a hug and kiss, and was pleased she allowed the kiss to linger before she stood up and walked out. Connor was left to wonder if she knew more than she was admitting. But if she did, why wouldn't Clara tell him? What could she be hiding from him?

Clara was relieved Connor was already gone when she returned to the kitchen with the children. Reese was discussing what he believed would happen during his day.

Throughout the day, Clara would not admit, not even to herself, that she purposefully avoided Connor. She was not aware that he saw her when she dropped off the kids at the daycare, and when she picked them up. Connor watched from the window of his office. When he went to the nursing home, Connor was suspicious she was avoiding him. He saw a glimpse of her walking patients in the hallway and heard her voice when she was in the room with a patient. He wanted to touch base with her about the evening plans, but she wasn't in her gym. Her laptop was gone from her desk, but her personal bag was still there, suggesting she was somewhere hiding. Connor decided to give her space, worried he may have overstepped the blurry line of discussing their feelings for each other and the mention of their future as a couple. It always made her tense.

Clara took her laptop and hid in the corner of Gigi's room as she attempted to complete her seemingly endless paperwork before she left for the day. Beside her was her cell, each of her friends agreeing to meet later that evening for a girls' night out. She had expressed her frustrations at not yet having an evening devoted to the girls. They each agreed, while they often hung out together, it was smaller groups for lunch, with couples, or the whole group.

It was still light out when they all walked together from Clara's house a few short blocks to the bar on the side street.

"Do you really think this place is a good idea?" Rachel asked. She had never been inside as she heard too many negative stories about fights and property destruction.

"Clara is right, the guys will never think to look for us here. With our cars all at home, they won't know where to look," Shannon chuckled.

"I have never been inside," Lila stated. She often saw the patrons injured in the emergency room. Of course, most were drunk injuries from stupid falls, nothing violent. It wasn't on the same level of crime and danger as similarly reputed bars in the city with stabbings and gunshot wounds.

"I've been inside before. I knew half of the people. Nothing to be afraid of. Come on, the first round is mine," Clara boldly assured her friends as she stepped inside.

trouble in paradise

Clara was right. Her friends knew many of the people there, either from their childhood or through work. They all shared a drink together before mingling among the crowd.

Shannon scanned the room. She was surprised to see a familiar set of brown eyes lock with hers. Shit, she thought, what the hell is he doing here? She tried to ignore her excitement as she approached him.

"Why are you here?"

"Just keeping an eye on you, making sure you're safe," Joel Montgomery said with a shrug. He missed her more than he would ever admit.

"Joel, I already told you, I don't know anything about what happened," Shannon found herself repeating.

"Yeah, you keep telling me that. I do not know how to make you understand the danger. He isn't going to simply walk away from this. He's convinced you have something on him," he explained with frustration.

"What can I possibly have? I only ever worked on my cases with my clients. I never had any idea anything illegal was going on until the day he called me into his office. He accused me of bringing in a corporate spy," she stated. "How can I possibly tell anyone what I don't know?"

Joel watched as she repeated what he heard before. She really isn't grasping the danger, he thought as he changed the topic. "You were certainly quick to get over your hurt and devastation, seeing that you're already shacking up with another guy. Regardless, I do think you're safer with him than with Clara," he commented. Joel wasn't sure what Shannon knew about her current guy, but if he were smart, he'd be honest from the start. But, not his problem. He was still in love with her and understood what he did wrong, but ultimately, he wanted her alive. Happy, sure, but she couldn't be happy if that bastard got his way. If she had that with this guy, then so be it.

"Did you hear about what happened to Jason?" Shannon asked, shifting the topic as she sat beside him. Both looked over towards Clara, as he told her what he knew and what he speculated. He didn't mention his run in with Clara in the city.

Shannon only worried about Clara recognizing him. While Lila knew all about him as the relationship progressed and burned, she never actually met the guy. Rachel was also aware of him but only met him once or twice in the beginning. Clara was the only one that got to know Joel as the two had double-dated many times the previous fall since the guys hit it off.

At the bar, Clara was talking to an older gentleman whose wife had been a patient of hers when she first arrived in town. She was happy to hear his wife continued to progress upon returning home and was now walking without her walker.

"Clara! I am surprised to see you here! Since you have your clothes on, Connor must not be around," a familiar voice teased from behind.

Clara turned around to see Matt was leaning on the bar beside her with a twinkle in his blue eyes. His eyes followed her hand as she looked down to her cell, immediately hitting decline when his brother's ID picture showed up. *Trouble in paradise?* he wondered.

"Matt, what are you doing here?"

"Apparently the same as you, hiding from my better half. Of course, in your case, you are the better half," he chuckled. He watched her seem to struggle with something as various emotions played across her face.

"What makes you think I'm hiding? I'm out here with my friends." Clara gestured behind her.

Matt had noticed her friends mingling among the crowd. He wasn't going to comment on the one snuggling up close in the shadows of the back room. There appeared to be too much comfort between them. He knew it was not Devan. Matt had yet to decide what, if anything, he would do about that. Devan was Connor's cousin, not his, which was his justification for staying out of it. He knew from experience, cheating always surfaced, sometimes sooner than later. Never pleasant when it did.

"Well, you are declining his calls and quite honestly, I don't think he would allow you to be in here without him. Connor couldn't possibly know you are here," Matt explained as he waved over the bartender. "I'll have my usual and get Clara another. Thanks, Chuck."

"Why wouldn't he approve of me being here? It's not as bad as I was led to believe, from the stories I've heard," she defended the place. "I've been here before."

Matt looked around. It wasn't clean, paint was peeling, and the seats were torn, but the atmosphere varied. You never really knew what to expect when you entered. He looked back at her green eyes, so like her mother's. He wasn't going to comment about her getting drugged the last time she was here. Devan and Josh seemed convinced it happened at The Lantern. "It's not as bad as it used to be. It's mellowed over the years."

When he turned his attention back, he noted she read a text, confident it was again his brother, before placing the phone in her back pocket. "What did Connor do?"

"He didn't do anything wrong," she answered sadly. Accepting her drink, she pulled it closer to sip, giving her hands something to do.

"If he didn't do anything wrong, did he do anything right?" Matt logically asked. He knew from experience it wasn't always the wrong things that doomed a relationship. Sometimes, the lack of the right words and actions caused it to burn faster.

"That's just it. Connor doesn't ever do anything wrong. He always does the right thing. He knows what to do or say before I even know what I need or want. It's like he knows the steps to the dance, and I just follow his lead," Clara blurted out. It could be the alcohol, but more likely he asked the right questions. He is a lawyer, she reminded herself.

Interesting analogy, he thought. Matt was very aware of his little brother's infatuation with the woman beside him. They had always been close, but nothing inappropriate when they were growing up. While Clara adored Connor as a young girl, he never sensed his brother's interest until the fundraiser. Since then, he remained on the sidelines, watching from afar as Connor appeared more smitten with her than she appeared to be with him. She was obviously comfortable with him. But again, he knew from experience, it was difficult to move on after the loss of a loved one, especially so tragically.

"You know, I met him," Matt stated as he looked down into his drink.

"Who?"

"Your husband," he answered quietly. Matt knew he had her attention when she gestured toward the newly vacated seat on her other side. Once he sat, he sipped his drink as he gathered his thoughts. "I was given the task of monitoring the funds in the trust. Our law firm already worked with his accounting company. My first meeting was shortly after you were married. My dad had mentioned in passing you had married, but I didn't make the connection until I saw your picture on Jason's desk. It was a crazy coincidence."

Matt sighed as he remembered mistaking her picture for Susi. She looked so much like her mother. But once he picked up the picture, he could see the subtle differences. It had to be her daughter. Matt once again felt the ache in his heart at the loss of his Susi. Upon hearing about her death this spring, he locked himself in his office for days, hiding under the guise of work. But his wife knew the real reason and kept her distance. While he knew she was dead, he did not know what caused the early death of his first love so long ago. He wasn't sure if he wanted to know. More accurately, he didn't know if he could handle the details of her final moments alive.

"Jason was so proud of you. He told me you had recently passed the boards and were working at the trauma center. I know your mother would have approved of him," Matt stated quietly as he squeezed her hand.

"You were close to my mother?"

"Yes, I grew up next to her, didn't I? I was her best friend, after Beth. We had many classes together, hiked the woods, and swam in the lake," he remembered.

He was in love with her, Clara heard clearly. How did they not end up together? Did she not love him back? How did her father win over her mother's heart? In the journals, her mother refers to M, that must be for Matt. That's right, he broke it off after her uncle was killed. And that left HG. Who was HG? That was when she remembered Josh's comments about his father never getting over her mother. Their fathers had forbidden the budding romance.

"Clara, she loved you very much and she would have been equally proud of you and your children," Matt grabbed her hand again and kissed it. "Take the time you need. Connor will wait for you. But if you don't love him, tell him. He will understand and step back."

"Why would you think I don't?"

Matt was quiet for a moment as he sipped from his drink, his blue eyes on her green as he organized his thoughts.

"I'm awakened frequently during the night to help bail someone out of jail. But I have never had a woman request me to bail out a man that wasn't her family member or current lover," he honestly answered.

Matt saw she understood his meaning. He had been both surprised and not by the call. Rob Foxwood did have a reputation as being a hothead. And the Thompson and Foxwood families did have a long history of exchanging blows. However, it did surprise him that the topic of discussion leading to the fight and arrest was Clara. A woman neither man had claims to defend as she was, he knew for an absolute fact, involved with his brother. It made him wonder if it was just old high school issues never resolved or if the Thompson guy just knew what buttons to push. Either way, it worried him to discover Susi's daughter was in the middle of such a violent dispute. The Thompson guy had a disturbing demoniac history. He remembered Connor, as a teen, sharing stories of what went on in the park over the years. And often he was left carrying home an injured little Clara.

"Rob and I are just friends," Clara stated a little defensively. "Always have been. He is the one that taught me how to drive a tractor, to swim, and to ride a horse. When we were kids, we all hiked the woods and helped with the chores. Rob was there when Connor was not. He always knew about Rob and who he is to me, just as Rob now knows who Connor is."

Matt remained silent as he watched her gather her thoughts.

Clara paused to process what she wanted to say, "I have always loved Rob, but I have always been in love with Connor."

"I'm not judging, as long as everyone knows where they stand, that's what is important. I believe Connor will wait for you. You have control of the pace and he will adjust," he smiled gently. Matt was tempted to touch her cheek but knew better. He winked instead, as she smiled softly and nodded. "I have kept you from your friends long enough, let me get you another drink. Hey Chuck, get my brother's girl a refill, will you?"

Lila and Rachel were approaching Clara when they heard Matt say, "Clara, it's always good to see you. Even if you have your clothes on."

"What does he mean by that?" Rachel asked, surprised by the

comment and her laughter.

"Oh, he walked in on Connor and me a couple of times," Clara dismissed.

"Oh, how awkward! I think I would just die if my brother caught Dallas and me together," Lila stated. Looking back, she could now admit they had taken some serious risks when they were in high school. It was easier when she left for college despite being in the same city as her brother and cousin. They were all in different schools in a very large city.

"How are things going with you and Dallas?" Clara asked.

Lila met her eyes and appeared to understand the unasked question. The expression on her face said it all, it was going great.

"I have a confession to make," Lila started just as Shannon rejoined the group. "You all have to promise me not to tell anyone. I mean it, especially you, Rach."

They all quickly agreed, "Do you remember when I went to the Florida Keys for vacation? Dallas and I got married and honeymooned there."

All the friends laughed and hugged.

Matt turned towards the contagious laughter and smiled as he watched Clara with her friends. He pulled out his phone to capture the moment of true friends together. Then he ordered a round of drinks for the women. He wasn't aware his son had quietly entered the bar, watching his father taking pictures of Clara with her friends.

After his drink arrived, Josh's eyes met with Clara's. He slowly made his way over to her group of friends. Rachel greeted him with a friendly hug before introducing him to Shannon. When everyone was distracted, he leaned over to ask her if her phone was off.

"Why?"

"Connor's looking for you," he explained.

"Josh, I like you so I'm going to ignore that. Let's do a shot," Clara linked her arm in his before leading him over towards the bar.

To his amusement, she placed money down on the bar as she ordered tequila shots. When they arrived, she handed him one while she lifted hers in a toast. "To friends."

Josh nodded his head as he clicked his glass to hers. As he was swallowing, he returned his shot glass to the bar when he heard his name being called.

"Josh! Where have you been? I've been waiting for you, come on." A man with blonde hair and sky blue eyes was standing behind him.

"Sean, I'm not late," Josh argued.

"It's happening right now, come on. We need to get those guys tonight!" Sean was about to pull his friend over towards the pool table when his eyes met Clara's. He came to a full stop and stared at her a moment before looking back at his friend.

"Am I interrupting something?" He asked as his eyes darted between them.

"Depends on where you are dragging him to," Clara answered as she signaled for another round.

Josh grinned at her protective tone as his friend's eyes widened in surprise and awe, "You and Clara Gibson? Really?"

"No," Josh laughed as he shook his head. "We're friends. She's with my uncle. Clara, do you know Sean Black?"

"Of the Thompson Clan?" Clara asked.

"Kind of but not really," Sean answered.

"What's the difference?" She asked, mesmerized by the sparkle in his sky blue eyes. Something was familiar about him but she couldn't place it. "When did you graduate?"

"With Josh, six years ago. You went to school with my cousin Danny. He's a Thompson. Not me, but my mother was a Thompson. Danny always had the hots for you," Sean stated. "It would be my honor if you'd be my partner tonight in the pool tournament."

Before Clara could answer, Sean grabbed her hand to lead her towards the back where the opposing team was gathering.

"Is he back there?" Clara stopped in panic, causing Josh to bump into her.

When Sean turned around, he saw fear in her eyes. "Hell no. He's still in jail for going after you and your friend with a knife."

"You were there?" Josh asked Clara. He had heard about the arrest the next morning from a nurse at the hospital. When he learned his father was the lawyer protecting Foxwood against Danny, he didn't bring it up to Sean. "My father didn't tell me."

"Forget I brought it up," Clara requested as she continued to the back room. "Bear!"

Bear Johnson turned and grinned when he saw Clara. He gave her a big hug as he yelled her name, "Clara Noelle! What are you doing hanging out with these delinquents in this hellhole?"

"Oh, they aren't too bad, are they?" Clara wondered as she turned to study them.

"Clara, you can't be fraternizing with the enemy!" Sean declared.

"Bear? He's the enemy?" She looked him over in amusement.

"Current champion of the pool tournament," Bear proudly announced. "Wouldn't you rather be on my team?"

"Clara's on ours," Josh declared. "First round with me and Sean. She'll play the final round."

An hour before last call, Clara was in a serious game of double or nothing with Bear Johnson. The back room was amazingly quiet as the crowd watched the petite woman with the wild curly hair slowly walk around the pool table as she contemplated what to do next. She leaned forward with the stick, gently tapping the cue ball into the two ball which, not what she planned to do, tapped the six and eight balls. All three went into pockets. Five minutes later, the game was over, and the room was cheering while money was exchanged.

Both Josh and Sean came over together, each with a hand in the air. She stood holding her stick beside her and slapped a high five with each of them.

"Damn it, Clara! I didn't know you were a hustler. Not fair," Bear complained as he towered over her.

"Bear, I swear, I am never this good!" Clara laughed as she accepted her winnings. She should have admitted to recently receiving lessons from Connor when they went to his lake house. The downstairs was set up as an ideal bachelor pad complete with the pool table and dart board. She looked over at Josh, "How did you know I could play?"

"Connor told me," he laughed. "He said you were getting pretty good. We just wanted to knock Bear off his perch."

"Why didn't you ask Connor to play?"

"Bear would never have agreed to it. Connor is the only one to ever defeat him," Sean laughed. "And besides, he's not here, you are."

Matt watched as Clara and his son continued to talk. He would never admit out loud, he had been concerned when he first saw Josh with her at the bar. But when Sean led her to the back room, he realized what the boys were up to. They had been scheming ways to beat Bear since the beginning of the month. He pulled out his phone again as he snapped another picture and hoped she would forgive him for what he would do next.

Lila stood to the side as she watched Sammy Black's little brother. He looks so much like him, she thought sadly.

please don't leave me

The next morning, the bedroom was bright with the summer sun when Clara's eyes opened. Oh shit, she thought as she looked at the clock. Connor can't be too happy with me. She rolled out of bed and into the shower. When she descended the stairs thirty minutes later, she stopped at the sight before her. Hailey sat on Connor's lap with Reese beside them while they played the memory game.

"Mama!" The young toddler was immediately up and running towards her followed by Reese. After they hugged, the children returned to their game.

Clara continued into the kitchen with the intent of getting a drink before joining them back in the family room. Instead, Connor followed her.

He remained in the doorway as she prepared her tea, waiting for her to acknowledge him. Instead of attempting to walk past Connor, Clara leaned into the counter, sipping and avoiding eye contact.

Connor walked towards the counter. He was less than a step from her as he prepared himself another mug of coffee. With his mug in hand, he tilted her chin and kissed her. He let his lips linger close to hers as he watched to see how she reacted. When she didn't pull back, he gave her another quick kiss before grabbing her hand to lead her to the table.

After they were sitting for a few moments in silence, Connor finally asked, "Want to talk about last night?"

"What is there to talk about?" Clara quietly asked.

"I don't know. We can start with why you were avoiding me. I don't think it was too much to ask you to answer a text about dinner. You could have simply told me you were going out with your friends. We aren't the couple that has to do everything together. Instead, I got here last night to find you are already out for the night with Michelle here with the kids." He had debated paying the sitter and staying in for the night but felt that was overstepping Clara, especially when she was avoiding him.

"You want to talk. Then tell me why you were texting and calling me all night?" She asked defensively.

"It would have ended once you answered me," Connor quietly explained. He leaned back in his seat, sipping his coffee, eyes still on hers. He wasn't reading anger in her tone. Over the years, Clara could never hide her fierce temper from him. She was almost indifferent. Or rather, she was trying to be. "Once you told me you were competing in the nightly pool tournament, I would have left you alone."

"No, you would have come right over and tried to pull me out. How do you even know about that anyway?" Clara demanded in a quiet tone.

Without a word, Connor placed his cell on the table with the picture of her and Bear together. She initially thought it came from Matt, but he was in the shadows of the background. When they all stepped out after last call, Connor was leaning against his SUV. Dallas and Devan were waiting beside him. Without a word, she went to the passenger seat when he opened the door. They continued home in silence and into the house. She was the one that turned to him for comfort during the night after dreaming of the shadow following her through the house.

"Do you want me to leave?" Connor asked.

"What? Why would you ask that?"

Connor gave a harsh chuckle, "You don't want to talk with me, you have been avoiding me the last few days, here and at work. If I make you unhappy, tell me. If you need space, say it. I'll step back, walk away, whatever it is you want, I will do it. Just tell me what it is."

Feeling a sudden restlessness, Clara was on her feet. She was busying her hands by rinsing out her mug without finishing it. She looked out the window and wondered if she could make it through a week or a month of sleepless nights. It would keep him a safe distance from Evil, she thought. Connor has always been her rock, her solid foundation of support which allowed her to grow. All her life, he was always there when she needed him. Even when she didn't know she needed him, he was there. Always. If he were gone, she would crumble. Clara was sure of it.

Connor wondered if he was causing her anxiety as he watched her stare out the window. Their relationship sparked fast. Barely a month in, reality was setting in. Was he once again pushing too much too soon? Should he step back and wait for her to make the next move? Wait for her to decide if she wanted this, him?

Clara turned around, wanting to talk but unsure if the words would form. She was startled to see Connor standing right behind her. He had paused to read a text from the hospital.

"I'm heading out," he started to explain as he returned the phone to his pocket.

"You are leaving me?" Clara asked in a panic as she grabbed his arm. "Please don't leave me."

"Clara, I am heading to the nursing home to check on someone then to the hospital," he explained. Connor wasn't sure which surprised him more, her sudden panic or her loss of composure when she closed the space between them, placing her arms around him. She held tight as she fought the tears.

"Will you be back?" Clara's voice was muffled into his chest.

"Do you want me to be back?" Connor asked. He leaned back, seeing the anxiety in her eyes. "You don't act like you want me here."

"That's not true," she said out loud, but could only think to herself. *I need you.*

"Mama, go go, Mama." Hailey suddenly appeared at their side, her arms around each of their legs.

"We want to go for a ride in the wagon," Reese announced from the doorway.

Connor reached down to pull her up as she held her arms out for her mother. He kissed her forehead before she went over to her mother's arms. He kissed Clara as Hailey hugged her mother. Then he walked out.

Next door, Shannon was slow to wake up as the sun brightened Devan's bedroom. Damn, she thought. I never sleep this late. She checked the time and noted messages left on her cell before she went to shower. An hour later, Shannon had a mug of coffee as she stood in the doorway of the room Devan used as an office. He always kept the door closed and rarely went inside when she was home. She slowly stepped into the room as she became aware of what she was looking at.

Devan didn't realize he was no longer alone when he heard Shannon gasp, he twirled around in his seat, "Shannon, you're up."

"What is all this? Are these people missing?" Shannon asked as she slowly walked towards the walls, covered with pictures and information regarding last seen and personal description. There were maps of the town, surrounding areas, and the federal park with pins of different colors strategically placed. She turned around in question.

"Some yeah. Others are people found or mysteriously dead in the last year," Devan admitted.

Shannon sipped from her coffee as her eyes scanned the room, she didn't know many people. Devan was relieved he hadn't had a chance yet to place Rachel's mother's face up on the wall. He stood up to stretch as he motioned her to follow him to the kitchen.

"Want me to make you some breakfast," he asked as he kissed her.

"You don't need to bother," she answered, as he refilled her mug.

"I'm hungry. I was getting ready for a break," Devan stated as he watched her check her phone. He didn't comment when he saw her ex-boyfriend's name appear next to the message. He figured she would tell him, when and if she was ready.

As he started to pull out items for the meal, Devan casually asked about the previous night. She talked about the music, the drinking, the pool tournament, and how Clara won the final round. He sensed she was leaving something out. While the omelets cooked, he leaned against the counter, sipping his coffee as Shannon once again checked her texts, responding before she returned her attention to him.

"So why all the secrecy?"

"What secrecy?"

"You ignored my text. In the morning, you mentioned meeting me at Memories for dinner during my break and then I heard nothing. Everything alright?"

"Yeah, everything's fine," she answered.

"So, why were all you girls on radio silence?" Devan asked.

"What are you talking about?" Shannon asked while she avoided his eyes.

"None of you answered any of our texts or calls all evening. It was like the girls-only evening meant no communication with the guys," Devan suggested. "Do we have a problem?"

"Why do you say that?" Shannon quietly demanded.

"Because I was worried about you, I reached out to you and you continued to ignore me all evening. We had plans together," he answered, watching her.

"I am sorry. I forgot we had plans. Clara started a group chat about us all going out for a girls' night. What's the big deal? It's not like we had real plans. You were working." Shannon minimized the issue. She really had intended to text him, but was distracted when Joel showed up at the bar. She honestly lost track of time.

"I don't know, I guess when someone initiates meeting me for dinner, I expect her to be there." Devan debated continuing but decided to drop it, for now. "I was concerned because of everything that's been going on lately. Missing women, dead bodies, and spiked drinks. I just wanted to be sure you were alright. Is that so bad?"

Shannon watched as he placed the food on plates and sat down with her.

"Dev, just because this town has had a few missing women and a body was found last month doesn't mean you need to be paranoid if I'm not at your bar every night," Shan dismissed. "You look at those walls all day, every day. It will make you lose perspective of reality."

"I don't think so. I happen to know more about what's going on than most. When we learned another body was found yesterday, all of us guys were feeling a little anxious, especially knowing Clara had her drink spiked. Connor freaked out when Josh mentioned he thought he saw Eric out in the neighborhood," Devan explained himself.

"What? What are you talking about? What body?" Her fork paused in the air.

"They found the body of a woman yesterday afternoon. Later in the evening, she was identified as the physical therapist from the nursing home. The one Clara replaced," Devan answered. He was relieved to finally have her attention.

"Why didn't you tell me?"

"I tried, you didn't answer your phone, remember?"

"Wow, I didn't know. No one mentioned it at the bar last night," Shannon stated.

"No, it wasn't released to the public until this morning. They needed to notify the family first," Devan explained.

"But what did you mean about the other part?" She further clarified when he looked up in question. "Clara having her drink spiked. I thought Eric was lacing her coffee with drugs. When did her drink get spiked?"

"Aren't you girls all supposed to be close? Don't you ever talk?" When she didn't respond, Devan further explained. "The evening you and Lila were late getting to Memories, Clara was out by herself at The Lantern. Her drink was spiked with a date rape drug."

"What?" Shannon dropped her fork. "Why didn't you tell me?"

"We weren't really together at the time. You didn't know I was an agent. I just figured she told you," Devan shrugged.

"Did something happen to her? How did you learn this?"

"Her behavior was off," he answered.

"Really? How so?"

"This was before she learned of her husband's death. She and Connor weren't really together either. She came into the place and kissed him. Let's just say, if he didn't pull back, she would have been fine with having sex right there."

Shannon laughed dismissively, "Clara is a very private person. She's never been big on public displays of affection."

"And yet she did that. I was blushing. Connor noted her pupils were pinpoint and pulled her out of there. I preserved her glass, then went upstairs to drop off food and pick up her blood sample. She was doing a little strip tease by the back door in front of both of us," he answered. "It was not a funny thing, having to watch a person you know totally uninhibited. She was purposely targeted and left vulnerable to harm. Imagine if she woke up the next morning, lost and alone, unsure of what happened, if she woke up at all. Multiple women are missing in the area."

"Why didn't you tell me all this sooner?"

"I thought she would have told you about it. Maybe she was embarrassed, but then within a week she was dealing with her husband's death. So maybe it was on the back burner," Devan stated as he brought the plates to the sink. "I am in a position where I'm not at liberty to share what I know from work. I just want to know you are safe and taking precautions." He grabbed her and kissed her before he continued, "And sometimes maybe I just want to hear your voice."

After lunch, the children were upstairs napping while Clara was busy cleaning up the house. She had been distracted while putting away her clothes. She sighed as she went through her drawers again. She couldn't find her shorts and t-shirt for volleyball. She sat on the newly made bed with her face in her hands as she sighed with frustration. I am losing my mind, aren't I? Who would be upset over something so silly as that? But she was also missing some of her lingerie. Could be at Connor's lake house, she thought. Something could have fallen to the floor and been kicked under the bed. Clara sighed again. Who actually knows how many pairs of underwear they have? She argued with herself as she went back downstairs. It'll all turn up.

She wished Connor would return. Clara worried he would leave her. She wanted to talk but didn't know what to say. She didn't know what she was feeling so how could he expect her to talk about it? And more importantly, is he in danger when he's with her?

Clara was startled by a sudden pounding on her front door accompanied by yelling. She cautiously went to the window to look out, once again surprised to see Felicia Thompson on her porch.

Good heavens, what the hell does the bitch want now, she thought. Worried the children would be awakened by her commotion, she opened the door. Before she could say a word, the woman started screaming at her.

"Where the hell is that bastard? You tell him I want to talk to him right now!" Felicia leaned to the side, trying to look around Clara into the home, "You can't hide from me! Do you hear me? I am not going away!"

"Ms. Thompson, what are you doing here?" Clara asked after a minute. She had never seen the woman this disheveled before. Her summer dress was wrinkled, her hair was uncombed, and her mascara was smeared beneath her eyes. In an attempt to calm her and allow the children to finish their naps, Clara stepped out onto the porch. That was when she smelled the alcohol. Oh great, just what she needed, a lively battle with a drunk Felicia Thompson.

"I am looking for that no good bastard father of yours," Felicia shouted. Stepping backwards, she looked up towards the second story windows, "Come out here and face me like a man you coward. Stop trying to hide behind your no good daughter. I'm not letting this go, not after all the time I've put into it!"

"Ms. Thompson, you need to leave," Clara demanded as the woman tried to push her away from the door.

"You let me in right now! I am here to talk to your father. I am not leaving until I see his face and give him a piece of my mind. If he thinks he can cut me out now that the money is coming, he'd better think again," the older woman yelled as she balled her fist and tried to punch Clara in the face. The poorly executed punch only succeeded in causing her rings to scratch Clara's cheek.

"Felicia, you get the hell off my porch. He is not here. It's only me and my children. There is no way in hell you are getting through that door. Go away!" Clara yelled back as she fought to maintain her footing in front of the door.

"You little bitch! You will not stop him from being with me anymore, you hear me? I will get inside, I am not leaving. Move out of the way!" Felicia tried to shove Clara again. First with her hands, then with her whole body. Clara didn't budge. No way was she letting this lunatic inside with her children.

Felicia, face red from alcohol and anger, grabbed Clara's neck as she continued to yell irrationally, "Move away from the door, you conniving little brat, or I will…"

"Or you will what?" Devan asked from behind. He had already called the sheriff's department and was currently recording the scene on his cell. Devan had remained in the background until she started to strangle Clara.

Clara clenched her fists and pulled them up between the other woman's arms, pushing them away to free her throat. Once Felicia's hands were off, Clara pushed her backwards, not intending to push the older woman off the porch.

Felicia fell with a loud scream just as the deputy cruiser pulled into the driveway with the lights flashing. She landed hard on her side with her right leg lying in an awkward position.

Devan stood over the woman as he instructed her to remain on the ground, "Don't get up. I will have you arrested for trespassing and assault, got it?"

He looked over his shoulder at Clara but before he could ask, she answered, "I am fine." Royally pissed off, but just fine, she thought. Her mind was racing with all the information she just received. Felicia was no longer with her father? When did they break up? Why did they break up? And what money was she talking about?

"Devan, what's going on?" Joe asked as he and his partner walked towards the porch. He took one look at the position of the woman on the ground and instructed his partner to call an ambulance.

"I have it all on my cell," Devan stated, keeping an eye on the woman as he handed his cousin the phone.

Felicia was crying, trying to play the victim. So intent on getting inside to talk to Carl, she wasn't aware of the neighbors gathering and taping the scene. In her mind, she didn't do anything wrong. "I was pushed! She pushed me!"

"Yeah, you certainly were, Ms. Thompson," Joe commented after reviewing the footage. Convinced the woman wasn't capable of going anywhere if she wanted to, Joe climbed the steps to the visibly shaking woman. "Clara? Let me see your neck."

He gently touched her chin to tilt her head up. Both Devan and Joe's eyes widened at the already inflamed red skin on her neck.

"Damn, Clara, that has to hurt. Walker, we are going to need another ambulance."

"Mr. Mancuso, I am fine. I don't need an ambulance," Clara started to say but Devan and Joe both chuckled.

"Clara, you can call me Joe. My father isn't here. Please, have a seat while I get a grip on all this." Joe instructed his cousin to assist her down on the first step.

"Ms. Thompson, please tell me, why are you here?"

"I am looking for that no good bastard that she's hiding inside. She wouldn't let me in," Felicia whined.

"Ms. Thompson, who are you looking for?"

"Carl Gibson," she whispered. It was starting to dawn on her the hole she was digging.

Oh, where to begin, Joe wondered. "First of all, you are under arrest for trespassing, assault, and violating a restraining order." He proceeded to read her rights as the ambulances drove up.

Three hours later, Clara was still in a hospital gown with curtains closed around her room. With Felicia Thompson's screaming and yelling, she had been tempted to remove her hearing aids. Clara was impressed she could hear what was being said over the yelling and identify the voices.

Devan had appointed himself as her security guard, and remained outside her curtain.

"Devan, what the hell is going on?" Dallas asked.

"Your mother paid Clara a visit. It didn't go well. Long story short, she attacked Clara. Clara defended herself, pushing her off the porch in the process. She has a fractured hip, I think," Devan explained.

"Why did she attack her?" Lila asked.

"No idea. Everyone has been wondering. Watch this," Devan said. Clara assumed he was playing the recording on his phone.

"I don't believe it. Is Clara alright?" Dallas asked.

Clara took that moment to peek out of the curtain. "Dallas, Lila, how is it going? Could either of you give me a ride home? Devan, I mean what I say, not one word to Connor." She ignored the hoarseness in her voice as she pointed a finger at him.

Dallas and Lila both stepped towards her. He lifted her chin, "She did this to you? Why? Are you alright?"

Both leaned in closer to examine the bruising on her throat and the scratches on her cheek.

"I am fine. You should see the other guy," Clara answered with annoyance.

"I'm getting started on a shift soon or I would take you home," Lila said apologetically.

"Is Connor home with the kids?" Dallas asked.

"I don't know where he is, nor do I want either of you talking to him. He doesn't need to know. But I can get myself home." Clara ducked behind the curtain when she saw Josh approaching the nurse's station. She knew Josh would immediately call Connor. Clara changed into her clothes, fully expecting to be discharged soon.

"What the hell is going on?" Dallas asked Devan.

"Not really sure which you mean. Between her and Connor? No idea. They've been a bit off lately. Between your parents? Again, no idea. Your dad has secured a restraining order against your mother. She is not to go near him, Clara or her kids. I am not privy to the reason, but apparently your dad saw potential concerns," Devan answered. He had also seen Josh enter the emergency department. Devan was half hoping the kid would mosey down this way.

"Is Shannon with the kids?" Lila asked.

"I have no idea where Shannon is right now. She went out this morning, I figured she was at work but she wasn't answering her phone," Devan answered. Lila detected a bit of annoyance in his tone. "And before you ask, I have no idea where Connor is either. I think he's due for a shift here which is why she's so anxious to get out of here.

Honestly, I'm surprised he hasn't just stumbled upon all this. Connor's usually very close by, especially since Eric's been out on bail. I saw his nephew a few minutes ago. I'm confident she will threaten HIPPA laws on him to keep him quiet. Since she's your sister, I think you should take her home. Connor can't fault you for taking her side but I'm his cousin and he's likely to skin me alive when he hears about this."

"I guess. Somehow, I think she's scarier than he is," Dallas commented as he stepped away to check on his mother.

Within thirty minutes, Dallas was escorting Clara to her car. She was relieved he was parked in another lot, decreasing the chances of walking into Connor.

"Thanks for driving me home, Dallas. I could just walk, it really isn't too far," she stated.

"Nonsense, I'm already driving by your place anyway. Do you have any idea what she wanted to see your dad about?" Dallas still wasn't comfortable calling the man Dad.

"I have no idea. I didn't even know they broke up, let alone that he filed for a restraining order. It makes no sense that Dad would feel the need to protect me when I haven't seen either of them in twelve years," Clara answered as they reached the car.

Wanting to find a more pleasant topic, Clara changed the subject. "I hear congratulations are in order. You and Lila are married! That's great."

"You aren't upset about this?"

"Why would I be?" she asked. "One of my best friends is married to my brother. Lila is my sister-in-law! You are one brave dude."

"I was thinking lucky dude," Dallas answered.

"Lila told you to tell me we were siblings, didn't she?"

Dallas nodded as he kept his eye on the road.

"When did you tell her?"

"High school," Dallas answered softly, glancing her direction for a moment before looking away.

Then it clicked. Clara saw a few pieces of the puzzle form together as she quietly asked, "You were with her the night the theater blew up, weren't you?"

Dallas simply nodded as his eyes remained on the road.

The small town boasted its own movie theater. It was open only on the weekends, beginning Friday evening, and showed movies that were already out, but delayed to the smaller communities. During the fall of their freshman year, Lila and Clara were dropped off at the movie theater by Rob as he went to pick up Shannon. Lila went to their seats while Clara stopped in the bathroom. Within minutes of Lila entering the theater, there was an explosion.

They later determined that a gas leak in the restaurant next door caused the explosion. Thirty-two people were injured. Miraculously, only one died, Sammy Black. Sean's older brother, she realized belatedly. And Dallas's cousin.

Clara was trapped alone in the bathroom. She was knocked unconscious when her head hit the floor. She only remembered bits and pieces. The search and rescue team found Clara within an hour. She was one of the first ones out.

Lila was along the exploding wall. She was trapped through the night and one of the last to be rescued. She never talked much about it except to say she wasn't alone. She was easily claustrophobic and never set foot inside a movie theater again.

"I'm sorry I didn't know sooner. I wish I did. I would have tried to be there for you. That was a horrible week. Lila never wanted to talk about it, but I guess she did with you," Clara stated as she reached over to squeeze his hand.

"Lila always encouraged me to tell you, but I didn't know how you would react. You and Rob always seemed so close, and he never let me near you." Dallas shrugged.

"Yeah, you know what was funny? He once saw you purchasing a box of condoms. He kept warning me to stay away from you. Don't take this wrong, but I never looked at you like that. It makes sense now. Rob said you were a player. Of course, he fails to mention he was also buying condoms. He was warning me to stay away from you while you were actually doing his sister!" Clara fell into a fit of laughter.

"And who was he doing?" Dallas asked quietly as he pulled into her driveway. He didn't bother to explain he was actually making the purchase for someone else.

"No idea, probably half the school. All I know is it wasn't me," Clara answered cheerfully.

As they headed up the steps, he paused as he turned towards her. "Is everything alright between you and Connor?"

Clara simply shrugged before she went up the steps, leading Dallas to think there was an issue.

Anthony Mancuso stayed with the children while Clara was at the hospital. She had been surprised Shannon wasn't next door. Clara was about to call Rachel, but Joe suggested his brother stay with the children in case her father showed up. Blizzard in July would have been more likely, she thought.

"Everything going alright? Any visitors?" Clara asked the deputy.

"No, your father was spotted a few towns over. How are you? She really got you good," Anthony remarked when he saw her neck. "Clara, will Connor be home soon?"

"No, he is working the evening shift at the hospital. I am fine," Clara answered as she started to head towards the children in the family room.

"Anything new on the body found?" Dallas asked.

Clara turned around, "What body was found?"

Anthony and Dallas looked at each other. "There was a body found late yesterday. It wasn't until later in the evening that we were able to identify her." The deputy paused for a moment while Dallas shrugged. "It was the physical therapist you replaced."

"What? I didn't know she was missing. I thought she moved back to her hometown," Clara whispered.

"She didn't seem to have many friends. Apparently, she had given notice at work and at her apartment. No one had a reason to suspect she was missing, until her body was found," Anthony explained.

"Didn't Connor tell you? He was understandably freaked out when he heard last night. Especially when Josh claimed to have seen Eric out," Dallas commented as he watched Clara's response.

Clara looked back and forth between the men then turned around to leave the dining room. She needed to get cleaned up.

An hour later, the smell of delicious food was in the air. Feeling better after a shower, Clara followed the scent into the kitchen. Dallas and her kids ate baked chicken with mashed potatoes, gravy, and carrots.

"Mama!" The little girl yelled from her booster seat. Everyone turned.

"This looks really good," Clara commented, kissing each child on the head before getting herself a plate.

"I saw the chicken was out. I hope you don't mind, I put a few things together. Reese was starving," Dallas explained.

Clara sat with her plate, "And you really can cook. Impressive. How did you get Anthony to leave?"

"I promised I'd stay," Dallas admitted. When she looked about to argue he continued, "I'm picking Lila up after her shift so why not. I get to hang with these two silly beans." He rubbed their hair and was rewarded with giggles.

Against Clara's wishes, Connor did indeed find out about the incident. But it wasn't one of her friends that informed him, it was Felicia Thompson. When he arrived at the emergency room, Josh had been initiating her admission. She was too intoxicated for surgery. Connor was nearby when she explained the cause of her injuries. She was the one who gave the details, playing the role of victim to the doctor, not knowing his relationship with Clara. He was furious.

It was Lila that talked him down. She assured him Clara was alright, had already been assessed at the hospital, and got a ride home with Dallas. He demanded to know why he wasn't notified, especially since Devan and Joe were at the scene.

"Connor, she didn't want us to call you," Lila quietly explained. She hesitated a moment before asking, "Everything alright between you two?"

"I don't know. She's been having these nightmares. She's been distant and avoiding me this last week. When I push, she just clams up," he said. "I think maybe I am pushing too much too soon."

"Possible. She's had a rough couple of months. She was good last night. She talked with your brother at the bar for a bit, danced, and won a pool tournament," Lila laughed at the memory.

"She's never ignored me before," Connor stated, annoyed that she hung out with his brother while ignoring him.

"Possibly because your relationship has changed. Before, you were friends in and out of each other's everyday lives, not living and working together around the clock. Give her some space. She's not going to let you go," she commented before getting called away by another doctor.

Connor was able to leave the hospital fairly early for a Saturday evening. He debated returning to Clara's but texted his brother instead. As he drove by Clara's street, he saw Dallas' vehicle still in front of her house before continuing to Memories.

Once seated, Devan showed him the video of the earlier incident. Again, Connor kept his temper contained. He was relieved she was able to remember her training. Then his brother sat down beside him.

"Did I pull you from your office?" Connor asked.

"No, date night," Matt replied. He nodded when a beer was placed in front of him.

"Oh, so I did you a favor."

Matt looked at his brother a moment before answering, "I thought you two kissed and made up already."

"No, you are thinking of your first wife," Connor answered.

"Dianne? When did you ever have contact with her? Hell, I haven't seen her since the divorce was finalized," Matt commented.

"True, it made the kissing and making up part a lot easier. I ran into her in the city a few years back," Connor paused as he sipped from his beer. "She seems to be doing well."

Matt was silent as he found himself thinking of Dianne for the first time in years. They married young. Both were pre-law majors from wealthy families. He later admitted that he married her in reaction to Susi's marriage. He needed a distraction with an anchor to keep him in the city, away from his family home where Suzi lived next door with her husband. It worked for a while until they were both sent home for the summer to work as clerks at the smaller law office. Dianne was smart, and she learned two important things that summer. First, she would never be happy as they would eventually move to the small town permanently. Second, she would never be able to make her husband smile at her the way he did when he saw the woman next door. A week before they started law school, he was served divorce papers.

Matt was shocked. He requested she meet him for coffee. That was when he learned the difference between loving and being in love. She had him nailed perfectly. The divorce was simple enough. Within a year, he was secretly seeing Susi. When his father became aware of the secret romance, he laid down the law. Once again, Matt felt he was back in high school as he was listening to ultimatums. He ended the affair and focused all his energy into law school.

He met his second wife, Jordan, at the courthouse when he was clerking at the city firm during the summer. She pushed for marriage early into the relationship, and his father encouraged it. Matt was overruled, and he was once again a married man.

But when he ran into Susi unexpectedly in the city, he was not properly prepared to defend himself against his feelings. The affair was rekindled. This time, he worked harder to keep it a secret from his overbearing father. Unfortunately, the relationship once again proved to be doomed, as her husband learned of the affair and begged her to return to their marriage. She agreed and privately announced she was pregnant. Matt returned to his own marriage. Within a year, he and Jordan welcomed a baby boy. But Susi lost her baby in an early miscarriage.

Matt and Susi occasionally saw each other, but the affair was kept light, never planning anything beyond the moment. Until his wife and son were in an accident. He totally pulled away from Susi with all his time spent working and caring for his family. Three months after everyone recovered from their injuries, he learned that Susi was preparing to file for a divorce. When he went home to the Emerson House for a visit, she was already gone. He never learned of her plans and believed maybe someone else did exist. During all their time together, Matt was aware of a relationship Susi kept hidden, even from him.

More devastated than he would ever admit, Matt returned home to his wife and son. Instead, he was served papers to dissolve their marriage. They initially had joint custody of their son, but eventually, he was awarded full custody as Jordan's work brought her overseas too many months of the year.

About a year after his second divorce and Susi's disappearance, he met Talia. For the first time, Matt was able to devote all his attention to a relationship without the distractions of a forbidden affair. Talia was different in many ways from his Susi. She was many years younger than he was. She was an extrovert that often spoke her mind. She had dark, almost black, long wavy hair with bright blue eyes. She spent hours keeping herself in shape, always dressing to enhance her curves. She was the opposite of those he previously loved. And yet she loved only him and no other man. This time, the marriage worked. Matt eventually grew to understand, Susannah Hawks was his first love, but Talia Jensen was the love of his life. When his father was ready to turn the Emerson House over to him, she was more than willing to relocate to the small town with their family of boys. Initially, they had one from his previous marriage, but it further grew to four.

Matt studied his little brother, remembering Connor's current issue with his wife. Connor accused Talia of leading a previous girlfriend to believe their relationship was heading towards the aisle. Talia said she only commented that the current woman seemed to be in the running, as she had lasted longer than the others. In turn, the girlfriend took that to mean that she and Connor would soon be engaged. As a result, she believed she had the right to use his accounts and credit cards without asking his permission. When Connor received the next bank statement, he called the police. He was shocked to learn the thief was his current girlfriend, Amanda. Matt and Talia both talked him out of pressing charges, but the relationship was obviously over.

Matt had concerns about his younger brother not finding someone. At that age, he was already in his third marriage. But when he saw Connor with Clara at the fundraiser, he realized Connor had already met his soulmate. He tried to prevent his brother from the long road of misery, as he well understood the effects of women from the Hawks House. But his brother's path proved to be different in many ways.

"Talia didn't give Amanda permission to use your accounts," Matt defended his wife. "Hell, the woman's premature actions simply sped up your decision to break it off."

"Possibly. I was already thinking of ending it when she started talking about rings and houses. Made me realize being cooped up in a house with her, no matter how big, was too confining," the younger brother answered.

"How is Clara?" Matt asked, thinking to bring the conversation to a more pleasant topic.

Connor wondered how long before he would bring up Clara. It made him realize how often their discussions were centered around her. If she weren't in the picture, they would have nothing to talk about.

Bringing to point the question at hand, what was his brother's interest in his girl?

"Did you hear about the incident today?" He glanced at his brother.

Matt's arm paused as he lifted the beer up. "What incident?"

"Felicia Thompson attacked Clara on her front porch this afternoon."

The beer came back down onto the bar as Matt turned his body toward his brother. "She attacked her? What the hell happened?"

Connor simply shrugged as he explained what he knew.

"Clara isn't hurt?"

"As far as I know, she has scratches on her left cheek and bruising on her neck. They already released her from the ER," Connor said.

"Why are you here with me instead of home with her?" Matt asked, not understanding.

Connor was playing with the beer bottle as he shrugged. "Clara didn't want me to know. She swore everyone to secrecy. She's been distancing herself from me these last couple of weeks."

Matt was quiet for a moment before he commented, "She's been struggling with the emotions of losing her husband and being with you so soon after his death. It takes time."

"Time?" Connor looked at his brother. "Why are you suddenly so interested in me? You barely paid any attention to me my whole life, and now you're meeting up with me multiple times a week? Letting me ruin date night? Why?"

"Well, date night was already interrupted by someone else and will resume when I return home. But I've always been interested in you. I just didn't like having a baby brother around when I was in middle school, but you grew on me," Matt explained. "You've never been receptive to me until now."

Connor admitted, as he grew older, their relationship became less strained. Especially after he returned home permanently. "So what's your interest in Clara? She's too young for you. Are you her..."

Matt firmly interrupted before the words were out. "No, I am not.

If I were, your relationship would have never evolved."

Connor had always been aware of Matt's on/off relationship with Susi, even when he was too young to understand the significance. "And how do you know?"

Matt didn't say anything for a moment, though he felt his brother's eyes staring him down. His affair was always a taboo topic. After a moment he sighed and said, "We had never been together like that until after she was born. But it never mattered. Despite who her father is, I've always loved that little girl. When she was sick at six months, she was in the hospital for weeks. When she returned home, she was still such a happy baby, but fearful of strangers. Yet, she still allowed me to hold her. I used to occasionally tuck her in bed, and check in on her before I'd leave."

He was quiet as he remembered various times together with both mother and daughter. "I'll always love her and give her anything she wants. Clara only needs to ask. As long as it's not harmful, it's hers. No questions." Matt paused for a moment as he pulled in the emotions he had never spoken. "But you don't need to worry about me trying to win her from you. Our relationship is what it is. Besides, she told me last night, she has always been in love with you. I would never be able to compete with that. Nor would I ever have the strength or interest. I am content and happy with my life."

They sipped their beer in silence before Connor asked, "Can you find out why Carl has a restraining order against Felicia Thompson? And why it includes Clara and the children? He hasn't seen her in years."

Matt shrugged. "The man's actions never made sense. The bastard had the most loyal woman in town as his wife and he chose to stray. Why would it help you to know about the restraining order?"

The younger brother chose his words carefully, "It's something Clara wants to know."

"Alright, I'll see what I can find out," Matt immediately answered as he finished his beer, not caring he was obviously being manipulated.

Connor returned to Clara's by midnight. He thanked Dallas for staying before he locked up the house. He first stopped in Hailey's room. The little girl's room had a pink tint from the princess night light. She was curled up on her side with her little baby doll. He reached down to touch her hair as he kissed her forehead and pulled up her blankets. Next, he checked in on the boy. Connor smiled when he saw Reese sprawled out on his bed, his stuffed animal hanging over the edge but still in a firm grip. He pulled the blanket over him as he kissed his forehead.

When he turned away, Clara was standing at the doorway. Connor paused to give her a kiss before gently tilting her chin up to examine her neck. Without a word, he kissed her scratched cheek and bruised neck.

Clara was relieved he didn't make an issue of it. She allowed him to look over the marks in the dim light before she reached for his hand to lead him across the hall to the bedroom.

• • • •

Evil paced in his home office as he debated what to do. He felt a slight panic at the idea the bitch would touch his girl. He wanted to go visit her, make sure she was alright, but her friends had closed the ranks protectively around her. He glanced out the window into the shadows as he debated what to do. Should he allow her to survive the surgery tomorrow? He debated his options, killing her off now would be too easy. She would not even be aware of her punishment. But he will make sure she pays for crossing the line, not only laying her hands on his girl but leaving a mark…

50 carl gibson

Dallas was up early the next morning, dressed in shorts and an old t-shirt. He was drinking coffee out on the front porch while debating what to make for breakfast before the long day ahead. It wasn't unusual for him to be up at sunrise, but it was very unusual to have an unexpected visitor this early.

Well, it was unusual for Dallas to have visitors any time of day. His home was his secret hideaway that he shared only with his wife. Until the other night, no one knew of the marriage. The relationship itself had been kept secret for so long, very few people had ever been invited over. The cabin was difficult to find, set back in the land close to two acres away from the road. Various trees hid it further and provided natural coverage to the long winding driveway. The entrance to the driveway was hard to find during the day and close to impossible after dusk.

Thus, Dallas was surprised when he heard someone driving up towards the house. He did not recognize the car. Dallas almost dropped his mug when the driver finally exited the vehicle. Walking up the path to the porch was his father.

Carl Gibson was still an attractive man in his early fifties. The years had been kind. He still had a full head of brown hair, prone to curls when it grew long, with only a bit of sprinkled gray. He had a few wrinkles around his blueish green eyes. Women had always told him his eye color changed depending on what he wore. His wife was the only one that declared his eyes changed with his mood. When he was angry, they were a violent blue, and when he was jealous, they were greener than hers. But when he was happy and satisfied, they were a soft blue. Susannah claimed that was how she knew when he was cheating on her. The accusations angered him. Mainly, because she was always correct, no matter how he tried to hide it. Keeping secrets from an intuitive wife was nearly impossible. A trait, Carl knew without a doubt, was handed down to their daughter.

Carl was always known as a charismatic, easy-going guy. He was not known for having a strong work ethic, but he did have a reputation for working hard to please whoever he was currently infatuated with. His current love interest was not Dallas' mother. He had a love/hate relationship with Felicia that started in high school and followed him throughout his adult life. It was a constant on and off. Every time he broke it off, he swore it was over for good. But something about her always pulled him back into her evil web. Felicia claimed he was her first love, and they were soulmates meant to be together forever, in this life and the next. He believed otherwise.

"Good morning, Dallas," Carl greeted his son. He was always aware of the child's true parentage but never openly admitted it, sober anyway, until now. He believed Felicia allowed herself to get pregnant by him on purpose. She later claimed she had stopped using birth control in preparation of her pending nuptials. He had been relieved when she announced her engagement to Zachariah Thompson. Carl saw it as a permanent end to their relationship. He really expected the night before her wedding to be their last time together. When she informed him two months later that she was pregnant with his child, he did not know what she expected him to do. Felicia was the one in a marriage, not him. Believing he was in the clear, he had already proposed to Susannah Hawks, her nemesis. Despite how it looked, it was never meant as a way of getting back at her. Carl always had an unexplainable attraction to Susannah from the first moment he saw her in high school. He wished he could say it was mutual, but he had reasons to believe that was unlikely.

When Dallas just looked at him, still shocked to see his biological father standing before him on his property, Carl's easy-going personality came through. "It's a beautiful place you picked out for yourself here. I heard you did most of the building yourself. I never had a chance to tell you how proud I am of all your accomplishments. Your hard work is shining through in this magnificent home."

Carl made a point of turning and looking around the area. He loved the privacy the isolated area provided. He could hide out here when the renovations at Clara's house reached the third floor. The rustic home was off everyone's radar, even his damn cousin's. He could be safe here, he thought. Who would ever think to look for him here? Not Felicia. Her needs were too regal, something he understood from the beginning. Carl was never able, or maybe just not interested enough, to meet her dreams of grandeur. Because she dated Aaron Hawks her senior year, Felicia felt entitled to the estate. Well aware of her motive, his refusal to marry her was an ongoing strain in their relationship. And when Susannah's death was confirmed, he realized he was being played like a fiddle. He kept hidden until he could decide what to do next.

"Why are you here?" Dallas asked, finally able to express his suspicion.

"I heard about the trouble your mother caused yesterday. I just wanted to come out and talk with you. Say a few things I should have said before. Things that need to be said before it's too late." Carl shrugged. "I want to apologize for not being able to help her."

Dallas was not sure what he was trying to say. Was Carl asking for forgiveness? Why now? Or even at all? And who was he unable to help, Felicia or Clara?

"I understand you've told Clara. I hope that has not made things too awkward for either of you, being siblings. Please give her my love and good wishes when you see her again," he stated.

"I think she would appreciate hearing it from you," Dallas answered back.

"No, I don't think it's safe to be around Clara right now. She has enough to deal with between work and her young children. They are beautiful, aren't they?" Carl stated, inadvertently admitting he had been watching her.

"They are. When was the last time you talked with them?" Dallas asked, confident he knew the answer, but curious if he would lie.

"Just pass it on. I need to get going before the sun is too high. Have a good day and good luck with your mother," Carl stated with a nod before turning around.

Dallas drank his coffee as he watched the man walk to his car and drive away. He heard the screen door open behind him, but continued to watch until the dust behind the moving car settled.

"Was that who I think it was?" Lila asked as she stepped out wearing only her nightie.

"It was," Dallas answered as he finished off his coffee.

"What did he want?"

"Not really sure," he admitted.

"Are you going to tell Clara?" She wondered.

"Not really sure," he repeated as he turned around. He smiled when he realized what she was wearing outside on the porch for anyone driving up to see...

Shannon woke up alone in the bed, but when she stepped out of the bathroom after her shower with only a towel wrapped around her, Devan was standing there. "Want to tell me why your ex-boyfriend has been texting and calling you all morning?"

"Why are you going through my phone?" Shannon demanded.

Her defensive tone immediately alerted him she was up to something. Something he didn't want to deal with as he explained, "You left it on the table. Every time he calls, his picture pops up for all the world to see. Is there something going on between you two again?"

Shannon was suddenly agitated. She didn't know how to explain what had happened over the weekend. She never imagined Joel would show up here in her hometown, so far from the city. Until Friday night, she had not been aware how much she missed Joel. And yesterday, Shannon never expected he could still make her feel the way she did. Her agitation made her defensive. "What makes you think that?"

"Well, things have been off between us. At first I figured it was the whole girls' secrecy thing. But now he's contacting you. I thought it was about the case in the city. You haven't mentioned it. Instead, you are being secretive and defensive. I can make this really easy for you," Devan looked her in the eye while he talked. He could see the wheels turning in her head.

"Devan, I don't know why you think I would go back to him," Shannon said as she stepped closer, placing her hands on his chest as she leaned up to kiss him, allowing the towel to fall off.

Against his better judgment, Devan allowed himself to be kissed and kissed back as his hands gently caressed her bare back…

A bit later, Shannon slowly eased from the bed. Convinced Devan was asleep, she quietly reached for her phone while she grabbed her towel from the floor and returned to the bathroom for another shower.

Devan was awake the second she got up. When he heard the water running, he was out of the bed and dressed. He grabbed his cell and keys as he headed out the door. In his vehicle, Devan drove around the block. He parked a few houses down from his own place and waited. He figured he'd give her an hour to see if his gut was correct or if he was turning into a possessive, jealous boyfriend. Something he swore he would never be.

Less than an hour later, Shannon stepped out of his front door. She was dressed casually but nice. Her hair was already dry and styled with her makeup just right. She climbed into her car.

Devan slowly followed behind her, careful to keep his distance. He was disappointed when she didn't turn towards Lila's farm or Rachel's house. His irritation climbed when he realized his suspicions were correct. Shannon pulled into a motel a mile out of town and parked near room twenty-eight. Before she could knock, the door opened. She was greeted with a very passionate kiss before she stepped into the room. Joel Montgomery quickly glanced around the parking lot before he followed her in, closing the door behind them.

Devan was quick to take pictures with his cell before they disappeared inside. He was shocked to see the woman, who an hour before was lying naked in his arms, was already in the arms of another man. Shit, he pounded his dashboard in anger as he debated what to do.

Do I go storming inside and catch them in the act? Call her on it when she comes home? He pulled away as he debated what to do. He usually loved it when a hunch played out, but not today.

51 wham bam, thank you, ma'am?

Lila sat with Dallas in the waiting room as his mother underwent surgery for her fractured hip. They both looked up at the sound of the elevator ding. Dallas was surprised to see Clara and Rachel stepping off the elevator. Lila was confident Clara would make an appearance, regardless of the incident the day before. She was supportive and loyal to her close friends, why would she be any different with her brother?

Both were wearing summer dresses, but Clara had a light scarf around her neck. It had taken her a long time to find something to wear that covered the bruises, now a deep purple color. Rachel was the one to suggest the scarf. After she found the appropriate one, she went through the closet to find a matching dress.

"How is she doing?" Clara asked after the greetings.

"Still in surgery. The surgeon had an emergency delaying hers," Dallas answered.

"Yeah, Connor was called in early this morning. There was a bad farming accident at dawn," Clara commented. "You know, your mother will need rehab after this. Send her to my place and I'll get her back on her feet."

Dallas chuckled at the thought. "I don't see that happening, especially after yesterday."

"You never know. Dallas, what is going on between her and Dad?" Clara asked, noting the looks he exchanged with Lila.

Dallas gestured with his head as he touched her elbow, leading her out into the hall. He told her about his unexpected visitor that morning.

Clara tried to hide her disappointment when she learned that her father was hiding from her. Why didn't he want to see her?

Dallas, never having any connection with the man, was indifferent to the early morning meeting. He almost regretted sharing the conversation when Clara's eyes teared up. Without giving it a thought, he pulled her in for a hug as she asked why her father would not want to see her.

Connor came around the corner just as Dallas pulled her into his arms. He debated turning around, but his eyes met Dallas'. Reluctantly, he approached them. "Everything alright?"

Clara shook her head as she wiped the tears away. "No it's not. Nothing is right and Dallas' mother will most likely need rehab to help recover from surgery."

Connor suspected there was more to her tears than Felicia Thompson's current predicament. And since she was talking to Dallas, he assumed it had to do with their father. Always a touchy topic with her, regardless of her age. Aside from Lila, that was their primary connection. But if she wasn't going to tell him what it was, he was going to tell her what he knew.

"Well, she won't be accepted at our place, sorry Dallas," Connor firmly stated.

"Oh, don't be, I wasn't even considering it," he answered. When Clara glared at him, Dallas explained, "Clara, how can she go to your place? She has a restraining order to stay away from you. You wouldn't even be able to go to work."

Connor nodded in agreement with the explanation.

Clara turned her angry green eyes on his brown, "How can you deny Dallas' mother the care she needs?"

"Easy, I talked to the case manager and told her absolutely not," he answered with a slight edge to his tone.

"Connor, be reasonable," Clara requested.

Dallas, never comfortable around other people's disputes, slowly stepped away from the lively discussion.

"I am being reasonable. Not only is there a restraining order against Felicia, but she violated it. She has demonstrated she is capable of violent behavior. Would you want her sitting next to Rachel's grandmother in the dining room? My priority is you and the kids, always; then it is the safety of our residents. I will not jeopardize your safety and well-being by allowing you to be in a position where she can harm you again."

"You are overreacting! She didn't harm me," Clara stated as she fought to control her temper.

"She didn't? Are you kidding me? If I remove this scarf, what will I see on your neck?" Connor held one end of the scarf but released it when she grabbed it, preventing him from removing it. He felt his point was made.

"You aren't the only one that approves admissions," she remarked.

Two weeks ago, Connor would not have believed she would play this card, especially over Felicia Thompson, of all people. But in light of recent events, he realized this would be a common argument between them. If she didn't get what she wanted, she would go to his brother. It hurt Connor that Clara had confided in his brother about her issues and feelings when she wouldn't open up to him. He was still undecided how he felt about that, trying to remind himself he was not the jealous type. Last night's conversation with his brother confirmed Matt's adoration for Clara.

"You may think you have him wrapped around your finger, but on this matter, he is in full agreement with me. Anyone that goes after you is not welcome," Connor answered forcefully, suggesting the end of the discussion. Instead, it threw her off.

"What the hell are you talking about?" Clara asked, totally confused.

Connor was momentarily distracted by his cell. He was reading a text and replied before he answered her. "This thing you have going on with Matt needs to stop. Don't abuse it. I'm being called down to the ER, I need to go."

He tilted her chin up to kiss her forehead before he walked away. She grabbed his hand and waited until he turned back to her. "What thing are you talking about?"

Connor studied her face for a moment before answering, "Matt will always give you what you want, you only need to ask. Unless it could potentially hurt you, he will never tell you no."

Still puzzled, "Connor, there is nothing going on between us. I don't ever want to do something that would upset you or make you jealous. I am sorry if I hurt you. That was never my intent."

It was then Connor realized she didn't understand Matt's feelings for her, reflecting off her mother. Why would she? She was only nine when she disappeared. Clara was simply turning to those she trusted. For some reason, she trusted his brother. His words from the night before echoed in his head, *she's always been in love with you.*

Connor pulled her into an embrace and held her tight as he whispered, "You haven't done anything to hurt me nor make me jealous. You are just being you, loyal, caring, and supportive to those important to you. Don't change."

Clara was almost teary eyed again by his words, but her temper flared when he continued, "Which is why you are irrationally feeling guilty for what happened to Felicia, so get over it. Accept that we, being me, Matt, and Dallas, all agree, you are not getting near her."

Connor could feel the lasers from her glaring eyes burning into him as she tried to pull away. He tilted her chin again and kissed her on the lips. As he backed away from her, he stated, "I'm likely to be late again tonight. I'll text when I have an idea how late. Please stay out of trouble until then."

It was dark when Shannon let herself into Devan's home. She placed her keys and purse on the table as she stepped into the family room towards the stairs. Suddenly, the light turned on. Shannon pivoted around, shocked to see Devan sitting on the sofa in the dark, surrounded by multiple boxes on the floor.

"Devan, what's going on?" Shannon asked as she looked down into the boxes.

"I took the liberty of packing up your stuff," he stated as he slowly stood up.

"Why are you doing this?" Shannon pleaded.

"Why? Because I'm not sharing my woman with another man. It's just not my thing." Devan shrugged. His hands were in his pocket to keep him out of trouble. If she touched him, he worried his love for her would melt his temper and he would again give in to her.

"So, you just go ahead and pack up my things without even talking to me?" She demanded.

"Well, that's where I disagree. We talked yesterday and today. I specifically asked you about him and you denied anything was happening. I figured maybe he was contacting you about his case as a witness. Made sense. But now I realize why you weren't answering your phone all weekend, you were with him!" Devan's anger was evident in his tone, despite his voice being low.

"So that's it? Wham bam, thank you, ma'am? Because he calls me, I must be with him? If you want to break up with me, then why can't we have a simple conversation?"

"I never treated this like a casual fling. You chased me. You all but moved in with me. I even told you what I do for a living and you think you can sneak around without me getting suspicious? I tried talking with you all weekend. Then this morning, you decide to worm your way out of an adult conversation by getting passionate with me, then an hour later you are off fucking another guy!" Devan's voice was slowly increasing.

The look on her face would have been amusing if he weren't so angry. "Are you going to tell me you have not been face to face with him before today? Because that greeting this morning suggested otherwise. Oh yeah, I followed you and I have pictures." Devan was about to leave but his cell chimed. He answered it, keeping his hazel eyes on her green as he listened and then answered. "Yeah, no problem. Just give me a few minutes, and I'll be on my way."

As he was replacing his cell, Shannon stepped towards him. "Devan, please."

He retreated backwards. "Don't even try. It won't work again. I felt things were different between us Friday night when you didn't answer my texts, but this morning you confirmed it. You know, for someone who doesn't like being lied to, you sure aren't very honest yourself. I need to go. I want your stuff out of here before I get back. Leave your key on the table and lock the door."

Devan gave a wide path as he circled around her. As he suspected, she attempted to reach for him again.

"Devan."

Against his better judgment, he paused, looking over his shoulder.

"I am sorry. I never meant to hurt you," Shannon stated quietly as she slowly walked towards him.

"Yeah, so am I. I was falling in love with you," Devan declared before he stepped out of the door.

Shannon remained still for several minutes with tears streaming down her face as reality sank in. She just messed up one of the healthiest relationships in her life. What did she do? Why? Why did she lie? Devan was right, Shannon thought, as she started to pack her car. She had lied to them both. She did spend a lot of the weekend with Joel. And because of that, she didn't answer Devan's calls.

Once she was in the car, Shannon drove around town. She had no interest in returning to Clara's, especially with Connor practically living there. It wasn't fair to them. Plus, she would be too close to Devan. She sighed as she wiped the tears from her face. Without thinking, she drove to where she always went when her heart hurt.

52 irrational

Felicia's surgery was successful, however her post-op was complicated by severe alcohol withdrawal symptoms. She was in the ICU for two nights before transferring onto the surgical floor. Dallas was already in her room on Tuesday afternoon when the case manager stopped in to discuss discharge plans. Being in a rural area limited her options. Pending assault charges due to violating the restraining order further complicated things.

Of course, being irrational didn't help either, Dallas thought.

"I just don't understand why I can't go to the nursing home across the street. My boyfriend's daughter is a therapist there," Felicia explained to Teri, the case manager.

"Mom, they will not accept you there." Dallas felt he was on a merry-go-round that would not stop as the conversation appeared to continuously repeat itself. He didn't even attempt to correct her on her relationship status with Carl. "Connor Emerson has made it clear you will not be allowed there."

"Well this would never have happened if Eric Howell still ran the place," she stated with authority.

"Mom, Eric's not there anymore because he was arrested for

drugging Clara," Dallas clarified. What the hell is wrong with her? Does she have her head in the sand? He was reminded of her weird obsession with the Howell family.

"That was her word against his," Felicia informed Teri.

"Mom, he yelled it out for half the town to hear. She didn't make the accusations, Eric bragged about it!"

Teri was beginning to understand what the nurses had been saying, about Ms. Thompson. She was not an easy person to get along with. She had an unrealistic view of everything and believed herself to be above those around her. And despite being the one to break the restraining order and being intoxicated while attacking another woman, Felicia truly believed herself to be the victim. Knowing the son understood the situation, Teri decided to leave. She put the papers on the table and excused herself.

Dallas nodded his understanding as she left.

"Well, the whole thing makes no sense. I always thought he and Clara would end up together," Felicia was stating.

"Really? Why? They were never close. I can think of at least ten guys in line ahead of him," Dallas counter argued against his better judgment. Again, wondering what her relationship was with the Howell family. "Listen, you don't have many options. You are likely to be discharged by Friday. It looks like the best bet will be home health."

"Maybe I'll go stay with my sister."

"Fine by me. When was the last time you saw her? Has she been here to visit?" Dallas was aware of the estranged relationship she had with most of her family. He had run into his Aunt Charlotte a few times. She didn't even recognize him at first and was pleasantly surprised with his success in life. Dallas had not informed her of his mother's surgery because it wasn't his place and he didn't want her to feel obligated to visit. It would not end well. "When was the last time you had a civil conversation with Charlotte?"

"What other options do we have? You are too busy trying to

impress the wrong girls. I mean, really? Of all people, you are dating Lila Foxwood? And what is going on with you and Clara anyway?" Felicia demanded.

"Mom, what is your problem with Lila? Have you ever talked with her before this week? What do you know about her?" Dallas was curious about how she would answer.

"She's a Foxwood! Your father cannot possibly be approving of this relationship either," she stated expertly.

"I don't see what he has to do with this. His opinion has no weight on what I do with my life. Oh wait, are you talking about your ex-husband or your ex-lover?" Dallas rudely asked. Controlling his temper when dealing with his mother was always a challenge, but insulting Lila, regardless of who it was, always brought out a side of him that proved he was biologically related to the ruthless person before him. Something he was not proud of.

"What are you talking about?" Felicia quietly asked.

"Is that how you are going to play it? Clueless?"

"Who told you?"

"Seriously?" Dallas paced the small space as he fought to control his voice. "It could have been the many drunk visits into my bedroom late at night when I was a child. Or it could have been I was no longer allowed in Zach's house when I was twelve. Oh, wait no, it could have been the visit to my place the other morning! Take your pick. We've all known for years! Why are you bothering to hide it now?"

"I just never wanted it to be like this," Felicia yelled.

"You never wanted what? No one to know you tried to hide your illegitimate son behind an honest hard working man?" Dallas shouted back.

"I never wanted to be left alone," she screamed back.

Dallas simply stared at her. "You were the one cheating, lying, and bouncing back and forth."

"How would you know?"

"Hello? I was there, remember? The short person always cleaning up your mess before your husband came home! The one you never had time for because you were too busy planning your next rendezvous!" Dallas lowered his voice. "Where are they now? I am the only one still standing here."

He turned around in disgust. When he opened the door and stepped into the hall, Lila was leaning against the wall. Dallas had no doubt she heard the conversation.

Without a word, she greeted him with a hug, and immediately his temper was gone. He didn't like her seeing this side of him, but she did on occasion and still loved him anyway.

the shadow

August 7

Father continues to lock himself in the office and Mother no longer sings. I wanted to go to a party next door but father forbade me. I was so upset, I yelled at him and then ran up the stairs. He yelled for me to come back down the steps. When I didn't he paused at the bottom step, his face was so red, his anger so evident but he didn't say a word. He fell to the floor as he clutched his chest. What have I done???

August 28

Labor Day is coming up. Father was discharged from the hospital last night. The heart attack has changed him. Well, I guess A's death is what really changed him. Nothing will ever be the same again.

September 5

Today is the first day of school. My sophomore year. A should have been off starting his freshman year at the university in the city. He will never again sneak into my room to scare me, tell me the dress I have on is all wrong, or simply sit on the floor and hang. I never thought I could miss anyone so much.

September 6

School is alright. It does help to keep me distracted from the gloom that hangs over our house. M is in 2 of my classes. He initially didn't talk to me, but stares when he thinks I'm not looking. E told me to just leave it alone, but at the end of the day, he offered to carry my bag home. I reminded him he wasn't supposed to be with me and stormed away. Later in the evening, he found me in the rose garden and we talked. He said he still loves me and will always love me, but we can't be together. Maybe sometime in the future. I told him I didn't know. Maybe I would, but I could never tell him how much he hurt me. I can't even talk to E about this because she might tell her parents. Oh the mess!

November 26

HG was home from the university for Thanksgiving break. He looks great! He smiled at me when I stopped in the pizza shop, and offered to take me home when he got off from work. He has the most charming dimples when he smiles!

December 21

It's the evening of the Hawks Christmas party. Seems so strange, preparing for the holiday without A. I miss him. Despite the whole town preparing for the season, it's not the same at the Hawks House, nor will it ever be again.

December 22

The Christmas party was fabulous! HG was there! He even kissed me under the mistletoe out on the back porch, but M saw him and told him to stay away from me. There was a bit of a pushing fest before L broke it up. M later reminded me L and HG are related and I should stay away from HG. I wouldn't want to be related to Evil, would I? I told him the joke was getting old. A was the first one to tell it, and it made me miss him even more.

December 26

Christmas was not the same. Later in the day, I went ice skating with E at the lake. So many people were there! Of course, I stayed away from M, but I can't shake the feeling of being watched! Then I realized it is likely M which annoys me. He doesn't want me, nor will he let anyone else near me.

November 24

I can't believe it's been so long since I last wrote! There's been nothing to write about except the B is back. Apparently, she didn't do well in school so her parents wouldn't pay for another year. I would laugh, but that means she's back in town. She's always acting so high and mighty, as if she can tell me what to do, but I have to remind myself, she is likely still hurting. Granted A dumped her before he was killed but isn't it possible they could have gotten back together if he didn't die? God, that seems so sad! But I think A could have done WAY better than her! She's such a BITCH!! She told me to stay away from HG. I told her she didn't own either of us. Heck, it's not like he talks to me all that much.

January 1

Another new year. I hope it's better than the last two years. Father's stroke last week has certainly changed him. I didn't think he could be any more passive than he's already been. Mother is talking of putting in an elevator, using the closets. Not a bad idea, really.

September 9

It's been so long since I've written. Not much really to write any more. My life is that boring! It's senior year, and not one fun, attractive guy in my class that I'm allowed to see anyway. M and I have decided to be friends. Now that he has his own car, he does drive E and I to school. E has her own HG from a neighboring town. He's nice and friendly. She seems to be head over heels for him.

December 26

Another Christmas has come and gone. Father has refused to use the elevator and had a bad fall. He broke his hip and was in the hospital. He came home on Christmas Eve. Now he has no choice but to use the elevator since he's basically wheelchair bound. He was not a good patient and difficult with the therapists. There was talk of him being placed in the nursing home but Mother would not have it. Now, there's a nurse with him around the clock. I miss the family dinners we used to have every night.

December 31

I am sooo excited! Going to a New Year's Eve party! Friends are picking me up! It's here in town so if things are bad, I can always walk home.

January 1

Party was great! So many of the college kids were home. It was sad seeing some of A's friends living their lives while he's no longer with us. I don't know if I told you, there were 4 guys in the car. All were killed. T told me my brother was alive after the crash. He was injured, but alive. He had a chance to survive but passed anyway during the night. It was later determined he may have thrown a clot, but we will never know for sure. As the driver, he was the only one sober and wearing a seatbelt. The other guys were all thrown from the car when A missed the dangerous curve and flew down into the ravine, hitting a tree before it rolled further down the hill. T knew all this because his uncle was working at the scene. T felt bad about telling me this and offered to take me home. I told him I was alright. It was stuff I needed to know. I mingled a little and good thing I stayed! HG came in just before the New Year rang in! He gave me a kiss and a hug!

January 4

I feel weird lately. I don't know why. I feel like someone is watching me, which is ridiculous. Who would care what is going on with me?

January 16

E and I snuck out of the house to go to a party in the woods. When I woke up this morning, I was in my bed. I have no idea how I got home. I must have had a lot to drink. I feel weird, but I can't explain it.

January 30

I feel so different, but don't know why. After blacking out at the last couple of parties, I have decided to stop going, but I still feel like I am missing hours. I don't want to say anything because everyone will think I'm nuts and we already know we have enough crazies in the family! I don't want to end up like that, stuck in the crazy bin to die.

February 2

Groundhog's Day, Phil saw his shadow so there will be another 6 weeks of winter. I can't wait for spring! This winter has been so dark and creepy! The shadow seems to move in on me after the sun sets, not that it's up long in the winter, especially in the valley.

February 8

I tried to avoid the shadow last night by keeping all the lights on. But when I woke up during the night, my room was dark and I think the shadow was moving around my room. I felt weird, my head was spinning and my body felt so heavy. I thought I heard a door opening and closing. But when I woke up this morning, everything was in its place, the lights were even on. I must have been dreaming. It felt so real. My next home address will likely be the looney bin with my grandmother.

February 12

I feel anxious and I don't know why. I wanted to hide from the Shadow, but it always seems to find me in the night and I wake up with missing time. I found blood on my clothes this morning.

March 4

I am late but I don't know how that is possible.

never leave you

Clara believed everything between Connor and her was back on track, but she continued to avoid him during the daytime hours. If she were confronted, she would have denied it.

But Connor thought differently. He believed she was unconsciously distancing herself while she silently grieved her loss. During the nighttime hours, she continued to turn to him for comfort. Sometimes she cried in her sleep, and other nights seemed to pass without emotional outbursts.

Neither was aware Clara was usually in a drug-induced sleep, unable to awaken from her repeated nightmare as her younger self huddled close to the banister, looking down into the kitchen. She watched the violent blue eyes emerging from the shadows. Fear kept her frozen in place as she mentally willed the familiar green eyes to open and fight back. And in the morning, her brain would be hazy with scattered images of her dreams slowly forgotten. Clara was left mentally drained and emotionally withdrawn.

Clara was never able to comprehend her frequent brief interactions with the shadow were actual moments prior to succumbing to her drug-induced sleep. As was her habit of preparing for bed after the children were asleep, she often curled up with a journal to read in her pajamas, hoping to still be awake when Connor returned home.

Instead, the drugged tea initially made her drowsy and hyperalert of her surroundings. She woke to the temperature change in the room, always the first warning. She felt the light touch to her hair, the smell of cologne mixed with sweat and the warm breath on her ear. And when the shadow faded, she would stagger around the house, looking for it.

• • • •

The shadow appeared more often during the last month of summer. Evil was overjoyed with the increased interaction. If she followed him, he would merely wait until she fell into a deeper sleep before carrying her to bed. He loved the game of hide and seek, not realizing it was a game she played as a child when he was visiting her mother. To him, they were one and the same. He loved holding her close. He would whisper his thoughts and express his love, never understanding the severity of her hearing impairment. The words were literally lost on deaf ears.

He was initially concerned when the younger child occasionally stood in the doorway watching him, but she never sounded the alarm. For this, she was rewarded with gifts. He would bring her something small, a book or a treat. And while her mother slept, he would rock with the child as he read a book of her choice.

Clara was often already asleep when Connor arrived home. She was usually in bed, but occasionally on the sofa or even a chair in one of the children's rooms. At first, he was relieved she was finally getting the sleep her body required to heal emotionally. But he became wary when he continuously came home to the alarm system being off and Clara already asleep at eight in the evening. He often remained home later in the morning, waiting for Clara to drag herself up out of bed in preparation for the day. Connor began dropping the children off at daycare.

It wasn't until the evening of the last volleyball game when Devan made a few comments, triggering the alarm to go off in his head. Devan had inquired if Clara was alright, stating she looked worse than when she had the fever. When Connor arrived home, later than expected, Clara was already home from the game and asleep. He carried her up from the sofa to bed. He decided he would make a point of talking with her during work the next day.

The next afternoon, Clara was looking through her briefcase. She was surprised to see one of the children's books mixed in with her files. She smiled as she picked it up. Looking it over quickly, she realized it was one of her favorites from when she was a child. Clara hadn't been aware Hailey had a copy. Puzzled, she returned it to her bag. After she found what she was looking for, she placed the file on her desk.

She felt better today, possibly because she had her first cup of coffee since Eric's arrest. Nothing like a cup of caffeine first thing in the morning. This time around, she drank it black. No sweetener or creamer to hide the taste of something not supposed to be there.

Clara was unaware someone was watching her review papers until she felt a hand on her shoulder.

Matt had been looking over a few potential candidates for the therapy department and decided to head down the hall to touch base with Clara. He paused at the doorway, momentarily surprised to see Susi sitting at the desk. When she shifted slightly, his brain told him it was only her daughter. Matt shook his head at his foolish thoughts. He quietly entered the room, not aware his brother had seen him pause to watch her. Despite being aware of her hearing loss, he often forgot how severe it was until he reached out to touch her shoulder, and she screamed.

"Clara, I am sorry I startled you," Matt apologized as he stepped back, looking into her green eyes. "I just wanted to drop off some possible applicants for you to look over. I'll be in touch."

Clara simply nodded as she accepted the file he was handing over. Her eyes followed him as he stepped away, thinking of something she read in her mother's journal earlier in the week. As he walked through the door, her eyes met with Connor's brown.

"Connor," Clara happily smiled.

"Clara," Connor acknowledged as he closed the door behind him. He walked closer. Even though he slept beside her almost every night, their last face-to-face conversation was at the hospital when Felicia Thompson had her surgery. When he saw her at night, the lights were often dim. Connor was shocked by the paleness of her face and the dark circles under her eyes. "What's going on?"

"Nothing much, I have all this paperwork to get finished before my new budget can get approved," Clara answered with a wave towards her desk. "I have interviews set up for later today and next week."

"No, I mean why do you look tired? You look like you've lost weight and haven't been sleeping. I know for a fact you've been getting at least ten hours a night. Please, tell me what's wrong," he softly demanded.

"What the hell are you talking about? You don't get to come and go as you please then finally come in here and expect me to fall all over you by telling me I look like crap! It doesn't work that way," Clara quickly became defensive.

"Whoa, wait a minute. You're the one not answering my texts and avoiding me at work, and on weekends. I figured you needed your space. The ball was in your court for when you were ready for something more," Connor responded. "I see you're still not ready to talk with me. I'll leave you to it. But please, start using the alarm system. It doesn't do any good if you don't activate it."

Connor turned to leave, but stopped when she said his name. He sighed as he quickly debated what to do. He heard her step towards him. Connor looked down as her hand rested on his arm before he looked into her green eyes.

"Connor, you always talk about what I want and when I'm ready, what about you? What do you want?"

Connor leaned back into the door as he tried to keep it simple, "I want you."

"That's it? You only want me? You don't want anything else? Marriage? Kids?" Clara challenged.

Connor stepped closer to her, "Are you seriously ready to have this conversation? Right here and now?"

"What are you talking about?"

"Every time I vaguely make a reference to the future of us, you stiffen up and pull back. That's why I've stepped back. I don't want to push you too soon into something you haven't decided you want or are ready for. I am good with you and the kids as things are." Connor considered reaching out to her but stopped, reminding himself he was waiting for her to make the next move.

"I do not pull away," Clara stated defensively while unconsciously stepping back as she crossed her arms over her chest.

Connor looked at her with raised eyebrows, ready to call her bluff, "No? Alright, good. Let's schedule a trip to Disney with the kids during the holidays."

"Connor, that's a big expense. I don't have the funds or the time off to plan for something like that," Clara quickly dismissed.

"It's just a week, we could go Wednesday to Wednesday so you're missing less days and the kids get in free. Now's the time to do it," Connor challenged as he stepped towards her. "I would only have to pay for you, me, and the hotel."

Clara unconsciously stepped back again as she shook her head, "Connor, I can't have you paying for the whole cost of a trip like that. It's too expensive."

"You don't pull away? You literally just stepped back away from me and threw out the whole idea altogether. There was not even any discussion or compromise," he argued. When he saw the tears, Connor felt horrible at pushing the issue. He was relieved he didn't offer to go shopping for an engagement ring.

"I wasn't dismissing the idea. I don't think you should always be covering the cost of everything," Clara stated softly as she leaned back onto her desk.

"What difference does it make who pays for what? I have the money. I enjoy spoiling you and the children. I haven't actually purchased anything for you besides dinner or drinks when we go out. I've not assisted you at all with the household expenses, and yet I stay at your place more than my own," he said.

"You bought car seats for the children," she challenged.

"Yes, I did because I was constantly moving them back and forth between our vehicles. It's more practical than playing musical cars every day," he answered. Connor chuckled before he continued, "You are so different from anyone I've ever been with. Most women want flowers, jewelry, and surprise weekend getaways. I have really restrained myself these last couple of months. I walk by the flower shop or the jewelry store and have to force myself not to go inside. I miss spoiling you."

After a moment of silence, Clara looked up. "You are right. I do pull back. I feel like I'm still processing so much. When I first moved back, I thought my husband left me. Like my mother, he left me without explanation or discussion. He literally packed his things and left. I didn't think I could be loved for the long term. I was attracted to you, I always have been, but I hid behind the façade of my marriage to keep you at arm's length."

When he stepped closer, Clara held out her hands to keep him from touching her. She shook her head as she took a deep breath before she continued, "I didn't want you to fall in love with me and then leave me when you realized I wasn't what you wanted, like the ones before you."

"Clara, they didn't leave you. They both loved you," Connor was relieved she finally talked about her feelings. But, he was surprised by her insecurities, "I won't ever leave you."

"Maybe not, but what's to keep Evil from taking you?" She asked as the tears flowed from her green eyes down her cheeks. She finally said it out loud.

55 the dna results are back

Connor was relieved with the breakthrough. Clara was finally opening up and talking about her feelings with him. He was shocked she was not afraid of getting hurt again but of him getting hurt. Connor called his nephew to delay his evening rounds before meeting up with Clara and the kids for dinner. As a result, Clara was in a good mood when she arrived home later than usual that Thursday evening. She and Connor discussed going to the lake house for the coming Labor Day weekend to relax and regroup. They even discussed having a small get-together.

Clara had instructed the children to unpack their bags as she saw Shannon sitting at the dining room table. It was unusual since she had not been over for some time. Clara honestly had no idea about her current status with Devan. But she suddenly realized Shannon had not been parking out front. Connor was right, I have been in a serious funk. How could I not notice Shannon's relationship is different, too?

Shannon was looking perplexed. She had been over it many times and still she was in shock. Her DNA results were in. When she set up her account, she was informed she had a half-sister. That, by itself, wasn't the shocker. It was the fact she knew the person.

"Shan, is everything alright?" Clara asked as she joined her.

"The DNA results are back," she answered quietly as she looked up into the familiar green eyes.

"Yeah? What does it say? Do you know who your parents are?"

"I have a sister. I know who one of my parents is based on that," she answered in an odd tone. One that made Clara stop what she was doing as she turned to study her friend.

"Yeah? And?" Clara encouraged.

"It's you," Shannon stated accusingly.

"What? We are sisters? Carl Gibson again?" Clara wasn't sure why this upset her so much.

"No, you are my maternal half-sister," she clarified.

"It's you?" Clara whispered. She was convinced she would never discover the truth about the baby she read about in her mother's journals.

"You seem to be handling this a lot better than I thought."

"Yeah, well, there's a lot to the story."

"You knew all this time your mother gave up a baby?"

"No, at the beginning of the summer, Rob found a hidden compartment at the house. It was full of journals. My mother's journals. I've been reading through them, slowly as time allows. Just the other night, I read the passage where she was pregnant and carrying you," Clara explained.

"Alright. So, who is my father?"

"No idea, she doesn't say." Clara shrugged.

"She doesn't write who it was?" Shannon asked, disappointedly.

"No, she had no idea who he was," she answered, taking her newly found sister's hand. "I'm sorry."

"Clara, your mother didn't seem like the slut type playing around with multiple guys," as she said it out loud, another explanation came to her. "Oh, that's terrible!"

"I don't really know if that was the case. There's a reference to someone she calls the shadow. I don't know if she used the term to keep the name secret or what."

"Well, I have an appointment tomorrow with the lawyer's office in the city that handled my adoption. Is it alright if I stay here tonight?"

"Absolutely," Clara answered, realizing she had not spent a lot of time with her friends in the last month. "Do you want company on your trip?"

Clara spent the rest of the evening preparing the children for bed before making arrangements for the next day. With the distractions, she did not complete her usual nighttime routine of reading while she drank her tea.

• • • •

Evil paused soon after he entered the house. It was slightly later than his usual time, so he was surprised to hear her voice as she read to her children. He remained in the shadows as he listened to the musical sound of her voice. He patiently waited, hoping her friend would soon leave. But as the evening grew late, he realized the friend was staying for the night. So, he left early, fading into the night.

Connor came home late into the night. Clara was aware of him when he snuggled up close. But she never had a chance to explain what her plans were for the day as he was called back into work before dawn.

The next morning, Clara was up early with the kids. She dropped them off at the daycare, leaving her car for Michelle to bring the children home after work. She would stay with them until either Clara or Connor returned home. Clara left a vague message on Connor's voicemail. He returned her call when she and Shannon were meeting with the lawyer. Unfortunately, Clara was too distracted by the information to return his call.

At work, Connor placed his cell back into his pocket, slightly irritated to once again get Clara's voicemail. When he called her at work, they informed him that Clara had called off. Of course, he received a message from her after that saying she had hoped to talk to him. She was taking the day off to take care of something personal. When he tried calling back, he got her voicemail. Connor tried sending a text, but it sounded too controlling and needy. He thought they had worked things out, so why didn't she tell him she was taking the day off? As the hospital pulled him into another case, he felt his cell vibrating in his pocket, alerting him to another call. Shit, he thought, that's probably Clara.

When Connor came out of the room, he headed towards the nurse's station to check on labs for a patient in room four. Josh came over. "Connor, you have someone in room ten waiting for you. She asked for you specifically."

Connor looked over upon hearing his nephew's tone. "Are you going to tell me who it is?"

Without a word, Josh handed over the thin file. After reading the name, Connor attempted to give it back, "Seems pretty easy. You can see this one."

"I don't know, she's pretty determined to see you. I don't think I could stitch her up correctly. She's too much..." he paused as he searched for the proper word.

Connor chuckled as he leaned back onto the desk. "Josh, if you want to be a doctor, you need to start thinking of women as patients or even clients that come to see you because they are hurting or sick. Don't be thinking of ways to ask them out. You need to be professional at all times because if you cross the line, your career is over."

"I know, but I don't think I could be comfortable alone with her after the last time I saw her," he admitted.

Connor laughed, "Yeah, I forgot about that. She didn't leave much to the imagination dressed like that at my door, did she?"

Josh looked over at his uncle, "You aren't still going to make me do this, are you?"

"Why not? If it makes you feel better, I'll stand in there with you. Make sure she keeps her claws off you," he teased. "If the setting were different, I'd say go for it. But she's after your wallet and your house."

"I don't have any cash in my wallet nor do I have a house," he answered.

"Keep saying that. She will lose interest soon enough, especially when she learns the house is likely going to Hunter," Connor teased.

"Hunter's getting the house?" Josh stopped to look at his uncle. "How does the youngest son of four inherit the house?"

"She can't even try to get those sharp claws into a six-year-old. Talia would have a field day with her arrest," Connor explained. "It could be Alex, if you prefer."

He watched Josh's face as he processed the idea.

"Oh, ok. I get it," the younger man said with a nod.

"How are you your parents' child?" Connor wondered. When his nephew looked over in confusion, he continued, "You are the only child of Matt and Jordan Emerson. You have the genetic makeup to be one of the most intelligent, confident doctors of your generation. Don't let a mere gold digger throw you off your base."

"Just because my mom and dad are intelligent and confident, doesn't mean I am," Josh answered sadly.

"True, you have their other qualities as well, making you a potentially awesome physician. You have empathy, compassion, and charisma, to go with the intelligence and confidence," Connor quietly explained as he squeezed his shoulder. "You have all their positive qualities shining the most. They could not have had a better offspring if they tried ten more times. And yes, they are both confident and successful in their professions. But both had significant insecurities when it came to their personal lives."

"Oh, Uncle Connor, will you hold me?" Josh asked, laughing as he was pushed into the desk.

"Let's not keep Ms. Krause waiting any longer. I want to be home early tonight," he announced as they both headed into the room.

Josh knocked before entering the room, Connor followed, remaining just beside the entrance.

Sitting on the stretcher was Tiffany Krause, wearing a low cut summer dress with a short skirt. She had been slouched in her seat. At the sound of the knock, she leaned back on her hands, allowing her chest to stick out.

"Hello doctor," she whispered, but paused when Josh was the one to step closer.

After he introduced himself, Josh asked her how she cut her hand.

"Connor, what is going on? I specifically asked for you," Tiffany pouted as the younger doctor gently lifted her hand.

"He's been shadowing me, learning the ropes. I didn't think you'd have trouble with him examining your hand and giving you stitches if needed," Connor answered as his eyes narrowed at the blood on the cloth beside her. He was immediately suspicious after seeing her lean on her hand, it didn't add up.

"There's nothing here," Josh stated as he realized what happened. He dropped her hand as he stepped back. He could literally feel his uncle's anger as he attempted to step out of the small room.

"Why are you here?" Connor's voice was harsh.

Tiffany first looked over at Josh, then at him. "I wanted to see you. You haven't called me."

"I won't be calling you. I am not interested," Connor answered.

"But why not? I thought we had fun together," she whined.

"Maybe at first, but we have nothing in common. There's no future for us," he answered. He paused at the door before leaving the room. "Don't come here again with a false medical problem. It's a waste of our time and pulls us away from those that need our attention."

Josh was about to follow but a manicured hand grabbed his arm. "Wait, you're his nephew, right?"

He looked down at her hand before looking up into her sad face and nodded.

"Can't you help me win him back?" Tiffany pleaded.

"He's not interested. He's moved on, and I think you should too," Josh answered, patting her hand.

Tiffany looked down at his hand on hers and smiled sadly. "You really think he's moved on? Why are you so sure I can't win him back?"

"He's with someone," he answered honestly. "He's pretty serious about her."

"He's with someone? Why didn't he say that?" She demanded.

"He told you the truth. He's not interested in you," he said with a shrug. "If he said he was with someone else, it would imply he could be interested in you, IF she weren't in the picture. And honestly, I believe him. He's not interested."

"What makes you so sure he's serious?"

"He bought car seats for when he picks up her kids," Josh answered with a shrug.

The woman chuckled, "That's hardly romantic."

"Maybe not, but it speaks volumes for his commitment," he responded before turning to walk away.

She grabbed his arm again. "But wait, you're available, aren't you? I can move on to you."

Josh was so surprised by her comment, he laughed. His uncle was right. Damn, Connor called this one. He shook his head. "I know it won't work, I don't have money or a house."

"That's alright, you're still young. You're the oldest son, right? You'll eventually inherit it all," she said with a smile as she stepped closer, caressing his arm.

"Not likely. Hunter is my father's favorite. He's being prepped to take over his firm and the house," Josh stated, attempting to be slightly annoyed as he walked away.

He could hear Connor chuckle as he returned to the nurse's station. "You were right. She's only after my house and money. Since I have neither, she's likely to go research the little guy now. If Talia finds out about this, I'll be homeless!"

"That's alright, I have a couch," his uncle answered as he reached for the next chart.

56 questions and more questions

In the city, Detectives Andy Sanders and Jim Walters were at their desks reviewing what they knew about the death of Jason O'Reilly. There was evidence of a struggle. Defensive wounds, multiple stab wounds, and blunt force trauma suggested a significant amount of rage and a personal connection.

The theory that it was the wife could not be proven. Nothing existed to suggest she had a secret lover or an old jealous boyfriend that wouldn't let her go. No disgruntled clients that could not account for their whereabouts. They thought the cell phone would have led them to the killer, but even that yielded nothing. There wasn't a person in the city who they could prove wanted Jason O'Reilly dead.

"Do we have anything new on the O'Reilly case?" Captain Trey Shepherd asked from the doorway of their office.

"Nothing, Captain," Sanders answered miserably.

"Nothing?" The captain asked skeptically as he looked back and forth between the two detectives. "Tell me what you know about the wife. She's young and beautiful, nothing hidden? Do you think she could have been involved in his death?"

"Not finding anything," Walters admitted. "From everyone we

interviewed, she's as honest as they come. Jason and Clara O'Reilly were tight and totally devoted. We can't find anyone in this city that would have a motive to kill him. The wife inherits the life insurance. She would not have had the strength to do it herself, and we can't connect her with any secret lovers. There doesn't seem to be any connections with anyone."

"Maybe you're looking at this from the wrong angle," Trey said hesitantly as a thought came to him. "No one IN the city had motive, but what often happens when someone suddenly becomes a single parent with young children in a large city with limited support?"

The captain looked at his detectives before he answered his own question. "They move back home. Who had motive to get the wife back home? In her small town? I bet that's where you will find O'Reilly's killer."

"Damn, it's certainly something to look into. We don't have any other leads to pursue," Sanders agreed. "We should head back now and talk to the wife and her friends."

"It's Friday afternoon, traffic will be horrible. First let's see who she was in contact with before she moved." Walters started to sort through the files on his desk. "Where's the list of calls from the apartment landline and O'Reilly's job?"

"What are you thinking?" The captain asked.

"I saw a couple of calls from the town's area code to his work number," the detective answered. "Maybe this wasn't just about getting the wife back home, but some kind of coverup for money laundering or stealing."

When Rachel pulled into her driveway, she pulled out her keys and bags. She needed to call Clara to confirm when they were meeting up at Connor's for the holiday weekend and to help coordinate the menu. Once she placed all the bags on the counter, she pulled out her cell. Glancing at the clock, Rachel was surprised the call went to voicemail.

"Clara, just touching base about the details for Labor Day. Call me back when you get this."

Rachel decided that today was the day to tackle her mother's bedroom. It had been almost six months since her death. The time to start cleaning out her room was long overdue. Since she was now head of the house, Rachel would sort through everything and purge instead of hoarding it in the attic, basement, or garage like the generations before her.

And yet she found herself standing in the doorway, afraid of the shadows of the past. While she and her mother had a strong relationship, her mother was always very private. Elizabeth MacKenzie's room was her quiet haven, shared with no one. Rarely was Rachel ever in the room and never without her mother. She felt as if she was invading her privacy, disturbing what needed to remain hidden.

Baby steps, Rachel thought. Her mother would not have any issues with a simple cleaning of her room. It hadn't been vacuumed, dusted, nor the bathroom cleaned since before her death.

With her mind made up, Rachel went to retrieve the cleaning supplies and vacuum. She was compelled to start by moving the bed to tackle the dust bunnies underneath. When she pushed the bed over, she stepped back in shock at the sight before her.

Lying in the dust was an empty syringe.

Clara drove the final stretch home from the city in silence. It was a toss-up who was more astounded by what they learned. While they did not discover who Shannon's biological father was, she did learn about a half-brother. It wasn't a shock that Shannon had a paternal half-brother, it was who the half-brother was that had both friends, now sisters, reeling in shock.

As if that wasn't enough, the details of the adoptions were both the same. Each was a young teenage girl from a small town requesting to give up her child anonymously. In both situations, neither mother was able to provide the father's name. Not to protect his identity, but because they didn't know it. That provided plenty of understanding of the circumstances, causing Shannon to question her mission.

Did she truly want to know the name of her biological father? Knowing how she was likely conceived made her hesitant to seek answers. What good would come from searching the shadows of the past?

About twenty miles from home, the car suddenly began to wobble. Clara forced herself to remain calm as she struggled to control the car. She needed both hands on the steering wheel to avoid driving off the road into the ravine. Clara's foot was already off the accelerator as she prepared for the sharp curve ahead. Without warning, her side window shattered, and glass went flying everywhere.

Clara's ears rang with Shannon's screams as she tried to protect her face from the glass. She wouldn't remember the pain, likely due to the excessive adrenaline as she fought to maintain control of the vehicle. A task that became impossible when Clara's left arm fell helplessly into her lap. Unable to move her arm, she lost control of the steering wheel.

With two tires blown and no way to control it, the car continued straight, completely missing the tight turn as it sped off the road into the ravine. Clara's mind fleetingly realized the irony of missing the same fatal curve as her uncle when the car bounced into the same tree head-on, causing the airbags to engage as the momentum pushed the car into a roll down the hill.

To Clara, the car seemed to roll in slow motion. She had flashes of those she loved. The first time she met Jason, the first time she held each of her babies in her arms, and Connor as he danced with her around the dance floor. Then everything went black as she closed her eyes...

coming soon

Small Town Secrets Book 2
SHADOWS OF THE PAST

acknowledgments

So many people in my life have supported me on this long journey of completing my first book. In the beginning, I sat at the table with my family as we debated the names of the original characters. I've kept them all. And when I finally got my act together to start the first chunk of the book, everyone was immediately available by text or in-person to list names or listen to a scenario. I thank you all for your help.

My children, growing up listening to their mother tell anyone and everyone I would be a best selling novelist. And as time went on, each of you had doubts a book would ever be completed, let alone published. You both have been patient, helpful and understanding, laughing at me when I made stupid mistakes on the computer and listened as I bounced ideas: Cody and Hannah, you are my IT people! The ones who suffered the most because I was too busy writing to start dinner, among other things.

Marcey, a great friend, the first one to say yes, finish it up and get it published. And the comment of, "Wow, this is actually pretty good" kept me going. As a true friend, most of our get-togethers were discussing the book. And my urgent but simple text messages: "Scenario A or B?" Thank you for your time and patience. I promise to get the second book done faster.

Theresa, my travel buddy! You listened to me talk about the book and allowed me to write on our trips and talk about my ideas while driving around Ireland on the wrong side of the road. I know deep down you and John had doubts I would ever get this done. That has helped to push me along.

Many of my co-workers who patiently listened to me sort out a scene and allowed me to process which path a character would take, thank you.

Aunt Barb, I can't forget you! You listened as I read the first draft to you, initially over the phone and later in person, you gave me suggestions and encouragement. I hope you enjoy the final draft!

And many friends especially Lisa, Deanna, Traci, Heidi, Harpreet, Amber, Kim Valentine, and Pierre, you all listened to me talk about my book and even shared it with others, encouraging me when I was discouraged and getting excited with me, I love the support you have all shown over the years! And the many patients who also grew excited while I talked about my book. The one that stands out the most, asked me every week after my time off, when would I finally get it done so she could read it? Theresa, I'm sorry I didn't get it done in time.

Dr. Hanna, you opened my world in ways I can't even express! Working with you has increased my hearing and confidence, expanding my world to places I didn't think possible. Your excitement and support has helped more than you will ever know. And most importantly, you introduced me to Jodi. Thank you for everything!

Jodi and Amy at Two Penny Publishing, you are great! You have been very optimistic and helpful as you guided me through the process of finally getting this published. Your patience as I struggle with the easiest of assignments, dragging out the time it should not have taken me, I'll try to do better next time. I've looked forward to our Zoom calls and can't wait to someday meet you both in person.

And finally, to the people behind the scenes at Two Penny Publishing, especially Holly, who read the rough original, you helped polish it up, thank you all for everything.

about the author

Julie Ann Keady has been hearing impaired since an illness when she was an infant. She started wearing hearing aids when she was five years old. Despite wearing bilateral hearing aids, Julie Ann still relied on lip reading. As she grew older, the hearing aids became less effective since her sensorineural hearing loss was progressive. Her hearing became non-existent in her one ear. Later in adulthood, she had a cochlear implanted and reentered the hearing world with a different view on life including a new appreciation for music and background sounds. Julie Ann has since had a cochlear implant on her other ear. Today, Julie loves to read, write and travel.